In

Cheng's body was as beautiful to touch as it was to look at, and Nan felt herself savouring every contact. She was so aware of him: the slight changes in pressure as he breathed; the faint perfume that came from his shoulder-length hair, as though he'd washed it in something rare and exotic. The smell of him conjured up images of sweet-scented ginger, growing wild on the banks of a jungle river. The black silk of his hair made her think of panther skin, and the palms of his hands made her wonder what they would feel like moving across her body.

Intense Blue

LYN WOOD

BLACK
lace

Black Lace novels contain sexual fantasies.
In real life, make sure you practise safe sex.

First published in 2000 by
Black Lace
Thames Wharf Studios,
Rainville Road, London W6 9HA

Typeset by SetSystems Ltd, Saffron Walden, Essex
Printed and bound by Mackays of Chatham PLC

ISBN 0 352 33496 7

Chapter One

When Megan first suggested doing A level art at an evening class, Nan felt quite traumatised; it was a long time since she'd learned anything except the latest word-processing package. She and Megan had been friends since school. Megan seemed to have found a new lease of life of late – she'd hennaed her hair and taken to wearing the sort of floaty dresses Nan's daughter Cassie wore. Nan opted for trousers and shorts and dungarees, never skirts; she kept her curly hair short, and she had the sort of complexion that always looks newly scrubbed. She didn't wear make-up or jewellery, and she was a dab hand at changing spark plugs and fixing washing machines. In an affectionate kind of way, each thought the other slightly foolish.

The classroom phobia left Nan surprisingly quickly; before long she was laying on the charcoal and paint with gay abandon, and loving every minute. Whatever piece of work she brought home, however, Mike would say, 'Ah. Geraniums again.' The first three or four times it was funny. After that her husband's joke began to wear rather thin.

* * *

1

Daughter Cassie had gone off to college the previous September, so Nan reorganised her old room so that she could use it as a studio during term-time, and during a mad moment she bought an extension so that she didn't have to run downstairs every time the phone rang. She nipped home at lunchtime, plugged it in and sat there admiring it. Just as she was about to go back to work, she heard the front door open, and before she could call out to Mike and ask him why he'd come home she heard him pick up the telephone downstairs. Then she heard him say, 'Sandra? It's me.'

Sandra's that empty-headed secretary of his, thought Nan. Maybe he was out on a job this morning, and he's ringing in to tell her when he'll be back. Nan had met Sandra a couple of times, so she decided to surprise Mike by christening the new purchase and joining in the conversation.

As she lifted the receiver she heard Sandra say, 'What's that? It sounds like an extension being picked up.'

'We don't *have* an extension,' said Mike.

Sandra laughed. 'Unzip your flies, then.'

Files, thought Nan. I've misheard. She must have said unzip your files. He's probably got his laptop on the telephone table.

'What are you wearing?' Mike asked.

'A dress. Stockings and suspenders. Nothing else.'

There was a chuckle. Nan sat there, her knuckles white. This can't be happening, she thought. It's so tacky. Listen a bit longer: it's all a mistake. There has to be some sort of explanation.

'Put your hand on your knee,' said Mike. 'Then run it up your leg, over your stocking-top, until you can feel bare flesh.'

There was a moment of silence. Then, 'I've followed your instructions to the letter, Mr Tilson.'

'Lick your finger,' said Mike. 'Now open your legs, and slide it over you know where. One side to the other,

2

nice and slow; I want to hear your reaction as you feel it stiffen.'

There was a quick intake of breath. 'Mm,' said Sandra, 'that feels wonderful. There's no one in the office at the moment, but Ralph could come back at any time . . . He wouldn't be able to see what I'm doing, but he might wonder why I've got this dreamy expression on my face. I'm picturing him watching me, running his tongue over his lips, wondering why he's getting a hard-on. I'm getting very randy now, playing with myself, feeling the excitement building . . . Have you got an erection?'

'Oh, yes,' said Mike. 'I've got the Eiffel Tower in here. I'm taking it out now . . . running my finger up it . . . imagining your hand, remembering what you do with that oil, the way you watch my face, controlling me. The way you bring me to the edge and then take me back again until I'm gagging for it . . . I want to slip the finger of my other hand inside you, feel you squeeze it . . .'

'I'm opening my lips,' breathed Sandra. 'I think you know which lips I mean. Things are very wet down there . . . Good job I'm not wearing any knickers; they'd be soaking.'

'Oh, God, I can see you so clearly in my head, that single-minded expression on your face, that screw-me-senseless look. I'm not sure how much longer I can keep wanking before I lose it . . .'

'Not yet, darling, not yet. I'm starting to fuck myself with my finger, the way you do it. Slowly, sensuously, in and out, twisting it so that it catches the right place on the upstroke. Oh, that feels so good . . . My nipples have gone rock-hard in sympathy; they're pressing against my blouse . . .' A long sigh.

'I can picture them, all pink and pointed. Your tits are the stuff of fantasies, Sandra. I want to lick them, come all over them . . .'

'I'm imagining you standing there, the telephone in one hand, your cock in the other . . .'

'I've got your scarf here. The silk one, with the exotic

3

fruits on it. I'm rubbing it over my prick; it feels like you, it really does. I'm going to come into it ... very soon now ... I can't hold out much longer ...'

Sandra's breathing was stopping and starting, punctuated with little moans. Mike groaned, and then Sandra gave a strangled cry. 'Now,' she gasped; Mike cried out loud, and there was a sudden clatter – he seemed to have dropped the telephone receiver.

After a moment Nan heard him pick it up again. 'Satisfactory lunchbreak?' he asked.

'Very,' said Sandra. 'You?'

'I'll bring your scarf back, then you can see.'

There was a throaty chuckle.

'I'll see you at the team meeting, then,' said Mike.

'Right you are, Mr Tilson,' said Sandra, and she hung up.

Nan heard Mike open his brief-case and shut it again. Then he laughed quietly to himself, and left the house. Nan carried on sitting there for some time. What do I do, she thought, face him with it? I don't think I can. How long has it been going on? I need time to think about this; I'm in a state of shock.

She didn't tell Megan. It was too humiliating. She felt like a frump all of a sudden – Mike hadn't been interested in sex for ages. And in the days when he had, it hadn't been particularly spectacular.

The two women went to an exhibition which Megan said was a must. It was a one-woman show by Simone Garnier, *Landscapes of the Body*: paintings, photographs and etchings. Mostly figurative, mostly male, mostly erotic, mostly very good indeed.

'There's nothing recent, though,' said Megan. 'Look, the last one was painted seven years ago.'

The painting Megan was looking at had been lent by a collector. It was a large canvas, a reworking of Manet's *Le Déjeuner Sur L'Herbe*. Nan knew the original well: two men, dressed in stiff Victorian clothes are sitting on the

4

grass next to a naked woman. In the background another woman, scantily clad, is knee-deep in water, filling some sort of vessel. The men appear to be discussing politics, or evolution, or theology; the naked woman looks bored.

Simone had switched the genders. This time it was the women who were formally dressed and deep in conversation. The man in the background was bending over as the woman in Manet's painting had been; he was broad-chested and muscular, and hung like a donkey. The figure in the foreground was sitting sideways-on. He had a beautiful body, and a sensitive face. One knee was bent under him; the other made a triangular shape parallel to the picture plane. Nan looked closer. The man's penis was just visible in the shadow, half-erect. He was looking out of the picture towards her, and it was almost an invitation. He seemed to be thinking, these women don't want my body; how about you, the onlooker? Come and join us . . .

'It's clever, isn't it?' said Megan.

Nan agreed that it was.

'Megan?' said a man's voice behind them.

'Goodness,' said Megan, turning round. 'Brian. Fancy seeing you here.'

'Came up for the ceramics exhibition,' said the man. 'Thought I'd take a look at this as well.'

'Brian's in my pottery class,' said Megan. 'Brian, this is Nan.'

Nan and Brian dutifully said hello to one another. He was a middle-aged man with thin sandy hair and freckles, and he blinked a lot, as though even the light in the gallery was too bright for his pale-blue eyes. They all moved on to the next painting together, and before long Megan was deep in conversation with him and Nan felt like an accessory.

'I think I'll take a look at the prints and the etchings,' said Nan.

'OK,' said Megan. 'See you in the coffee bar at – what – half past twelve?'

Nan moved on to the prints and etchings on her own.

The photograph caught her attention as if a friend had waved to her from a crowd. A black and white image of a child, running towards the camera, wild, exuberant, her gypsy-style dress billowing out at the sides and her blonde curly hair flying in all directions. Nan stood looking at it for a long time; there was something about the child that was oddly familiar. The strangest thing was that the dress seemed familiar too; although the photograph was in black and white, she was absolutely certain that the squiggly design on the fabric was red, quite a dark red, like dried blood.

'Simone has a way with bodies, doesn't she, however she chooses to represent them.'

Nan glanced at the man standing beside her. He smiled at her. He was tall and thin, with a curiously old-fashioned look to him – grey flannels, and an open-necked shirt. He held out his hand. 'Hugo Forbes. I'm a photographer – reproductions, mainly. Of paintings, that is.'

'Nan.' They shook hands.

'Is this the first exhibition of Simone's work you've been to?'

Nan nodded.

'And what do you think?'

Nan took a deep breath. 'Well, it's . . .'

He grinned. 'Let me give you a guided tour. I work here part-time.'

The tour eventually ended in a room upstairs, which was marked PRIVATE. He opened the door with a key, and stood to one side to let her through. There was a large desk by the window, some bookshelves, a thick cream carpet, and two armchairs. A little kitchen area, with a sink and a fridge and coffee-making things. 'There are a few more prints in here,' he said, opening a drawer. 'Simone withdrew them at the last moment.'

Nan wondered why. They were just as good as the ones she'd seen outside.

6

Hugo Forbes seemed to read her mind. 'I've no idea either,' he said. 'Simone's an unpredictable woman. This one's my favourite. Lifelike, without being bland. Stylish.' It was a watercolour of two feet. One of them was wearing a sheer black stocking and a red stiletto, and the other was naked. There was something in the background . . . a hand? No, a penis.

'I like the shoe,' said Nan lamely, becoming acutely aware of the battered trainers she was wearing, the shapeless dungarees, the practical masculine watch clipped round her wrist.

'Yes, I like the shoe too. You look hot, Nan. Have a seat. I always keep a bottle of Chardonnay in the fridge this weather – may I offer you a glass?'

Nan nodded, and sat down. The wine was delightfully cold, and she drank half of it in one go.

'Hard on the feet, walking round a gallery in July,' said Hugo. 'If I were you, I'd take my shoes off for a bit while I had the chance.'

Nan considered for a moment; then the thought of air between her toes became very seductive, and she removed her trainers, and then her socks. After that she drank the rest of her wine, and Hugo refilled her glass. He talked for a while about Simone's paintings, but his eyes kept on straying back to her feet.

'Simone has this way of homing in on specific areas of eroticism,' he said, twirling the stem of his wineglass. 'She gets you to imagine yourself as one of her subjects. I picture myself massaging the sole of that unknown woman's foot. She'd be spreadeagled on a satin cushion, her eyes closed. With every stroke the sensitivity would increase, until her whole being would be centred in that foot. Her toes would be tingling, and so would a rather more sensitive area, as though there was an invisible thread between the two. I can imagine the man in the background taking her little toe in his mouth and running his tongue round it. Can you imagine yourself as the woman?'

7

Nan felt herself blush. The idea of someone taking that amount of time and trouble over a peripheral part of her anatomy was a real turn-on, but only in the abstract. She wanted passion, all right – but she wanted closeness and cuddles afterwards, poetry and chocolates, meanderings about the meaning of life. The things she'd never had with Mike. Feet seemed a bit disembodied.

'Of course,' Hugo Forbes continued, 'a lot of men would see the culmination of the act taking place in the shoe. I, on the other hand, would prefer to bend her legs at the knees and place the soles of her feet together. The arches make a little cavity.' He knelt down in front of her, took her feet in his hands in a strangely dated and courteous way, and showed her.

Nan swallowed; she hadn't expected him to actually touch her. Belatedly, she realised that this was a little naïve. She stiffened, and noticed at the same time that he had stiffened too – his erection was evident beneath his neat grey trousers.

'You do have beautiful feet,' he said. 'Has no one ever told you?'

'I really ought to get back to my friend,' hedged Nan. 'She'll be wondering where I am.'

'Your feet are still flushed,' he said. 'Let me massage them for you. It won't take long. There's a little tub of talcum powder in the desk.'

Before Nan could think of anything to say, he had found the talcum powder, swivelled the nozzle, and sprinkled some of it on her foot. She sat there as he smoothed the powder over her skin, at a loss for an appropriate reaction. He must have done it many times before; there was an expertise to it that was mind-numbingly effective. She drifted for a few moments, just enjoying it. Then she heard his breathing become ragged, and she snatched her foot away and said, 'No, I really must be off.'

He groaned, held his breath – then he relaxed, bit by bit, and she heard him sigh with pleasure.

'That was delightful,' he said. 'We must do it again some time. You can always ask for me at Reception.' The tone of his voice made it sound as though he was referring to afternoon tea, probably with cucumber sandwiches. There was a wet patch on his trousers, which he ignored. 'Simone won't show her latest work,' he said. 'The mind boggles – in a most aesthetic way, of course. Oh – here. Have a present.'

Nan stiffened. She had a bit of a thing about presents – no one had ever bought her anything she really wanted. He handed her a long thin strip of card. Nan looked at it. It was a bookmark, featuring one of Simone's paintings. She wanted to laugh. Closeness and cuddles and poetry and chocolates?

They parted company at the top of the stairs, and Nan found Megan and Brian in the coffee-bar. 'You look a bit hot and bothered,' said Megan.

'I don't feel too well,' said Nan. 'I think I'll go home.'

'Oh,' said Megan. 'I wouldn't mind hanging on a bit longer – will you be OK?'

'It's only a headache,' said Nan. 'I'll be fine.' She bought a postcard on the way out: a reproduction of the photograph of the child with blonde curly hair in the squiggly dress.

She didn't say anything about Hugo Forbes to Megan. The incident seemed to exist in a little glass box – divorced from reality, like Mike's phone call, and she felt slightly ashamed of herself for not putting a stop to it immediately. Nor did she say anything about the photograph – not until two weeks later, when she came across a snapshot of herself, a little older than the child in Simone's print, six years old perhaps. The likeness was astonishing, although the Nan in the album had a sullen expression, and the wild hair had been tied back and domesticated.

'My God,' said Megan when Nan showed her the two photographs, side by side, 'it *is* you.'

9

'It's *like* me.'

'It has to be you. It must have been taken when you were four – look at the date on it. When your real mother was still alive.'

Nan had no memory of anything at all before the age of eight. The first thing she could recall was her father's wedding – but after that the memories followed thick and fast, and by the age of thirteen she was only dimly aware that Frances wasn't her real mother. Like most children who sense something simmering under the surface, she made sure she never asked the wrong questions, and the woman who had given birth to her was never mentioned. As a result, Nan's first eight years were documented only by her birth certificate and a record of vaccinations.

'Aren't you curious?' asked Megan. 'I would be. I wonder where Simone took it.'

'I could write to her. Ask her.'

'She doesn't answer letters,' said Megan. 'She's a bit of a recluse. Lives in a bloody great mansion, Lavender Hall . . . Oh, wait a minute.'

'What?'

'She runs painting courses. Well, *she* doesn't run them exactly, they just use her house, but she has some really *wicked* people taking the classes. Hey. A week off, a week away from homes, husbands, hassles. Cool.'

'I can't just go off for a week.'

'Why not? Darren moved out two years ago, and Cassie's got a field trip over the summer. A fortieth birthday present. To us, from us. And with any luck you'll bump into Simone and you can ask her about the photograph.'

'I'd feel silly.'

'I don't see why. Your father died ages ago, and you've no brothers or sisters. You don't have anyone who might remember anything – like the dress, for instance.'

'That's the weird thing,' said Nan. 'That dress . . . The wiggly bits were red. Dark red. I'm sure of it.'

'Wow,' said Megan. 'We *definitely* have a mystery now. I'll get them to send me details of the courses.'

Nan showed Mike the print. He laughed and said, 'You've probably just seen some material like it.'

She let the subject drop. She felt on the edge of a precipice these days – as though one unwise remark could lead to disaster. When she told him she had booked a place on the course, he was surprisingly enthusiastic about it. Well, he would be, wouldn't he? she reasoned; he'll spend the time with Sandra. But she still couldn't make herself say anything to him about it.

Just before she was due to leave, Mike surprised her by saying, 'You don't seriously think that photograph's you, do you?'

'You've seen it,' she snapped. 'It's awfully like me.'

'I don't think so.'

Nan scowled.

'I know what's going through your mind,' said Mike. 'You think that Garnier woman may actually have *known* your mother. Oh, come on, it's not very likely, is it? Simone Garnier's a really famous painter. And your mother was . . . Well, just a housewife.'

'So?'

'You'll only get upset,' said Mike, 'when it doesn't lead anywhere.'

'I'm not five,' said Nan icily. 'I can handle it.'

'It's going to be really nice,' said Mike, 'having a week on my own.'

You won't be on your own, though, thought Nan, her eyes narrowing. If she was going to say anything, that was the moment – but then Megan tooted the horn, and Nan heaved her rucksack on to her shoulder and slammed the door behind her.

* * *

11

'Just get a load of this atmosphere,' said Megan, climbing out of the car and sniffing the air like a pointer. 'Wow.' She tried to open the gate, but it wouldn't budge. She rattled it, annoyed. 'Give us a hand with this, Nan,' she said. 'It's stuck.'

Nan got out of the passenger seat. The beech trees met overhead, and the woods to either side of the track were dense and dark and unkempt. She could just see the house, big, old, sprawling in the evening sunlight; she caught a glimpse of a conservatory, a greenhouse, some outbuildings. There was a powerful smell of vegetation, not the same as a garden at all: wild, uncontrolled, too much of it. They opened the gate between them, then Megan drove the car through and waited for Nan to close it again. The catch snapped shut like a gin-trap.

'A whole week,' said Megan, 'and no husbands. Bloody marvellous. Three miles to the nearest pub, unfortunately.'

'I thought we'd come here to paint,' said Nan.

'Some of the time.' Megan grinned. She parked in front of the house, and they both went inside. There was a small office marked RECEPTION, with no one in it. 'We're a bit early,' said Megan, glancing round the oak-panelled hall as though every section of wood might conceal a secret passage. 'D'you think there might be a ghost?'

Nan smiled. Megan was thoroughly into ghosts and crystals and astrology at the moment; she looked the part, as well, with her waist-length red hair and her diaphanous clothes. Definitely alternative, with signs and wonders wrought out of silver on a chain round her neck and a small tattoo on her shoulder, of which Nan disapproved, although she couldn't quite say why.

They walked to the other end of the hall, which was lit by a stained-glass window. A wide staircase rose in front of them, and tacked to the banisters was a sign saying PRIVATE. NO ADMITTANCE UPSTAIRS.

One of the oak doors leading off the hall was ajar.

Megan stuck her head through the opening. 'There's nobody about,' she reported. 'Let's take a look.'

The room turned out to be a library. A window looked out across the back garden, which was enclosed on three sides by buildings; there were people on the lawn, arguing. One of them glanced towards the house, and saw Megan. He nudged someone else and the group broke up immediately. The man who had first spotted them walked over to the window, which was open. He was in his late fifties, maybe: white hair, a trim white beard, eyes that turned down at the outside corners, hooded, careful. Nan had the feeling that she'd seen him before somewhere. He was wearing jeans and a rough cotton shirt, half unbuttoned with the sleeves rolled up. There was something very physical about him, although he wasn't a big man. He leaned his arms on the window sill and looked at them.

'Small mammals, watercolours or short stories?' he said to Megan.

Megan smiled. 'Watercolours.'

'I'll come through and give you a hand. You're in the coach-house.' He glanced at Nan, and did a double-take. For a moment he stared at her; then he said, 'What's your name?'

'Nan. Annette. Annette Tilson.'

He gave a slight shake of the head and smiled, as though he'd realised he'd been badly mistaken about something.

They walked back to the car and hauled their cases out of the boot. The man didn't introduce himself; he simply took them to the coach-house, carrying a couple of bags, and told them to take their pick of the rooms. 'Supper at nine tonight – seven o'clock the rest of the week – in the building next to the conservatory.' After that he vanished.

There were four twin bedrooms in the coach-house, and they chose one upstairs that looked out over the courtyard. Megan rummaged in her bag and said, 'Now

13

we *are* on holiday,' and they drank warm gin and tonics out of their toothmugs.

A car pulled up outside. Megan peered out of the window and said, 'Hurrah.' Then she said, 'Oh.'

'What do you mean, oh?'

'Take a look.'

Two elderly ladies were climbing out of a battered Range Rover. One of them was big and busty and the other was tiny and delicate. They lifted item after item out of the vehicle, and distributed the things around them, on the ground. Nan stared in amazement – there were easels (two sorts each), canvases, boxes of paints, butterfly nets, photographic equipment, suitcases, a violin, binoculars, walking boots . . . She started to laugh.

'I hope it's not going to be painting for geriatrics,' said Megan sourly.

'They look like fun,' said Nan.

A man appeared from the direction of the conservatory. He was tall and dark-haired, big-boned, tanned; the hair was tied back in a ponytail. A gardener, perhaps, with his faded denims and his two days' stubble. He moved with the loose confidence of the physically fit, and although he wasn't classically good-looking he had an interesting face – strong features, expressive, mobile. 'Ye gods,' he said, glancing at the clutter, 'how long have you come for?'

'Just the week,' said the larger of the two women. 'My name's Imogen. Imogen Mulholland.'

'Tad,' said the man, holding out his hand.

'Sorry?' shouted Imogen. 'I'm slightly deaf.'

'Tadeusz,' said the man. 'Tad for short.'

'Oh,' said Imogen. 'You're our tutor, then. Gosh. I mean . . . Gosh. Pleased to meet you.'

They shook hands. 'You're in the coach-house,' said Tad. 'I think I'd better get a wheelbarrow.' He disappeared.

'Damn,' said Megan.

'What now?'

14

'Can you imagine getting plastered with those two? Mind you, the tutor looks all right. What do you think?'

'What about?'

'Tadeusz Kalinowski. Rather dishy, in a rugged kind of way.'

'I didn't notice,' said Nan.

'No, Miss Goody Two-Shoes,' said Megan, with a definite smirk, 'I don't suppose you did.'

Nan bridled inside. Goody Two-Shoes? Was that the image she gave off? They went back downstairs and out on to the drive.

'Lettie,' Imogen was saying, balancing a large box against her ample khaki-clad bosom, 'take this, will you?'

'The stereoscope?' said Lettie. 'Oh, honestly, I thought this was meant to be a bit of fun. Chatting up the OAPs, getting pissed every night.'

'I've come here to dissect owl pellets,' said Imogen. 'When I'm not painting.'

'I know.' Lettie sighed.

Tad appeared with the wheelbarrow. Nan and Megan stood by the front door, feeling superfluous. He glanced behind him and noticed them. 'You in the coach-house as well?' he asked.

They nodded.

'Good. You can give these two a hand, then.' He let the rear end of the wheelbarrow drop, and rubbed his palms together as though he were washing his hands of the whole business. He studied the Range Rover, said, 'I'd park it in the field over there, if I were you,' and went.

'Helpful soul,' said Nan.

'He's the bee's knees, my girl,' said Imogen, 'if somewhat taciturn. That's why we're here. That and the bats and the owls.'

'We've heard he's a fantastic teacher,' added Lettie. 'As long as he likes you, that is.'

They trundled the two women's belongings over to

the coach-house. Imogen revved up the Range Rover and reversed into the field as though she were taking part in a rally.

They went back for the rest of the things. Another car had arrived and an elderly couple were standing in the drive, looking helpless.

'Do you work here?' the woman asked Megan, through gritted teeth.

'No,' said Megan.

'Calm down,' said the man, 'we're here now.'

'I am calm!' shouted the woman.

'Gerald Grey,' said the man apologetically, 'and this is my wife, Gladys.'

And suddenly there were three more cars and nowhere to park them. Megan and Nan bundled the last of the luggage on to the wheelbarrow, and made themselves scarce. They watched the mêlée from the bedroom window. One of the cars reversed into the field next to the Range Rover, and the others eventually followed suit. The people dispersed, all except for one man who had obviously found something of interest on a bush and was peering at it through a hand lens.

'They're all going to be nut-cases,' said Megan. 'Nut-cases or senior citizens. Shit.' She yawned. 'I think I'll have a pre-dinner doze. Get my strength up for the evening.'

'I think I'll go for a walk,' said Nan.

The grounds were extensive and there was no sound of distant traffic, none at all. Nan wandered among the gardens and the outbuildings, breathing in the scent of lavender and roses, listening to the birdsong. She turned a corner, and found herself confronted by a barn. She'd always wanted to climb over bales of hay, and had never had the opportunity. She went inside, climbed to the top of the haystack and sat there, smelling the sweetness and looking round. An ancient tractor, a pile of tarpaulins, a full-length mirror (cracked), some rolls of netting, an old chest of drawers ... She leaned back and closed her eyes. The gin had got to her, as well.

A faint rustling woke her. She peered over the top of the nearest bale and saw a man, standing in front of the mirror. He was young – early twenties, maybe, nationality indeterminate: Asian, Burmese perhaps. He had shoulder-length black hair, flat as silk, and a face so exotic and so perfectly proportioned that he was, quite simply, beautiful. She had a sudden feeling that she wasn't meant to be there, so she kept very still and watched.

He was wearing a pair of loose white trousers, tied at the waist, and some sandals. He kicked off the sandals, untied the trousers, and slipped those off as well. He was now completely naked, and as well endowed below the hips as he was above them. He stood very straight and still for a moment; then he began to move, slowly, so slowly that to begin with she wasn't sure that he was moving at all. T'ai chi, she thought, that's what he's doing. He made one shape after another, limbs weaving in and out, muscles rippling, perfectly co-ordinated, perfectly controlled. Nan watched, entranced – it was like a ballet, but with an edge to it. An erotic edge, for she had gradually become aware of his erection. It hadn't been there at the outset; it had arrived as slowly and smoothly as his movements. She saw his left arm brush against it as he twisted his body, and then the right arm did the same. The next time the palm of his hand travelled all the way up the shaft, and then out into the air in a wide sweep. He twisted in the other direction, and the other hand mirrored the arc. By this time Nan was quite sure it wasn't accidental; it was part of a ritual. She caught a glimpse of his face. No clues there; it was quite expressionless.

It was a titillating display. Initially, Nan had just been captivated by the sheer elegance and symmetry of the performance, but as the routines became more sexual she found herself getting turned on by them. It wasn't a

17

reciprocal sort of lust. She didn't want his body against hers; she just wanted to watch.

He bent and curled, touched himself, uncurled and stretched, touched himself, stood on one leg, perfectly balanced, and raised the other leg at an angle. She could see the sinews under the golden skin, taut as wires. He began to caress himself more deliberately, but still with that iron self-discipline, letting go of his cock every so often to complete another sequence of actions.

Nan imagined herself trying something similar. Beneath the grey asexual dungarees her own body was still slim-waisted and full-breasted. She pictured herself standing in front of the bathroom mirror, running her hands across her skin the way he was doing, touching herself in all the places that hadn't been touched for far too long. She shivered.

He bent one leg, stretched the other, and ran his hand all the way from his ankle to the tip of his penis. Then he changed position, and ran his hand all the way up the other leg. A droplet of moisture glistened on the head as he grasped his cock in his hand and slowly moved the foreskin up and down, watching his reflection in the glass.

She wondered whether she would be able to manufacture the same sort of control, if she tried it. The way she was feeling she doubted it, somehow. It would be hell for leather towards orgasm by now.

When he did finally come it was a silent affair, although the black irises of his eyes rolled upwards and she glimpsed the whites for a moment. His mouth opened in a soundless scream of victory. After a moment or two he put his trousers back on again, and went. The whole episode seemed like a dream. Then someone started to ring a hand-bell in the building next to the conservatory. It sounded quaint and anachronistic; it was getting dark, and it was time for the evening meal.

Chapter Two

*T*here were four tables in the refectory; the watercolour group sat at one, the creative writing people at another, and the naturalists at a third. The tutors and other members of staff sat at the fourth. There was a brief introduction, given by a rather severe woman who seemed to be the administrative manager. It was explained that all the courses were interchangeable; if a watercolourist wanted to study bees for the day, he or she was perfectly entitled to do so, and vice versa. There would be several evening trips out to look for bats and owls, which were open to all.

The woman sat down, and Nan looked at the others on the staff table. She recognised Tad, and the man with the white beard. And there, sitting beside him, almost hidden, was the Asian youth. She moved her eyes quickly to the next figure. A woman with either a bad cold or hay fever, and next to her another man who reminded her of a hamster – ginger whiskers and thick sandy hair. Nobody was talking to anybody else. The man with the white hair was miles away, Tad looked irritable, and the Asian boy looked inscrutable. It didn't seem to be a happy team. The hamster didn't look anyone in the eyes, and he fiddled and fidgeted with his food and left early.

'What we all want to know,' said Gladys Grey, clipping each word as though she were tackling a topiary, 'is when do we get to meet her?'

'Simone Garnier, you mean?' said Imogen, helping herself to more bread.

'Yes.'

'You don't,' said a prim-faced girl with dark hair. 'Simone doesn't do any teaching.' Her name was Jocelyn.

'I didn't expect her to,' snapped Gladys. 'But I thought she might give a little talk or something.'

Jocelyn shook her head. 'No. I saw her in the distance, once. She doesn't mix at all.'

'Have you been here before, then?' Nan asked her.

'Several times,' said Jocelyn, but she didn't seem inclined to elaborate.

'Simone never has her photograph taken,' said Imogen. 'Got something against it.'

'But she uses photography herself,' said Megan.

'Not any more,' said Imogen, reaching for the tureen. 'If you've seen anything, I bet it was taken a long time ago.'

Nan began to feel very apprehensive about trying to meet Simone, and asking her about the picture of the child with the unfettered hair. Her initial curiosity had turned into something that was more like an itch, an irritation, something disagreeable that needed to be scratched.

It was only after she'd married Mike and was expecting her first child that the niggles had started – she was eighteen, and she knew nothing about her medical background on her mother's side. She had more sense than to ask her stepmother; she waited until she could get her father on his own.

He wasn't very forthcoming. Her mother had died of cancer when Nan was four. It had been very sudden.

When she asked him what sort of person her mother had been, he simply said, 'Look in the mirror.'

'I want to know what was she like as a person,' said Nan. 'Placid, volatile, academic, practical, happy, sad . . . You know.'

'She was very ordinary,' he said, tight-lipped.

What a legacy. 'Was she nice?'

'It's a long time ago,' he said. 'Let sleeping dogs lie.'

'That's not fair,' said Nan. 'She was my mother.'

'Frances is your mother,' said her father.

In the end, all she got from him was her mother's date of birth and her blood group. There was nobody else to ask, and then Darren was born and Nan's attention went elsewhere.

Nan gave herself a mental pinch to get back into the conversation. 'It's quite something though, isn't it,' Gerald was saying, 'to say you've actually stayed at Simone Garnier's house? I love her work.'

'I don't,' said Gladys.

Gerald looked at her. 'You never said.'

'I did, Gerald.'

'Do you think they do cocoa?' mused Imogen. 'I want an early night.'

Megan glanced at Nan. Nan smiled.

Four of them ended up in the library, drinking coffee and talking: the vivacious Lettie, the reserved Gerald, Megan and Nan. Megan seemed on edge about something; she kept glancing at the door. When she saw Nan watching her she didn't do it again.

'Klimt was a pornographer at heart,' Lettie was saying. 'All those women wearing lovely chiffon dresses – he painted what was underneath all that pattern and glitter first.'

'Really?' said Gerald, obviously wanting to pursue the conversation further, but not quite knowing how.

'I often wonder,' said Lettie, with a long slow look in

21

Gerald's direction, 'what women would have painted if they'd been allowed to.'

'What do you paint?' asked Gerald, fiddling with some coins in his pocket.

Lettie laughed. 'I like figurative stuff, which is why I like Simone's work. You remember that Asian boy at dinner, sitting at the table by the window? I wonder if he's her current model.'

Megan looked wistful. 'Do you think she lends him out?'

'On rainy days?' said Lettie, laughing. 'I doubt it. It'll probably be flowers or fruit in the studio.'

'Would you want to paint him?' asked Gerald.

'Oh, yes,' said Lettie. 'Those cheekbones, that hair. And the eyes. Quite expressionless. Devastating, in that face.'

Gerald leaned forwards slightly, took his hands out of his pockets and folded them on his lap. They looked oddly superfluous, as though they were unused to such exposure. But his face was less guarded; the air of a retired bank manager was beginning to leave him and he was coming to life. 'Why?' he asked.

'Because you don't know what he's thinking,' said Lettie, 'and that's exciting.'

The door at the far end of the library opened, and Megan looked round. Tad came in, accompanied by a pale middle-aged man with thin sandy hair and freckles.

'Hello, Megan,' said Brian. 'Fancy seeing you here.'

'Brian's in my pottery class,' said Megan to everyone, as though that explained everything.

'It's a very small world here,' said Tad. 'Sometimes I think it actually shrinks as you watch it.' He glanced at his watch, scowled, pulled up a chair and sat down.

'Who's the Asian lad?' asked Lettie.

'Cheng,' said Tad. 'He's a student.' He talked about the surrounding countryside for a while, and the most picturesque places to paint.

Gerald and Lettie seemed to go off at a tangent at

22

some point, and Nan only heard snatches of their conversation from then on – Gerald said, 'Without a codpiece?' rather loudly at one juncture, and Lettie got quite expansive about muscles a few minutes later.

'I think you have to be a tactile sort of person to do pottery,' said Megan to Brian. 'It's basically a physical thing.'

'There's a splendid pot in the entrance hall,' said Brian. 'Did you see it?'

Megan shook her head, although Nan was quite sure she *had* seen it.

'Oh,' said Brian, 'you must. Excuse us for a moment,' and they both got up and left the room.

Tad had sprawled himself across one of the leather armchairs. He had very long legs, and bits of him seemed to turn up in unexpected places. He looked at Nan. 'What's your name?' he said. 'I never remember names.'

'Nan.'

'Nan. And are you?'

'What?'

'A grandmother.'

'No,' said Nan, annoyed. 'It's short for Annette.'

'Oh,' said Tad. He looked bored, and started to flick through a magazine.

Nan felt slighted, but she couldn't think of anything to say. Lettie and Gerald seemed to have disappeared as well, now. She wished Megan would come back. He suddenly seemed to notice and said, 'Sorry. Tiring day.' He shut the magazine, stretched out his legs in front of him, closed his eyes and put his hands behind his head.

'Well,' said Nan after a moment or two, 'I think I'll turn in.'

'Oh, right,' said Tad. He opened one eye. 'Night.'

'Goodnight,' said Nan.

She left the library, and decided to take a short cut through the conservatory. This wasn't really allowed,

23

but everyone else seemed to have gone to bed. She tiptoed barefoot across the quarry tiles, moving from one patch of moonlight to another and hoping she wouldn't kick over any flowerpots hidden in the shadows. It was a big conservatory, Victorian probably, with little paths leading through a jungle of palms, lemon trees and succulents. Stone statues appeared here and there like ghosts, pale intertwined Grecian figures, doing disgraceful things to one another. Sappho, her arms around another woman, her head buried in her neck, their fingers laced together. A satyr, slant-eyed, leering, his hand round his erection. There wasn't a single sculpture that didn't have a sexual theme. She emerged from a tunnel of bougainvillaea, and saw the other door at the far end of the path.

The sigh stopped her in her tracks. It was a woman's sigh, low, drawn-out, languorous – and spine-chilling, because it sounded as though it were coming from one of the statues. She stood there, frozen to the spot, trying to adjust her eyes to the night.

'Oh, yes,' breathed a voice. 'Do that again . . .'

Another sigh.

'Oh, Sappho,' murmured the voice, 'your mouth really is sheer poetry. Don't stop. Oh, yes, lick me there . . .'

Nan felt an icy trickle of sweat at the nape of her neck. This was ridiculous; there had to be some logical explanation. A giggle. Some rustling; more moaning sounds. Then some of the foliage moved slightly, and she caught a glimpse of something white, over by the hibiscus.

'Faster,' said the voice. 'Oh, God, that's incredible . . . I don't know why women bother with men, I really don't.'

That voice . . . She'd heard it before. *Jocelyn*. That's who it was, the snooty one with the dark hair. Nan heaved a sigh of relief, and banished the supernatural from her thoughts. So Jocelyn was gay, and she was acting out an erotic little Grecian scenario with someone else, right here in this highly appropriate Mediterranean

24

setting. The sigh turned into a moan, then into a series of indrawn breaths, punctuated by tense silences.

'Yes,' moaned Jocelyn, 'oh, yes, keep doing that. Oh, deeper, deeper, right inside: oh, yes, there ... You can fuck with your tongue like no one else.' There was a gasp and then a muffled shriek, which subsided into a long groan of pleasure. 'Wow,' said Jocelyn eventually, 'that was spectacular. OK, Sappho, tell me what you want and I'll do it.'

'Run your fingers through my hair – yes – like that – then lick my nipples and play with them, blow on them, so they harden ... Tease the tips.'

'Like this?'

'Exactly like that.'

To Nan's surprise, she felt her own nipples harden.

'Now run your hand down my body. Open my legs. Touch me everywhere, so that I can't predict which orifice you'll tickle next ... Oh, yes, like that, as light as a feather ...'

'You're getting very wet.'

'You're getting very good.'

'I've been here before.'

'I know. Last year.' A giggle.

Nan was getting rather wet as well. She'd never fancied women but this eavesdropping was different – forbidden, wicked. The whole thing was making her as horny as Cheng's performance had made her feel. She just wanted to listen – and maybe touch herself a little at the same time. She slid her fingers inside her trousers and started to rub herself. It was a long time since she'd done that – after all, she shared a bed with Mike, even if nothing much went on in it apart from sleep.

'I'm going to put my finger inside you now,' murmured Jocelyn, 'but which hole am I going to choose?'

'I don't care,' said the other woman, her voice low and husky. 'Finger-fuck either of them and you'll get a result.'

'How about both at once?'

25

A strangled inhalation, a sob of ecstasy.

'Oh, you like it when I get really dirty, don't you? That's right, Sappho, squeeze me hard. I want to feel it when you come . . .'

A hand appeared in a pool of moonlight, reaching for the stars. Nan stepped back quickly into the shadows, not wanting to be seen. Something rigid was pressing against her, in the crease between her buttocks. She turned her head, and saw the leer of the satyr. The something rigid was his stone penis – the ultimate hard-on. She imagined him flesh and blood, and moved tentatively against him. Even though the friction was through her clothing, it was as arousing as any other sort of friction, and she let the sculptured phallus slide back and forth between her legs, from her clitoris to her anus, pressing a little harder each time.

'You love this, don't you?' whispered Jocelyn.

Yes, thought Nan.

'I can't take much more of this,' said the other woman. 'Finish me off.'

'Tongue or finger?'

'I don't care. Just do it.'

'Both, then.'

Nan imagined the satyr throwing her on her back and licking her like an animal, and she rubbed herself against him more forcefully. The feeling began to build, that delicious tingling sensation deep inside; her knees went weak, and she knew she was going to come. She caught hold of the statue's other hand to steady herself, shut her eyes and went with it.

There was a muted cry from the hibiscus; she hadn't climaxed alone. She just stood there afterwards, feeling a bit shaky and wondering what to do. She didn't think she could reach the door without being seen. Eventually she heard the other two get up; the door she'd entered by opened and closed, and she was free to leave.

* * *

26

She went back to the coach-house, wondering who Jocelyn's partner had been. A student from one of the other courses, maybe, for there was no one in the water-colour group of the right age or sex. But someone who'd been to Lavender Hall before ... She was so wrapped up in her thoughts that she barked her shin against an aggressively carved chair standing in the passageway. She could hear Imogen snoring in the downstairs bed-room, even with the door shut. The stairs creaked and the upstairs landing light wasn't working. Nan went to bed, feeling mildly appalled at her own behaviour, and fed up with Megan, but she couldn't get to sleep. She noticed a dog-eared paperback by Megan's bed, so she switched on her bedside lamp and picked it up. The cover was missing, but the title page revealed that it was called *Beyond The Estate*, by someone called Nicholas Cross. She'd heard of him, although she couldn't quite recall the context.

She flicked through it until the word *erection* caught her attention. Hm, she thought, so this is the sort of stuff Megan's reading these days. She settled herself against the pillow, turned back a page, and started to read with more attention. The author was writing from a woman's point of view, and doing it rather well.

I stood there at the carriage window, watching London turn from a grey ubiquity to a smudge on the horizon. The train was practically deserted. I glanced up as the man came through the intercon-necting door from the carriage in front. I suppose I registered that he was tall, dark, good-looking. When he came level with me, I squashed myself against the window to let him pass. I felt our bodies make contact, and something tugged at my sweater.

'Whoops,' he said, 'my belt buckle's got caught in your jumper. Don't move – you don't want it unrav-elling, do you? Just hold still, and I'll disentangle us.' He had a sexy voice. He was the sort of man I

27

might have wanted to know better, if we'd been properly introduced.

I couldn't turn to face him; I was stuck against the window, my back pressed against the front of his body. That was when I felt his erection through his trousers. I've always viewed an erection as a compliment to my femininity. And compliments are a turn-on, as long as they come from the right person.

He must have registered my sudden intake of breath. And the reason for it, because he said, 'What a pity we haven't been properly introduced.'

I laughed. I couldn't help it, the way his words were echoing my thoughts.

'I sometimes think things are more interesting without any introduction at all,' he said.

I felt his hand on my hip. Do I stop this now, I thought, or do I let it continue? Common sense said stop, but my body was saying something else altogether. His hand slid down my hip to my thigh, and then up again, building to an ebb-and-flow rhythm through the thin silk of my skirt. I felt myself respond to the pressure, moving into the stroke as it approached my crotch, moving away slightly as it receded. I felt his other hand lift the hair away from the nape of my neck, and the light touch of his lips. A small explosion of arousal took place somewhere below my waist. I tried to turn to him.

'No,' he whispered, 'we're going to stay as we are. Faceless. Nameless.'

I felt him swivel my skirt round on my hips, so that the side opening was now at the front.

'Unbutton your blouse,' he said. 'I know you're not wearing a bra. Press your breasts against the glass. No one inside the train will be able to see.'

I felt a surge of excitement at the prospect of this exhibitionist behaviour.

'Do it,' he whispered.

I did it. The chill of the contact was strange at first, but not unpleasant. My nipples hardened. I now had my face pressed against the window as well, sideways on, and I could see the green blur of the countryside flashing past.

I felt him unzip his flies. Then he took my hand in his, and guided it to his cock. The compliment was huge by now, and I ran my fingers up and down it, circling the head. I heard him gasp. He slid his finger through the opening in my skirt, and stroked me through the silk of my underwear. I felt myself getting very, very wet, and I squeezed his prick and increased my stroke. His hand slipped beneath the last shred of clothing between us, and I felt his finger enter me. He placed his thumb over my clitoris, and massaged it at the same time. My knees buckled, but I was supported by the window on one side, and his body on the other.

His breathing grew harsher, and his fingers more insistent. The carriage was still deserted, but the train was slowing. It wasn't a station; it would be another ten minutes before we reached Reading. The train shuddered slightly, and came to a stop.

There was a man on an old black bicycle, stationary, one foot on the path, the other foot raised as he adjusted his cycle clip. He was a middle-aged man, muscular – a farm worker maybe. He had a streak of white in his hair, like the crest of a cockatoo, and he was wearing a red vest with a picture of an anchor on it. To the left of the anchor was the letter W. There was a couple of days' growth of stubble on his chin. He looked up, and saw us. Instead of a dash of cold water at this sudden lack of privacy, I felt a rush of desire. The cyclist did a double-take; then he realised what we were doing, and he couldn't take his eyes off us. He laid his bicycle on the ground and unzipped his flies. His erection was quite apparent, even from this distance. He started to masturbate urgently, his eyes fixed on my breasts.

My nameless partner thrust his finger deeply inside me and, as I felt the tingle of approaching orgasm, his cock jerked in my palm.

All three of us came together. We stood there for a moment, sated. Then the cyclist zipped himself up again and got back on to his bike. The train pulled away.

Nan put down the book. Sex seemed to be on every agenda she encountered here – and where the hell was Megan? It was gone midnight. She turned off the bedside lamp, and went to sleep.

Monday. Nan filled a small bowl with cereal, left the refectory and sat on the low wall surrounding the herb garden. Megan had come back after Nan had fallen asleep, and she was still in bed. After a while the man with the white beard came out, accompanied by a woman with short blonde hair and thick glasses. They were both holding mugs of tea, and were deep in conversation.

Nan heard the woman say, 'How do you go about it?'

The man laughed. 'It's different every time. I'm sorry. I've forgotten your name.'

'Faith.'

'Faith. Have you read *Beyond The Estate*?'

'Yes.'

Nan pricked up her ears. It was the book she'd been reading the previous night.

'That one came from a couple of lines in a newspaper about a man who killed cats and kept them in the freezer – plus a snipe at someone I don't much like.'

Nan gulped. If this man had written *Beyond The Estate*, he must be Nicholas Cross, and presumably he was taking the creative writing class. His last book had won some prize or other. She just hadn't connected the name

30

with the man she'd met the previous day because the cover of the book had been missing, and with it the photograph of the author. She was surprised he did any teaching; he was quite a big name. It also explained why his face had seemed familiar – she'd probably seen a photograph of him in the newspaper.

'Did the someone you don't much like know it was him?' asked Faith.

Cross laughed. 'I doubt that he reads much. And certainly not my sort of book.'

Nan got up and went back inside. Neither Faith nor Cross noticed her go; perhaps they hadn't even been aware of her presence in the first place. She began to feel invisible.

Back inside the refectory there was now a definite air of anticipation. Megan had finally arrived, breathless and perfumed, her hair damp from the shower. Imogen was adjusting her army-style water bottle, and Lettie was tying the string on her sunhat. Gerald was sitting next to his wife. Nan saw him steal a quick glance at Lettie, and she saw Lettie smile impishly in return. Tad was leaning morosely against a pillar, ticking off names in a folder.

'Brian,' said Tad. 'Do we have a Brian?'

'Sorry,' said Brian, opening the door and sidling through it. He was festooned with so many different pieces of equipment that he had to negotiate narrow spaces in a crab-like fashion. He blinked at everyone, smiled, and stood next to Megan.

'OK,' said Tad, 'we're going to the top of the little hill this morning, to do some skyscapes.'

'It's just blue today, isn't it?' said Imogen.

'It'll cloud over later,' said Tad. 'It always does.'

They trooped out of the refectory and started off down a path towards some woods. The hill rose up about half a mile away. There was a pile of stones on the top, a cairn maybe, and gorse bushes dotted here and there as though someone had been throwing cadmium yellow

31

around. Brian stopped to take a photograph, screwing on lenses and fiddling with filters. Tad didn't slow down. Megan stopped to help Brian, and the two of them dropped out of sight as the rest of the party rounded the next bend. Tad glanced behind him, and saw Nan on her own. He slowed down and allowed her to catch up with him. 'I thought you came with a friend?' he said.

'So did I,' said Nan.

Tad grinned. It was the first time she'd seen him smile and it transformed his face; she saw someone who might be fun under different circumstances. Perhaps he just hated teaching.

'Whose idea was this painting holiday?' he asked.

'Megan's,' said Nan.

'Uh-huh. Married, is she?'

'Yes. We both are.'

'Why didn't you bring your husbands, then?'

Nan bit her lip. 'The only thing Mike can draw is money out of the bank,' she said, rather more bitterly than she'd intended.

'And thingummy's husband?'

'Megan's? He's into model aircraft. Spends his weekends swearing at little bits of machinery on the common and shouting at any children who get in the way.'

'So how long have Megan and Brian been having an affair, then?'

'What?'

He laughed. 'Happens all the time here. Perfect cover.'

She didn't know what to say.

'Don't tell me you thought they'd met up by accident.'

She shrugged, annoyed at having been used as an alibi. If it were true.

'Oh, well,' said Tad, 'there's always the bats and the owls. If you want something to do in the evenings.'

They lapsed into silence.

* * *

32

'Just spread yourselves out,' said Tad, when they reached their destination.

Nan glanced round. Neither Brian nor Megan had caught up yet, and everyone else seemed to be pairing off. Imogen teamed up rather surprisingly with Jocelyn, and just as Gladys got herself settled with Gerald, Lettie came by and said, 'There's a much better view from over there.'

'I'm not moving now,' said Gladys.

'I think I will,' said Gerald, and he picked up his stuff and followed Lettie, leaving Nan with Gladys.

Nan beat a hasty retreat.

She found herself a secluded spot surrounded by gorse bushes; she was feeling thoroughly resentful and not at all in the mood for delicate blue washes. A couple of clouds had appeared on the horizon, so she imagined them over the whole sky, drenched the paper and dropped in as many browns and greys as she could. The colours bore no resemblance to what was in front of her, but it was an excellent sky, the best she'd ever done.

'You're annoyed about something,' said Tad from behind her.

She turned round. He'd been standing there watching her and she hadn't realised.

'It's a good sky,' he said, 'angry. But you'll have to change the lighting on the landscape underneath.' He sat down on the grass, got out a notebook and started to sketch the view with a pencil, using it to shade the appropriate areas and give a tonal feel to the whole thing. 'You need to darken it up quite a lot here,' he said, accentuating something. He glanced up at her, sitting on her stool. 'Did you do much drawing as a child?'

'I don't know,' said Nan.

'You don't know? You don't remember?'

'I don't remember anything before I was eight,' said Nan.

'What happened when you were eight?'

She was surprised at his directness. 'My mother died when I was four,' she said. 'Then my father remarried. When I was eight.'

He stopped drawing, and Nan looked at the sketch. She knew she didn't have a hope in hell of getting anywhere near the atmosphere he'd achieved with just the pencil on its own.

She said, 'You drew a lot, presumably. As a child.'

'All the time. Look, you mustn't mind me. I'm just pissed off about a lot of things at the moment. Not the best of company.'

'Do you live here all the time?'

He laughed. 'No, thank God. I don't like teaching very much. Well, not these classes, anyway. I do it as a favour to Simone, really.'

Nan wondered whether she ought to confide in him about the photograph. She was going to need someone's assistance, that was clear; her chances of just bumping into Simone were looking increasingly remote. 'I suppose,' she said, 'everyone asks you what Simone's like.'

His face darkened, and she realised she was going to have to tread carefully. 'And you're another one of the paparazzi?' he said.

'No,' said Nan, 'because I have a personal reason for asking. Have you known Simone long?'

He hesitated. 'Eleven years.'

'You don't know what she was doing thirty-six years ago, do you?'

He looked surprised. 'No. No idea. I would have been ten. She would have been ... what, twenty-two. Just finished college. Why?'

'That exhibition she had. There was a photograph.'

'A photograph? She doesn't –' He stopped. 'I don't usually discuss Simone's –'

Megan's head suddenly appeared above the gorse, followed by Brian's. 'Sorry,' said Megan breathlessly. 'We got a bit lost.'

Tad stood up. 'You can set up here with ... sorry, what was your name?'

'Nan.'

'Oh, yes. Nan.' He smiled mischievously and she got a momentary flash of the other Tad; then he was back to his lugubrious self. 'I'd get a move on, if I were you,' he said dourly to Megan. 'It'll probably be raining by lunchtime.'

Megan started to unpack her belongings, and Brian put down his equipment.

'There's not enough room in this clearing for three,' said Tad. 'You'd better come with me, Brian; there's an excellent view from the other side.' Brian picked up his stuff and followed Tad off down the path. Nan smiled to herself.

Megan looked put out.

'Are you having an affair with Brian?' asked Nan.

'What?'

'You heard. You've used me to give a bit of credibility to your week away, haven't you? You don't care about the photo.'

'I do care about it,' said Megan, neatly avoiding the first question. 'And guess what, Nan – Brian and I actually saw Simone in the distance. She was walking across the field, with Nick. She looks a lot younger than fifty-eight.'

'Nick?'

'Nicholas Cross. He's the man who wrote –'

'I know,' said Nan shortly.

'Are you miffed about something?'

'Of course I am!' shouted Nan. 'I've hardly seen you. And you didn't answer my question. Are you having an affair with Brian?'

'Don't be silly,' said Megan. 'Are you going on the wildlife trek, this evening?'

'Yes,' said Nan.

'I don't think I will,' said Megan.

Somehow Nan wasn't surprised.

Brian came over later to share his lunch with them. He was pleasant enough but Nan felt like a gooseberry, although neither of them gave her any cause. He was a nice man, but nothing to get excited about.

It did cloud over for the afternoon, and Nan did some good skies, although she never quite matched the first one. She couldn't quite work out whether she was annoyed with Megan for not confiding in her and treating her like a fool, or whether she was just plain jealous. Not of Brian himself, but of the relationship she imagined they might have, which included sex and pottery and art galleries. But then, she hadn't confided in Megan about Mike's infidelity, the incident with Hugo Forbes, *or* the goings-on in the barn and the conservatory. Strange, the way they suddenly seemed to be growing apart after all these years.

Chapter Three

*I*t was raining by the evening, and the walk was postponed until it cleared up. Nan sat in the library, drinking red wine and leafing through the art books. Neither Brian nor Megan was there. Imogen was enthusiastically explaining the structure of owl pellets to a girl called Denise from the creative writing group, and after a while Nicholas Cross came in.

'Faith was looking for you, Nick,' Denise said to him, and he smiled.

Then he saw Nan, and he walked over and sat down next to her.

'On your own?'

'Apparently,' said Nan, 'though theoretically I came with a friend. Megan.'

'She's gone to bed early, has she?' Nick laughed. 'You want to say, yes, but not in her own room, don't you? God, this place has a strange effect on everyone.'

Nan stared at him. 'How do you mean?'

'The atmosphere. It just begs for stories to happen. Makes them happen.'

Nan looked sceptical. 'I'm a practical sort of person. I don't go for the supernatural.'

'I didn't really mean that.'

'So what's so special about the atmosphere here?' said Nan.

'Describe what you've picked up so far,' said Nick.

Nan thought for a moment. Then she said, 'Sort of . . . secretive, but intense. A collection of people thrown together by the vagaries of enrolment cards. Unexpected alliances. A mysterious guru-like figure who never meets the *hoi-polloi* . . .'

'Ah,' said Nick. 'There's the key. Are you familiar with Simone's work?'

'A bit.'

'What do you think of it?'

'It's very good,' said Nan.

'And the subject matter?'

'Interesting.'

He laughed. 'Interesting. What a terribly English thing to say.' He had a very sexy voice. There was a roughness to it, a grittiness, something only just held in check with BBC vowels and manicured consonants.

'All right,' said Nan. 'Erotic.'

'There's a lot of stuff she doesn't show.'

'What sort of stuff?'

He looked at her for a moment. Then he chuckled. 'Come on,' he said. 'You must know what I'm getting at. Klimt. Know anything about Klimt?'

'Oh,' said Nan, remembering what Lettie had said about Klimt painting his models nude before he dressed them. But after the first flush of embarrassment, she began to feel intrigued. What exactly was Simone working on? How far did you have to go these days before something was considered too risqué? 'Cheng,' said Nan, 'the Asian boy. Is he her model?'

'When it suits him,' said Nick. 'He's a postgraduate student. Very good, actually.'

'I didn't think Simone did any teaching.'

'She doesn't.' Nick filled her glass again. 'I'm not sure you can teach Cheng anything, anyway. It's a reciprocal arrangement. He gets to see her working; she gets to paint him. When he's in the mood.'

Nan decided it was safer not to ask what he meant by *in the mood*. She changed the subject. 'Why has Simone got a thing about photography?'

'Who told you that?'

'Everyone seems to know about it. She doesn't like having her photograph taken.'

Nick smiled. 'Do any of us, past forty?'

Nan felt irritated. First Tad had asked her if she was a grandmother, and now Nick was assuming she was over forty. She was, but only by three weeks.

'Some of us,' said Nick, the smile widening, 'are a lot further past forty than others.'

She laughed.

'That's better,' he said.

Nan studied him as she drank her wine. He was rather good-looking. The silver hair suited him, gave him a veneer of authority that was intriguingly at odds with the casual way he dressed. The veiled eyes were very light blue, analytical yet dissolute; there was a lazy confidence about his movements that suggested a younger man. There were a lot of contradictions about him. He could have been as old as sixty.

'When you first saw me,' said Nan, 'through the library window, you behaved as though you'd seen me before. Then you changed your mind.'

'You reminded me of someone.'

'Who?'

'An old flame,' said Nick. 'A very long time ago.'

She didn't quite know what to say. He was old enough to be her father, but this reference to a lover was like letting one drop of paint fall into a jar of water; the effects were minimal at first, but gradually permeated everything.

'Oh,' said Nan.

He laughed. 'This is the first time you've escaped, isn't

it? Your first taste of freedom, and you've forgotten how to flirt.'

She blushed.

'It's quite simple,' he said, 'and extremely good fun. I say something ambiguous, and you take it the wrong way. Then you say something and I misinterpret it. After that, we indulge in a bit of innuendo and a few metaphors. I invade your personal space on some pretext, you invade mine, we tell the odd tall story; then, if we're not too drunk, we have a brisk and witty exchange and say goodnight. Beats television.'

'You start,' said Nan, knowing by her answer that she'd had too much to drink.

'All right,' said Nick. 'How responsive do you think contemporary women artists should be to traditional male domination?'

She was surprised. 'Artistic domination?'

'All domination. At work, in government, in the home, in bed . . . How much control do you really have?'

She hesitated.

He smiled. 'Perhaps you don't really know. Do you usually feel that life just happens to you?'

'I didn't think real questions were allowed.'

'It wasn't a real question,' he said. 'Get into the part.'

She looked at him, a little uncertain.

'Invent a character.'

'I'm doing watercolours, not creative writing.'

'All right,' he said, 'I'll give you one.' He leaned back in his chair. 'Bored wife, undemanding job, nest empty, dull sex-life, no intellectual stimulation. Then that quiet sort of horror that creeps over all of us in mid-life, and a blind stab at doing something about it.'

'Right,' said Nan, thinking, to hell with it, I can be whoever I want to be here. 'I'd better have a blind stab at inventing yours then, hadn't I?'

He poured them both another drink and waited.

She tried to remember what she knew about him. Not a lot, really. He'd had his first novel published when he was in his early twenties; then a long period of obscurity, followed by a string of best-sellers.

'Successful author,' said Nan, 'tutoring on a creative writing course. Odd, really, because he can't be doing it for the money.'

The smile left his face, and Nan realised that she'd hit on something important almost by accident.

'Therefore,' she went on, 'he's probably been a friend of Simone's for some time. Divorced,' (guessing now) 'a grandfather,' (he grinned) 'and between novels. At a loose end, maybe.'

'Very good,' he said. 'That's stage one.'

'What now?'

'We switch the order around a bit.' He leaned across her to reach the bottle of wine. He didn't touch her, but he came very close and she knew that an invisible barrier had been crossed. She was now far more aware of his physical presence than she had been before. 'So,' he said. 'Tell me about watercolour. Is it an approachable medium?'

'I'm not sure,' said Nan. 'I'm not very experienced. If you get things in the wrong order it can cause a lot of problems.'

'So what have you been painting for the last twenty years?'

'Skirting board. Picture rails. Cots. Bikes.'

'Satisfying?'

'Occasionally.'

'But there has to be more to life than a coating of gloss.'

He was a bit too good at this for her comfort.

'Gloss is an excellent protective covering,' she said.

'Wrong answer,' said Nick, 'for your character.'

'You want to see her undercoat, I suppose,' said Nan.

'You're a very able pupil,' said Nick, raising his glass. He looked as though he was enjoying himself.

The library door opened and the hamster came in. 'It's

41

stopped raining,' he said. 'If anyone's interested, the walk's leaving now.'

Nick looked at Nan.

'I'm game,' she said.

They went outside. Faith spotted Nick immediately, and manoeuvred herself with great skill so that they left together. From then on she seemed to be attached to him by a piece of elastic. The hamster's name was Dominic; he was the leader of the expedition, and he was a zoologist. He fell into step with Nan, as though anxious to get away from his own students.

'Watercolours or stories?' he mumbled into his cagoule.

'Watercolours,' replied Nan.

'Ah,' said Dominic to his left sleeve. They walked for a while in silence. 'Bush cricket,' he remarked suddenly, and with evident relief, pointing his torch at a small green insect on a leaf. He started to search his pockets for something. Nan crouched down and peered at the cricket. It was rather cute, with a face like a horse and very long antennae. She watched it for a while, thinking that it would be fun to paint.

'Use this,' said someone, and an arm appeared over her shoulder, offering a hand lens. She turned round, looking up. Dominic had disappeared; the arm belonged to Nick. She thanked him, and focused on the cricket. It had golden eyes and a carapace that reminded her of the collar on a highwayman's cloak – apart from the fact that it was bright green.

'Actually,' said Nick, 'it's Dominic's lens. He's probably forgotten I've got it.' He turned to Faith, who was standing at his shoulder, her pale hair white in the moonlight, her eyes hidden behind the thick glass of her spectacles. 'You couldn't run on and give it to him, could you?'

Faith looked confused for a moment, as though she was unsure whether he'd given her an important task or her marching orders. 'Right,' she said, 'see you in a minute.' And she took the lens and walked away from them.

Nan could see that Nick was smiling. He noticed her looking at him and said, 'There's always one.'

'One what?'

'One disciple.'

They started to walk along the path after the others. There was a barbed-wire fence to their left, presumably denoting the perimeter of Simone's domain.

'You and Tad don't get on, do you?' she said.

'Nope.'

'Why?'

He shrugged.

'There seem to be a lot of secrets round here,' said Nan.

'What do you expect,' he said, 'with someone like Simone in the background?'

'What *is* she like?' asked Nan, hardly believing her luck at the opportunity she'd been given.

He took a deep breath and let it out slowly. For a moment, it looked as though he was going to back out of answering, the way Tad had, but then his face softened, and he smiled at her. 'Obsessive, unstable, self-centred, brilliant, bloody-minded, fascinating . . .'

'What does she look like?'

'Small, slim, brown eyes, waist-length hair, sort of honey-coloured; her skin is as well, she looks as though she's all one colour. As though she's been made from one piece of wood. And she's paranoid about her privacy, which is why – as a rule – we don't talk about her. Will that do you?'

She smiled. 'Yes.' At least she would be able to recognise Simone if she bumped into her.

They were quite a long way behind everybody now, and when the shriek came they must have been the only ones to hear it. Nan stopped dead in her tracks; the cry tore into her body like fingernails and tightened like a noose around her neck.

'Oh, shit,' said Nick, 'the bastard's caught another one.' He glanced up and down the length of the fence.

'Another what?' whispered Nan.

'Fox.' He found a slight dip in the ground, and lifted the strand of barbed wire as far as it would go. 'If you hold it here, I can get underneath.' He smiled briefly. 'Don't let go, will you.'

'Whose land is it?'

'Some industrialist. He has a very dodgy gamekeeper, though. Ex-army.' He wriggled under the wire.

'I want to come,' said Nan. If Megan was off into her own adventures, Nan felt she was entitled to a bit of excitement as well.

'It won't be very pretty,' said Nick. He lifted up the wire. 'Are you insured?'

'Third party, fire and theft.'

He grinned. She scrambled through the opening, stood up and brushed the leaves off her clothes.

'We are now the wrong side of the law,' said Nick.

'You're making it sound very dramatic,' said Nan.

'I can make boiling an egg sound dramatic,' said Nick. 'I'm a writer.'

They started off through the woods. Nan felt more alive than she had for a long time. She was looking and listening as hard as she could; there was a definite frisson of danger, and it was exhilarating. She hadn't really been scared of anything except an overdraft for years, and she suddenly realised that this was a minus, not a plus. She followed where Nick walked; occasionally they snapped a twig, and they spoke in whispers. The cry hadn't come again. The real danger was the gamekeeper.

Nick swore quietly, and held up his hand for her to stop. Then he broke off a small branch, and thrust it forwards. There was a sudden flurry of foliage and the branch shot up into the air, held in a loop of wire. 'Spring snare,' said Nick. 'Bastard.'

They started forwards once again, but with more

caution this time. Everything began to look more sinister: a holly bush mimicking a crouching giant, the stem of a creeper twisted snake-like round a tree-trunk, ferns coiled like cobras ready to strike. Nothing moved; it was as though everything was holding its breath just to watch them, for even the trees and the bushes seemed to be equipped with hidden eyes.

Then the animal screamed once more, very close, and Nick held up his hand. She heard a faint panting sound, and then all of a sudden Nick was smiling. 'Come here,' he whispered. 'You don't get to see this very often.'

Nan took a couple of paces forwards, and stood at his shoulder. There were two foxes, not one. The bigger of the two was sitting down, just like a dog, its tongue hanging out; the smaller was standing a few yards away, its back towards the other. After a moment or two, the bigger fox got up and approached the other. They sniffed one another rather delicately. Then the big fox mounted the little one and thrust like crazy for a few seconds, an expression of mindless ecstasy on its face.

'I don't speak fox fluently enough to distinguish between "Come and get me out of this," and "Come and get me, big boy,"' whispered Nick. 'The shrieks aren't that dissimilar. And they're very private about clickitting as a rule.'

'Clickitting?' queried Nan, equally softly.

'Foxes don't fuck, they clickit,' murmured Nick, his mouth brushing her ear. Nan suppressed a shiver, in case he misinterpreted it. But the sensation hadn't been at all unpleasant; quite the contrary.

The dog fox broke away and sat down again. The vixen sniffed herself, and looked thoughtful. Two minutes later, the dog fox mounted the vixen again, and repeated the procedure. How strange, thought Nan, watching two animals having sex. It feels a bit voyeuristic. But Nick's so matter of fact about it – it's one of the sights of nature, and we're privileged to have the chance to see it.

45

They watched for another twenty minutes, losing count of the number of times the animals mated. Then Nan sneezed, and the foxes vanished.

'Sorry,' said Nan.

Nick smiled. 'It doesn't matter. They couldn't have gone on much longer, surely? Makes an old man feel decidedly inadequate.'

She laughed. 'You're not old.'

They started to retrace their steps, and Nan stepped in a rabbit hole and stumbled. She swayed for a moment, trying to keep her balance and feeling like a fool. Nick caught her by the elbow before she could fall, and put his arm round her. There was something very welcoming about his body; she felt herself sinking into it, enclosed by his arms, safe. She had never felt like that with Mike. After a moment or two, she said lightly, 'I'm OK now,' and he let go.

They carried on walking, not speaking. Something sinuous crossed the path in front of them.

'Weasel,' said Nick. 'There's a lot of them round here.'

'Oh,' said Nan.

He held the wire for her, and she slithered back through. Then she did the same for him.

She realised that she was covered with dead leaves. He started to brush her down, fairly briskly at first, just her back and shoulders. Then he picked a few out of her hair; the touch of his fingers made her scalp tingle, and she caught her breath. He slid his hand down to her arm, and turned her to face him. She was struck once again by what a very attractive man he was: the soft white hair against the weathered skin, the expressive mouth and the secretive eyes. There was a slight smile in them, or was it a dare? He started to brush her down once more, his eyes never leaving her face. The palm of his hand smoothed something away from her shoulder, then trailed lightly across her breast and dusted it. Then he took his hands away, folded his arms and surveyed her from head to toe.

'Squeaky clean,' he said.

'On the outside,' said Nan.

He laughed. Then he said, 'What's the most difficult thing you've ever done?'

'Trigonometry.'

He shook his head in reproach.

'Oh, I don't know,' she said, resisting the temptation to give him another flippant answer. 'It's like the thing, the most difficult thing, it's still going on: it's been going on for the last twenty years and it never lets up. A sort of back-seat existence, never really being in the driving seat. The sickening bloody selflessness women have to go through, year after year. Making all the right decisions, and gnashing their teeth in private.' She stopped, surprised at herself. She'd enjoyed being a mother – loved it, in fact. She hadn't resented any of it.

'That was rather bitter,' said Nick.

'It just came out a bit –'

'No,' said Nick, 'it came out the way it should have done.' He glanced down at his clothes; he was covered with leaves as well. Then he looked up at her and smiled.

She started to brush them off, knowing full well what she was doing. He let her do it for a while; then he caught hold of her arms, pulled her towards him and started to kiss her. She put her arms round his neck and he pushed her back against a tree-trunk and pressed the length of his body against hers. What she'd done with Mike for the last twenty years suddenly seemed rather innocent; then jaded, boring and unimaginative. This was someone who knew very precisely what he was doing, someone who only needed the tiniest of signals to guide him. The kiss went on for some time, and the spangled imprint of the treebark was still on her shirt the next day.

He walked her back to the coach-house. 'We've got some gin,' said Nan, but her voice was tense and slightly unsteady.

47

He laughed and said, 'I think you need a tonic more.'

Everything seemed very focused and sharp: the pre-dictable squeak of the doorhandle, the staccato click of the latch moving back. Their shadows on the stairs, the creak on the top step, the smell of beeswax and lavender, the softer click as the bedroom door closed behind them. Megan, predictably, wasn't there. Nick glanced at the lock, then questioningly at Nan. She nodded, and he turned the key.

She was shaking. He turned her towards the open window, so that he could see her face in the moonlight, and said, 'You haven't done this before, have you?'

She shook her head. Unfaithful. The word sounded archaic, silly. Then deeply meaningful. Then silly again.

He held her at arms' length, his hands on her shoulders. 'Are you sure?' he said.

She nodded, although she didn't know how much of it was plain physiological desire, and how much of it was desire for revenge against Mike.

He started to unbutton her shirt. 'At this juncture,' he smiled, 'as you'll be a little out of date, we say things like, "I have no known diseases," and "as luck would have it, I've got a condom in my pocket".'

She laughed, but a voice inside her head whispered, does he carry them round with him all the time, then? What do you think you're *doing*, Nan?

He slipped her shirt down off her shoulders. She ignored the voice and started to unbutton his.

Everything seemed to drop a couple of gears. She unbuckled his belt, unbuttoned his jeans, unzipped them, moved them slowly down his legs. He stepped out of them and did the same for her. When there were no more clothes to take off, he lifted her on to the bed and spread her out like a starfish. Then he sat back on his heels and looked at her, his intentions written in his eyes – and it was so sexy that she wanted him to touch her, badly, and she reached out. He caught her wrist and placed her arm back on the bed beside her, above

48

her head. 'No,' he said, 'you're not to do anything. Just lie there, and don't move. Close your eyes.'

She closed her eyes. He took a long, long time arousing her, and he was very skilful. First one arm, then the other, stroking her lightly, skirting round the sensitive places at the outset, then touching the insides of her elbows and her armpits almost by accident. After that he dealt with each of her legs in turn, leaving the crooks of her knees and her feet till last. He sensitised area after area, avoiding the obvious ones and turning her hips and her shoulders into unexpectedly erogenous zones. Then the more naturally susceptible places – her scalp, the nape of her neck, her ears; only after that did he allow himself to touch her breasts, and once again it seemed almost accidental. Then she felt the tip of his tongue on her nipple; it was like a shock of effervescent water, and she writhed with pleasure. He put his hands on her hips and stilled her, and after a while his fingers travelled down and started to caress the folds between her legs, opening them a little further with each movement and tracing delicate patterns in the creases with his nails. He still hadn't touched her clitoris, and she wanted him to more than she had ever wanted anything in her whole life. Finally she couldn't fight the urge to move her hips any longer, so he rolled on top of her and entered her in one well-judged movement.

The sudden friction in the right place had a dramatic effect. She felt her body gather as though it were about to leap a hurdle – and then she came, clenching round his cock like a vice, relaxing, clenching, relaxing; the fizzing sensation even reached her fingertips.

He kissed her on the tip of her nose and stayed where he was for a little while. Then he started to move, very slowly at first, bringing her back, reminding her what they were about. She opened her eyes and watched him. There was a slight smile on his face; he was looking at her, gauging the pace, winding her up like an old-fashioned gramophone. Then faster, then very fast and hard, and she closed her eyes again and dug her hands into his back. She heard him groan as they both climaxed more or less together – syncopated percussion. They slithered apart and lay there, the breath knocked out of them.

After a couple of minutes he rolled on to his side and looked at her. 'You don't regret it, do you?' he said.

'No.'

'Good.' He was still looking at her, but his expression was strange; wistful. 'I think we ought to go back to the library,' he said finally, 'before we're missed.'

Lettie and Gerald were the only ones in there. They all smiled at one another, but stayed separate. Nick poured Nan and himself glasses of wine, and they sat in the deep leather armchairs and talked about literature.

After a few minutes, the door opened and Tad came in. He stood there silently for a moment. Then he said to Nick, 'She wants to see you.'

'Oh,' said Nick. He didn't move.

'Right,' said Tad, too quickly, 'I'll tell her you're busy.'

'No, no,' said Nick, standing up. 'I'll go.' He turned to Nan. 'Shame we didn't get on to poetry,' he said. 'Another time.' He left the library.

'You did quite well today,' said Tad conversationally. 'Those skies.'

'Thanks.' Nan felt extremely disorientated; the abrupt change of company had thrown her.

He looked at her. 'Why did you come back later than everyone else from the walk?'

She elaborated and extended the fox incident.

'That was bloody irresponsible, taking you in there,' said Tad. 'That gamekeeper – and he's not a proper one – he's a nut-case. It's only a matter of time before he shoots someone.'

'I did ask to go.'

'Why?'

'Oh, I don't know. I'm just trying not to be me, I suppose.'

He seemed to know exactly what she meant, for he smiled and nodded and spread himself out in his customary fashion, limbs everywhere.

'Listen,' said Nan, 'I'm not being nosy about Simone. I just need to find out about this photograph I saw.'

'The ones in that exhibition were lent by private individuals. Simone wouldn't have shown them. They don't belong to her any more.'

'I need to meet her,' said Nan.

He put his feet up on the table. 'Then you need to tell me more.'

'All right. Simone's photograph – the one of the child with the mad hair.' She could see from his face that he knew it. 'I think it's me. Aged four.'

He looked thoughtful. 'And you don't have any memories before the age of eight.'

She was surprised that he had remembered.

He got up and went over to the bookshelves. 'Yeah, I can see why it's important. Tricky, though.'

'You'll help me?'

'Mm.' He was running his finger along the spines of a row of large books. He stopped at one, pulled it out, flicked through the index and turned to a page. He held the book at arm's length and looked from it to her and back again. Then he covered part of the page with his hand, and looked at her again. 'Christ,' he said.

'Let me see.'

He handed the volume over, and got out his notebook. There was a reproduction of the photograph, smaller than the print she'd seen, but still clear.

Tad held out his hand for the return of the book. She gave it to him. He glanced at the picture, and started to draw. She watched the girl in the photograph emerge on his page, line by line. The likeness was exact. Then he shut the book and turned to Nan.

'Come closer,' he said, 'and watch.'

51

She went across to the leather chair and sat on the arm, so that she could see what he was doing from over his shoulder.

'As people get older,' he said, 'the proportions of their faces change. In a child, the features occupy a smaller area of the skull. There's more cranium. So the size of the forehead decreases in relation to the rest of the face as the subject ages.' He rubbed out the lines denoting the child's hair, and made the head smaller. 'The chin becomes stronger,' he said, altering it, 'and the bone-structure more evident.' He shaded inside the eye sockets.

She could see herself appearing on the paper; every additional line made it all the more obvious.

'Then we just need a change of hairstyle . . .' He glanced round at her, then back at his drawing. A few more lines, and it was finished. 'Yeah,' he said, 'reckon you're right. Unless you've got a twin.'

'I've never had any reason to think so.'

'What do you know about the time you can't remember? You must have asked some questions.'

'Not many,' said Nan. 'It wasn't a subject anyone was willing to discuss. I know next to nothing about my real mother. All my father ever said about her was that she was very ordinary.'

He laughed, but there was an edge to it, as though he understood how she must have felt about such an unflattering description. 'You don't know where your family was living, anything like that?'

'No.'

'I'll see what I can do,' he said. 'There's one thing you should know, though.'

'What?'

'That photograph of you was the last one she ever took. I don't know why. She's touchy about the past.'

'What will you do? Ask her about it, or engineer a meeting?'

'Play it by ear,' said Tad, 'like I always do.'

'Am I right in assuming that Nick is an old friend of Simone's as well?'

He made a face. 'He's known her longer than anyone.'

'So I should have asked him about it.'

There was a brief flash of annoyance. 'Do you want my help or not?'

'Yes,' said Nan. 'Why do you dislike one another so much?'

'Why do you ask so many questions?'

'Why are you so touchy?' Then she instantly regretted it and added quickly, 'I'm sorry.'

'If two of us start asking her about it,' said Tad, 'you'll never find out anything.'

'All right. I won't mention it.'

'And don't go asking Cheng, either.'

'I've never spoken to Cheng.'

'Good.'

It was as though they'd had an argument about something, although she had no idea what.

'I think I'll go to bed,' said Nan.

'Good idea,' said Tad.

Chapter Four

She took the short cut through the conservatory again, feeling perverse, but this time it was deserted. As she opened the door at the far end she realised that the window directly above her was part of Simone's private wing, and she could hear voices.

'You could have been a bit more diplomatic,' Nick was saying.

'Oh, *pouf*,' said someone. It was an exclamation, not an accusation; the voice was husky, with a slight trace of a foreign intonation. 'I need another woman, Nick. Someone less . . . you know.'

'I'm not your pimp, Simone,' said Nick.

There was silence for a moment, followed by the sound of something soft being stabbed with a sharp instrument; then the sudden rushing hiss of ripping canvas. Then footsteps, something thrown, wood splintering. Nan just stood there, half in and half out of the conservatory door, listening, not knowing whether to stay or go. The end result was that she just carried on standing there, her mouth slightly open, her hand on the doorknob.

'What do you expect me to do,' said Nick, 'pull another one out of a hat? Don't throw that –'

There was another thud.

She heard him shut the window and pull down the blind.

A crash, and splintering glass. *'Merde,'* said Simone, muted but still audible; then, *'Salaud.'* Nan could hear the sound of a struggle and a lot of heavy breathing.

'Right,' said Nick. 'I'll see you in the morning, when you've sobered up.'

Nan heard his footsteps cross the floor. She shut the conservatory door as quietly as she could, and made her way down the path. She felt a bit shaken at first; then she began to realise that Nick's voice had sounded more resigned than anything else, as though this was a scene that had been played out many times before.

It was very dark. She picked her way along the shrubbery and down a couple of steps – and bumped into someone. The someone switched on a torch and shone it straight in her face. Nan put up a hand to shield her eyes, and the light flicked over to the shrubbery. After a moment or two, she realised that the other person was Gladys.

'Sorry,' said Gladys viciously.

'Why didn't you have the torch switched on before?' asked Nan.

Gladys glared at her.

'What were you doing?' said Nan.

'None of your business,' said Gladys, and she stomped off, leaving Nan in the dark.

Megan wasn't back at the coach-house. Nan got into bed, picked up *Beyond The Estate* with a lot more interest than she had done the previous time, and carried on reading.

The second time we met was at a party. I saw him on the opposite side of the room, and everyone else blurred out of focus. Then he glanced up and saw me, and it was just a question of finding somewhere to do it. We both made our separate ways to the door.

'Bathroom,' he said.

We found it, went inside and shut the door. There was no lock.

'Oh, well,' I said. 'Another time.'

'Uh-uh. I want you now.' He glanced around – then he grinned. There was a broom standing in the corner. He wedged it under the doorhandle. Then he turned to me and said, 'Strip.'

'Are you sure that's wise? A quickie's one thing, lifting a skirt –'

'I said, strip.'

There was a dangerous glint in his eyes, and I liked it a lot. I stripped. He watched me, expressionless.

'On your knees,' he ordered.

I knelt.

'Fellate me.'

I took his cock in my mouth.

'You're good at this,' he said, after a while. 'But then, I expected you to be.'

He sounded far too composed for my liking. I wanted to make him really lose it. I speeded up.

'Enough,' he said suddenly. 'Now I want you on your back.'

I lay down on the floor.

'Open your legs.'

I opened them.

He lay down beside me, his feet level with my shoulders, and got going on the cunnilingus. This man had a PhD in oral sex, no question. It was like a game of chess – I moved one way, he countered the other. I feinted in one direction, he anticipated it. He began to circle my clit with his tongue, never staying long enough in one place for me to out-think him. I pushed against him but he retreated; he wasn't going to give me satisfaction just yet. My whole body was as tense as a bowstring. If he'd plucked me in the right place he'd have got an instant bulls-eye.

'Please,' I whispered.

'Ssh.'

He teased me for a few minutes more. Then he rolled on top of me and started to fuck me. The hard surface of the floor only accentuated his thrusts, and each one took me closer and closer to the point of no return. I was thrashing my head from side to side, and the room was a kaleidoscope of colour – the blue of the shower curtain, the pink of the tiles, the brilliant white of the swan-shaped linen basket . . . A look of triumph crossed his face, but I could tell he was near the end of his self-control. I squeezed him as hard as I could, and then we both –

Megan opened the door. 'Good walk? Brian and I spent the evening in the library.'

'Really?' said Nan, closing the paperback as quickly as she could. 'All evening, eh? Anyone else there?'

'No.'

'Just you and Brian, looking at books.'

'And having a drink.'

'*I* was in the library,' said Nan. 'First with Nick. Then I went on the walk. Then I went back to the library and talked to Tad.'

'Ah,' said Megan, kicking off her shoes. Then she said, 'Nick? Nicholas Cross? I knew he was teaching here, this week. I brought one of his books with me – oh, you're reading it. What's he like?'

'Where were you?' demanded Nan.

'Playing dominoes.'

'In Brian's room.'

'Yes.' Megan was struggling to keep a straight face.

'I'm not stupid,' said Nan.

'It's just a bit of fun,' said Megan. 'Don't go all prudish on me. I'm not about to leave Terry or anything.'

'You used me.'

'I wanted you to have a good time as well. Come on, Nan, you've just spent one part of the evening with a famous author, and the other with a well-known painter. Tell.'

'Why didn't you tell me about Brian?'

'I didn't think you'd understand. Lighten up, for goodness' sake. You're on holiday. Behave like it. Hasn't the atmosphere of the place got to you yet?' Megan started to take off her make-up. 'It's all topsy-turvy, here. Brian and I have been ferreting around. Nightcap?'

Nan shook her head. Megan poured herself a gin in her toothmug, and stood it on the dressing-table.

'It all goes back to centuries of women being painted by men. Simone's trying to redress the balance. You know Rob?'

'The randy social worker on our A level course?'

'Mm. I went out to lunch with him. There we were, in this café – enclosed on all sides by glass, no sound at all from outside – and all these secretary-types walking through the concourse eating their crispbreads. I asked him which women were a turn-on, him being the expert. Narrowed it down to high heels, tight skirts and long hair. Entirely visual. It got me thinking, though. What would happen if I started looking at men like that?'

Nan laughed.

'I'm serious,' said Megan. 'We don't, we women. We're well trained. We go for humour, intellect, power, money: sensible things. I think what Simone's doing in her painting is trying to make us look again. You ought to try it. It's fun. I started doing it in the street, but there wasn't enough time. We don't respond to visual things the way men do, instantaneously. So I began watching Brian, during pottery. It got really addictive. Wet hands moulding clay, naked arms, sinews, tendons, pots rising up from the wheel in long cylindrical shapes, that sort

58

of thing. He noticed me watching him, of course. He sort of jumped on me in the clay-store, we were both grey from head to foot by the time we'd –'

Nan bit her lip.

'Bloody hell,' said Megan, 'you've never slept with anyone except Mike. Haven't you ever wondered what it's like with someone else?'

'Of course I have,' snapped Nan. Why couldn't she just *tell* Megan what had happened? Was it because she felt guilty? Or was it because the experience with Nick had become too precious already, and she was scared it wouldn't happen again?

Megan squeezed something out of a tube and started rubbing it slowly into her forehead. 'Well, try undressing Tad tomorrow,' she said, 'and see how you get on. Drop-dead gorgeous, that one.'

'I don't think he is,' said Nan.

Megan turned out the light. Nan lay there in the moonlight, unrelated images flitting through her mind in the surreal way they did just before sleep overtook her. Megan's car turned into the linen basket from the bathroom scene in Nick's book; she could see it so clearly, the painted wickerwork, the way its neck arched, the buttercup-yellow of its beak . . .

Tuesday. Nan woke early and went for a walk on her own. As she turned the corner by the barn she saw Tad carrying something that looked like a torn canvas. He spotted her, and stopped. For a moment he looked ill-at-ease. She waved, and carried on back to the coach-house. At the last moment she glanced behind her, and saw him going into the barn.

Megan missed breakfast again. Only the ginger-whiskered hamster and the administrator were sitting at the staff table this morning. Gladys was smashing up a banana with the back of a fork, and Gerald was poking moodily at his toast. Finally he pushed his plate away from him and said, 'I went down to the stream, Gladys.

59

That's all. I listened to the frogs, saw a water-vole, and came back.'

Gladys glanced at Nan and said icily, 'Nice weather today.'

Nan could take a hint. 'See you later,' she said, and left.

There was still half an hour to go before they all met up and went off to their venue for the day. Nan slipped out of the refectory, and made her way over to the barn. She finally found what she was looking for in a corner, covered with tarpaulins – Simone's mutilated rejects. She glanced round, ascertained that she was on her own, and started to smooth out the creased pieces.

Everything had been cut and slashed and muddled up. She picked up a scrap of canvas and examined it. Half a face, the eye unfocused, dreamy. Nan realised it was the woman she'd seen the first evening, the one with hay fever. Without the swollen eyes and the runny nose she was very pretty, but the fragment had decapitated her, and there were no clues as to what the rest of her body was doing. She put it down and picked up another piece. A man's foot, the bones looking fragile and delicate beneath the skin. It had been torn off above the ankle and she wanted to stroke it, it was so lifelike – and she knew she would have half-expected a response.

She went through the other fragments, but they were just as obscure. She counted seven elbows in one triangular piece, but she couldn't decide which bits of anatomy belonged to whom. It was like a jigsaw puzzle. Then she realised that something she had taken for the stem of a plant was, in fact, a ponytail, and the naked shoulder and sliver of neck probably belonged to Tad. She wondered whether she'd come across other bits of him without knowing.

Again she glanced round, for there was something so voyeuristic in what she was doing that she felt uncomfortable, but her curiosity was more powerful still. And there was nobody watching her; she was quite safe.

Another piece, another hand. This one had to be Tad's, surely? It was big and square and sensitive, awkward and practised at the same time. She'd watched him when he'd been drawing, and she remembered it well.

In the end, she only found three fragments that would actually fit together. She spread them out on the ground. Initially, it was rather confusing. Then she identified an arm, a wrist, a hand. The brushwork was very precise but the colours were unexpected, blues and greens, flesh by neon-light. Simone had a way with bodies, no doubt about it. The skin was cold velvet, veins and muscles suggested beneath.

One of the slashes had cut right through a hand, a female hand. Nan peered closer, wondering what the hand was holding. She turned the piece of canvas this way and that, trying to work it out. Then she realised that the painting must have had more than one model, and it all began to make sense. The other model had been a man, and what the woman was holding was his erect penis – she could make out the milky droplet of moisture glistening on the end of it. Had someone modelled for this? It looked too accurate to have been painted from imagination. She sat back on her heels and tried to imagine the whole thing. The more she tried to place the two intertwined figures in her head, the more difficult it became. The man could have been Cheng. His body was absolutely beautiful, one curved muscle inter-cut with another. For the first time she found a work of art visually erotic, but it was like looking at an inkblot – one moment it worked, the next moment it didn't.

A tiny shred finally, just an eye. Black, slanted, expressionless – definitely Cheng's. But whichever way she held it, it watched her; she put it back rather hurriedly, for it seemed to have a malevolent life of its own.

She sat back against a bale of hay, deep in thought. She wanted to see the rest of Simone's work very badly now. But what was more astonishing was the fact that she wanted to do it herself. Why paint a sky when you could be painting skin? Why bother with bushes when you could be tackling hair? The mood of the weather seemed tame and two-dimensional compared to the mood of a human being. She glanced at her watch, and realised with a shock that it was half past ten.

By the time she had located her class it was nearly a quarter past eleven, and the sun had become very hot. Megan and Brian had parked themselves under a tree, and Brian had stripped to the waist. He looked pale and middle-aged and suburban, and Megan was watching him with ill-concealed lust. Nan sidled off down the path a little way and set up on her own. To begin with, nothing went right; her trees looked lifeless and dull. Then she noticed Jocelyn in the distance, perched pixie-like on her stool. She started to draw her, remembering how her hand had looked in the conservatory, reaching for the stars. Or had it been the other woman's hand?

Tad came over and stood behind her, looking over her shoulder. 'You had a rake through the barn, then,' he said finally.

There was no point in lying about it. 'Yes,' said Nan.

He walked round in front of her and sat down on a tree-stump, resting his arms on his knees. His shirt was open to the waist, and she could see the skin creasing where he leaned over, describing muscles rather than flab. He must have been about the same age as Brian, but they could have been fashioned from entirely different materials. She tried not to look, but Megan's words and Simone's painting were a powerful combination.

'You ought to think about texture a bit more,' he said.

I am thinking about texture, thought Nan. Skin.

'Try doing some plant studies. Comfrey, that's a good one. Or would you rather be doing figure-drawing?'

'I would now,' said Nan.

'Go on, then.'

She stared at him. 'Draw you? I couldn't.'

62

'Why not? A blurring of boundaries?'

She didn't know what to say.

He smiled. 'Simone's work can have an odd effect on people.'

Nan put down her brush. 'I wish I could see what she's doing. Properly. The bits I saw were incredible.'

'Last night wasn't the right time to ask her about the photograph,' said Tad. 'But I will. I'll try and get her to see you up there, in her studio.' He opened his rucksack, took out a can of beer and offered it to her. She shook her head, but she couldn't take her eyes off his hand, for it was definitely the one she'd seen in Simone's painting.

'So why don't you want to draw me?' he asked.

'There's not enough time now,' said Nan.

He grinned. 'Rubbish.'

'You're quicker than me.'

'Race you.' He got out his notebook and pencil. 'Come on. How much can you do in two minutes?'

'Two minutes?'

'Chicken?'

She laughed, and got out another sheet of paper.

He glanced at his watch and fiddled with it. 'Go.'

She started to draw. There wasn't time to check things or rub anything out; she just scribbled over the top, harder, and the drawing became tonal without her even thinking about it. Their eyes met from time to time, cursory, businesslike; then the alarm on his watch went off.

'Time's up,' he said, and they put down their pencils.

She looked at what she'd achieved in amazement. It was, without question, the best figure-drawing she had ever done. The body was solid, real; there was hardly any detail, but what there was counted. She gave a little laugh of disbelief.

He held out his hand and she passed it over. She watched his eyes roam over the page. He looked up, smiling. 'You don't need me to tell you it's bloody good, do you?' he said. 'You know.'

'I want to see yours.'

He handed her his notebook. The previous drawing he'd done of her had been almost entirely linear; this one was exclusively tonal, and very powerful. She saw a side of herself she'd never seen before: someone determined, excited, uninhibited. But it was her, no question, and an extremely skilful piece of work.

'I'm envious,' she said.

'But you were quicker than you thought you'd be.'

She smiled. 'Yes. A very successful demonstration, all in all. Does that happen to everyone when you set that exercise?'

'I haven't done it with anyone else,' he said. 'Except Simone.' He took a drink from his can of beer, and wiped his mouth with the back of his hand. 'And that's a bloody nightmare,' he added, 'because she's absolutely ruthless. You never like yourself very much afterwards.' He stood up. 'I suppose I'd better go and see what the others are up to. Imogen's been painting some nice broccoli.'

'Broccoli?'

'Trees,' said Tad, and went.

She joined Megan and Brian for lunch again. Then Jocelyn came over, and Gladys, and before long everyone was there except Lettie and Gerald.

'Birds of a feather, your Gerald and my Lettie,' said Imogen to Gladys, slicing a cucumber with a Swiss army knife.

Nan could see Tad smiling into his sandwich.

'Well, he won't get any lunch if he doesn't turn up soon,' said Gladys, 'I'm not wasting it.' She took another hard-boiled egg.

'I've finished,' said Nan. 'I was going to go for a walk. I'll see if I can find them.'

'I'll come with you,' said Tad. 'I can show you some of that comfrey I was talking about.' He stood up in his rather untidy fashion, tucked his notebook into the back pocket of his jeans and glanced at the sky. There wasn't a cloud anywhere. He took off his shirt, and stuffed it in his rucksack.

'Maybe you should be hoping for a change in the weather,' said Tad, as they followed the path through the gorse bushes towards the other loop of the stream.

'Why?'

'If we have to stay in, we could do some life painting.'

'Who would we use as a model?' asked Nan.

'Well,' said Tad, 'there's always Sniffle.'

'Who's Sniffle?'

'The woman with hay fever. She's a horticulturist: supervises the greenhouses and teaches botany, but she doubles as a model.'

'Bit of an unkind nickname,' said Nan.

'Don't blame me,' said Tad. 'Blame Simone.' He stopped suddenly. 'Hey, hey,' he said, 'supper. Chanterelles.'

Used to a supermarket, Nan felt really apprehensive at the idea of just picking toadstools and eating them. On the other hand, she didn't want to question Tad's expertise, because he looked as though he knew what he was talking about. He picked one and handed it to her. 'Smell it.'

She smelled it. 'Apricots,' she said.

'*Cantharellus cibarius*,' said Tad, 'in case you're worried.'

Nan gave him a watery smile.

'We'll get them on the way back,' said Tad. 'If you're really paranoid I'll show you how to do a spore print.'

'No,' said Nan, finally convinced. 'I trust you.'

'Oh, do you?' said Tad.

They walked for a while without saying anything. Then he stopped again, and Nan realised that something was moving in the ferns to one side of the path, less than a stone's throw away. He turned to her and put his finger to his lips. She looked questioningly at him. He spread out his hands as if to say, it's not my fault, but she could see he was struggling quite hard not to laugh out loud.

'What?' whispered Nan, wondering if more wildlife was copulating for her amusement.

'Sh.' He took her by the arm and moved her to a slightly different position so that she was standing in front of him, and she could see through a gap in the ferns.

The first thing she saw was Lettie's sunhat, lying in the shade. Then she saw Gerald's shirt, folded quite neatly on a stone by a dead branch. The patterns of the shadows made it difficult to discern one shape from another at first glance. She leaned forward slightly to see better, but Tad pulled her back, and she found herself pressed against him, her half-naked back against his bare chest. They just stood there, both facing forwards, his arm still round her, holding her wrist – and then she realised what she was watching.

What she'd thought was a patch of sunlight was, in fact, Gerald's right buttock. And the dead branch wasn't a piece of wood at all, it was Lettie's left leg. And the way the ferns were moving had nothing to do with the breeze. There wasn't a breeze.

'I think we ought to . . . well, go,' whispered Nan.

'Why?' said Tad softly in her ear. 'When elephants do it, the whole herd gathers to watch.'

'Elephants,' she repeated, unable to think of anything else to say. She wanted to move but she couldn't; any step forwards would have given them away, and any step backwards was impossible.

'And I've got my sketchbook with me,' whispered Tad.

She turned her head to look at him, aghast. He grinned, and she had no idea whether he was serious or not. But the position of her neck was uncomfortable, and she couldn't hold it for longer than a couple of seconds. She had little alternative but to look at Lettie and Gerald, although she couldn't see their faces.

'Think of it as another lesson,' he murmured. 'What material are you prepared to use, and what material aren't you prepared to use?'

Lettie's leg was at full stretch now, toes pointed, foot twisted slightly inwards. The ferns were speeding up.

'And what material,' whispered Tad. 'Are you prepared to research?'

It was the strangest art lesson she'd ever had. She was very aware of the physical contact between them, although their positions were unconventional as neither of them could see the other's face. All communication between them was either tactile or aural; he had made sure she could only see in one direction. Straight in front of her, just like the woman on the train in Nick's book.

'When people start painting,' he said, his voice very low, 'they see it as a separate activity from the rest of their life. It isn't. If you don't paint what arouses you, in whatever sense, you might as well not bother.'

She could hear Gerald's breathing now; there was a sort of whistle with every inhalation, ending with a catch in the throat. Lettie's foot moved convulsively, and knocked over a bottle of lemonade. Neither of them seemed to notice. Nan watched the lemonade froth on the ground before it seeped away.

'Details,' said Tad. 'Remember the details. Nice little visual metaphor for semen there.'

The way Nan was standing was putting a strain on her calf-muscles; if she leaned back a little it would ease, but if she leaned back she leaned right into him. She leaned back, and the connection spread in two directions like a ripple, from the small of her back up to her shoulders, and then down to her thighs. He brought his other arm round her and moved his head very close to hers so that he could talk softly in her ear.

'Look at the shadows cast by the trees,' he said. 'The patterns describe the form of the bodies; convex, concave. The arm, look at the arm . . .'

With her slight change in position Nan could now see

67

Gerald's back. Lettie's arm was thrown across it, her fingers practically in spasm, but it was a delectable curved shape, dappled with sunlight, surprisingly youthful.

Tad ran his finger up the inside of her wrist to the crook of her elbow. 'This is the important bit,' he said, 'this shape here.'

Nan knew that if he touched her like that once more she would go to pieces completely. Every bit of her body seemed to be ten times as sensitive as usual – the slightest pressure had a corresponding effect between her legs, as though the nerves had decided to link up in one great sexual conspiracy. She knew she was wet, so wet that it might even show if you looked in the right place. It was one hell of a struggle just to keep her breathing sounding normal. What's happening to me? she thought. It's as though all the years of denial have been swept away, and I'm getting turned on by absolutely everything.

And then she thought: this activity I'm watching is actually incredibly beautiful, taken in isolation like this: moving shapes, fragmented images, rhythms and patterns. It's only the years of conditioning that make me not want to watch.

'Curiosity,' whispered Tad. 'Lose it and you might as well be dead.'

Lettie's hand was stroking Gerald's spine in time with his thrusts, starting from just below his shoulder blades and ending in the crease between his buttocks. 'The reason this is so suggestive visually,' said Tad, 'is because you can only see bits. The whole scene would be too explicit; no leeway for the onlooker's imagination.'

She really didn't trust herself to say anything at all now. There was an ache in her groin that could only be relieved by one thing, and keeping still required a supreme effort of will. Then, with one final flurry, the ferns stopped moving, and she heard both the protagonists sigh. Tad stepped back and pulled her with him, and after a few more paces they were out of sight and he let go.

'I can't believe we just did that,' said Nan.

He grinned. They carried on walking along the path towards their original destination. The track was over-hung with brambles, and it twisted round fallen trees and dipped suddenly from time to time. Occasionally they bumped into one another, but it didn't seem to matter; the relationship had changed subtly in some way.

'There is no shame in this place,' said Tad. 'That's what makes it so different. You leave your morals at home.'

'Do you have another home?'

'Yes,' said Tad. 'But when I'm here I'm someone else.'

'Who?'

'Simone's lover,' said Tad. 'Didn't you realise?'

'No,' said Nan. 'I didn't.'

'Coo-ee!' The voice cut through the woods like a chain-saw.

'Christ,' said Tad, 'it's Gladys. We don't want her to find them, do we?'

Nan thought about poor downtrodden Gerald, enjoy-ing himself for once. She shook her head. Gladys spotted them, and started to walk over. Tad and Nan met her halfway.

'Any joy?' asked Gladys.

'You bet,' said Tad. Then he smiled charmingly and added, 'They went that way,' and pointed in the opposite direction.

'I wonder why,' said Gladys, but she went.

They had only walked a few metres further when Lettie appeared, slightly dishevelled and faintly flushed. But her eyes were sparkling, and she couldn't stop smiling.

Tad bowed from the waist.

'Thanks,' said Lettie.

'Don't mention it,' said Tad.

'I'm not very likely to, am I?' said Lettie.

They all laughed. Nan felt part of a completely different world, one where the usual rules didn't apply: a looking-glass land, a fantasy country. It was as though a sexual undercurrent ran beneath the grounds of Lavender Hall like an underground river, irrigating everyone into an unwitting state of slight arousal, seeing everything differently as a consequence, and not quite knowing why.

'So what are you two up to?' asked Lettie.

'Nature studies,' said Tad.

'Chanterelles and comfrey,' added Nan quickly. In the distance she could see Gerald above the ferns, now that he was on his feet; he had his back towards them, and he seemed at a bit of a loss.

'See you later,' said Lettie.

Tad and Nan carried on down the track to the stream. They fingered the comfrey, stroked the foxgloves and fondled the mud, looking for ever more ridiculous examples of textures. Then they took their shoes off and dabbled their feet in the stream.

'You told me to be curious,' said Nan, 'so I shall be. How much of the year do you spend here?'

'Six months,' said Tad.

'And the other six?'

'We don't talk about out there,' said Tad, 'not when we're here.' He wriggled backwards and lay down on his back in the grass.

She turned to look at him. He had closed his eyes; she let her own eyes wander, unobserved, and she tried to see him Megan's way. He had a strong face with a wide mouth and high cheekbones: not conventionally handsome but sensual, sexy. His black hair was scraped back into a ponytail – quite thick hair, shiny. His body looked well used but hard, and he was evenly tanned. Slim hips, long legs, a scar on his forearm, big bones, an awkward grace. Was that what Simone saw, too?

He opened his eyes and smiled at her. Then he glanced at his watch, and sat up. 'Back to work, then,' he said.

They collected the chanterelles, and when they got back to the group everyone was suitably impressed. Imogen extolled the virtues of shaggy parasols and inkcaps. Gerald said he'd never dared to eat anything he'd found himself, Lettie said there's always a first time, and Gladys said that as far as Gerald was concerned the first time was likely to be the last time. He couldn't tell a mushroom from an aubergine unless it had a barcode on it.

Tad looked up at the sky, which was clouding over, and said, 'Thunderstorm later.'

Nan settled down as well as she could for the afternoon, but nothing seemed to go right and she packed up early. When she went over to Megan and Brian she found them preparing to leave as well; the sky was very dark now, and there was an occasional gust of wind. They walked briskly back to the house, and got under cover just as the first drops of rain started to fall.

'We're all going out tonight,' said Megan, after dinner. 'There's a super little pub in the next village.'

'Oh,' said Nan sarcastically. 'I'm going to get some of your company this evening for a change, then, am I?'

'Unless you've got other plans,' said Megan. 'Nice walk with Tad, was it?'

In the past, Nan would have told Megan everything that had happened; they'd have had a giggle, said good for Gerald and then dismissed it. But somehow she couldn't, not now; she didn't want to turn it into a joke. She realised that Tad really had been trying to teach her something, and he had succeeded. Simone, Tad, even Megan – they had permanently altered the way she looked at the human body.

Chapter Five

*I*mogen packed nine people into the Range Rover. Gladys had taken one look and pleaded claustrophobia. Gerald pretended not to hear, and Imogen drove off. It wasn't a very comfortable ride. Imogen slewed the vehicle round the bends and accelerated away from them as though the hounds of hell were after her. By the time they reached the pub, everyone except Lettie was as white as a sheet.

'You really are a brick, Imogen,' said Lettie cheerfully, 'not drinking so that you can drive us back.'

Faith went over to the payphone and peered intently at the minicab numbers.

Nan found herself sandwiched between Damon and Trevor, two of Nick's students. They seemed to find her presence mildly irritating so Nan stood up and excused herself, and went to the washroom. When she came out, a group of men had taken over the tables outside the door, and she couldn't get past them. Most of them had their backs towards her, and they were talking so loudly she couldn't make any headway.

'Bloody good ratter, that dog o'yourn,' said one of the group.

'He's an artist, is old Monty,' said a big man with

72

black hair. There was a streak of white in it, and an image of a badger shuffled into Nan's head.

As though the subject had been raised out loud another man said, 'How is old Monty with badgers, then?'

'Butch ain't got no badgers *left*,' said someone else.

There was a scattering of laughter.

''Ere, Cotter,' said one of the men, suddenly noticing Nan, 'there's a nice young lady as wants to come past you.'

Cotter turned to Nan and smiled slowly and unpleasantly. 'Dunno about that,' he said, 'she's one of them from that house.'

'There's some funny things as goes on up there.'

'There's rumours – ain't there, Mickey.'

'Very free and easy, so we're told. Know what I mean?'

'She's gone there to paint men with their clothes off.'

'What about me, then, darling? Come outside and I'll give you a preview.'

'Excuse me,' said Nan levelly, trying to push past Cotter's legs. Then Butch was in the way, and she was caught between the two of them.

'Hey, Butch, make her press herself against you to get past,' said one of the men.

Butch leaned across the table and grabbed the speaker by the throat. 'Shut up, you,' he snarled, 'Bloody smut, that's all you lot think about.'

Nan slid past Butch, went back to her own group and sat down next to Brian. Although Brian made a valiant effort to include Nan in the conversation, they didn't seem to have the same tastes in anything. The conversation limped along from one topic to another with all the goodwill in the world – and the most inert chemistry imaginable. Lettie and Gerald were sitting huddled in a corner; at half past nine a minicab turned up for Faith, and three others went back with her. The rain trickled down the windows as the evening dragged on, and when it was time to go Nan was heartily relieved. She knew she'd been hoping Nick would turn up, and she knew she was disappointed that he hadn't.

The lights were still on in the library when they got back, and Brian and Megan elected to join whoever was in there for a nightcap. Nan trailed along behind them, unwilling for the moment to brave the dash through the storm across the courtyard to the coach-house. Gladys was drinking cocoa, and Faith was reading one of Nick's books.

Jocelyn started to talk seriously about Simone's work. She was very clued-up, and mentioned such diverse sources as Egon Schiele and Georgia O'Keefe. Nan poured herself a white wine and listened, although her mind's eye kept doing reruns of Jocelyn in the conservatory and she had trouble keeping a straight face. Megan played footsie under the table with Brian; Gerald had abandoned Lettie and was sitting next to his wife, looking edgy. After half an hour or so, Nan excused herself to go to the loo. The one in the main building was next to the studios the painters used on rainy days; she hadn't seen them yet, and she was curious. She opened the door, and fumbled for the light-switch. It wasn't anywhere obvious so she went inside, feeling her way round the easels. She could see the silhouettes of a couple of plants, a row of pots, some chunks of driftwood. She edged her way round them and headed for the doorway to the second studio.

A rustling sound, distinct from the rain that was lashing at the windows. Then a sigh. Bloody hell, thought Nan, who have I stumbled upon this time? She moved as silently as she could to the doorway, and peered into the gloom. There was a faint flickering light; it was coming from an oil lamp, the old-fashioned Aladdin variety. She could see a sort of dais at the far end of the room, covered with drapes. There were two figures on the little platform, one standing, one kneeling, and after a moment or two she realised that the standing figure was Trevor, one of Nick's students she'd met in the pub. He seemed to be wearing a toga.

She heard him say, 'Listen, slave, unless you want a good whipping, you do as I say. Now suck me, nice and slow – and then, if you've done a really good job, you can fuck me.'

'Whatever you say, master,' replied the other figure. And the other figure was a man – Damon.

I don't believe it, thought Nan. First Jocelyn and whoever it was, and now these two. What a syllabus: short stories, small mammals, watercolour and voyeurism. But she was intrigued, in spite of herself. What did men do to one another? She found the prospect of watching them disturbingly erotic. As silently as she could, she edged forwards until she was standing behind a huge cheese-plant, hidden by the leaves, but still able to see.

She saw Damon part the toga with his fingers. Trevor's cock appeared as if by magic, pointing at the ceiling. Damon bent forwards, and licked it from the root to the tip.

'I said suck it.'

Damon put his mouth round it, and sucked.

Trevor seized Damon by the hair and started to move his head for him; Damon put his hands on Trevor's hips to steady himself. Gradually, Trevor's grip loosened. After a little while, a glazed look came over his face, and he let go of Damon's hair and just stood there. 'By the nine gods,' he said huskily, 'you know how to make a man come.'

Damon moved a little faster.

'I don't want to come in your mouth,' said Trevor. 'I want to come all over your face.'

Damon stopped sucking. 'Whatever you wish, master,' he said. He started to wank Trevor, sliding his palm round the shaft in a circular motion. There was a mischievous smile on his face; it looked as though both participants were thoroughly enjoying themselves.

'Faster,' ordered Trevor.

Damon wanked him faster, cupping Trevor's balls in his other hand and gently caressing them.

Trevor threw back his head, arched his back, and came. The spunk shot out, spurting over Damon's face, and trickled down his cheek. Nan felt an accompanying tingle of arousal. A man's orgasm was a man's orgasm, however it was achieved.

'Did I please you, master?'

'Not quite enough, minion,' said Trevor. 'Take off your toga.'

Damon did as he was told, sliding it down his body as provocatively as possible. He had a stiff erection, and his eyes were bright with anticipation.

'On your front, across the dais.'

Damon lay down, his buttocks slightly raised. Trevor picked up a thin supple switch that was lying beside him, and brought it down on the right cheek. Damon jerked, and sighed. Trevor struck the other buttock. Damon groaned, but it was a groan of pleasure, not pain. Trevor hit him again. 'No more master, I beg you,' pleaded Damon, but the tone of his voice implied something else entirely.

Trevor whipped him a few more times, although Nan suspected that he wasn't putting a great deal of force into it. Then he said, 'You're enjoying this far too much, slave. Stand up.'

Damon stood up, his cock arcing out from his body.

'Now you can fuck me,' said Trevor, throwing off his toga and lying down in the same position Damon had adopted.

'Whatever you say,' replied Damon. He spat on the palm of his hand and ran it round his dick, sliding the foreskin back and forth experimentally a couple of times. Then he smeared Trevor's puckered arsehole with saliva, very carefully and delicately, and slid his cock into him. After a moment or two he began to move – slowly at first, then faster.

'I'm going to fill you with spunk,' growled Damon. 'Hot and wet, just the way you like it. Your wish is my command. Your wish is always my command.'

Trevor gasped and clung on to the dais, his fingers clenching around the fabric. With each thrust, he moved a little further forwards.

Nan watched, fascinated. Seeing two men at such a pitch of excitement was making her feel astonishingly horny. The two figures were locked together in front of her, lit by yellow guttering oil-light, their shadows strange and unearthly against the drapes. Damon raked his hands across Trevor's sweat-speckled back, and Trevor moaned. The fingermarks were long red lines in the lamplight. Nan could hear both men panting, as though they were taking part in a race. Then Damon's ragged breathing stopped for a moment; a series of grunts followed, and Nan realised that he had climaxed.

'We must try that again some time,' said Trevor after a moment or two.

'Practice makes perfect,' replied Damon, 'and Rome wasn't built in a day.'

They both laughed, and kissed each other affectionately on the lips. Nan tiptoed back through the doorway, back through the first studio, and back into the hall.

She returned to the library, sat down, and carried on listening to Jocelyn talking about contemporary art. Her mind kept drifting back to Trevor and Damon – and every time it did, she experienced a little start of surprise when she remembered how turned on she had been by it.

Suddenly there was a rumble of thunder, and Gladys stiffened.

'She doesn't like thunder,' said Gerald.

'I'd have an early night, if I were you,' Lettie said to Gladys. 'Take a sleeping tablet or something.' Her white hair was tied back with an Indian scarf, and she was wearing a pair of really gorgeous dangly earrings, lapis lazuli and filigree silver. Gladys looked ten years older by comparison, although it was Lettie who was the elder of the two.

'When I want your advice,' said Gladys, 'I'll ask for it.'

Gerald swallowed hard and smiled weakly at Gladys. Gladys started to talk about delphiniums in a tight, high-pitched voice.

Then the library door opened, and at the same time there was a theatrical flash of lightning. Nan saw Tad silhouetted demonically in the doorway, one arm against the architrave, the other holding open the door. There was a crash of thunder; the floor shuddered and Gladys whimpered. The lights flickered, and went out for a moment. Tad was still in the same position when they came on again, although Gladys was now under the coffee table and Lettie was laughing.

Tad beckoned to Nan. She could see that he was soaking; he was wearing a white shirt that was semi-transparent with water, and his jeans were so wet they looked as black as tar. He beckoned again, and she went over.

'Don't mention the photograph straight away,' he said, 'Simone thinks you're going to see her for something else. Come on.' The lightning flickered across his face.

'Why are you so wet?' asked Nan.

'Because I thought you were in the coach-house,' said Tad irritably.

She followed him out into the hall as the thunder did its stuff again, and then up the staircase. His arrival had been so sudden that she hadn't had time to be nervous. He steered her along the landing, and then through a curtained door that led to the wing that was above the conservatory.

'What other reason?' asked Nan suddenly.

'She needs a model,' said Tad.

'*What?*'

He laughed. 'Got a better idea?'

She glared at him. 'No.'

The moment they were through the door, the bohemian atmosphere intensified. There was a faint smell of incense, and the walls were crammed with paintings: large ones, small ones, drawings, screen-prints – a frieze of bodies, one painting dissolving into another, a succession of lovers scrambling for her attention. The door at the other end of the passage had been reinforced, and it was festooned with locks. Tad took a bunch of keys out of his pocket, and opened it. She heard music, faint, strange – Gorecki or Glass or someone like that – and voices. Then she was in Simone's studio, and the voices stopped.

It was a huge room with angled windows in the roof. The walls were painted white, and plastered with sketches and colour tests, all tacked up in a random fashion, some of them overlapping, some of them swinging at crazy angles from drawing pins. There was a set of shelves down one side, overflowing with oddities; she saw a carriage-clock, a human skull, a bunch of honesty, a pile of drapes, jam jars, a stuffed platypus ... Against another wall there was a jumble of enormous embroidered cushions – the only furniture, apart from a brass coffee-table on which stood a bottle of vodka and some glasses. The ceiling had some sort of tracking system from which hung a number of stage-lights, but they were all switched off. A dim pink glow issued from a lamp standing by the window, and its base was made from two intertwined bodies. In the centre of the studio there was a dais, with a sheepskin rug on it. To one side stood an easel, and a bench covered with brushes and tubes and bottles and tubs. Three people were sitting on the cushions, drinking: Nick, Cheng, and a woman wearing a long brown dress. Her feet were bare, and her hair hung over her folded knees, the same colour as the dress. She looked up, and for a moment she just stared. Then she smiled.

'Hello,' said Simone.

She waved a hand at the cushions, and Nan sat down. Nick smiled at her with real warmth and she felt singled out, special. Cheng got up, went over to the shelves and found another glass. He poured Nan a vodka without asking her if she wanted one, put some ice in it, gave it to her and sat down again. Tad took off his shirt, grabbed a towel from the shelves, and untied his hair. Nan hadn't seen him with it loose before; he shook it back from his face and started to dry it.

'Tadeusz says you want to see my paintings,' said Simone.

The full name took her by surprise. Tad had no accent, she'd forgotten he wasn't English.

'Yes,' said Nan.

Simone was looking at Nan in a very appraising way, and it felt extremely odd because only men had ever looked at her like that before. If Tad hadn't told her about himself and Simone, she probably would have thought Simone was gay. Then it suddenly occurred to her that Simone might be bisexual. Was Simone the one who'd been Jocelyn's Sappho in the conservatory? *'I've been here before.' 'I know. Last year.'* But Jocelyn's Sappho hadn't had the slight French accent; it had to have been someone else.

'Relax,' said Simone. 'Whatever you've heard about what goes on up here, it's probably ... true.' She laughed.

Tad dropped the towel on the floor, and sat down next to Nan.

'Oh, for God's sake, Tadeusz,' said Simone, 'you're soaking. Take them off.'

Tad stood up again, took off his jeans, then his underpants. He looked wryly amused, and he didn't hurry it. Then he strolled over to the shelves, took a sheet of printed cotton material, tied it round his waist like a kanga and sat down again. He was suddenly transformed into someone very exotic, black hair spread over his shoulders, bare-chested, tanned legs crossed. He reached behind him, and passed Nan a plate. 'Have a chanterelle,' he said. 'They're a bit cold now, but they're nice.'

Nan took one of the tiny orange mushrooms and tried it. It tasted slightly peppery, and there was a fragrance to it. She felt rather daring.

'What were we talking about?' asked Simone.

'What we waste,' said Nick.

'*Ah, oui.*' They began to talk about ideas that didn't go anywhere, at what point you knew you were flogging a dead horse. Tad and Nick seemed to disagree about almost everything. Nan felt as though she was in rather exalted company so she just listened, and watched Simone at the same time. The moment her glass was empty, Cheng refilled it.

Simone had a striking face: a hooked nose, a sharp chin, and deep-set light-brown eyes. In anyone else the combination would have been a disaster, but her eyes flashed and her mouth was full and sensual; there was an electric charge to her, spicy, dynamic, sexual. Her laughter was so suggestive, it bordered on the obscene.

Cheng said very little. Nan wondered how on earth she was going to broach the subject of the photograph. There didn't seem to be any way to steer the conversation in that direction. She glanced at Tad. He didn't seem inclined to help. Cheng filled her glass again, and she knew she was beginning to feel a bit tipsy. She hardly ever drank at home, and she'd consumed more alcohol in the last two days than she had in the previous two months.

'If you don't try out different things,' Tad was saying, 'you don't move on.'

'I experiment. Of course I experiment,' protested Nick.

'No, you don't,' said Tad, 'I read your last one, and you're not doing anything different. Same old characters.'

'Spotted yourself, did you?' said Nick.

'If you mean the git with a fridgeful of cats,' said Tad, 'yes.'

Nick laughed. 'That was the one *before* last.'

'I enjoyed it,' said Simone.

Tad looked at his feet and twiddled his toes. 'Are you going to show Nan your paintings,' he said, 'or am I?'

Simone turned to Nan. 'Are you pissed enough?' she asked.

Nan nodded.

Simone stood up. 'Come with me.'

Nan got to her feet. The room tilted for a moment, then righted itself. She followed Simone into another room. The thunder carried on rumbling in the distance, right on cue.

Simone shut the door, leaned against it and laughed. 'They'll sit and trash one another's work for hours,' she said. 'It's mock-fighting. I love it.' There were paintings stacked all round the walls, facing inwards so that they couldn't be seen, and folders of drawings on a bench: a sort of store room. 'Tadeusz says you're rather good,' said Simone. 'He doesn't often say that. Most of the time he just whinges about his students.' There were a couple of bentwood chairs standing in a corner. Simone pulled them out, picked up one of the folders, sat down, and indicated to Nan to do likewise. Nan sat down, torn between wanting to get the business of the evening over, and wanting to see Simone's work and hear her talk about it. If she mentioned the photograph straight away, she might not get to see anything.

'I show you these on the understanding that you don't discuss them with anyone,' said Simone. 'Tadeusz spent a long time convincing me you needed to see them, but he did convince me, so here we are. *Voilà.*' She opened the folder and handed Nan the first sheet of a set of drawings. 'I started off oh-so-very-tentatively,' she said, 'playing safe: you know?'

Nan looked at the drawing with something approaching awe, and went on to the next. They were anatomical studies of men's bodies, fearfully accurate and yet strangely evocative, with real definition between hard and soft structures. There were a lot of hands. Gradually the male hands were joined by female ones, and the juxtapositions became more suggestive. The last in the series was of a man's hand on a woman's breast, with obvious reference to Bronzino's painting in the National Gallery. But the man's hand was big and square instead of white and delicate, the tone a lot darker, the fingers powerful. This was the female version of the painting: for what woman would want to be touched up by a pre-pubescent Cupid when there were other alternatives?

Simone was smiling at her. 'You understand that one, don't you?' she said. 'Thank God for that.' She put the drawings back into the folder, and got out a portfolio. 'I went on to these,' she said. The drawings were still accurate and textural, but now they were of men's hips and thighs and genitals, different bodies in various states of arousal. The pencilwork was unbelievable, and the designs intricately beautiful: Arthur Rackham behind closed doors.

'They're fantastic,' said Nan, with such feeling that Simone laughed.

'But oh-so-stilted,' she said. 'I was just acquiring the vocabulary. Then I started to put it all together. I wanted to paint pictures for women. Men have had it their own way for far too long. We've had to be content with what they think is beautiful, or erotic, or pornographic. You think they painted all those naked women for the glory of God?' She laughed. 'I don't think so. And how about *Le Déjeuner Sur L'herbe*? *Le Déjeuner Pour Les Hommes*, more like. Now it's our turn. But unfortunately it isn't as simple as that, is it?'

'No,' said Nan. 'There's a huge difference between the way men see women, and women see men.'

'*Voilà*. It's a time-difference.'

'What do you mean?'

Simone stood up and went over to a stack of paintings. 'Men want a snapshot. Women need a narrative.'

'Is that why,' said Nan, her heart in her mouth, 'you went off photography?'

'Partly,' said Simone, but she bristled and Nan could see that Simone didn't want to go into it. She decided to bide her time.

Simone turned the first painting round, and Nan caught her breath. It was big and very dark, a semi-abstract forest. There were lots of thorns and briars and tangled shapes, which partly obscured the two figures Nan eventually made out in the foreground. Once she'd spotted them, she didn't see how she could have missed them. Then she realised that the painting was a reworking of *The Sleeping Beauty*. But the handsome prince had decided to wake the princess in a rather more direct fashion, and the kiss wasn't on the lips. Nan knew she was smiling; the idea was so funny and so appropriate.

'You see,' said Simone, 'it's easy when you already have a story. You just slot the new information into it, so; the motivation of the subjects is already there.'

'Men did that as well, though. The judgement of Paris was a particular favourite.'

'*Oui*,' said Simone, pulling out another painting, 'but you still get that freeze-frame feel to it, that the story is incidental, and the exploration of female flesh paramount. The women in the paintings have no right to reply. They're just there for male consumption.'

The next few were also reassessments of well-known tales. There was one of Red Riding Hood seducing the wolf, and another with Prince Charming as a foot-fetishist; Nan realised it was a development of the watercolour Hugo Forbes had found so arousing.

'These are all old themes,' said Simone. 'I did them, what, fifteen years ago. I had to get them out of the way before I tried something new; I'd never exhibit them. But they're not rejects. They're just stages in a process.'

Nan thought they were wonderful; she hadn't

84

expected the dark humour that ran through these paintings. Prince Charming looked rather like an El Greco Christ, wearing just a towel and washing Cinderella's feet. The dwarves all symbolised different aspects of sexuality, but they were part of the forest; they grew out of the tree-stumps and boulders.

Simone leaned the paintings back against the wall. 'So,' she said, 'I then had to start thinking about writing my own stories.'

And that's where Nick's involved, thought Nan. Do the two of them work together? Is that it?

'I wanted to paint something for Everywoman,' said Simone. 'Something for you and me, the woman next door, the traffic warden, the checkout girl, the granny – all just as capable of having an orgasm as the pin-up girl. No?' She glanced round the room as though she'd lost something. 'I need another drink,' she said. 'Go and get some more vodka from the studio, and I'll prop these up. They're fairly recent ones.'

Nan went back to the studio. One of the spotlights had been switched on now; Nick was reading, Cheng was lying naked on the dais and Tad was drawing him. 'OK?' said Tad, without looking up.

'Drinks,' said Nan, feeling slightly unsteady but determined not to show it.

'Oh, bloody hell,' said Nick. 'Not two evenings on the trot.'

'Bad luck,' said Tad, still drawing.

'Where are you spending the night, then?' said Nick.

Tad put down his pencil. 'Where the fuck do you think? Picking up the pieces. Unless you're volunteering.'

Nick glanced at Nan. 'I'll sort the drinks out,' he said. 'You go back in with Simone.'

'Thanks,' said Nan, and she went.

When she opened the door to the store room, she saw that Simone had arranged the paintings all the way round the room, next to one another and with no gaps. She looked pointedly at Nan's empty hands.

'Nick's doing it,' said Nan.

'Suitably diluted with tonic, I think,' said Simone. 'Oh, well. Start at the left, and work your way round.'

The references to well-known stories and other artists' paintings had gone. These canvases were harder to take in; it required time to disentangle the complexities of shadow and pattern. There were no women in the first few of the series. All the subjects were men, their eyes directed out of the painting and straight at the onlooker. To begin with, Nan found the inclusion of women's clothing and jewellery odd, although the combination of lace and muscle was a powerful contrast; gradually she noticed that the clothes had in fact been discarded, and left draped around the painting as though they belonged to somebody else. With a jolt she realised that the somebody else was *her*: the onlooker.

She looked more closely at the last one along the second wall. The sitter was black, tribal scars on his face, hair intricately woven, painted designs on his chest and arms. His eyes seemed to focus on her, urgent, intent. Swathes of bright printed materials surrounded and partially covered him: beads and leather, shells and feathers, a riot of colour and design. The man was naked, one hand caressing what at first seemed to be part of a necklace; then she realised it was his erection, head on. The effect was electric – the subject was reacting to *her*.

'I like that one, as well,' said Simone. 'But it still doesn't go far enough. What came before and what will come after is suggested, but I'm still leaving too much to the imagination.'

Nan turned to the paintings on the third and last wall, and now she was looking at people she knew. Sniffle featured in one; Tad in another; Cheng in several. These were more dynamic, interactions between two people, fairly explicit foreplay but with an odd twist – the faces were looking out of the painting, enticing her in.

The door opened, and Nick came in with a tray. He smiled.

'They're incredible,' said Nan, 'absolutely incredible.'

Simone looked pleased. 'You'll do it, then?'

'Do what?'

'Pose for me.'

Nan's mind raced. She hadn't been able to turn the conversation the way she'd wanted, and if she didn't pose for Simone she didn't know whether she'd get another opportunity. If she did say yes, she was in with a real chance. And underneath it all ran a little strand of vanity she never knew she had, whispering – to be painted by Simone Garnier. To live on, in paint. *Oh, yes.*

'*Bon,*' said Simone, as though Nan had agreed. 'Bowl of cherries. Know what I mean?'

Nan didn't. She suddenly realised that Simone was very drunk: she just disguised it awfully well.

'Tomorrow evening, then . . .'

'OK,' said Nan.

'Going to bed,' said Simone. 'Stay and rummage. *Bonne nuit.*' She walked out of the room with great deliberation, hit the doorjamb on the way past, swore in French, and vanished.

Nick sat down on one of the chairs. 'You've never posed for anyone before, have you?' he said. 'Simone isn't just anyone, either.'

'I realise that.'

'No,' he said, 'I don't think you do. She's moved on from those.' He waved at the paintings on the last wall.

'Do you work together?' asked Nan.

'Yes.'

'How?'

'It's difficult to explain. We sort of throw ideas at one another, fight over them, rip them to pieces, reconstruct them . . .'

'Does she work with Tad as well?'

'Ah,' said Nick. 'You've touched a nerve there.'

'He wants to and she doesn't?'

'No,' said Nick. '*She* wants to and *he* won't. It's rather an emotive issue.'

Nan couldn't quite see why.

Nick noticed her perplexity and said, 'Simone couldn't have children, Nan. Her paintings are her kids, she cares passionately about each and every one of them. It's as if Tad has consistently refused to father a child on her. She keeps trying to persuade him, but he won't budge. Oh, he helps out from time to time with the rest of her brood, but he won't embark on a proper just-the-two-of-them project with her.'

'Nick,' said Nan, 'what *is* the set-up here? I can't work it out.'

'Complicated,' said Nick.

'I gathered that much.'

'You're going to be staying on next week, aren't you?' he said thoughtfully. 'If you're modelling.'

This hadn't occurred to Nan. 'I can't,' she said. 'My job.'

'Take some time off.'

'We need the money.'

'Simone throws money at people like confetti,' said Nick. 'Don't worry about it.'

Stay on. The idea appealed a lot. She went over to the last set of paintings, as she hadn't had a chance to look at them properly. But it was different looking at them, with Nick there. 'I really would like to know what's what around here,' she said.

'Simone was my French pen-friend,' said Nick, 'when I was at school. Then she came to college over here, and stayed. We've been lovers on and off for nearly forty years. More off than on.'

'Oh,' said Nan, unable to think of anything else to say because all of a sudden she seemed to be hurting somewhere.

'I don't see a lot of her,' said Nick gently. 'I come

88

down here to teach a couple of times a year; Simone was left the house by an admirer on the condition that it was used for educational purposes. Why don't you give the watercolours a rest tomorrow and come to my class instead?'

'I don't know . . .'

'Loyalty to Tad?'

'He's taught me a lot,' said Nan. 'I don't always get on with him, though; he's a bit touchy at times. You don't like him, do you?'

'No. And it isn't just because he's younger than me. He's Simone's lover, too, and he doesn't like it when I turn up. You're not shocked, are you?'

'No,' said Nan, 'although I would have been this time last week.' You liar, Nan, she thought. You knew about Tad already – and don't pretend you're not upset to learn that Nick and Simone are an occasional item, as well. She decided to keep quiet about enlisting Tad's help; Nick wouldn't be pleased.

'It's a state of mind, this place. You do what you feel like at the time. Something either leads to something else or it doesn't, and many threads get entangled. Once in a while, we need some new blood.' He looked at her rather directly. 'And this year – you're it.' He got up, went over to her, turned her to face one of the paintings and stood behind her, his hands resting on her shoulders. 'What do you see?'

The painting she was looking at was one of Nick. The whole thing was very misty and atmospheric; he was standing behind a woman, someone she didn't recognise, with one hand gripping her wrist and the other on her thigh. They were both looking directly at her. She shivered. Nick slid his hands down her arms, and took hold of her left wrist. The other hand carried on down the side of her body and stopped at her thigh.

The door opened. Nan glanced over her shoulder. Tad was standing in the doorway, still wearing the cloth; he looked them both up and down. Nobody said anything.

Then he glanced at the painting, smiled nastily at Nick and said, 'A closet Post-Modernist, and I never guessed.'

'She's gone to bed,' said Nick, annoyed.

'I know that.'

Nan disentangled herself. 'It's probably time I went.'

'See you in the morning, then,' said Tad.

'No you won't,' said Nick. 'She's coming with me tomorrow.'

'Suits me,' said Tad, and he went.

'That wasn't fair,' said Nan, feeling guilty. 'I hadn't decided.'

'We're working together,' said Nick. 'I want to find out how you think.' The hooded eyes were smiling at her, and the prospect of collaborating with him felt really exciting. He ran his finger up her thigh. 'Which one of Simone's paintings turned you on the most?'

'There were several,' said Nan, determined to be honest. 'The black guy, the Sleeping Beauty ... the one in front of us.'

'Masturbation, cunnilingus, and mirrors. I think I can handle that.'

He walked to the other side of the room and moved a couple of canvases, behind which was a mirror. He turned to Nan and beckoned her over. Then he took off her shoes, and moved them both into the same positions they'd been in when they'd been looking at the painting. She saw herself standing there, Nick's head resting on her shoulder, one of his hands holding her wrist, the other on her thigh. She glanced at the open door.

Nick smiled at her in the mirror. 'They've all gone to bed. There's only you and me.'

The hand on her thigh slid round to the buttons on her dungarees and started to unfasten them, quite slowly, one by one. Each little thump of released material felt like another step down a one-way street, and each little patch of newly bared flesh felt like one more step towards a cliff-edge. When he had finished unbuttoning her, he let go of her wrist, and slipped the

90

garment off her shoulders. It crumpled around her ankles. She stepped out of it, and then she was standing there in just a pair of plain white briefs and her bra. He removed the bra with practised ease, hooked his thumbs under the waistband of her briefs, slid them off and sat her on the bentwood chair, legs apart. She could see herself in the mirror, the brown bush of hair between her thighs, the tiny slash of pink peeping through. She had never looked at herself quite like that, and she felt a twinge of arousal.

Nick stripped. He had a wiry, muscular body, very neat and symmetrical. He arranged all the discarded clothes in a pile, and sat down in the middle of them, facing her. She could see his cock, head-on, exactly the way the African guy's had been in Simone's painting. He touched himself, making it look almost accidental. Then he did it again, and his cock jerked slightly. He started to play with himself more deliberately, his hooded blue eyes never leaving her face. They were several feet apart, and the distance that separated them only heightened the sexual tension. She wanted to reach out and touch him; she wanted skin. She wanted to run her fingertips through his soft white hair, letting it drift between her fingers. He smiled slightly, his hand moving up and down his cock slowly and sensuously, his eyes saying, It's you that's making me do this, I can't help myself. She wriggled on the chair, and the friction of the seat made her feel randier than ever. His smile widened a fraction, but he didn't speed up. There was a hypnotic quality about what he was doing; she felt quietly dreamy yet strongly aroused, the way she sometimes did on waking. There was a clock ticking somewhere in the background, and he was keeping time with it. She saw a bead of moisture appear on the end of his prick. He slowed to a stop; then he stood up, walked over to her, took her by the hand, led her over to the scattered clothes and lay her down on them, opening her legs wide.

'And now for the Sleeping Beauty,' he said. 'Close your eyes.'

Nan closed her eyes. She felt his lips brush her nipples; first one, then the other, and she felt them tighten. His tongue, just on the very tip, making her wriggle. His beard, stroking her breast; his fingers on her thighs, light as feathers. They travelled up between her legs and gently opened out all the folds, stroking lightly in between them, making her squirm with pleasure. His tongue began a long slow journey down the length of her slit, soft and warm and wet, lingering here and there, lapping at her one moment, delicately teasing her the next. Then back to her clitoris again, harder this time, making her catch her breath and fight to control her hips. He caught hold of her with both hands and immobilised her, his nails digging into her. His tongue slid inside her and he started to fuck her with it, raising her to a new pitch of wantoness. She heard herself groan. She felt his tongue slide back to the important bit; then he was finger-fucking her as well, and it was all too much. The orgasm rushed at her like an angry swan. She was helpless in its path, and the intensity of it finally gave way to cramp in a calf-muscle. She sat up, half-laughing, half-grimacing, and Nick stretched her leg out and flexed her foot. The cramp went.

'I think it's bedtime,' said Nick. 'Off you go.'

'What about you?'

Nick glanced down at himself. His erection was subsiding. 'Keep it for tomorrow,' he said.

Tomorrow. Nan felt a surge of happiness. 'I'll see you in the morning, then.'

'Night.' He kissed her briefly on the lips; she floated back to the coach-house, and tiptoed up the stairs. Megan was snoring.

Chapter Six

Wednesday morning. 'Where did you get to last night?' demanded Megan.

'You noticed,' said Nan.

'Everybody noticed. Tad appears in the middle of a thunderstorm, and you disappear with him. And you don't come back. We stayed in the library until two o'clock, Nan. *Two o'clock.*'

I'm not accountable to you, thought Nan. You certainly didn't play straight with *me*. 'I'm not going out with you lot today,' she said.

'Oh, ho,' said Megan. 'And why not?'

'I'm going to do the writing. Just for one day.'

'Oh, yes? Why don't you want to see Tad?'

'I don't not want to see him,' said Nan, 'I'm just going to Nick's class today.'

'You didn't chicken out, did you?'

'Chicken out of what?'

'*You know.*'

'I'm sick of this,' shouted Nan. 'I am not the slightest bit interested in Tadeusz Kalinowski, nor he in me. Why don't you just get on with your own affair – share a room with Brian and have done with it?'

'Fine,' said Megan. 'If that's how you feel.'

And when Nan went back to the coach-house after breakfast, she found Megan's things gone. It was a relief, really; behaving as though nothing was going on was becoming increasingly difficult. She grabbed a couple of pens and a notebook and went over to the house, as the writers' group met in the library.

Faith was the only one in there. 'Hello,' she said, surprised. 'I thought you were one of Tad's.'

'Not today,' said Nan.

'You may find it difficult, coming in on the third day,' said Faith. 'We've done lots of different things. Nick's really inventive.'

Everyone else drifted in, and then Nick arrived. He sat down and surveyed the group. 'We've got two newcomers today,' he said, indicating them. 'Nan, from the watercolourists, and Derek, from the nature group. So instead of pursuing the haiku, we're going to do something different.' He flicked through some papers. 'I want a childhood memory of a parent. If possible, I want the women to remember their mothers, and the men their fathers.'

'Fan*tastic*,' said Faith.

'I'm going to come round to each of you, and discuss what you're doing. Right then, scatter. Back here in half an hour.'

They all picked up their things and headed for the door. 'Where are you going?' Faith asked Nan.

'The conservatory,' said Nan. 'How does he know where we are?'

'I've no idea,' said Faith, 'but he usually seems to find us.' She walked briskly away in the opposite direction.

Nan settled herself in the conservatory. I can only write about my stepmother, she thought. But I can't refer to her as anything except *mum*; giving her another title seems like a betrayal. The woman had done her best. Nan started to describe her, a well-meaning muddler who liked polyester cardigans and finishing other people's sentences for them.

About twenty minutes later, Nick strolled into the conservatory. But he was very businesslike; he read what she'd written and then he started to ask her questions about her background.

'So your mother wasn't like you at all,' he said. 'You're reacting against her, not emulating her.'

'I emulated her for twenty years,' said Nan. 'I even do my washing up in the same order.'

She told him about her childhood, the unspeakable wallpaper and the plastic flowers round the mirror in the hall. She didn't go back as far as eight – there was no point. What he wanted were the memories that had made her what she was. And all the time she was thinking, supposing I mention the photograph? Will he know anything? Why should I keep my mouth shut, just because Tad told me to?

'OK,' said Nick suddenly, 'what's on your mind?'

'A photograph,' Nan blurted out.

'What photograph?'

'One of Simone's. I saw it at that –'

'I don't know anything about her photography,' said Nick shortly. 'We didn't see much of each other at that stage. Sorry.'

They walked back to the library, and then everyone broke for lunch. Faith cornered Nick and Nan browsed along the bookshelves, trying to find the book with the photograph in it, but it didn't seem to be there any more. She did find one on contemporary women artists, however, which said that Simone had gone to Hornsey School of Art, and had stayed in the area for several years afterwards.

Nan smiled. At last she had a place. Simone had definitely lived in North London around the time Nan was four.

During the afternoon, she tried to write something about her feelings as a child, but they didn't seem logical any more. Why hadn't she asked more questions? Why had she toed the line so assiduously for so many years?

95

She didn't understand herself any more. She decided that even if the photograph did turn out to be a red herring, she wasn't going to stop looking. She would find out about her mother some other way.

Brian made a real effort to be nice to her, over dinner. Gladys pointedly ignored her, and Megan was very distant. Lettie wasn't there. When Nan got up to leave at the end of the meal, she saw Nick stand up as well, and they went out of the refectory together. As she turned to close the door, she caught the look on Faith's face, and she didn't like it.

'Come up about eight,' said Nick. 'Just go up the stairs, the way you did before, and into the studio. It won't be locked this time.'

'What shall I wear?' asked Nan innocently.

He turned to look at her with such an expression of dismay that she couldn't keep a straight face.

'Whatever I wear, I won't be keeping it on for long, will I?' she said. 'Gotcha, though. Just for a moment.' She knew she was glowing, almost fizzing; his presence did something inexplicable to her.

'How do you feel about posing with Cheng?'

'I hadn't thought about it.'

'Think about it,' said Nick. 'I'll see you later.'

Nan went back to the coach-house and took a shower. She rubbed her hair dry with her usual vigour, and looked at herself in the mirror. Her body wasn't bad, although there were stretch-marks across her stomach. Her breasts sagged a little, but they were still full and very white against the tan on her shoulders. She hadn't analysed herself so intently for years, and she was slightly surprised at what she saw – for, unclothed, she wasn't the mother-next-door who was good at fixing washing machines at all. She wasn't slouching; the frown-lines between her brows weren't quite so pronounced; and her face seemed livelier, more awake. She rummaged through her chest of drawers for something

96

to wear. Everything was severely practical – jeans and shorts and T-shirts. She threw them back in disgust.

Then she noticed that Megan had left something behind – one of her floaty dresses, in pale bright greens and turquoises, really pretty. Nan put it on, and stared at herself. It was wonderful, slinky and seductive, frivolous and feminine. She twirled, laughed at herself for being so silly, and then twirled again. Then she got a fit of the giggles as she thought, I may have to pose with Cheng. What do I think of *that*? He is achingly beautiful, with that satin amber skin; you can't help wanting to touch him.

She sneaked over to the main building at eight o'clock, hoping she didn't bump into Megan. She didn't see anyone, and she scampered up the stairs, opened the door and walked down the corridor to the studio. She knocked, but there was no reply. She knocked again, and when nothing happened she opened the door and went inside. Cheng was sitting meditating on the dais.

'Oh,' said Nan. 'Sorry.'

He looked up. 'It's OK.' He uncrossed his legs and got to his feet. He was wearing some light cotton trousers and nothing else. 'Drink?' He poured her a vodka and tonic. 'It's all we've got,' he said, 'but we've got lots.'

'It's fine,' said Nan, drinking half of it in one go.

'You're nervous, aren't you?' said Cheng. 'Don't be. Like actors and actresses, playing a part. Easy.'

'I haven't taken my clothes off before,' said Nan.

Cheng smiled, and simply took off his trousers. He was beautiful everywhere: symmetrical, tidy, exactly the same colour all over, just the way Nan remembered him from the barn. 'See?' he said. 'Easy. Now you.'

Sod it, thought Nan. I've sunbathed topless before. She kicked off her sandals and pulled off her knickers; then she unzipped the dress and slipped it off her shoulders. It tumbled all in a rush to the floor, a green-and-turquoise sea suddenly frothing at her feet.

'Ice?' asked Cheng. He went over to the bench and

brought over an ice-bucket. Nan held out her glass. He dropped in two cubes, and then topped the whole thing up with vodka.

'Get a bit pissed,' said Cheng. 'Then you won't mind in the slightest. And make sure you're comfortable, if it's a long pose.'

She smiled. He was little more than half her age, but he was behaving like a fussy old teacher. She stepped out of the circle of the dress, and they both sat down on the dais. He talked a bit about life drawing, and then he said, 'We'll put our clothes on again now. The next time you take them off, it won't be so difficult.'

She smiled as she put the dress back on. She was beginning to like Cheng a lot.

Nick and Simone came in together a few minutes later. Nick stopped dead in his tracks and just stared. Blimey, thought Nan, maybe I ought to wear a dress more often.

'Oh, good,' said Simone, 'we can get started.' She took a huge sketchbook down from the shelves. 'What I'm trying to do now,' she said, 'is to get some dynamics into it. So what I want you to do is to follow a sequence of actions, five-minute poses – no more. *Bon*?'

Nan nodded.

'You don't mind Nick being here, do you?' said Simone. 'We're working on this together. He provides the script – which I can alter – and you do whatever he describes. OK. Let's go.'

Nan slipped off the dress. The first few poses were no problem – straightforward positions that Nick explained, sometimes walking over to her and moving her limbs accordingly. Cheng watched from the cushions, impassive, as she hunched up her knees and hung back her head, screwed herself up in a ball, stretched herself full-length on the rug. She began to feel quite abandoned, on to her knees, on to her stomach, hugging herself, clutching her ankle.

They had a break. Simone showed her the drawings,

and Nan saw what she was doing, superimposing one figure over another, creating a feeling of movement, and she could have cried with envy.

'So,' said Simone, 'how do you feel about posing with somebody else?'

'Fine,' said Nan, now quite sure that Cheng would be an easy and considerate person to work with.

'Good,' said Simone. She turned to Nick. 'Strip.'

Nick blinked. 'What?'

'I'm changing the script. I want you in it, not Cheng.'

Nan could see that Nick really had been taken completely by surprise.

'Cheng and I had a better idea,' said Simone, 'that's all. Strip.'

Nick slowly took off his shirt, tight-lipped. Then he took off his shoes and unbuckled his belt. Simone turned to a new sheet of paper, and indicated to Nan to stand on the rug. Nan stood up, and did as she was bidden. Nick took off his trousers and his underpants, and got up on the dais. He stood there, quite relaxed though not happy, hands on his hips, looking at Simone.

'Cheng,' said Simone, 'you take the script.'

Cheng picked up a sheaf of papers, and ran his finger down the first page. 'OK,' he said, 'just facing one another, to start.' They went through half a dozen different positions, nothing very taxing, about a metre apart. She was aware of Nick's eyes on her because she glanced at him from time to time, but she couldn't make herself look at him for long. She was beginning to get excited by the idea that he was watching her.

They stopped for another drink.

Nan was really enjoying herself; she was feeling terrific, appreciated, needed. Cheng patted her on the back. 'You're very good,' he said, 'in case nobody else bothers to tell you.' She wanted to hug him.

They went back to their positions. Nick's initial anxiety seemed to have gone, and he smiled at her. Cheng turned to the next page, and so did Simone. Her eyes were shining, and she was tapping her toes in anticipation.

'This time,' said Cheng, 'Nan has her head on Nick's shoulder, and he has his arms round her.'

They slotted themselves into place. She felt Nick's hands slide round her back and hold her in position. The five minutes passed rather enjoyably. There were a few variations on that position, concentrating on triangular spaces, and then Simone clapped her hands.

'*Magnifique*,' she said, stepping back from her work and looking at it.

They broke the pose, and went over to see.

The drawing was light and flowing. Nick looked serious, and Nan looked dreamy and distant. She hadn't been glamorised – she was definitely a woman of mature years – but she had a glow, a kind of dawning awareness that her body was her own again.

'You're not going to draw on top of that one, are you?' said Cheng.

Simone nodded.

'No,' said Cheng.

She stared at him.

Cheng separated the page with his fingers, and tore it out of the sketchbook. 'Do it again if you have to,' he said, 'like you tell me. But don't touch this one.' He took it over to the shelves and laid it flat.

Simone shrugged. They went back to the same pose, and she drew them again. But it wasn't as good as the first one; Simone knew it, Cheng knew it, and even Nan knew it.

'That one,' said Cheng, 'you can scribble over.'

The atmosphere felt as though it had gone slightly askew. Cheng was asserting himself in a way that seemed to have taken everyone by surprise. Nick went over to Cheng and they began to talk in low voices.

'I'm so happy,' said Simone to Nan. 'You are just what I needed. Tadeusz has a good eye.'

'Do you mean he selected me?'

'Oh, yes,' said Simone.

'Tested me to see if I was broad-minded enough?'

'I don't know how he goes about it.'

'He's done it before?'

'Sniffle was the last one; there were others before that. Sniffle was the only mistake.'

'I see,' said Nan. Nick's words to her in the store room were ricocheting like a bullet in an enclosed space.

Once in while we need some new blood. And this year, you're it.

And she thought she'd been calling the tune, finding a neat way of seeing Simone and asking her about the photograph. Tad had been playing his own game all along, cold-bloodedly capitalising on her curiosity about her own past. She felt angry, gullible and manipulated.

'We'll just do one more,' said Simone. 'Then we'll pack up.'

Cheng went over to Simone and conferred about something on the sheet of paper. Nan heard Simone say, 'Change it, then.' Nick had disappeared, presumably to go to the loo.

Cheng took Nan by the arm, and stood her back on the dais. He moved her this way and that, and Simone got him to modify the lighting; the room darkened, and the spotlight intensified. Cheng slid a sheet of something in front of the bulb and the room went blue, apart from the small pool of white light thrown by the lamp Simone kept suspended over her drawing board to illuminate her work. She discarded her pencil, and got out a set of pastels. Then she went over to the shelves, poured herself another drink and got out a sheet of grey Ingres paper. She framed Nan with her fingers and said to Cheng, 'Stand in for Nick for a moment.'

Cheng put his arms round Nan's waist. Simone indicated what she wanted him to do, and the pair of them made tiny movements towards her, away from her, half a pace here, a five-degree turn there. It could be a minimalist dance, thought Nan, for the two of them synchronised their actions perfectly. Simone suggested another pose, finished her drink and poured the next one.

Cheng dropped to one knee and bent Nan backwards across it. His thigh was taut and smooth; she was reminded of a Doberman she'd once stroked, solid muscle covered with a deceptive lick of velvet. She felt his hand on her stomach, steadying her.

'Move it down a little,' said Simone, 'and bend over her as though you were about to kiss her.'

Cheng moved his hand down, and Nan fought back a shiver of excitement, remembering his hand in the barn, and the way he had caressed himself.

'Bit further,' said Simone, and then Cheng had his hand right between her legs and Nan felt herself begin to get wet.

'Don't worry,' whispered Cheng in her ear. 'We're all made of flesh and blood. I am, certainly.' And when they changed the pose again, Nan could see that he had an erection. He smiled at her as though it was just another pair of underpants. Then Nick came back in, and Cheng went and sat on the cushions again.

'Right,' said Simone, 'this time, I want . . .' She stopped and looked at Nan, suddenly perplexed. 'What was it I wanted?'

Nick took a deep breath. 'Time to pack up for the night,' he said.

'What's the matter with you?' said Simone. 'Stage fright? *You*?'

Nick said something very quickly in French. Cheng laughed, and Nan felt stupid, uneducated, excluded.

'Oh, for God's sake,' said Simone, 'this is work.'

'Yes,' said Nick, 'but I don't know what you're getting at now, and I'm meant to be the damned writer.'

'*Pouf*,' said Simone. She put away her pastels and stood up rather unsteadily.

Nan saw Nick and Cheng glance at one another. Simone turned pointedly to Cheng, and Cheng got up.

Nick just sat there, expressionless. Simone held the door open for Nan, and Nan left the studio behind Cheng and Simone.

'It wasn't too bad, was it?' said Simone. 'You'll come back tomorrow night?'

'Yes,' said Nan, 'but there's something I desperately want to ask you.'

'What?'

'It's important. Your photograph of the little girl running towards the camera, the one in the exhibition . . .'

Simone's eyes narrowed slightly. 'Felicity.'

'Felicity?'

'That was the little girl's name.' There was a guarded expression on her face, as though she expected Nan to start grilling her about photography.

'Oh,' said Nan.

'What about it?'

'I just thought . . . she looked a bit like me at that age. I don't know anything about my childhood before I was eight and I wondered . . . I wanted to know her name.'

'Felicity,' said Simone. 'Felicity Trent. Her mother was a friend of mine.' Then she said, 'Is that why you came here? To ask me that?'

'To begin with,' said Nan.

'Are you disappointed?'

'Sort of.'

'You just need to think of it,' said Simone, 'as one of those ideas that didn't go anywhere. But those ideas can become catalysts for something else. It brought you here, and now you're into something else entirely. The good accidents – new ideas spring from accidents.' She was so lucid that Nan didn't realise how drunk she was until Cheng grabbed her by the elbow to stop her falling over. They said goodnight, and Nan left the building. To her disappointment, there was no sign of Nick.

And so that was that. The girl was called Felicity Trent – not Annette, or Nan. She stood for a moment by the shrubbery and cried, for the disappointment was acute.

Then she wiped her eyes as efficiently as she could with the hem of the dress, made her way back along the path at the side of the building and bumped into Megan going in the opposite direction. It was dark, and Megan couldn't see what Nan was wearing. 'Night, Megan,' said Nan, struggling to keep the misery out of her voice but not wishing to fuel the enmity by not speaking at all.

But Megan wasn't so easily fooled. 'You've been crying,' she said. 'What on earth's the matter? Come here.' She pulled Nan out into the light. The dress fluttered like something out of *Lawrence of Arabia*, and Megan let Nan's arm drop and just stared.

'I'm sorry, Megan,' said Nan, cringing inside.

'I don't give a bugger about the dress,' said Megan. 'What happened? Was it something to do with Tad?'

'Oh, for God's sake,' said Nan, 'I haven't seen Tad all evening. No – I found out about the photograph. It wasn't me at all.'

'How do you know?'

'I asked Simone,' said Nan.

Megan's mouth actually dropped open. 'You what?' she squeaked. 'You've *met* her? Listen, let's have a drink and bury the hatchet.'

They went back to the coach-house and sat on the beds with their feet drawn up like a couple of school-girls, drinking gin and lemonade out of their toothmugs.

'So what's she like?' asked Megan.

'Simone? Friendly. A bit eccentric. Drinks like a fish.'

'Where did you meet her?'

'Tad took me up to the studio yesterday.'

Megan stared at her. Then she said, 'That was nice of him.'

No, it bloody wasn't, thought Nan, but she couldn't say anything, so she sat there, looking annoyed.

'You know,' said Megan, misinterpreting Nan's expression, 'I really am sorry about the photograph. I didn't realise it was that important to you.'

104

'I'm not sure it was until I came here,' said Nan. 'But now I need to know who I am, if I really want to paint.'

'You're really into it, aren't you?' said Megan wonderingly. 'I'm just a teensy bit jealous.'

Nan laughed. Then she said, 'Megan. Do you think I could be any good?'

'You already are,' said Megan, 'you cow.'

They smiled at each other.

'You don't regret coming here, then?'

'God, no,' said Nan.

'I thought maybe – Brian and I – we've excluded you, haven't we?'

'What's it like, Megan, having a proper affair?'

Megan laughed. 'I feel ten years younger.'

'What if Terry finds out?'

'He won't.'

'Are you in love with Brian?'

Megan hesitated. 'Not really.'

Nan stared at her.

'What did you expect, Nan?' said Megan. 'I'm forty. Brian's forty-seven. It's a meeting of bodies, not a meeting of minds. It's fun, dammit, and it's exciting. What else have I got to look forward to? Weekends on the common with Terry, holding the thermos and the sandwiches? Radio-controlled planes are the pits and so are the people who fly them; you've no idea. Anoraks with attitude.'

'So you're unhappy with Terry.'

'Not all the time. And that's the best that can be said for most marriages, in my experience.'

Nan didn't reply.

Megan sighed. 'Oh, Nan. When have you had a chance like this before?'

'Tad's screwing Simone,' said Nan. 'And I don't fancy him anyway.' She was still furious with him for his sly undercover reconnaissance.

'I would, if it wasn't for Brian.'

Nan fleetingly pictured Tad and Brian next to one

105

another, and they could have been members of two different species. However much Tad annoyed her, Brian was no competition by comparison. There was something of the slug about him.

'Why do you think I moved into Brian's room?' said Megan. 'I was thinking of *you*.'

This was so unlikely that Nan turned her head away to stop herself laughing.

Megan stood up, made her way to the door and stood there for a moment, leaning against it. 'Remember,' she said, 'opportunity is the greatest aphrodisiac of the lot.'

'Sweet dreams, Megan,' said Nan.

Megan grinned. 'If I get the chance.'

The foxes' screams woke Nan at ten past three. She lay there, disorientated, wondering if she had dreamed them. Then the cry came again, and the memory of the last time came flooding back. Sleep was impossible after that, so she slipped on Megan's dress, grabbed her torch and went outside. She walked across the courtyard and then round the perimeter of the house, wondering which window was Nick's, and whether he was alone. And then a window opened and his head emerged.

'They woke me as well,' he said. 'But it's a braw bricht moonlicht nicht – perfect for a walk. Would you like some company?'

'Yes,' said Nan.

Nick came out of the house a couple of minutes later. 'Seen the lake?'

Nan shook her head.

They walked all the way to the lake, and sat on the bank in the moonlight. Nick cast a sidelong glance at Nan and said, 'Fancy a skinny-dip?'

Nan had never swum in the nude. They took off their clothes, and stepped tentatively into the water. It was cold enough to take her breath away.

'You just have to plunge straight in,' said Nick, and he swam away from her with long easy strokes. Nan submerged herself more slowly, but the cold quickly

106

wore off and she and Nick paddled round one another, touching every so often.

'Simone's sleeping with Cheng as well, isn't she?' said Nan. The sensation of the water on her bare skin was wonderful, a feeling of total freedom.

'Yes. Tad doesn't approve; but then, he's a jealous bugger, and I'm not.'

'Tell me about your background,' said Nan, floating on her back, watching him.

'I was born in India,' said Nick. 'Moved to England when I was eleven. I told you Simone was my pen-friend, and that she came over here to go to college. After I graduated I started teaching, and I got a job near her. We became lovers almost immediately, but it was a very on-off sort of thing. Simone collected lovers like stamps. There was a group of us – writers and artists, mainly. John Fox, Harriet Trent, Alan Marshall.' He mentioned a few more names, some of which were very famous by now. 'We had one recurrent topic of conversation – which is the more truthful, art or literature?'

'Does it have to be one or the other?' said Nan, feeling a current of water move between her legs as she changed position.

'That's like saying it always takes two partners to break a marriage, whereas my appalling track-record has been entirely my own fault. Why should truth be equally distributed between the arts, just because it would be nice if it was?'

'But surely,' said Nan, 'art and literature are about different things?'

'No,' said Nick, immersing himself in the water again, 'they're not. Not fundamentally.' He started to float beside her, their shoulders touching. 'I think literature's more truthful; Tad thinks it's art, so does Simone. We work together to prove one another wrong. Anyhow, after the group broke up, I went abroad . . .'

'Why did it break up?' asked Nan.

'Harriet died,' said Nick.

'Oh,' said Nan, taken by surprise and not quite knowing what to say. 'How?'

'She drowned.'

'Oh, God,' said Nan, 'how dreadful.' The water suddenly felt very cold. She shivered, and they both swam to the bank and climbed out.

Nick put his arms round her, and they slithered against one another like seals. He started to kiss her, dribbles of water running down his nose and on to hers; then he seized her buttocks and pulled her against him, hard. She broke away from the kiss. He took hold of her face with both his hands and turned it back towards him, and they struggled playfully for a moment.

'Someone else might be going for a walk,' Nan pointed out.

He moved his hands to her arms, and marched her over to a little hollow surrounded by ferns. Then he pushed her down on to the grass, so that she was on all fours. 'Right, my little vixen,' he said, 'this dog-fox will now give you a good clickitting.'

He got down on his hands and knees and sniffed her all over, his nose touching her lightly now and again, his breath warm. It felt divine; she had her back to him, and she couldn't see which bit he was going to investigate next. Each time he managed to surprise her, switching from her spine to her nipple, the nape of her neck to the crook of her knee, her thigh to her ear. She growled softly. He growled in return, and butted her on the behind with his head. She opened her legs wider, and he began to lick her with long strokes of his tongue. She knelt there, feeling the excitement building as she got wetter and wetter. She twisted her head to look at him and he glanced up, his beard glittering with saliva, and smiled. Then he nipped her sharply on the buttock, and she bit him back. He cuffed her, his hand curled into a paw. After that the licking became more relentless; the downstroke gave her one sensation, the upstroke another. He lingered at the end of each lick, pressing her clitoris, then he would veer off again until he reached the other end, where he also lingered, teasing the little puckered hole until it contracted with pleasure. The rhythm of it was almost hypnotic; then he changed the tempo and she was catapulted into the orgasm, shuddering.

When she'd recovered a certain amount of composure, she thought, my turn now, and she flipped herself round and butted him. He rolled on to his back and lay there like a dog waiting to have its stomach scratched. Nan took a deep breath, and bent over him. Fellatio was something she had little experience of; she'd done it a few times in the early years with Mike, but he hadn't reacted with particular enthusiasm, so she'd stopped. She suspected it was because he felt he would have to reciprocate, and cunnilingus didn't turn him on at all.

Nick's cock was as white and erect as a toadstool in the moonlight, and when she ran her tongue down it there was the same velvety texture. He made a little whining sound of pleasure. Encouraged, Nan started to play with him, darting from here to there with little flicks of her tongue, controlling him, making him gasp. His reaction was the best aphrodisiac of all, and she began to really enjoy herself. She ran her tongue all the way round him, and then did some vibrato work on the sensitive underside. He groaned, and grabbed hold of her breast. She took his cock into her mouth properly and moved up and down, enjoying the rigidity of him, sucking him every so often, feeling the tension in his body grow, savouring the tiny leakage of spunk on the end of his cock.

He sat up suddenly and said, 'Any more of that and you won't get fucked,' and he pushed her so that she overbalanced. They wrestled on the grass, snapping at one another and making fox-noises.

She loved the sudden unexpected pressures of arm against breast, leg against chest; the weight of him, the smell of him, the urgency, the little cuffs to the side of the head, the shoulder. Then he hauled her on to all fours again, and mounted her from behind. This time there was no gentleness; they both knew what they wanted, a good hard fuck. With each thrust he moved her nearer to the point of no return; then that slow fizz of the blood, the gradual conversion to champagne, the inexorable build to overflow . . .

'Now,' hissed Nick, and she knew that this time they were going to come in absolute unison. She cried out as it happened, it was so intense – and the afterglow reached right to the tips of her fingers. Nick stroked her face a few times and then they lay together for a while, not speaking.

Eventually he said, 'I'm going to be knackered tomorrow. And, Nan – I think we'd better keep things on a professional footing in front of Simone.'

'You think she'd mind?' Nan couldn't quite believe the hypocrisy of it.

'Simone has totally illogical double standards.' He picked up Megan's dress, and slipped it over her shoulders; then he got dressed himself. When he sat down again on the grass to put his shoes on, she slid her arms round his waist and hugged him. He disengaged her and stood up. 'Don't get too fond of me, Nan,' he said. 'I'm bad news. I can't stop looking for someone I can't have, and you've come so close I'm not going to be able to keep away.'

She wondered what he meant, but it didn't seem like the right time to ask. They walked back arm-in-arm and said goodnight.

Chapter Seven

*T*hursday, and the handbell was ringing for breakfast. She got dressed, deliberately selecting the roughest T-shirt and the most rugged shorts. There were some things about her personality she'd decided to keep.

She went over to the refectory and helped herself to some muesli. Dominic was the only person seated at the staff table, and he was buried in a copy of *Nature*. There was something that looked like a large metal mouse-trap on the table beside him, and an opened tin of dog-food. As she watched, Dominic absently put his knife in the dog-food instead of the marmalade, and transferred some to his toast. He ate it without a second glance, turning the page of his magazine as though absorbed in the most gripping of thrillers. A minute or two later, he suddenly looked perplexed, glanced at the marmalade, shook his head and went back to his journal.

'Coming with us today, then?' said Brian cheerfully.

'Yes,' said Nan, tearing her eyes away from Dominic.

They all trooped outside. Tad was leaning over Imogen's Range Rover, looking at something under the bonnet. 'God knows,' she heard him say.

Imogen looked up. 'It just cuts out,' she said to Nan.

Nan didn't really want to get involved, not with Tad

there; she was still furious with him. But Imogen had addressed the remark directly at her, and Nan couldn't just ignore her. 'Let's hear, then,' she said.

Imogen started the engine, and after a moment or two it spluttered and gave up. 'Fuel blockage,' said Nan.

'We know that,' said Tad irritably, fiddling with a feeder pipe.

Nan glanced at it. 'There hasn't been any fuel through there for a while,' she said. 'The problem's further back. When did you last have it serviced, Imogen?'

Imogen looked guilty. 'Can't remember.'

'I'll look at it, lunchtime,' said Nan, 'it's probably something silly like a bunged-up filter.'

'Ah,' said Imogen. 'Last time I had it serviced they said I needed the filter thingy replaced.'

Tad dropped the bonnet with a loud bang, picked up his register and walked off.

They set up in the woods, and Tad left her until last. When he finally did appear she'd nearly finished. She didn't say anything; she just sat there, stiff-backed, wondering how best to attack him.

He looked at her painting and said, 'Not bad, but it's a shitty composition.'

'I know,' said Nan, gritting her teeth.

'Enjoy yourself last night?' For a moment she wondered how he knew, then she realised he must be talking about the modelling session.

'Yes, thanks,' she said.

Tad sat down on the grass, legs everywhere like a tarantula. 'I hear Nick's very good,' he said.

'What at?' snapped Nan.

He laughed.

She glared at him, caught out.

'So you did enjoy yourself.'

'Twice,' said Nan, looking him straight in the eye.

'My, my,' said Tad, 'and I thought I'd picked another mouse.'

His bald admission of the thing of which she was

112

about to accuse him annoyed her intensely. 'So how many times have you pimped for Simone?' she said.

He didn't even attempt to evade the question. 'Too many to remember.'

'Cheng one of yours?'

'No,' said Tad. 'He came by a different route.'

Nan laughed. 'Oriental plumbing's different, is it?'

He turned his head away so that she couldn't see him smile, but he didn't quite manage it.

'Anyway,' said Nan, 'thanks for trying to help over the photograph, though I can see you were in fact helping yourself –'

'I never,' interrupted Tad. 'I was very restrained, back there in the woods the other day.'

'I thought you only had eyes for Simone,' said Nan.

'Oh, yes? What's Nick been saying?'

'He called you a jealous bugger.'

Tad looked surprised. 'I'm not.'

She shrugged.

'You can love more than one person at a time, you know,' he said offhandedly.

'Simone obviously does.'

'Oh,' said Tad, 'I wouldn't call what she and Cheng get up to *love*.'

'I found out about the photograph,' said Nan.

'Did you?' said Tad. 'I assume it was you who took the book out of the library?'

'No,' said Nan. 'I thought it was you, actually. But it doesn't matter now. I did manage to ask Simone about it, and the girl wasn't me. It was someone called Felicity Trent.'

He didn't say anything.

Nan felt very annoyed at his lack of response. 'Have you read Nick's script?' she asked him.

'Nick's script? I think it's Cheng's.'

'No it isn't.'

Tad smiled patronisingly at her, and glanced at his watch. 'Lunchtime.'

113

Nan went back to the house so that she could take a look at Imogen's fuel filter, but there wasn't very much she do could except suggest that Imogen rang the nearest stockist and asked them to deliver one. 'I can change it for you,' she said, 'but I can't conjure one up out of thin air.'

'I didn't expect you to,' said Imogen. 'Why are you and Tad so ratty with one another?'

'Just incompatible, I guess,' said Nan. But she didn't want any more questions, so she went over to the library to see if there were any more of Nick's books there.

She found several, one of which had quite a long introduction. She sat down in a corner and started to read. Apparently he'd been married three times and had three children and five stepchildren.

'Hello,' said Faith, walking through the door with Denise, the large woman from Nick's class. 'Joining us for the afternoon session?'

'No,' said Nan. 'Just getting out of the sun for a bit.'

'I quite liked that piece about your mother you wrote yesterday.'

'Thank you,' said Nan. 'But I don't think writing's my thing.'

'No,' said Faith.

Nan felt slightly put out. It's one thing to say you're not as good as you'd like to be at something, quite another to have someone else agree with you. 'I'd better be off,' she said. 'We're doing trees today.'

Nan knew that she would have to telephone Mike sooner or later about staying on for another week, and she'd also have to ring her office. She went into the main building and rang them from the payphone. No problem, said her boss. Then she stood there for ages, looking at the phone with the rest of the coins warm in her hand. Finally she picked up the receiver, and punched in Mike's number at work – but it was Sandra who answered.

'Oh, hello, Mrs Tilson,' she said brightly. 'Are you having a good time?'

Nan felt the anger boil up like a pan of milk, but all she said was, 'Is Mike there?'

'Sorry. Can I take a message?'

Why not? 'I'm not sure which day I'm coming back,' she said, feeling vindictive.

'Would that be sooner or later than you originally intended?'

'Sorry?'

'Sooner or later?'

'Yes, I'll be back sooner or later,' said Nan.

'I think Mr Tilson needs to know *when*, Mrs Tilson.'

'This is an appalling line,' said Nan, 'you sound like a sea-lion.'

Sandra was losing her cool. 'Which day are you coming back?' she shouted.

'I'll phone tomorrow,' said Nan. 'Bye.' She hung up, smiling. That would give them both something to think about. She leaned back against the wall and shut her eyes, and she stayed there for a while.

'You all right?' asked a voice. There was something about the voice that rang a bell. Nan jerked round. Sniffle was standing there, watching her.

'Just tired,' said Nan.

Sniffle smiled. 'I'm not surprised.'

Denise came out of the library. She glanced at Sniffle. Sniffle seemed to nod her head very slightly, and then she glanced at Nan as if saying to Denise, *this is the one*.

'Will you be joining us this evening?' asked Denise. 'We're going to write rengas.'

'No,' said Nan, wondering what a renga was but determined not to ask.

Denise and Sniffle looked at one another and smiled. Nan wondered how much they knew, or had guessed. She would have liked to ask Sniffle what her experience of modelling for Simone had been like, but all of a sudden it didn't seem wise. She picked up her things

115

and walked back to the woods. As she ducked under a creeper, she suddenly knew where she'd heard Sniffle's voice before – in the conservatory. Jocelyn's mysterious female partner had been *Sniffle*. Was that why Sniffle had been no use to Simone, because she was gay? What had Simone wanted her to do?

Nan left the path and ducked under some rhododendrons, hoping to find a small clearing where she could set up. When she emerged the other side she saw just what she'd been looking for, but it was already occupied. Faith was sitting there, her pad of paper on her lap, looking thoughtful, presumably waiting for Nick to come and find her in a nice secluded setting. Nan stepped back into the rhododenrons – Faith was the last person she wanted as a working companion. Then she heard a rustling sound on the other side of the clearing and Faith looked up, her face alight with excitement.

Dominic appeared, carrying some small plastic containers. Faith's face fell, but she said, 'What have you got there, Dominic? Something good?'

'*Araniella cucurbitina*,' said Dominic helpfully.

'Oh,' said Faith.

'Spider,' explained Dominic.

Faith went over to him; he gave her his hand lens, and she looked at it. 'It's beautiful,' she said. 'Like pale-green silk.'

Dominic looked pleased.

'Nick knows a lot about spiders,' said Faith. 'There are several references to them in his books.'

'Look at this one,' said Dominic, holding up a glass test-tube. Faith squinted through her glasses, so Dominic moved the test-tube a lot closer. Then he dropped it, and looked round on the grass in a distracted manner. Faith started to scrabble at her blouse. 'Oh,' said Dominic, noticing, '*that's* where it went,' and he helped her to undo the buttons. She wasn't wearing a bra. Dominic's eyes widened – then the test-tube fell out, but the lid was missing – and so was the spider. 'Just keep still,' said Dominic. 'I'll find it.' He moved his head close to Faith's breasts, and his whiskers brushed them in passing. Faith shivered. 'There it is,' said Dominic, and he pressed the test-tube against her nipple, neatly trapping the spider inside. Then they just looked at each other, and Nan could see that Dominic had an erection.

'I've always wondered,' said Faith, 'what it would be like, kissing someone with a beard.'

'I wouldn't know,' said Dominic. 'I'm not that way inclined.'

Faith laughed.

Dominic bit his lip. Then he said tentatively, 'Would you like to find out?'

'Oh, yes,' said Faith, but to Nan it was obvious she was thinking of Nick.

Dominic grabbed her, pulled her against him and started to kiss her. For a moment, it looked as though she was trying to push him away – then she seemed to relax, and after a minute or two they subsided on to the grass.

Nan took a step back, intending to make her escape – and stepped straight into Cheng. Once again she was stuck – unable to go forwards, because Dominic and Faith would see her, unable to go back, because Cheng was blocking the way. 'This we have to see,' whispered Cheng.

'Rub your beard all over me,' instructed Faith, pulling off her skirt and briefs. Dominic made a swallowing sound, and complied. 'You can rub your prick against me as well if you like,' she added.

'Faith,' said Dominic – then he hesitated.

'What?'

'I've never . . . you know . . .'

'He's a virgin,' whispered Cheng. 'Simone's going to be jealous as hell when I tell her about *this*.'

'Never mind,' said Faith to Dominic. 'Just do what I say but don't *talk*, okay?'

Dominic nodded.

I'm going to watch someone lose their virginity, thought Nan, and the thought aroused her far more than she was prepared for. She could feel the warmth of Cheng's body on her back, and she made a firm resolution not to press herself against him.

Faith undressed him quickly and efficiently, then she took a condom out of her purse and smoothed it down over Dominic's rather undecided cock. Dominic's mouth opened as though he was about to say something; then he remembered and shut it again. 'Keep on rubbing me with your whiskers,' said Faith. 'All over my body, and then end up between my legs. And if you feel like licking me, do it.' Dominic started to nuzzle her, and she closed her eyes. It was a curiously silent affair, just the occasional catch of breath and the odd snuffle. Faith lay there, occasionally stroking Dominic's cock, which jumped to attention every time.

Nan could feel Cheng's breath on her neck, and smell the faint exotic perfume that hung around his hair. It reminded her of something, but she couldn't quite decide what. He was breathing slowly and evenly, but every so often he would change his position slightly, and his skin would touch hers.

Faith must have realised how close Dominic was to orgasm because she suddenly flicked him with her finger, and he wilted slightly. He rubbed his beard against her abdomen again, and she seized his head with her hands and said, 'Lick.' Dominic opened her legs and began to lick her. 'Left a bit,' ordered Faith, then, 'harder.' Then, 'No, not there ... *there.*' He seemed to get it right then, and for a while there was just the sound of his tongue against her body. His erection was back up to full power, and he was trying to rub himself against the grass at the same time.

'OK,' said Faith, 'you can fuck me now.' There was some awkward manoeuvring, and Faith finally grabbed hold of Dominic's cock with the obvious intention of easing it inside. Her eyes widened, and she bent her head to look.

'What's the matter?' Dominic sounded worried.

'Nothing whatsoever,' said Faith. 'A donkey could be proud of that.'

Dominic suddenly got lucky with his aim, and he pushed his cock inside her and started to thrust like crazy. Faith screwed her eyes shut, but before she could get anywhere Dominic came; then he just lay there, as though he couldn't believe what had happened and the slightest movement might turn it all into a dream.

Cheng laughed quietly.

'Oh, bloody hell,' said Faith, 'what a waste of time.'

'It was wonderful,' said Dominic.

'Not for me,' snapped Faith. She got up and started to put her clothes back on. 'Why the hell couldn't you have been Nick?'

'We could try again,' suggested Dominic.

'You've got to be joking,' said Faith, and she picked up her things and went.

'Oh, well,' whispered Cheng, 'back to work,' and he melted into the shrubs. Nan followed him, and after a couple of minutes she found herself in a glade.

Cheng had set up his stuff there, and he had been using Chinese brushes and an inkblock; she could see the pestle he used to grind the ink, and the little bottle of distilled water. He'd covered sheets and sheets of paper with very simple line-work, but each one was a perfect composition on its own, beautiful.

'I wish I could do that,' said Nan.

He sat her down, gave her a new sheet of paper and pointed at a tree. 'That one,' he said, 'has character.' He showed her how to use the brush, guiding her hand a couple of times; then he sat cross-legged on the grass and watched her.

She got the hang of loading the brush properly, experimented with a few strokes, and started on the tree. Although she thought she was doing as she'd been told, it didn't seem to go right; she could manage the shapes, but the picture as a whole didn't work.

'It's the composition,' said Cheng.

'Tell me what to do, then.'

'Focus on that branch, then don't move your head or your eyes. How much of the rest of the tree can you see in focus?'

'Very little.'

'OK,' said Cheng. 'When you look at a painting, you can't take it all in at once. So your eyes dot around, and you think you see the whole thing clearly, but you don't, just a little bit at a time. Your brain builds up the composite, and lies to you.'

Nan nodded.

'So,' Cheng went on, 'you *have* to look at one small area first. The bit you look at first is the focal point. Engineer a focal point, and you can make people look where you want them to, lead them round by the ear –'

'Nose,' said Nan, smiling.

'Nose. So. How do you attract someone's attention?'

'You just make the focal point that bit different from everything else,' said Tad, coming up behind them.

Cheng's expression didn't change one iota. 'Hello, Tadeusz,' he said.

'Hello, Cheng,' said Tad, with exaggerated politeness. He glanced at Cheng's drawings, and smiled bitterly. 'Too fucking clever for your own good.'

Cheng didn't say anything. Tad looked at what Nan was doing, but he didn't comment on her prowess.

'I was only trying it out,' said Nan.

'Suit yourself.'

'I'll go and set up somewhere else now.'

'Whatever.'

'I've finished,' said Cheng. He picked up his things, and Nan caught a glimpse of a book inside his bag. She wasn't absolutely certain, but it looked like the one that had gone missing from the library. He rolled up his drawings, and went.

'Do you want a lesson on composition,' said Tad, 'or do you know it all?'

She wondered what he meant by lesson. 'Of course I don't think I know it all,' she said. 'Do you?'

'No.'

'I'll still take the lesson,' said Nan.

'Don't feel obliged.'

'I don't,' said Nan. 'Shall we get on with it?'

'Leave your stuff under the tree, then,' he said.

'Why?'

'Rule number one. When being taught by me, you do as I say.'

Nan put her things under the tree.

'Right,' said Tad, 'we're going hunting.'

'What?' She laughed. He raised an eyebrow. 'Sorry,' she said hastily.

'I explain things better visually,' said Tad. 'You'll just have to put up with it. Right. Hunting and gathering. What are we looking for?' He strolled off, glancing around him.

'Chanterelles.'

'Yes, all right,' he said irritably, 'what else?'

'I don't know . . . rabbits?'

'Rabbits,' he repeated, as though her reply were a bitter disappointment to him. 'See any?'

'No. But we're talking. We'd frighten them.'

He laughed. 'Rabbits are big-time. We'd be looking for anything, Nan, absolutely anything. Seeds, carrion, snails, insects . . .'

'*Insects?*'

'Mm-hm. See any?'

'No.'

He turned over a leaf. Half a dozen tiny green things leaped off it as though on springs. 'Leafhoppers,' he said. 'Start looking, woman. You've got a family to feed.'

She started to get into it. After a while she was spotting all sorts of things, from toadstools to shield bugs. They had walked quite a way; she hadn't really been paying attention to the direction, and she had no idea where they were. She found some early blackberries.

'Uh-huh,' said Tad, 'why did you notice them?'

'The shape. And the colour.'

'What colour?'

'Black,' said Nan.

'Black's not a colour. It's a tone.'

'All right then, tone.'

He drew her attention to the corpse of a decomposing bird. 'We'd have that – maggots and all. How's it different from the background?'

Both the bird and the dead leaves it was lying on were brown. The edges of the shape were lost in the substratum. 'Texture, I suppose,' said Nan.

He smiled. 'OK. End of part one. Now then . . . what else might you be looking for?'

'Predators.'

'Good. See any?' He glanced round. They were standing in a small clearing, but the woods were dense on either side.

Nan laughed. 'No.'

He looked at her, not smiling. 'Do you know where we are?'

'No.' The smile left her face.

'We're in enemy territory. The storm blew down part of the fence; you didn't notice when we crossed it.'

She stared at him.

'There's a mad gamekeeper out there somewhere, and I know for a fact that he's got a shotgun. We'd better be a little more circumspect, hadn't we?'

She swallowed. Unorthodox teaching methods was right.

'Right,' said Tad brightly, 'what are we looking for now?'

'How the hell would I know?' snapped Nan. 'I've never even seen the guy.' And then she remembered the incident in the pub. 'What's his name?'

'Oliver Mellors,' said Tad.

Nan felt relieved. Although the name sounded oddly familiar, at least it wasn't Butch.

'I'll tell you what we're looking for,' said Tad. 'We're looking for something – *anything* – that doesn't fit in with the surroundings. Tone, colour, shape, size, texture. Only now your life may depend on it.'

'Don't be so ridiculously melodramatic,' hissed Nan, 'and just get me out of here.'

'Which direction do you suggest?'

'Don't wind me up,' said Nan. 'This isn't funny.'

'I'm not laughing,' said Tad.

'If you don't start walking,' said Nan, 'I will. And I may get it wrong.'

He pointed through a small gap in the trees. 'That way.'

She took the lead – but she was really frightened, despite the fact that she was fairly sure Tad was exaggerating. Why would anyone hire a gamekeeper who wasn't very good at his job, and a nutter to boot? 'Why doesn't he get the sack,' asked Nan, 'if he's so unstable?'

'You're hoping I'm going to give you a nice comforting answer, aren't you?' said Tad cheerfully. 'Sorry. He's the owner's brother. Ex-army; couldn't adjust to normal life – there's not a lot of call for explosives experts at Tesco's. This keeps him happy; he can do his torturing and mutilating and disembowelling away from prying eyes. Neat solution all round.'

'Thanks,' said Nan. 'You're a real comfort.'

She had never been so aware of her surroundings in her life; she noticed everything, checked every shape, every inconsistency, every anomaly. As one false alarm gave way to another, she began to relax a little.

And then she saw him.

The wrongness of him, his blue jeans against the green, his verticality among the horizontal pieces of timber he'd been stacking. He was a powerful man; in a bygone age she'd have expected him to be a blacksmith.

123

He was holding some implement, his back towards them. She stopped dead, and held up a hand. Then she backed slowly along the faint path until she bumped into Tad and, without turning round, she whispered, 'It's him. He's got an axe or something. He hasn't seen me.'

Tad pushed in front of her and looked for himself. Then he grabbed her by the arm and pulled her back along the path until they'd turned a bend. 'Christ,' he said quietly, 'what the hell's he doing here? It's market day. He's meant to be getting rat-arsed at the pub.'

Although it registered that Tad hadn't been quite as lunatic as she'd thought, it didn't make the situation any better. 'Do we have to go that way?' said Nan. 'Or is there an alternative?'

'We could go across the stream,' said Tad. 'Yes, we'll do that.' He veered off at about forty-five degrees, and they began to walk downhill. The path twisted and turned, and every so often there were fallen trees and brambles. 'He ought to learn to manage these woods a bit better,' said Tad. 'This is a mess.' He slipped, caught hold of a branch and hauled himself back to his feet. A blackbird rose out of the bushes, giving its alarm-call. 'Damn,' said Tad, ducking, as something swung in front of him. Then she saw it was a loop of wire, dangling from a branch. 'I bet that was bloody Nick,' said Tad. 'Every time he comes here, he goes out at night and springs the bastard's traps. Old Mellors will think it's us, mind you.'

'His name isn't really Mellors, is it?' said Nan, with a sinking feeling as the name Lawrence suddenly popped into her mind.

'Of course it isn't,' said Tad. 'His name's Rupert Braithwaite.'

'Oh,' said Nan, cheering up slightly.

A dog started barking in the distance and they heard a voice call, 'Monty! Here!'

'Frequently known as Braithwaite The Butcher,' added Tad.

' "Butch" for short?'

Tad looked at her sharply. 'Yes.'

'I saw him,' she said miserably, feeling a little sick, 'that night I went to the pub with Imogen and the rest. He was a bit . . . intense.'

'Come on,' said Tad, 'let's get a move on.'

They slithered down the last part of the path to the stream. It was wide and shallow, with large flat stones here and there that projected out of the water. On the other side of it was the fence, a row of hawthorn bushes and something that looked like an old air-raid shelter. Behind the shelter was a field, stretching uphill towards the house and safety. They sat on the bank, protected by the overhang, and caught their breath.

'It's very exposed,' said Tad. 'I think I'd better go first.'

'And leave me here?' said Nan. 'No way.'

'If he takes a pot shot at us,' said Tad, 'we can go in the shelter. If we get across.'

'What do you mean, *if* we get across?'

'*When*, then.' He glanced at her. 'Why are we sitting here, arguing about bloody words, when we could be having a whale of a time getting shot at? No sense of adventure.' He leaned out slightly and looked along the stream. The dog hadn't barked again. 'All clear,' he said. They stood up gingerly and started to make their way from stone to stone. He held out his hand and she took it, for some of the footholds were slippery. When they were halfway across, a voice shouted, 'Oi! You! Halt!'

'Jesus,' said Tad, and he speeded up, pulling her with him.

'You're trespassing!' yelled Braithwaite, and he fired the gun over their heads. There was no mistaking the voice on a second hearing. Braithwaite was Butch, all right. Nan glanced back over her shoulder and saw him at the top of the rise, the white badger-streak in his hair and the gun in his hands.

Hop, jump, one foot, the other foot, steady ... she slipped. Tad slid his arms under her armpits and pulled her back up. They swayed on one stone for a moment, then he swung her to the next and they were balanced again.

'You're the bastards that keep springing my traps, aren't you?' yelled Braithwaite. 'You're from that sodding house!' He let off another shot in the air.

They were three-quarters of the way across now. The water was a little deeper, and the stones were a little sharper.

'I warned you,' shouted Braithwaite, and this time he fired *at* them. Nan heard the buckshot pepper against the trees in front of them. Tad slipped this time and nearly fell but he managed not to drag her down with him, and he twisted his body like a cat to regain his equilibrium. He changed hands, holding her with the left one rather than the right. Three more stones to go.

'And again!' yelled Braithwaite, sounding even madder than anyone had suggested. She heard the shot spattering in the water behind them like giant raindrops.

Tad leaped the last bit to the bank, dragging her with him. Her feet slid into the water, but he manhandled her out, lifted the bottom strand of wire on the fence, pushed her to the ground and shoved her through. She scrambled to her feet and dived for the shelter, and he followed. The moment they were under the corrugated iron, Braithwaite fired again, playing a tinny tattoo on the roof. They scuttled down the steps and sat at the bottom behind a brick pillar.

'He won't follow us, will he?' said Nan.

She saw Tad shake his head in the gloom. 'No. With any luck he'll forget all about us, and go and kill something instead.'

'This is all your fault,' said Nan.

'Sorry.' There was no apology in it.

126

She glared at him. 'How long do we have to stay here?'

'My company that objectionable?'

'Yes.'

'All night, then,' said Tad viciously.

She laughed. 'Like hell.'

'If you're in such a hurry,' he said, 'why don't you stick your head outside and take a look?'

'Shut up,' said Nan.

He shut up.

'This is going to get awfully boring,' said Tad eventually.

'Didn't bring a book,' said Nan. 'But then, I was under the impression I was doing a watercolour course, not survival training.'

'In your case, it's probably the same thing.'

'What's that supposed to mean?'

'Nothing.'

'Nothing,' said Nan. 'No, I'm not accepting that.'

'All right. You won't like it. Either you find something to do with your life, something that gives it purpose, or you die. You carry on walking and talking, but you're dead.'

She felt very cold all of a sudden, and she shivered. Her clothes were damp from the splashes they'd taken crossing the stream, and her shoes were sodden. She took them off.

'You think my life is that empty?' she said.

'You tell me.'

She thought for a moment. Then she said, 'It just didn't have a focal point. Now it has.'

Time drifted. On more than one occasion Nan caught herself nodding off, and came to with a jerk. Once Tad said, 'I had a look outside. He's still there,' and she realised she must actually have been asleep.

Then all of a sudden it was dark, and she was very cold down one side, and bits of her didn't feel as though they were there any more. She was lying down, but she

127

couldn't work out where she was at all; the warm side of her was against someone else's body. 'Mike?' she said, disorientated.

The body stirred, and she realised it wasn't Mike. 'Nick?' she tried, and then she remembered.

'Carry on,' said Tad. 'It was just getting interesting. How many more to go before you get to Tad?'

'Mind your own business,' said Nan irritably. She tried to sit up, but bits of her had gone numb, and she couldn't see anything at all, it was pitch black. They bumped heads, and said sorry at the same time.

'Hands and knees up the steps, I think,' said Tad, 'wherever they are.' He started to grope around – she could see the tiny light on his watch moving. She felt his arm brush her thigh.

'What's the time?'

The light shot up into the air. 'Ten past nine.'

'No wonder I'm hungry,' said Nan.

'This'll go down a storm with Simone,' said Tad. 'Both of us missing.' The light climbed a little. 'Found them,' said Tad. 'This way.'

As they ascended the steps, they began to see dim shapes, then they were in the main area of the shelter with the gaping end opening on to the field. It was just light enough to see the rabbits, dotted about the field like giant mushrooms. They stood outside, the shelter between them and the stream, and breathed deeply. Nan started to laugh.

'What?'

'You're a mess,' she said. 'Filthy. Your jeans are torn, your hair's full of vegetation and you . . . hang on.' She stared at his arm. There was a thick dark line crossing the old white scar. The rest of the arm was streaked with dark as well.

He glanced at it. 'Oh,' he said, 'that.'

'Braithwaite hit you, didn't he?' said Nan. 'Just before we got to the other side of the stream, you stumbled, and you never said anything.'

'Of course not.'

'What do you mean, of course not?'

He grinned, then said in an American drawl, 'It's just a scratch, kid. Now tell me, how many people get the opportunity to use a classic line like that?'

It was his painting arm; Nan didn't smile. 'I think we'd better get back and have a look at it. Is it safe now, d'you think?'

He nodded. As they trudged back up the hill to the house a faint, irritating whine began to increase in volume. Eventually Nan realised that it must be Imogen playing her violin, for it certainly didn't sound like any recording of *Jesu Joy of Man's Desiring* that Nan had ever heard. The notes slurred around like a switchback at twice the normal speed, cutting corners every so often. Tad was laughing like a lunatic. Just before they reached the drive he sobered, caught her by the arm and said, 'What are we going to say?'

'What happened, I suppose.'

'And you seriously think Simone and Nick will believe us?'

She touched his arm. 'You've got proof.'

'Anything could have done that.'

'You're actually worried what Simone's going to think, aren't you?' said Nan. 'Well, well.'

'No I'm not.'

'She really has managed to reverse everything, hasn't she?' said Nan. 'Long live the double standard. She's got three of you, and none of you are allowed to play away from home.'

'You're wrong,' said Tad.

'Just because you say I am?'

'You *are* wrong,' Tad repeated.

'No.'

'I have to prove it, do I?' He pulled her against him with his good arm and kissed her, hard. Emphatic would be the word to describe it, rather than erotic. She was so

129

surprised she just let him. Then he let go and glared at her. 'Satisfied?'

'After ten seconds?' said Nan, and then regretted it because it wasn't what she meant at all.

'What precisely *is* this focal point you've discovered?' said Tad. 'Anatomical, is it?'

'I meant painting,' said Nan, wanting to hit him.

There was a faint roll of thunder in the distance.

'Let's stop this carping,' said Tad. 'I'm enjoying teaching you; you understand what I'm on about. I am not about to tread on Nick's toes and I wasn't making a pass at you. You'd just annoyed me, that's all. I'd like to carry on teaching you, if you want me to. Truce?'

'OK,' said Nan.

'I'll see you upstairs, then,' he said, and they went their separate ways to get cleaned up.

Chapter Eight

When she entered the studio, she could see that Simone and Tad had been arguing. Nick was sitting on the cushions, reading a book, ignoring them. He looked up and smiled at her. He was wearing a djellaba, white cotton, long-sleeved, very Arabic. Cheng was nowhere to be seen. She could see Tad's arm under the spotlight; there was a savage mark that went from his elbow almost all the way to his wrist. It was much worse than she'd imagined. Although the shot hadn't broken the skin at either end, the middle had opened up again, and he was holding it together with a piece of kitchen roll.

'It might need stitches,' Simone was saying. 'You're right-handed; you can't just ignore it.' She glanced up and saw Nan. 'You've been having fun,' she said. But there was no animosity in it.

'It doesn't need stitches,' said Tad. 'Give me the script and we'll get on with it.'

'I didn't think you were staying,' said Nick.

'Give me the script,' repeated Tad.

'Cheng's doing it,' said Nick.

Tad glanced pointedly round the studio.

Nick looked at Simone.

'Oh, for God's sake, give it to him,' she said.

Nick picked up the script from the floor and handed it over. Tad started to flick through it, but before he could really get into it Cheng walked in, and held out his hand. 'Hang on,' said Tad, reading something and looking puzzled.

Then Cheng very delicately lifted the script out of his hands and said, 'OK. Let's go.'

Nan took her clothes off, and so did Nick. They got up on to the dais as before, and Cheng asked her to lie down on her stomach across the rug. Tad got out some paper and a pencil, but she could see him wincing every so often.

'Right,' said Cheng. 'One figure stays still as a visual anchor, but the other one moves. Nick, prowl round her, one side then the other; keep your face towards Simone if you can.'

Tad sharpened his pencil. Cheng leaned back against the cushions, expressionless as ever, and Simone did her little foot-tapping routine in anticipation. Nick began to circle her like a predator, slowly, carefully. She could hear both Simone and Tad sketching them, the sudden flurries of the pencils, the pauses when they stopped to look. They held the pose for twenty minutes, and then they did another. Tad started this one, but gave up after half a minute and just sat there, looking depressed.

'Right,' said Cheng, 'on your knees, Nick, crouching over her.'

'I didn't write that.'

'Just do it, Nick,' said Simone.

Nick looked as though he was about to argue, then he seemed to change his mind. They completed that one, then Cheng arranged them into something far more suggestive, Nick sitting astride Nan and holding her down by her wrists. There were a couple of quick variations on this one, until Nick was lying on top of her, and Simone was demanding so many slight changes

132

in position that the friction of Nick's body started to have the inevitable effect on her.

'Keep going,' said Cheng, and he changed the lighting.

Nan felt Nick's lips brush her ear. 'They want us to go further,' he whispered.

Nan stiffened slightly. She'd known all along that it wasn't going to be simulated sex, hadn't she? And she'd still said yes. But her mind wasn't ready yet, even if her body was.

Nick sat back on his heels and left his hands resting lightly either side of her waist. Simone was scribbling furiously. 'Time for a tea-break,' said Nick cheerfully.

'Nick!' screamed Simone, really frustrated. 'It's going like a dream. *Please.*'

'Have a heart,' said Nick. 'I'm not as young as I used to be.'

Simone threw down her pencil in a temper and walked out of the studio. Nick stood up, and slipped on the djellaba. He handed Nan the dress.

Cheng stood up. 'Do you really want tea?' he asked.

'Yes,' said Nick, whereupon Cheng left the studio as well.

Tad flexed his fingers. The blood on his arm had dried, but he didn't look frightfully happy. Nan went over to Simone's drawing and looked at it. She'd used pastels again; the blue lighting had thrown up warm shadows and there was a sense of real movement in the picture. She wanted to see what Tad had drawn, but he'd turned it over. He glanced round, saw her looking, and shook his head.

Simone reappeared with Cheng and the tea, all smiles. The tea came without milk, in little oriental bowls, and with an unfamiliar flavour. Simone downed hers in one go, but Tad declined altogether. Nan found it rather refreshing after a while, although she would have preferred the usual sort. Cheng tried to refill her bowl, but she shook her head.

Simone clapped her hands. 'Break over,' she said, and

133

Nan and Nick slipped off their clothes and went and stood on the dais as before. Cheng brought over a pile of drapes and scraps of material, and substituted them for the rug. There was velvet and brocade, cheesecloth and leather, gingham and mohair. Fine gold threads caught the light, every texture and colour she could imagine jumbled together, folds and creases, Klimt in a messy mood. 'Lie down,' said Cheng. 'On your back this time, knees drawn up, arms folded across your breasts.'

Nan did as she was told. Tad leaned back against the cushions, watching. The lighting was the same blue lamp that Simone had used before but this time she was standing up, an easel in front of her. This time she was going to paint.

Cheng told Nick to place his hands on her knees, as though he was about to force them apart. Suddenly, the silky touch of Nick's skin was as welcome as a glass of sparkling water on a hot day, and she felt a thrill travel through her, like a bubble rising to the surface. There's no doubt about what my body wants, she thought. It's my mind that's the problem. But as one pose ran into another and he slid his hands across her, the mental reserves started to melt away. There was something different; she was more aware of his touch, more aware of the differences in pressure. Everything was heightened. The feathery strokes of his fingertips were more feathery, the tingle in her scalp more tingly, the pleasurable ache of desire more pleasurable. How beautiful his face is, she thought. Those secretive eyes, exactly the same blue you get just above the horizon on hazy mornings in July. That beard, as neat and controlled as the rest of him. The line of his cheekbones, the waves of his hair falling across that high brow, white as a clean sheet.

A few poses with Nick's hands on her breasts. It was freeze-frame sex, a movement here – pause – another movement there. His fingers caressing her nipple, then stop, hold it, carry on . . . the little bursts of arousal, then the moments of breath-holding anticipation until the next sequence. His erection touching her here and there as he changed position, the stern expression that came over his features as now and again he struggled to keep himself under control. He seemed to be having as much difficulty keeping still as she was. The urge to rub herself against him was becoming unbearable; she felt like a bitch on heat, desperate for him. Nothing else mattered but getting shafted; nothing else was important – there could have been an earthquake and still they'd have carried on regardless.

'Now,' said Cheng, 'you hold her hands above her head, both wrists with one hand.' He stepped over and organised it. Nick was now on top of her. Her knees were either side of his hips; she could feel him between her legs. 'Hold her down,' said Cheng, 'as though you think she might struggle – but don't kiss her. We need to see your face.'

We, thought Nan fleetingly. Cheng really has taken over, hasn't he?

'I can't keep this position up for long,' said Nick.

'Then don't,' said Simone. She was watching them with an expression of real excitment, her brush poised, her eyes blazing. 'Go with it. She's got hang-ups about this, Nick. Overcome them.'

Nick held Simone's eyes for a long moment. Then he switched to Nan, looked at her slightly apprehensively and said, 'Yes? Or no? Just say stop, and I'll stop.'

His voice was so sexy, it seemed to penetrate her all on its own. He slid his hand down her body, and it was as if he were painting her with a wash of crimson, burnishing her skin into one great area of lust. Every nerve ending was twice as sensitive, twice as responsive. He slid his finger inside her, twisting it so that the knuckle caught her where it mattered, and her body arched in response. She could see Tad watching, expressionless; and that was when she finally said *yes*.

She opened her legs wider, felt him enter her as

135

smoothly as if he were inserting a key in a well-oiled lock, but her eyes never left Tad's face. Nick had one hand on either arm now, holding her captive; she could feel his nails digging into her and the knife-like pressure was wildly erotic. He started to fuck her, long deep strokes, right the way in, then nearly all the way out. She could hear Simone's brush whisking across the canvas. She saw Tad swallow, and shift his position. He looked physically uncomfortable. This, in its turn, aroused her even more. As she watched him she realised that she'd never kept her eyes open before; with Mike she'd needed every ounce of concentration to come. This was a different plane of awareness entirely. She wouldn't have been able to stop herself if she'd tried; the orgasm built and built and still their eyes stayed locked together.

She heard Simone say, 'That's brilliant. She wouldn't look at him would she? She's captured it, the whole thing. She's the best bloody model I've ever had. You're a genius, Tad . . .' And the brush moved faster and faster, and Nick seemed to be moving in time with it, and Tad seemed to have turned to stone . . .

And then Nick upped the tempo, fast and hard, and she couldn't hold back any longer. Her whole body went into spasm and her toes clenched as the pleasure spread through her. She heard Nick make some sort of sound, swept along by it and ejaculating with her, thrust and contraction perfectly synchronised, a textbook copulation. She heard Simone say *yes*, and Cheng turn the page. Tad closed his eyes, as though he had a headache. Nick kissed her softly on the cheek, and withdrew.

'Nan,' said Simone, 'that was absolutely out of this world. Thank you. *Incroyable.*'

They sat up, and put their clothes on. There was no embarrassment, nothing; it really was another world. Nick ruffled her hair affectionately, as though they'd just won a doubles match, and Cheng cleared away the tea things. He was smiling.

136

Tad stood up. Then he went very white, swayed slightly, and grabbed hold of the shelving. A terracotta pot of dried honesty toppled to the floor and shattered. Simone simply stared at the shards of pottery as though they were some sort of jigsaw puzzle, and Cheng looked at the tea-tray he was holding as though he was debating whether to put it down and clear up the mess. Nick merely looked thoughtful. Nan couldn't understand their lack of concern. The strange heightened intensity of the last half an hour was dissolving away now, and she felt a bit like the only responsible adult in the room.

She went over to Tad, caught hold of his wrist and looked closely at the cut. He must have been flexing his arm at the time, for the shot had incised a line through where the muscle had been raised, and just grazed him at either side of it. The skin surrounding it was an angry red.

'It does need stitches,' she said. 'Someone should take you to casualty.'

Tad turned to Nick.

'Don't look at me,' said Nick. 'I'm in no state to drive.'

'I haven't got a car,' said Nan.

'Take Tadeusz's,' said Simone. It was no surprise by now that she didn't offer to drive him herself.

Nick looked worried. 'Do you think you're up to it?'

'I'm fine,' said Nan. 'I've only drunk tea.'

'Cheng hasn't got a licence,' said Nick helplessly, 'and I don't think we ought to ask any of the students. Would you be so kind: one of the tutors got shot this afternoon, happens all the time round here, minor hiccup . . .'

'I *am* one of the students,' said Nan.

'Only on paper,' said Nick. 'You're one of us, really.'

Despite his indifference towards Tad's predicament, Nan could have hugged him. She had wanted to be part of something else – some other way of being – for so long; she knew that now. She'd been invited into their world, Nan Tilson, Mrs Average from suburbia, and she felt a wild surge of euphoria. She was *someone*.

Tad picked up his jacket and said curtly, 'Come on then. Let's get it over with.'

They went downstairs and round the back of the building to some garages. He took a set of keys out of the jacket pocket and threw them to her. There were several cars there. To her surprise, he pointed to a very flash Mercedes and said, 'If you reverse it out, I'll shut the door after you.'

Nan had never driven anything like it. It was like being in control of a guided missile made of silk. He shut the door and climbed into the passenger seat. 'This wasn't what I'd imagined at all,' said Nan.

He smiled with a complete absence of humour, winced, looked miserable again.

'It really hurts, doesn't it?' said Nan. 'Why didn't you say anything? I didn't take you for the stiff-upper-lip macho masochist type.'

'Dunno,' he said.

She stopped him getting out of the car to do the gate, and opened and closed it herself. Then she drove very gingerly along the track until they reached the open road. She put her foot down, and the car responded like a lover.

'How far is it?'

'About fifteen miles. Turn left when you get to the roundabout.'

'God,' said Nan, 'this is weird. You don't seem to belong in normal surroundings.'

'Thanks.'

'You know what I mean.'

She turned left at the roundabout. He leaned his head back against the rest and closed his eyes. They travelled for a while in silence.

'It's funny,' said Nan eventually. 'I've just realised that I know absolutely nothing about you.'

'Rubbish,' said Tad, without opening his eyes. 'You know how I behave when I'm scared, you know what

138

I'm like when I'm working, you're driving my car and I've kissed you. There you go.'

She laughed. 'I meant that I know nothing about your background.'

'Oh.'

'Why the reticence?'

'I'm not being reticent.'

'Yes you are.' Was he just being his usual awkward self, or was there more of an edge to it?

'Age forty-six,' he said irritably, 'born in London, Polish parents, only child. Chelsea art school, then the RCA, then a couple of years in the States. Juggled teaching and painting ever since, but the teaching's taken a back seat for a good few years now. Met Simone when we had an exhibition together with a couple of other people. Never really wanted to do anything much except cover things with paint.'

'Sketchy,' said Nan.

'What do you want,' snapped Tad, 'my O levels in oils?'

They travelled the rest of the way in frosty silence. Eventually a hospital sign loomed before them, and Nan turned into the car park. They got out.

'I hate hospitals,' said Tad morosely.

'I'll see if they sell Smarties anywhere,' said Nan.

They went over to the desk, and Tad started to give his details. He gave Lavender Hall as his address, and the woman behind the desk looked at him a little oddly. Then she said, 'You're the painter, aren't you?'

Tad scowled, discouraging any further questions.

The woman glanced at the third finger of Nan's left hand. 'If you'd like to wait in there, Mrs Kalinowski,' she said, directing Nan to the waiting room.

'I'm not Mrs Kalinowski,' said Nan, 'I'm a –' and she hesitated. What was she? A student, a model, a chauffeur?

'She's a friend,' said Tad shortly.

The woman sent him off to triage, and Nan went and

sat in the waiting room. She sat there for the first half-hour, puzzling over her identity. She felt like a fish out of water in the hospital; it belonged to another world. She got up and went over to the coffee machine. There was a sweets machine there as well, so she got a packet of Smarties. Then she saw the telephone. She suddenly remembered telling Sandra she would call Mike, so she picked up the receiver and rang home.

'What's up?' he said blearily. 'It's gone midnight, for God's sake.'

She was shocked. She hadn't looked at a clock for hours.

'I didn't realise,' she said. 'Sorry.'

And then, so quietly that at first she wasn't sure that she wasn't imagining it, she heard a woman's voice whisper, 'Who is it?'

There was a rustling, as though Mike had put his hand over the mouthpiece. Oh, to hell with it, thought Nan, I don't care any more. 'I'm staying on for another week,' she said. 'I've cleared it with work.'

'Oh,' said Mike. 'Enjoying yourself, then?'

'Even more than you,' said Nan, and hung up.

Tad emerged at two o'clock, looking fed up and with his arm bandaged. 'He doesn't want me to do any painting for a few days,' he said. 'And he asked some bloody awkward questions, as well. I told him I was stretching a canvas and he said what with, a shotgun?'

'It's OK, though? He didn't want to call the police or anything?'

'He said my sexual hang-ups were my business, not his. So I went along with it and said I'd invite him to my next private view.'

They walked out to the car, and Nan gave him the Smarties. He suddenly brightened up and ate all the orange ones first. She drove out of the car park and back on to the main road.

'Tell me about Sniffle,' said Nan.

He looked out of the window. 'She turned up on my

140

watercolour course. Simone was into lighting at the time, fairly tame stuff; she was trying out different effects. Sniffle really got off on it, changed her approach to botanical stuff as a result – massive improvement. She stayed on, started doing some tutoring, identifying woodland plants, that sort of thing. She's quiet: doesn't say what she thinks, bottles it all up. When Simone wanted her to move on to rather more explicit poses with Nick, she refused.'

'Did you sleep with her?'

He stared at her. 'Why on earth would I want to sleep with Sniffle? She's got less conversation than a bulrush. Which is what she's mainly interested in. Bulrushes. And besides that, she's gay. Simone thought she was bisexual, and when she found out she just told Sniffle she didn't want her any more. Sniffle had burned her boats: left her partner, had nowhere to go back to. She models for the students, sometimes, but she doesn't speak to Simone any more. I think she's looking for another job.'

'Did you ever draw her? She's very pretty.'

'You can't have understood any of my paintings,' said Tad, annoyed. 'Does my work look that superficial to you? Christ, I spend my bloody life trying to get *under* the skin, not skate over it like Simone.'

'I haven't *seen* any of your paintings,' said Nan. 'Only the two drawings you did of me, and the landscape.'

'Oh,' he said.

They drove for a while in silence, and then she realised that he'd fallen asleep. He didn't wake up again until they were just about to leave the main road.

'Do you want to see my work?' he said abruptly.

'Of course I do.'

'You're not to make rude remarks.'

'Fucking hell,' said Nan, 'I wouldn't dare.' The new Nan seemed to have a new vocabulary as well. She turned down the track and the trees closed above them like a living creature, blotting out everything else.

'Back to unreality,' said Tad.

She drove the car quickly and accurately into the garage.

'Impressive driving,' said Tad, retrieving the keys.

They went into the house and up the staircase, but this time they turned left instead of right, and went into another wing. Tad opened the door to a large room, and switched on the light. There was a double bed in one corner, the quilt still rumpled. A few canvases against the wall, and piles of drawings everywhere. The drawings were much more dramatic than Simone's, although they weren't as erotic; he seemed to be saying that the relationship between his subjects was more important than the figures themselves. It was a more balanced viewpoint, and a more complicated one, and she was surprised. His drawings made you think, rather than react. She'd had him down as someone who went for an emotional response rather than an intellectual one, and she'd been wrong. She started to ask him questions about why he did things, what he'd aimed at, how he'd achieved a particular effect. He answered her seriously and in depth, and she found herself liking his work more and more. Once again she found herself thinking about what she wanted to paint herself – but this time she was thinking *why*, not what or how.

He began to ask her questions about the way she would have dealt with a particular problem herself. Then he said, 'I don't know how you'd feel about this . . . there's something I've been working on, and I don't want to stop in the middle of it. You wouldn't try to impose your ideas on me like Simone, and I need someone receptive.'

'What are you asking?'

'I'm asking you to work with me, just for a few days.'

'You want me to pose?'

'No,' he said, 'I want you to paint.'

She was astounded. 'I'm not good enough,' she said.

'You can hold a brush. I can't at the moment, can I?'

'Honestly, Tad, I don't think I'm up to it.'

'You don't want to?'

'I'd love to,' she said. 'I just don't want to let you down.'

'We're not dodging bullets here,' he said. 'If something doesn't work, it just goes in the bin. Let's give it a try.'

She looked at one of his drawings, and felt very inadequate. 'This isn't just another one of your highly original teaching methods, is it?' she said.

'You can look at it that way, if you like.'

'All right, then,' she said. 'Extra lessons.'

'And no surcharge,' he said. 'Bargain. We finish – what – about half past four. Dinner's at seven. We can talk about it, try a few things out, really get going next week when I'm not teaching.'

She took a deep breath. 'OK.'

'Now go and get some sleep.'

When she got back to the coach-house, the things she'd left under the tree and forgotten about were neatly piled on her bed.

Friday. She overslept, and woke up at midday. There was a note tacked to the door. 'Down by the lake. Tad.'

This time they were all grouped together, just a few yards separating one from the other. Tad was talking to Lettie. Imogen was trying to rescue an utterly hopeless sky, and Megan and Brian hadn't finished their lunch. They were drinking wine out of plastic beakers and laughing a lot. Jocelyn was doing quite well, and Nan was surprised to see that Denise had joined them for the day. She didn't seem to have much idea what she was doing.

'Lie-in?' asked Gladys nastily as Nan put down her things.

'Headache,' said Nan.

'Everyone's under the weather,' said Gerald. 'Tad cut

143

his arm stretching a canvas, and Gladys has a dose of piles.'

'Oh, dear,' said Nan. Gladys was glaring at Gerald in a way that made Nan fear for his safety later.

'All right,' said Megan, as soon as she got Nan on her own, 'what happened yesterday? You go off with Tad, and I don't see you again until now.'

Then Jocelyn appeared, and set up next to Megan and Nan. Megan looked annoyed, but there was nothing she could do about it. The conversation dried completely.

Nan started to sketch in the view. She quickly established her focal point and how she was going to accentuate it, and the sky went on in under thirty seconds; this time she knew what she was doing. She darkened the trees and started to make them suggest things, other viewpoints, other themes, using their shapes instead of just copying them. Jocelyn glanced across. Then she stood up and walked over. She stared at the painting for a full minute; then she smiled faintly and went and sat down again.

Tad came over some time later and just stood there, grinning. 'Aren't you going to say anything?' demanded Nan.

'Nope. Nothing *to* say, except keep going.'

She felt really pleased.

He went over to Jocelyn, and began to explain something about perspective. Jocelyn started to argue, and Tad eventually said, 'You can't have your lake on two levels, goddammit. Water doesn't behave like that. Where's your eye-level?'

They scrapped for a while longer, Jocelyn determined not to be told anything, and Tad determined not to give up. Megan went off to see how Brian was doing.

'I thought perspective was about railway lines and buildings and things?' said Jocelyn. 'I don't see how it's important out here.'

'It *is* important,' said Tad, 'because your lake is a topographical impossibility.'

144

Jocelyn looked put out. Then she said, 'I think I'll pack up now.'

'Suit yourself,' said Tad.

Jocelyn went.

'Did you understand all that?' asked Tad.

'I'm not sure,' said Nan. 'I can see that her water was wrong, and how she could have put it right, but I'm not sure I can reason out why.'

'Fair enough,' said Tad. 'Want another lesson, then?'

She grinned. 'Yes.'

He glanced round, then took her to the edge of the trees, well away from the others. 'Right,' he said. 'What shape is the lake from here, standing up looking at it?'

'It's a sort of squashed oval – and there's a spit of land breaking it up that goes about a third of the way across.'

'Now lie down on your stomach, and describe it again.'

She lay down. 'It's just a thin strip of water, I can't see any shape to it at all really.'

'Good. Now we climb that tree.'

'What?'

'Up you go,' he said. 'I've selected a reasonably easy one.'

It was a horse chestnut, and it was big. Nan was glad she was wearing her customary shorts and T-shirt, and she started to climb without too much difficulty. She glanced down. Tad was following her, climbing one-handed whenever possible. She went about three-quarters of the way up, and stopped when she reached a rather neat platform created by the junction of several branches with the trunk. There was a gap in the leaves, and she could see for miles. She waited for Tad.

He joined her on the platform, and sat astride one of the branches. 'OK,' he said, 'what shape is the lake now?'

She looked at it and laughed. Seen from above, the oval had nearly become a circle, and the spit of land cut into it like a mouth. There was a tiny island to the right,

145

which became an eye, and the whole thing now resembled a fat little fish, with a rather silly expression on its face. 'That's wonderful,' she said, 'it's a piranha that's just had dinner.'

'So,' said Tad, 'you'll agree that the perspective affects the way you see the lake?'

'Oh, yes,' said Nan.

'But why is it important?'

She thought about it. He leaned back against the trunk and watched her, his eyes half-shut. 'Oh,' she said suddenly, 'I see. It's all to do with the observer, isn't it? The perspective you put in the picture tells the onlooker where they are in relation to everything in the painting. It's the connection. Artist to audience, you are here. You are me.'

He smiled. 'But then you take it further. You can manipulate your audience, make them believe they're a dwarf or a giant. Perspective is a tool, not a restriction.'

He brushed an insect off her arm. She found a half-finished packet of peppermints in her pocket, and they scoffed the lot. The leaves cast wonderful five-pointed shadows across their bodies, which danced with each puff of breeze. She could have stayed up there for hours.

'What's the difference between linear perspective and aerial perspective?' asked Tad, trying to scratch under his bandage.

'I give up,' said Nan. 'And stop that, it's bad for you.'

He made a face at her, but he stopped.

'What's the difference then?' asked Nan.

'Blue,' said Tad.

'That's a big help.'

He smirked. 'Aerial perspective is the effect atmosphere has on colour and tone. Atmosphere – and foreign particles in the air, let's be accurate – they scatter light, except for blue light, so things in the distance look bluer and lighter than they do close up. A touch of blue gives depth.'

'I knew that,' said Nan, 'I just didn't know the name for it.'

'Does knowing the name make a difference to what you see?'

'No.'

'Does what you see make a difference to what you describe?'

'Of course.'

'Quite,' said Tad. 'Images take precedence over words.'

Nan looked across the lake to the line of trees on the other side. When she compared them with the trees, close to, there was a pronounced difference, and the longer she looked the more of a contrast she saw. The trees had become a cold pale turquoise, a halfway house between the green of the foliage and the blue of the sky, and anything but that precise colour would have been garish and wrong. From her vantage point she could see Imogen and Gladys and the rest, tiny figures now – but she couldn't see Lettie. Nor could she see Gerald.

'It's probably time we went,' said Tad, and they started to climb down. When they were halfway there, they heard voices. Nan looked down, and saw Lettie. Then Gerald moved into her field of vision as well.

'It's too risky,' she heard him say.

'Rubbish,' said Lettie, unzipping his fly.

'No,' said Gerald. 'I couldn't get my clothes back on in time, if someone came.'

'Someone *is* going to come,' said Lettie. 'You.'

Gerald made a strangled sound in his throat.

'You don't need to take your clothes off,' said Lettie.

'What are you going to do?' asked Gerald. 'Wank me? I can't go back to Gladys with spunk on my trousers.'

'There won't *be* any,' said Lettie. 'I'm going to suck you off. One swallow may not make a summer, but several might make yours.'

'Oh, God,' said Gerald. 'No one's ever done that to me before.'

'It seems to be his lucky day,' whispered Tad to Nan. 'I think we ought to keep very quiet. I'd hate to deny him his first experience of fellatio. And I bet Lettie's a past master at it.'

'Back against the tree-trunk,' said Lettie. 'That's it. Oh, my, what a stiffie we have all of a sudden.'

Lettie knelt down, and took Gerald's cock in her mouth. 'Oh, Christ,' said Gerald, 'that feels unbelievable.' There was silence for a while, punctuated by faint licking sounds and Gerald's uneven breathing. 'Lettie,' said Gerald hoarsely, 'I think I love you.'

Lettie stopped what she was doing. 'None of that,' she said. 'This is just sex, Gerald. Don't spoil it. And once you're back home you'll see it that way, too.'

'Will I ever get to see you again?'

'I'm sure we'll be able to arrange the odd dirty weekend.'

'Thank God for that,' replied Gerald. Then, 'Oh, Lettie, yes, keep doing that. It's out of this world . . .'

More sounds, and even more uneven breathing.

'Talk to me, Gerald,' said Lettie. 'I love it when you go all incoherent.'

'What about?'

'Oh, for God's sake,' said Lettie, 'tell me what you like. Tell me what you want. Tell me what you'd like to do to me.'

'I want you to keep on licking me for ever . . . and that thing you do to my balls with your fingers – oh, yes – and . . . and the way you run your tongue round me . . . oh, Jesus, don't stop . . .'

'And what would you like to do to me in return?'

'I'd like to lick you, too. Down there.'

'Good,' said Lettie. 'Another time, though. Ever done it before?'

'No.'

'I'll teach you.'

Lettie resumed her fellatio, and Gerald tried to keep talking. 'Yes . . . more, just there. The tickly thing you do

... That butterfly effect – oh, God, I – never – oh, Lettie ...'

Nan glanced at Tad, and saw he was watching her. And then she didn't look at Lettie and Gerald again; she just sat very still and didn't take her eyes from Tad's face. They stayed like that, motionless, listening, their eyes locked together the way they had been in the studio, when Nick had fucked her in front of him. She had no idea what was going through his mind, but the sounds from below were very explicit, and she wondered if he was imagining her doing the same to him. And then she wondered what it would be like, giving Tad a blow-job, and what he would be like, doing licky things to her. He kept his face expressionless, and she did the same, but it was an effort.

'Oh, my God,' cried Gerald, 'I'm coming ...' His breathing tumbled into a series of jerks, and then he sighed deeply.

'Come on, stud, we'd better get back,' said Lettie.

Gerald laughed a little unsteadily, zipped himself up, and they walked off.

'How come you started sleeping with Nick?' asked Tad suddenly.

'He just turned me on, I suppose,' said Nan, looking away.

'So it was a spur-of-the-moment type thing.'

'No.'

'Why, then?'

'A blow for freedom, I suppose.'

'Really?' said Tad. 'A blow, eh? You were busy.'

She glared at him.

He laughed. 'You haven't fallen in love with him or anything?'

'No.'

'Good,' said Tad, 'because he's bad news.'

'That's what he said.'

'Coo-ee!' called a voice. They looked down. Gladys

149

was standing at the foot of the tree. 'I've finished,' she said.

They climbed the rest of the way down, Tad going first. He took it quite slowly and sensibly, and then behaved as though sitting up a horse chestnut was the most natural thing in the world. Gladys looked at him as if he were mad.

Chapter Nine

When they got back at half past four Megan said, 'Brian and I are going back to the lake for a swim, and so are some of the others. Grab a towel.'

'No, I don't think so,' said Nan.

'What on earth's the matter with you?'

'I've got things to do.'

'Something's going on,' said Megan.

'Please,' said Nan, 'not now.'

'All right,' said Megan, 'temporary reprieve, on condition you spill the beans later.'

'All right,' said Nan, suddenly tired of working things out on her own, and wanting someone to talk to about it all. She went back to her room and changed into some cotton trousers and a tatty T-shirt. Then she went over to the main building, and as she walked across the entrance hall Denise came out of the library. Nan didn't want to go upstairs while Denise was watching, so she took off her shoe and pretended to forage for a stone. Denise just stood and looked at Nan until Nan felt she had to say something – so she asked Denise if she was going back to Nick's class the next day.

'I expect so,' said Denise. Then she added casually, 'What's the painting like that Simone's doing of you?'

Nan stared at her.

'Come on,' said Denise, 'I'm not daft. I'm just surprised you agreed to do it, that's all. You don't seem the type.' Her tone was very lightweight, but the dark close-set eyes were far from stupid.

Nan didn't know what to say.

'Is it a single pose, or is there someone else involved? Cheng, for instance?'

Nan remembered Denise standing there with Sniffle, remembered their covert glances. Denise knew. It was perfectly obvious. 'No,' she said. 'Cheng's not involved.'

Denise smiled, and Tad came in through the main door. He stopped, and Nan saw him sum up the situation fairly rapidly. He nodded politely at Denise, turned to Nan and said, 'I suppose I've got to let you look at my arm and change the bloody dressing now, haven't I?'

'Excuse me,' said Nan to Denise, and she followed Tad up the stairs. As she turned along the corridor at the top, she could see Denise looking at them, the slight smile still on her face. She had a biro in her hand, and she was getting out her notebook. My God, thought Nan, she's writing about us. What's Nick going to say?

They went into Tad's room and Nan said, 'Do you really want me to see to your arm?'

'Tomorrow,' said Tad. 'It'll do for now.'

He got out some drawings, and spread them out on the floor. Nan looked at the first one and saw Simone looking back at her, her face full of concentration but also imbued with that subtle sexual glow that enveloped her when she was drawing bodies.

'The voyeur observed,' said Tad. 'It has a nice twist to it, don't you think?'

She moved on to the next. They talked about pencil control, directional shading, line weight, emphasis.

'How on earth can I help with these?' said Nan eventually. 'I couldn't begin to capture what you've got in them.'

152

'Studio assistant,' said Tad. 'I need backgrounds.'

Nan glanced at one of Tad's paintings, leaning against the wall. 'I've not used oils very much,' she said.

'Piece of piss,' said Tad, 'compared to watercolour.'

'For you, maybe.'

'Scrape it off, paint over it, move it around the canvas: it's malleable. None of this irrevocable business you get with watercolour.'

'Is this what you were drawing, in the studio? Why you wouldn't let anyone look?'

'Yes,' said Tad. 'The others are earlier.'

'This one ... I remember this, when Simone was rinsing out that pot, but it only took her a minute. How on earth did you get so much done? It's not possible.'

'From memory.'

'You did some of these from memory?'

'I've got a photographic memory,' he said. 'It's no big deal.'

'Has Simone?'

'Has Simone what?'

'Got a photographic memory.'

'No.'

'So who was Simone painting before me? Sniffle?'

'Cheng. And me.'

She gulped.

He laughed. 'She didn't get what she wanted, but she tried hard enough. She's so insidious: *just move this way a bit, Tad, brush against him – no, no, your hips, not your arm* ... Skin's skin, Nan; it feels the same, whoever it belongs to. *Nice erection, Tadeusz, turn this way a bit more ... Bend over, Cheng* ... No. Not my scene. Nick offered to write her another script. I think you were meant to have sex with Cheng instead.'

'*What*?'

'Nick wrote this before you came on the scene, remember.'

'So what was the story going to be about?'

'Christ, I don't know. The last temptation of the Bud-

153

dhist monk or something; don't ask *me* what goes on in Nick's mind.' He glanced at the clock on the wall. 'Dinner.' He locked the door of the room as they left, and pocketed the key. 'You have to stand up to Simone if you don't like what she's asking, Nan. She will always keep pushing; she never gives up. And the nearer she gets you to what you're not prepared to do, the more expression she gets out of you. She feeds off that.'

Much as Nan would have liked to pursue this topic of conversation, she didn't want to arrive at the canteen with Tad. 'I'm going to the loo,' she said. 'I'll see you later.'

When she opened the door to the refectory, a little while later, she saw all the watercolourists' faces turn towards her. She felt very isolated and conspicuous, and to make it worse Nick smiled at her. Sniffle had gone over to the writers' table, and was sitting with Denise. Tad was talking quietly to Cheng. Nan went and sat next to Megan.

'We had a fabulous swim,' said Megan. 'The water's really clear. Bit cold, but lovely.'

Nan finished her meal as quickly as possible and went back to her room. She was sitting on the bed, thinking, when Megan came in without knocking.

'Are you sleeping with Tad?' she demanded.

'No.'

'I don't believe you,' said Megan. 'I know a post-orgasmic glow when I see one, and you had it yesterday morning.'

Nan saw that she wasn't going to be able to fend Megan off much longer. 'I slept with *Nick*,' she said. 'Satisfied now?'

Megan looked pole-axed. 'Nick,' she said. 'Nicholas Cross. The biggest name of the lot. Bloody hell.' She shook her head a couple of times.

'What's so astonishing?' said Nan, faintly annoyed.

'*You*,' said Megan. 'I honestly never thought you would . . . not really. Shit.'

'Oh, so it's a bad idea now I've done it, is it?'

'I just didn't expect it to be *him*.'

'What's wrong with him?'

'Nothing,' said Megan, 'he's just a lot ... older than you.'

'So what?'

'I just thought – you seemed to get on so well with Tad.'

'It's you who fancies Tad, isn't it?' said Nan. 'You just want to do it vicariously, through me. Brian not living up to expectations?'

'Don't be ridiculous,' said Megan, but she flushed.

Nan laughed. Then she became quite serious and said, 'Megan, let's not scrap. I really need to talk to someone about this. I didn't know I was capable of such – well, lust.'

Megan smiled.

'He's slept with so many women,' said Nan. 'He never makes a wrong move. It's almost unnerving. He seems to know what I'm thinking.'

'That's his job, Nan,' said Megan, 'knowing what people think. Are you going to miss him?'

'I've no idea,' said Nan, 'I haven't thought about it.' She glanced at her watch. 'Look, I've got to go. I'm due in the studio.'

'In the studio? Why?'

Nan smiled. 'I'm posing for Simone,' she said.

Megan looked thunderstruck.

'I really am having a fantastic time, Megan,' said Nan. 'I just wish the photograph had led somewhere. I want to know who I am. And that means finding out about my mother, and I don't know where to look now.'

'How about asking your stepmother?'

'I couldn't.'

'Have you tried, since your father died?'

'No.'

'Well, then. She might be prepared to open up a bit now. You never know.'

'I might do that,' said Nan. 'Yes, I just might do that. OK if I borrow your dress again?'

'Keep it,' said Megan. 'It suits you.'

When Nan made her way back to the studio after dinner she found just Simone and Cheng, huddled over the script. Simone glanced up. '*Ah bon*,' she said, 'There's tea in the pot. Help yourself.'

It was the same pale green stuff she'd had once before. She poured herself a bowl of it, and overcame the slight initial repugnance. Cheng and Simone seemed to reach an agreement about something, and Cheng came over and poured her another, and one for himself. This time she sipped it a little more slowly and the bitterness turned to an odd sort of sweetness, lingering and fruity.

'It's an acquired taste,' said Cheng, and Simone laughed in her bawdy way.

'What is it, exactly?' asked Nan.

'Something I have sent over from South America,' said Simone. '*D'accord*. I'd like to do a couple of you and Cheng standing back to back.'

That sounded harmless enough. Cheng took off his trousers, and Nan slipped off the dress, feeling it slither to the floor like the caress of a lover. She was relieved to note that Cheng didn't have an erection, and they both stepped on to the dais and posed as instructed.

He was quite short, only an inch or so taller than she was, and their bodies made a shape that was very nearly symmetrical. Simone had them with their heads touching, which meant that their shoulders and their buttocks were touching too, and also their calves and their arms. Cheng's skin felt delightful, as smooth as a child's, but she could sense the sinews and the muscles beneath the deceptively delicate exterior. His body was as beautiful to touch as it was to look at, and she found herself savouring every contact like a fine wine, feeling the warmth seep into her. She was so aware of him; the slight changes in pressure as he breathed, the faint

156

perfume that came from his shoulder-length hair, as though he'd just washed it in something rare and exotic. She recognised the same heightened awareness she'd had before – but this was stronger, more intense. The smell of him conjured up images of sweet-scented ginger, growing wild on the banks of a jungle river. The black silk of his hair made her think of panther skin, and the palms of his hands made her wonder what they would feel like moving across her body with a more definite purpose in mind.

'How are you doing?' Simone asked Nan.

'Fine,' said Nan. Then she thought, no. I feel more than fine. I feel terrific.

'Lying down, then, side by side.'

They lay down. Cheng put his arm round her, and she nestled her head on his smooth chest.

'I need a bit more movement,' said Simone. 'Can you stroke her, Cheng?'

Cheng started to stroke Nan's back, very slowly and carefully, from the nape of her neck to the crease between her buttocks. It felt calming and reassuring, as though she were being groomed. Time did something peculiar, and she had no idea how long she lay there, Cheng moving his hand down her spine, stopping at the base of it, then starting at the top again. Her back had never felt so sensitive, so responsive. Each little area seemed to become magnifed as he touched it; she felt she could separate out every single nerve-ending by the pinprick of pleasure it gave her. And at the same time she felt almost sleepy; she didn't want to have to do anything energetic. She wanted things to be done to *her*; she wanted more of this dreamy languid love-making, and part of her wanted it to go further.

Simone moved them round again; this time Nan was lying face-down on the mattress, and Cheng was sitting astride her, his knees on either side of her hips. She could feel his balls resting in the crease between her buttocks, cool and soft and surprisingly heavy. 'Massage her shoulders,' said Simone, and Cheng leaned to one side for something; then he sprinkled her with talcum powder and it felt like he was showering her with refrigerated stardust. He started to knead her, gently at first, then harder.

Oh, he really knows what he's doing here, thought Nan. This is divine. Whatever tension was left just melted away under the pressure of his fingers, and her mind emptied of everything except the sensation. Up the middle of her back, his hands separating at the nape of her neck, round the shoulder blades, under the armpits – just glancing off the nipple in passing – then up the middle of her back as the cycle started again, until she felt like dissolving altogether. The sound of the door opening was a long way away.

'Nick,' she heard Simone say, as if she were in an adjoining room, 'just who we need. Have some tea.'

She heard Nick pour himself a bowlful. 'It's a bit strong, isn't it?' he commented.

'It's just fresh,' said Simone. 'Try it with blackcurrant. Takes away the bitterness.'

Nan heard Nick dribble something out of a bottle. After a moment or two he said, 'All I can taste is blackcurrant now.'

'Stop complaining and take your clothes off,' said Simone.

Nan felt Cheng's hands move further down her back. He carried on massaging her with little circular movements and she drifted again, dreaming of rain forests and orchids and brightly coloured birds, cool encounters with succulent vegetation, creepers, epiphytes, the gossamer breeze of butterfly wings. A whole jungle was making love to her; she was covered with honeydew, and humming birds were licking it off with their long thread-like tongues. Then she saw Nick kneeling beside her, naked.

'OK,' he said to Cheng, 'I can take over now.'

'*Non*,' said Simone. 'Just stay as you are, watching.'

Nick looked slightly miffed, but he did as instructed. The massage went on, but Cheng's hands were getting lower and lower. Now they were kneading her buttocks, his thumbs pressing into her as he circled round, his fingers echoing the pattern; he was getting closer and closer to the crease, opening her cheeks and closing them again, closer, closer . . .

'Open her legs, Nick,' said Simone.

Nan felt Nick take hold of her ankles and spread her legs wide. Cheng's hands moved down the outside of her thighs, then up along the insides. Her brushed her sex very lightly in passing. Then back to her hips and down the outside of her thighs again, then once more up the inside leg. The lightest of contacts, then back to her hips. She shivered. His finger became a little more daring each time, strayed a little further inside, lingered that little bit longer. She could feel the moisture on his fingertips when he trailed them across her thigh.

'Turn over, Nan,' said Simone.

Nan turned over. She could now see Cheng and Nick, one on either side of her.

'I want Cheng where he is, *oui, comme ça*, and Nick up by her head. Nick, you concentrate on her breasts. Cheng, you carry on with what you were doing. Faces towards me whenever possible.'

They moved round, and Nick brushed her ear with his lips. 'Are you OK with this?' he whispered.

'I'm fine,' said Nan.

He licked his index finger, then slid it across her nipple. She felt it harden in response. He pinched it gently between the finger and his thumb, and then he did the same thing to the other nipple. She swallowed. She felt Cheng start to massage her thigh again, getting higher and higher with each sequence of movements, and then he was there, between her legs, and the massage became extremely intimate. Her sense of smell seemed to be very acute; one moment it would be Cheng, with his mysterious eastern fragrance that suggested citrus and lily and a pinch of spice. Then Nick, his musky masculine scent mixed with soap and a hint of blackcurrant. Four hands and two mouths, and all she was required to do was to lay there and take it; she wondered if it was possible to drown in sensory overload.

'*Formidable*,' said Simone softly as her brush whisked to and fro, to and fro.

Both Nick and Cheng had erections now; she could feel their cocks touching her as they shifted position. Nick was nibbling her neck and playing with both her nipples, and Cheng was doing complicated twisting movements with his fingers that took her almost to the edge, and then let her down gently again. He was using his tongue on the inside of her thighs, sweeping up towards her clitoris and then veering away again. She wanted to come now; she didn't know how much more of this she could take.

'Cheng,' said Simone, 'fuck her.'

Hang on, thought Nan. No.

'Uh-uh,' said Nick. 'That's my department.'

'This is work.'

'It's a bit more than that, Simone.'

Nan twisted her head so that she could see better. Simone was biting her lip. 'It's not like you to be possessive, Nick. Why is this?'

'You know why,' he said.

'I can't see inside your head,' snapped Simone.

'That's the trouble,' said Nick. 'I think you can.'

'All right, then,' said Simone, '*you* fuck her, and Cheng plays with her tits.'

'I think that would be better,' said Cheng, sliding his hand up Nan's body and running his palm over her nipple.

'I'd prefer that too,' said Nan.

'You would, would you?' said Simone nastily. 'All right.' She put on some music: Peruvian pipes, breathy,

160

evocative, sexy. Then she laughed, her mood switching as unpredictably as ever. 'Right. All together now.'

Cheng began to stroke her breasts very lightly, as though he were brushing off feathers. He avoided her nipples to begin with, until they were aching for him to touch them. Still he teased her, dusting her delicately with his fingertips, making her long to grab hold of his hands and guide them to where she wanted. Nick was playing with her cunt, feeling it the way a blind man might: exploring it, learning it, going back to particular areas as though he needed to imprint them on his memory. After a while, the two men began to work in harmony, using the music as a guide. The rise and swell of the pipes led to increases and decreases in pressure, until her whole body became one with the music. She could tell that the tune was building to something, and she sensed that they were going to make her come when it reached its crescendo.

Nick stopped what he was doing, shifted his position, and entered her. That felt good, really good; he was hot and hard, and he was fucking her with real determination. Cheng had finally transferred his attention to her nipples; he was sucking in time with Nick's thrusts, and the added stimulation lifted her to the point of no return. As the music rose breathlessly to its conclusion and she felt herself clench for the first contraction of orgasm, she heard the door open. She had her eyes closed – she couldn't have opened them if she'd tried – but she knew that the newcomer had to be Tad, and that was enough to send her into one of the most explosive climaxes she could remember. She was vaguely aware of Nick coming inside her, and Cheng coming over her breasts. As she lay there afterwards, she heard Tad say, 'Cheng got the short straw, then.'

'*Pouf*,' said Simone. 'Look at the paper, Tadeusz. I captured it all.'

'Mm-hm,' said Tad. 'Why have you changed Nan's hair?'

'Not so very much,' said Simone.

'Enough,' said Nick, who had gone over to look. 'That looks more like Harriet than Nan.'

Cheng politely handed Nan a towel, and she wiped his spunk off her body.

And then the telephone rang. It was such an ordinary sound. It didn't seem to fit in with the surroundings at all, insistent, very much of its era, a reminder that there was somewhere out there beyond the studio. Cheng went over to it and picked it up. 'Yes?' he said. There was a brief pause as he listened. Then he turned to Tad. 'It's your wife.'

What? thought Nan. Tad has a *wife*?

Tad stood up and went over to the telephone. Simone stretched herself, puma-like, smiled and said, 'What's next, Cheng?'

My God, thought Nan, what does she mean, *next*? And at the same time she was trying to listen to what Tad was saying on the phone. She couldn't quite get her head round it; Tad married? It seemed so unlikely. He was such a law unto himself; it didn't make sense. And he was here for six months of every year.

'Hello?' she heard him say. '*Co to jest?*' Then, '*Tak.*' It was a shock to hear him speaking Polish; then he switched to English, and then a mixture of the two.

Cheng offered Nan some more tea, but this time she declined.

'No,' said Tad. 'I don't do any interviews over the summer; you know that. Not even for him. Forget it.' There was another pause. Then, '*Kto?*'

'I just want to do one more thing this evening,' said Simone, 'and then we'll call it a night.'

'Listen,' said Tad, 'if I bump into one of his fucking photographers round here, I'll break his bloody neck. Yes, you can tell him that.'

Simone looked up sharply.

'God, no,' said Tad, 'I leave all that to you. Yeah, see

162

to it, would you?' Then, 'Why?' Another pause. '*Dobrze.*
Do widzenia.' He hung up.

'What photographers?' queried Simone.

'Don't worry,' said Tad. 'I've sorted it.'

'Are you sure?'

'Yeah.'

He glanced at Nan. Nan looked away.

'Right,' said Simone, 'one more.'

'Whoa,' said Nick. 'Haven't we done enough tonight?'

'Not up to it?'

'No,' said Nick. 'And not ashamed to admit it, either.'

'Cheng?'

Cheng held up the script like a shield.

'Tad?' tried Simone.

'Oh, for God's sake,' said Nick.

'Tad?' repeated Simone.

'You're pushing it, Simone,' said Tad.

Simone laughed. 'I always do.' She got up and went
over to him, slid her arms round his waist and kissed
him on the neck. 'I just need to go that little bit further,
chéri.'

'You always do,' said Tad, not responding. 'Maybe
you should learn when to stop.'

'I was watching you, Tadeusz,' said Simone. 'You'd
have been on that dais like a shot if I'd suggested it.'

'No,' said Tad.

Simone put her hand down his trousers. He didn't
move. 'Who are you kidding?' said Simone.

Nick stood up. 'Come on, Nan,' he said. 'Time to go.'
He ushered her towards the door.

Nan saw Tad forcibly take Simone's hand away. She
hit him on his injured arm; he winced, and indicated to
them both with a slight movement of his head to get
out. They went.

'I want to talk,' said Nick. 'Let's go down to the lake.'

They started to walk. It was a clear night, but hot,
sultry, intense. She caught a whiff of honeysuckle as
they passed the coach-house, then lavender. A bat

skittered across the courtyard, and something rustled in the buddleia to their right. They left the buildings behind. Everything seemed more alive, more itself; the vegetation more vibrant, the moonlight more incandescent, the shadows pure Indian ink.

'How do you feel about what happened this evening?' said Nick after a while.

'I don't know,' said Nan. 'There's a sort of atmosphere that carries you along with it, saps your reason.'

'It was more than that,' said Nick. 'That tea Simone dishes out. She did a bit of travelling a while back, met this medicine man in Peru. He gave her some leaves that he used to brew up to get a heightened sexuality for some mystical nonsense. Oh, it's nothing to get alarmed about; it's not in the slightest bit addictive. But she should have told you what you were drinking.'

'I drove under its influence,' said Nan, horrified.

'I doubt it,' said Nick. 'It wears off quite quickly.' He put his arm round her and they walked like that until they reached the lake. Nan could feel a trickle of perspiration down her back; there didn't seem to be any way to get away from the heat. It followed them like a faithful dog, glancing the other way occasionally but never really letting up. They sat on the bank and looked across the water.

'It won't leave you alone, this place,' said Nick. 'It's there forever, somewhere inside your head. You keep coming back. God, it's hot. Let's go for a swim.'

Nan stood up and took off her clothes. They both stepped into the water and swam out to the middle. Once again it felt incredible, hedonistic, Bacchanalian. Eventually they swam back to the shore, and lay on the bank. He began to make love to her, slowly and delicately, as though each action was something to be perfected before moving on to the next.

'I thought you were finished for tonight,' said Nan.

'Quite possibly,' said Nick, 'but you're not.' He traced the shadows of the trees on her skin; then he picked a stalk of meadow barley, and ran it gently over her. It was the softest thing she could imagine, like being stroked by a lecherous moth. She watched his face as he did it, trying to work out why she found him so addictive. He was so beautiful in the moonlight, the white hair, the sensual mouth, the regular features. He discarded the barley, and picked a thistle-head. Nan couldn't help it, she gasped.

'It's all to do with pressure,' he said, 'I'm not going to hurt you.'

And the thistle-head was even more arousing than the barley-stalk; the little spines were that bit more intrusive, but not sharp enough to hurt. It was as though all of a sudden he had a hundred fingernails, each one of them dead set on arousing her. She began to squirm with pleasure; he grinned, swept it across her breasts in one last flurry, then threw that to one side as well. 'Now we move on,' said Nick, rolling on to his side and taking something out of the pocket of his trousers, which were lying beside him.

'On to what?'

He brandished a torch. It was about eight inches long and an inch and a half in diameter, and the silver casing gleamed in the moonlight. The business end looked just like any other torch but the battery end was rounded, like a cigar cylinder. He smiled, raised it to his lips, slid the rounded end into his mouth, and then out again. 'Open your legs.'

She opened them.

He slipped it inside her, and started to move it in and out. 'Not quite as effective as a vibrator, but more substantial than a finger. Oh, you like that, don't you?'

She did. The coolness of it was strange at first – but then that in itself became erotic, the image of a cold impersonal prick, as hard as stone. She felt it slide in and out, appreciating the firm solid resistance when she pressed against it. He nibbled her earlobe, then he ran his tongue round the shell and said, 'Ever used a vibrator?'

'No,' said Nan.

'Oh, we'll have to do something about that.' Then he was sliding the torch back and forth between her legs and massaging her clitoris at the same time and she couldn't think straight any more. When he started to fuck her with it properly and suck her nipple at the same time, the pleasure built rapidly, and she came easily.

'I could fall asleep out here,' said Nan afterwards.

'Not a good idea,' said Nick. He sat up and looked at her. 'I want to carry on seeing you. After.'

It was a sudden injection of the outside. The two worlds didn't mix; she couldn't envisage it.

'How?'

'I don't know. We'll think of something.' He stood up and pulled on his jeans.

She slipped on Megan's dress and he walked her back to the coach-house, but he didn't stay. She wondered whether his room was like Tad's; then she realised she knew just as little about him, none of the superficial details that go to make up the composite. Tidy or untidy, sentimental or practical, prudent or profligate. Perhaps she'd go over to the library the next day, and see if she could find an early book of his.

Chapter Ten

Saturday, and the last day of the course. A party planned for the evening, cheese dips and French bread and sangria. The weather had finally broken for good, as though someone had thrown it against the wall in a temper and left it to bleed quietly. The sky looked ashen, and there was a fine drizzle that penetrated everything. The walk from the coach-house to the refectory became a bit of an ordeal by water.

'I think we'll be in the studio, this morning,' said Megan.

'Flowers and fruit,' said Jocelyn.

'I thought we were going to have a model?' said Brian.

'Not all of us want a model,' said Gladys.

Tad and Nick came in together. There was no sign of Cheng.

'Tad,' called Lettie, 'bodies or beetroot this morning?'

'I'm having cereal,' said Tad morosely. He went to lift the milk-jug with his right hand, flinched and let go. Nick leaned across and did it for him. Tad recoiled slightly, but he didn't have any option; he couldn't reach the jug with his left hand. He barely acknowledged the gesture. Nick smiled, and offered to pour Tad a cup of tea in mime. This petty skirmishing went on for some time, neither of them speaking.

Sniffle came in and sat down. Nan heard Tad say, 'I need a model this morning.'

'Really?' said Sniffle.

'Don't piss me about, Sniffle,' said Tad. 'Not today. Just say you'll do it.'

'Try saying please,' said Nick.

'Try staying out of it,' said Tad to Nick.

'Oh, shut up, the pair of you,' said Sniffle. 'I'll do it.'

After breakfast, Nan went over to the telephone in the main house. She took a deep breath, and tapped in her stepmother's number. There was no reply, and Nan thumped her fist on the wall in frustration. It was so unfair, when she'd geared herself up for it. She walked down the corridor to the studio, and sorted herself out a position at the back. Sniffle took her clothes off and arranged her own pose on a stepladder. It was a good one – everyone could see her and, as she was above them, the eye-level was unusual and challenging. Gladys said she had a headache, and went back to her room. Gerald sat next to Lettie, and Nan set herself up next to Megan and Brian.

'Right,' said Tad, 'proportion. Measuring up.' He leaned over, and picked up Nan's pencil. He showed them how to scale it, emphasising the need to keep their arms straight. 'Now,' he said, 'before you actually do it, I want you to estimate how many hands go into an arm. Don't look, don't measure, guess.'

'Five.'

'Seven.'

Tad held Sniffle's arm out straight. Then he got her to move her other hand up her arm in a series of placements, counting. 'Three,' he said. 'What about feet?'

'Five.'

'No, more. Eight,' said Imogen.

'I bet it's three again,' said Nan.

Tad smiled, and got Sniffle to put her hand on his shoulder and stand on one leg. She became a stork. Then

168

she moved her foot up her leg the same way. It was three again.

'OK,' said Tad. 'Off you go: two short poses, just drawing, then a longer one.'

Nan started to sketch. Within a few seconds she knew that – for her – this was what it was all about. Representing what lay under the skin, that was the real issue: not just muscle and bone but individuality, essence. Lettie kept leaning across Gerald and showing him things, although Gerald didn't seem to be getting very much on to the paper. Sniffle had slim hips and full breasts and an ivory skin, as well as a voluptuous mouth and almond-shaped eyes. Her expression was a little unfortunate – reminiscent of somebody in a supermarket queue. The wet weather had got rid of her hay fever. Gerald loosened his collar. A fly landed on Lettie's arm and Gerald brushed it off. Lettie smiled at him.

Sniffle finished the two short poses and they started the long one. After about half an hour they had a coffee break, and Nan made a quick trip to the payphone. Denise was using it. She didn't see Nan; she was talking in a low voice and writing things down every so often. Nan realised she was giving someone directions to the centre. 'No, no,' she heard her say, 'right after the roundabout, not left.' She glanced up, saw Nan, and froze. Then she smiled tightly and said, 'I'm afraid I'm going to be a while.'

'It wasn't urgent,' said Nan, hiding her disappointment. She went back to the studio. Tad was sitting in a corner, looking like death.

'Arm,' said Nan. 'Show me.' He took off the bandage. The cut was infected. 'I think you need to see a doctor,' said Nan.

'I just need antibiotics. I'll ring the surgery.'

'Promise?'

'God, you do fuss,' said Tad. 'Why don't you ring him for me? You've got a nice wheedly voice. There's that bloody party tonight, as well.'

169

'Are you going to it?'

He looked miserable. 'I have to.'

At lunchtime she went back to the payphone, and tried her stepmother again. This time she was in luck.

'Nan? What a lovely surprise.'

Nan explained where she was, and what she was doing – with a few omissions – and then she said, 'Look, I know I've never asked you this before . . . but what do you know about my mother?'

'Goodness,' said Frances, 'that's a tall order over the phone.' But she didn't sound upset. 'I never met her, of course,' she went on. 'She died several years before I met your father. But they'd split up. Did you know that?'

'No,' said Nan, 'I didn't. I don't remember anything –'

'Before you were eight,' interrupted Frances. 'I know. When she died, your father hadn't seen you for a while. Quite an undertaking for a man, suddenly finding himself with sole responsibility for a child he hardly knew. It was one of the things I liked about him, the way he coped. Listen, I've got a chiropodist's appointment in half an hour – why don't you come and see me when you get back? I'll tell you everything I know – but it's not much, I'm afraid.'

'Do you know where my –'

'Mother was living? Hornchurch, I think. Or was it Horsham? No, I don't think it was Horsham . . . Oh, I remember. Hornsey.'

Hornsey. 'Are you sure? Hornsey in –'

'North London. Listen, Nan, I have to go or I'll miss my bus.'

They said goodbye. It could be a coincidence, thought Nan. And then again . . . There was still another half hour to go before the afternoon session, so she went over to the library to see if she could find out any more about Simone's early career. The relevant books had already been taken out, presumably by others who were interested in their reclusive host. She did find Nick's

170

first novel, however. She sat down on one of the leather chairs and started to read.

The book had a slow beginning. It was about a love affair between a young writer and a photographer. Nan skimmed through the narrator's childhood in India, and skipped to university. The photographer – Teresa – turned up shortly afterwards; she was French, and given to burning other people's possessions when she got annoyed. She had honey-coloured hair, and a hooked nose.

A woman artist – Marcie – appeared about halfway through, with a ten-year-old son. The boy was sensitively drawn, and the writer-character, John, seemed to be very fond of him. She flicked forwards, and found herself reading from the child's viewpoint all of a sudden, but with an adult's hindsight; the boy's name was Thomas.

It was a lovely day. We all sat in Teresa's garden and drank home-made lemonade, and John showed me a crab spider. It was really beautiful, pure white except for the little red stripe on its abdomen, and the yellow tinge around its eight eyes. He told me that spider silk was one of the strongest materials in the world, and that spiders aren't insects at all, they're arachnids. It held its legs out from its body, just like a crab. Its Latin name was . . .

Misumena vatia, thought Nan. She looked back at the text. *Misumena vatia.* How had she known that? She hadn't been very interested in natural history at school. Television programme, maybe. She carried on reading.

Mum hates spiders. She likes Donald, though. I don't. He wants me to learn the violin, but I'd much rather have a snake. John's seen loads of snakes, he's travelled all over the place; Africa, India, South America. He went to South America with Teresa, and they brought me back this beautiful shell – all white and spiky – and pink inside, like the inside of a mouth.

'Tell him what it really looks like, Marcie,' said Teresa to my mum.

'He's not old enough,' said my mum, laughing.

But I knew. I'd seen Vivian's private parts, when we played doctors down the end of the garden . . .'

Nan could see the shell quite clearly in her head. The chalky white exterior, slightly rough to the touch; the blush of the opening, getting pinker and pinker, the deeper you looked. She could picture the smoothness of that interior so clearly, and the wet shine it would have. And then she thought – maybe I *did* see it. Hornsey. Nan's mother had lived in Hornsey, and so had Simone. Supposing her mother hadn't wanted to be found: might she have changed their names? Could she still be Felicity, and could Felicity have been friends with Thomas, and seen the shell that way? She got up, put the book in her bag and went back to the studio. Sniffle had taken up the same pose again and Tad was sitting down, his eyes shut.

Nan went over to him and tapped him on the shoulder. He opened his eyes. 'Did you ring the surgery?'

'Yeah.'

'And?'

'They said to go down there.'

'I'll take him,' said Imogen, who'd been listening. 'I've made that nice young woman look like an orang-utan.'

Tad glanced round the class. 'You'll all be OK?'

The class nodded.

He stood up and followed Imogen rather reluctantly out of the studio. Nan sat down and tried to make some sense of Sniffle's body. After a while she got into it, and the time flew.

* * *

Tad and Imogen came back at four o'clock. Tad looked a bit white, and Imogen was grinning. Nan heard Lettie say, 'What's the joke?'

'He doesn't like my driving,' said Imogen.

'Maybe he hasn't been out with a rally driver before,' said Lettie.

'I was very restrained,' said Imogen, 'except for the bit along the track.'

Tad came and sat down next to Nan. 'Ye gods,' he muttered, 'the woman's a lunatic.'

'But very good,' said Lettie loyally. 'She might have done really well if she'd ever managed to grasp the basic principles of the combustion engine.'

'Or the violin,' Nan heard Brian say under his breath.

'Did you get your tablets?' Nan asked Tad.

Imogen started to laugh. Tad looked sheepish.

'The doctor gave him an injection,' said Imogen. 'He doesn't like injections, do you, Tad?'

Tad glared at her.

'He made all sorts of excuses,' said Imogen, enjoying herself, 'and he's got some tablets as well.'

Nan couldn't stop smiling. Tad was such a big man, hard and fit and tanned; his inconsistencies gave him an air of vulnerability that was very appealing. She wanted to ruffle his hair and say *never mind*.

'It took half a packet of chocolate buttons before he'd even consider it,' said Imogen.

Tad looked at Nan. 'Mention Smarties and you're dead.'

She smirked, and went back to her painting.

At half past four they packed up. Megan and Brian decided to have a little nap before dinner, whatever that meant, and Gerald asked Lettie whether she fancied a walk in the rain.

'What a lovely idea,' said Lettie.

Tad and Nan went over to the main building, and up to Tad's room. He shut the door, pulled out a large canvas, and spread the drawings across the floor. Then he handed her a palette and a large brush, and sat her down on a stool. 'I want something in the background,' he said, 'something oriental. Not Cheng. Something that suggests him.'

They started throwing words around.

'Pagoda,' said Nan.

'Bamboo.'

'Those stylised pine trees – Hokusai woodcuts.'

'Magnolia.'

'Cherry blossom.'

'Pointy mountains.'

'Dragons.'

'Yes,' said Tad, 'I like it. Chinese dragons.'

'Is Cheng Chinese?'

'Cambodian,' said Tad.

'How did he manage to get over here?'

Tad hesitated. Then he said, 'He's very bright, learned his English in Hong Kong. Cheng's a Chinese name, not Cambodian, so it won't be his real one. He earned his passage doing something very dodgy – don't ask me what, I'd rather not know. Simone finds him . . . exciting. I find him terrifying.'

Nan felt shocked.

There was a shelf on the wall jam-packed with books on art – huge books, shiny expensive books, everything from Michelangelo to Paul Klee. Tad found one on Chinese art, and they looked at it together.

'There's something about the expression on the dragons' faces,' he said, 'I'd like to capture that. A kind of surprise. The way you'd be if you looked absolutely terrifying, and didn't realise it, and then saw people's reactions to you. So the malice has to be there as well, at the same time. We can suggest it; we don't have to be too representational about it.'

He turned the canvas over and she saw Simone already there, sketched in.

'It needs to go behind her,' he said, 'as though she's casting him as her shadow. Start with the shape – use something dark, but make it slightly three-dimensional and have the light coming from the left.'

Very tentatively, Nan started to use the brush. He caught hold of her wrist with his left hand and made her use sweeping strokes, round and round for the shape of the head until it looked right. She became bolder, blocking in the dark side; he sat back and watched, nodding every so often. It only took her twenty minutes to cover a quarter of the area of the whole canvas.

He grinned, went to a fridge in the corner and got out a couple of beers. He had some of his colour back now; the injection appeared to be working.

'You can't,' said Nan. 'You're on antibiotics.'

'There are times,' said Tad, 'when you remind me rather powerfully of my mother.' He handed one can to her, put the other one back in the fridge and took a mineral water instead.

Nan laughed. 'What's she like?'

'Was. She died ages ago. Oh, very Polish. Obsessed with education and qualifications. Wanted me to be a doctor. All Polish mothers want their children to be doctors.'

'Was she disappointed?'

He smiled. 'No. She came to every exhibition, read every review, hung everything I'd ever given her on the walls. The house looked like a bloody art gallery.'

'And your father?'

'Dead, too. Bit more jaundiced about life; the most clued-up political observer I've ever met. She encouraged me; he made me think. Pretty good combination. Right. Let's have some red in it, over there.'

She dipped her brush into the cadmium red, changed her mind and went for the alizarin crimson.

'Good,' said Tad. 'Keep it dark, like that.'

They worked for a while longer and the dragon began to emerge, vague, shadowy, oddly profane. Tad made her lengthen the head and narrow the eyes a little and there was a sudden fleeting resemblance to both Cheng

175

and the administrator woman. He began to look quite excited and he got up and paced from side to side, squinting at the canvas from different angles.

There was a knock at the door.

'Go away!' shouted Tad.

The handle turned, but the door didn't open.

'Tad,' said Nick from outside, 'come on. Unlock it.'

Tad and Nan looked at one another.

'I'm working,' said Tad loudly.

'Pull the other one,' said Nick, 'your arm's buggered.'

'I can still sit and think, can't I?'

'Tadeusz. Stop pissing me about.'

Tad got up and went over to the painting. He leaned it against the wall, the back of the canvas outwards; then he gathered up the drawings strewn across the floor, rolled them up and unlocked the door. Nick walked in, saw Nan and stopped dead. Nan suddenly spotted another interpretation to the locked door, and squirmed inside.

'Well?' said Tad.

'Denise,' said Nick. 'She did one day with you. What did you make of her?'

Tad shrugged. 'She didn't say much.'

Nick was now looking at the palette on the bench where Nan had been working. The brush was still covered with paint. There was a smudge of alizarin crimson on her arm. 'Simone will go spare,' he said.

'Only if she knows,' said Tad.

'I'm not going to tell her,' said Nick, 'if that's what you're worried about.'

'Decent of you.'

'Oh, come on,' said Nick. 'You can't paint at the moment, and Nan's good. Listen, Denise writes a little too professionally for my liking. A little too *journalistically.*

'Ah,' said Tad. Then, 'Are you going to this bloody party?'

'Yes. And I think we ought to keep an eye on her, just

in case she decides it's good cover for having a peek at Simone's work.'

Nan was about to tell him about Denise and the payphone, but just then Nick picked up a rag and wiped the smear of alizarin crimson off her arm. He did it as sensuously as he did most things, and it had the inevitable effect. 'I think I'll go and have a shower,' she said.

'Have one for me,' said Tad. 'It's a bit difficult, with this arm.'

Nick stood up, and so did Nan. 'I'll see you later, then,' he said, and left.

Nan started to gather together her watercolour things, for she'd come straight from the studio.

'It is a bit of a problem,' said Tad.

'What is?'

'Having a shower. You have to stick the bandaged arm out of the curtain, and do everything one-handed. Takes forever. On your own.'

She looked at him.

He was smiling.

'What are you suggesting?' she said.

'We could combine it with an anatomy lesson.'

'You do have some strange teaching methods.'

'Effective, though. And supposing I slipped over and I couldn't break my fall?'

She smiled.

'Trade you a deltoid and a trapezius for a good lathering.'

Nan put down her things. 'You win,' she said.

They went down the corridor to the bathroom. It was huge, with great expanses of tiled floor and an old-fashioned bath on legs. The shower reminded Nan of the ones she'd had at school, just a faucet on the wall with an extensive white ceramic surround, and a curtain across the front. Tad opened the airing cupboard, and took out two towels.

'Two?' said Nan.

'I thought you wanted a shower as well?'

177

'Yes, but . . .'

'It'll be a lot easier for you if you don't have to worry about getting wet.'

There was no arguing with that. She felt cornered. He started to take off his clothes, wincing theatrically every so often. 'Oh, sod you,' said Nan, 'come here.'

She unbuttoned his shirt, and slipped it off. Then she took off his shoes and socks, pulled down his jeans, took a deep breath, slid her hands under the waistband of his underpants and rolled them down his legs, looking at some unspecified point on the other side of the room. Then she stood up, and started to undress herself.

He turned on the shower, and adjusted the temperature. He looked very dark against the white tiles. 'Right,' he said. 'We'll start with the head.'

She washed his face, and he named each muscle as she ran her hand across it. Then she untied his ponytail, and shampooed his hair. He bent and moved as she instructed, and she progressed to his neck, and then his shoulders. 'The trapezius is an important one,' he said. 'All muscles are essentially convex; they fold under one another, a bit like a parabola. So if you draw the line from the neck to the tip of the shoulder as a concave curve it will look wrong.'

She moved down to his chest. She already knew he had a very nicely defined body – after all, she had drawn him; she really could feel the shapes, and see where each one overlapped.

'The pectoralis major is a fan-shaped muscle, and the deltoid fits over it at the top of the arm. You've got breasts there, of course.' He ran his left hand down her chest, and felt for the sternum with his thumb. 'You need to be aware of the difference between representing soft tissue and muscle.'

His fingers moved sideways. She swallowed.

'So this part . . . this part can be concave, before you reach the nipple.' He took his hand away. She started on his stomach, and he named things as before. Even though she was trying not to look, she knew he had started to get an erection. He laughed and said, 'Good grief, Nan, don't be such a prude. Surely you expected it? You're going to have to wash it in a minute. I shall behave with all due decorum.'

She laughed, but she did his arm first, and then his legs. He conscientiously identified everything, and drew her attention to the places where the bone made the outline, rather than the muscle. She chickened out, turned him round and did his back. As she got to his coccyx, she began to wish she'd stayed on the other side. But she didn't skimp anything; she slid her soapy fingers between his buttocks and had the satisfaction of seeing him shiver. Then she took a deep breath, turned him round again and lathered her hands once more.

He was fully aroused. 'You're doing extremely well,' he said, smiling, and he started to talk about primitive art, and how men had been depicted in a rather upstanding condition for centuries. In fact, Leonardo had called a man's shadow on a wall – with erect phallus – the first painting. She gently washed his scrotum, and he discussed the profile of the male nude. He was erudite, amusing and incredibly self-controlled. She found herself wishing he'd just grab her and fuck her stupid, and then felt appalled at herself. Eventually she took hold of his penis, and soaped it up and down the entire length. His voice faltered for the first time, and he closed his eyes.

She couldn't stop. She found herself thinking, this is the last time, and then she'd do it again. There was almost an expression of pain on his face, but he managed an interesting paragraph on Indian art and Nepalese temples. Nan was full of admiration for his concentration, but she was so turned on she hardly knew what to do with herself. She moved her hand up and down again.

'Karnak,' said Tad unexpectedly.

'What about it?'

He took a deep breath. 'Shrine to divine masturbation,' he said. 'The guide books are a little reticent on the subject.'

'Oh,' said Nan, carrying on with what she was doing and wondering why she seemed to have so little self-control these days.

'The thing about erotic art,' said Tad, 'is that it's a reciprocal process. It requires a physical response . . .'

'You could say that about all art, surely,' she said, her voice now decidedly unsteady. 'Masks. Fear. Adrenalin.' She was losing her syntax.

'Not to quite the same extent. And the other aspect . . .'

She forced herself to slide her hands back down his thighs. He let his breath out slowly. 'Yes?' she said.

'Fear is different,' he said. 'The artist who depicts fear . . . doesn't feel frightened of his work himself. Herself. Whatever.'

He still had his eyes shut. She let her hands move upwards again, almost of their own volition, following the sartorius muscle. She smiled; she'd actually remembered the right name.

'However,' said Tad, 'erotic art doesn't work unless the artist gets aroused by his work . . . himself. Herself. Whatever.'

She ran her fingers across his testicles, and up the shaft of his penis. 'Left some soap there,' she mumbled, circling the head with her thumb.

The third time she did it, he suddenly took a deep breath and turned abruptly away. He leaned his head against the tiled wall, his back towards her, his arms above his head, and ejaculated against the tiles.

'Sorry,' said Nan.

He didn't say anything for a minute or two, just stood in the same position, breathing hard. She noticed that the bandage was soaking; neither of them had paid much attention to keeping it dry.

'Don't mention it,' he said eventually, turning round again. 'Performance art never sits very happily with decorum.' He looked at the bandage. 'Ah, well,' he said, 'I might as well do you, then. One-handed, I'm afraid.'

He started at her head, and followed the same general plan. He talked about how eroticism had often been seen as the compensation for old age and death and had therefore been celebrated rather than suppressed; the frescoes at Pompeii, the explicit paintings on the amphorae of Ancient Greece. He talked informatively about the sexual content on the pediments of Gothic churches, Japanese pillow books, how Watteau and Fragonard had been asked to depict certain scenes for the education of young kings. How the vaults and store rooms of galleries and museums held countless pictures that never went on general display.

She listened, fascinated. He sketched things on her body by way of explanation and she had to split her concentration; it was like learning to ride a bicycle. He began to talk about male artists and female models, treating her as an object, but finding the most erogenous places to demonstrate some point or another.

'Orifices,' he said, as though he was talking about another set of muscles. 'Very important.' He ran his finger round her ear, then across her lips. She didn't even try and pretend she was unmoved; it would have been pointless. He soaped her back, and then down to the crease and between her legs. 'Henry Moore liked to move orifices around,' he said, and he slid his fingers round and twisted his hand so that she had to move her legs apart. Then he demonstrated the possibilities of interchange, sliding from one opening to the other and back again.

When he finally reached her clitoris, she was practically writhing. 'Keep still,' he said. 'You're like a bloody eel,' and he placed his thumb over it, slid his finger a little way into her anus and started to talk about Rodin. She was shocked into an instantaneous orgasm; she felt herself contract around his finger, and it seemed to go on for ever. She had to lean against him; she couldn't have stood up on her own, her whole body jerked and the pleasure spread everywhere, blanking out everything. After a moment or two the white noise of the water gradually filtered through again, and she remembered she was still under the shower.

'That's a new one on you, isn't it?' said Tad, grinning.

She stepped back, annoyed. 'I don't know why we did that.'

He raised his eyebrows. 'Really?'

'You know what I mean.'

'What's all the fuss about?' said Tad. 'It was only performance art, not an installation.' He turned off the shower and threw her a towel. They dried themselves, and got dressed. She didn't help him, and it took him a while.

'Oh, come on, Nan,' he said, 'it takes two. What do you want me to say, I'm sorry? I'm not. And I can't fix this bandage myself.'

'You need another one,' said Nan. She unwound it and took off the dressing. The wound still looked red and painful, but it did seem rather better. He pointed to a medical cabinet in the corner, and she played nurse for a few minutes.

'Right,' he said, 'all ready for the party, then?'

She was feeling absolutely furious with herself. 'You were just trying to get at Nick, weren't you?' she said. 'And I fell for it.'

'You're making it sound as though it was a thoroughly miserable experience,' he said. 'Didn't look that way to me.'

'Oh, shut up,' said Nan, and she walked out and slammed the bathroom door behind her.

Chapter Eleven

When Nan walked into the library about twenty people were gathered there already, talking animatedly about the last week. She was wearing Megan's dress again, and Lettie smiled at her in an oddly maternal way. Sniffle and the hamster were talking to one another, but neither Nick nor Tad were there yet. Nan rather suspected that Tad was having a rest before he came down.

'Hello,' said Faith. Her eyes were different sizes behind the thick lenses of her glasses, and it was hard to ascertain their expression. She brushed a lock of very straight blond hair back from her face, and refastened it with a tortoiseshell clip.

'Hello,' said Nan.

'You've met Simone, haven't you?' said Faith.

'Yes.'

'And – what was his name – Cheng?'

'Yes.' Why on earth couldn't she think of something else to say?

'Hi,' said Denise.

Nan began to feel cornered. She wished Nick would arrive; then she hoped he wouldn't, because she didn't know whether she could look him in the face. She didn't know if she could look Tad in the face, either.

'You've seen Simone's work, haven't you?' said Denise.

'I saw the exhibition,' said Nan. 'Landscapes –'

'I meant her current work.'

'Why would I know anything about that?'

'Oh, come on,' said Denise. 'I *know* you've seen it. What's it like?'

Nan couldn't think of anything to say.

'What are they like?' repeated Denise.

'Erotic. You *know* what her work's like.'

'Not the recent stuff,' said Denise. 'No one does; it's a closely guarded secret. What's she into, Nan – bondage?'

'No.'

'Lesbianism?'

'Oh, for God's sake,' said Nan – then she realised that, by denying things, she was narrowing the field.

'Hasn't the week flown?' interrupted Megan, coming over as Brian went off to fetch more drinks. Nan had rarely been so pleased to see her.

'Nan's been modelling for Simone,' said Denise. 'Haven't you, Nan?'

'I know,' said Megan, with just the right matter-of-fact intonation to take the wind out of Denise's sails.

'What sort of poses has she asked for?'

'All sorts,' said Nan.

'With anyone else?' Denise glanced at her watch. 'She likes group studies. I remember a drawing I saw once, two men and one woman. Both the men were –'

'I think I'll get a drink,' said Nan.

Megan followed her. 'What on earth have you been getting up to?'

'Listen,' said Nan, 'I'm not coming back with you tomorrow. I'm staying on for a few days. It's OK with Mike.'

For once, Megan was completely lost for words.

The door opened, and Nick came in. Faith buttonholed him immediately.

'I got hold of my stepmother,' said Nan, deciding that

a change of subject was called for, and she told Megan about the phone call. Then she told her what she'd read in Nick's book.

Megan looked at her quizzically. 'What are you saying, Nan? That Felicity was you, after all?'

'Maybe,' said Nan.

Then Tad arrived. He'd changed his clothes, and he looked very different. He was wearing a black silk shirt, black trousers and a waistcoat. His hair was tied back with a thin red scarf, and he looked very sexy in an arty sort of way. He spotted Nan, and flashed a smile with a slightly lecherous edge to it at her. Jocelyn arrowed over to him. Nan turned away.

'What was that about?' said Megan, never one to miss an innuendo, whether verbal or visual.

Nan felt herself blush.

'Nan,' hissed Megan, 'what's been going on? I'm getting worried about you, really I am. Going off the rails is one thing, but you're steaming off towards Timbuktu. What's between you and Tad?'

Nan made a non-committal movement of the head.

Megan looked sceptical. Then she said, 'Listen, Nan. I've had a bloody good time here, as have you by the look of things, but it isn't going to affect the rest of my life. I shall go back to Terry, and Brian will go back to Maureen. We shall all carry on as before – until the next time. Nobody gets hurt, no recriminations, no regrets. No burned bridges. Can you really go back to Mike and pretend nothing's happened?'

'I don't give a toss about Mike's attitude,' said Nan. 'He's having an affair with his secretary.'

Megan looked pole-axed. 'Mike? *Mike's* being unfaithful?'

'I didn't tell you about it,' said Nan, 'because it made me feel like a frump. And to cap it all, you kept on needling me about only having slept with one man. And you were having an affair and you didn't tell me,

185

because you were hoping I'd make you feel less guilty about it by doing the same.'

'I've had lots of affairs, Nan,' said Megan. 'Brian isn't the first.'

Nan stared at her.

Megan shrugged. 'Brian simply reminds me of the first boyfriend I ever had. Tony.'

'I remember him,' said Nan. 'The one that got away. You were inconsolable. Does Brian know?'

'Yes.'

'And he doesn't mind? I think I'd feel . . . second best.'

'A lot of things in life are second best, Nan.'

Nan shook her head. 'No. I'm not settling for that any more. So why are you getting all puritan with me, Megan? I don't understand. I really don't.'

'Because they've taken you over,' said Megan. 'You don't even sound like you any more.'

'I'm *not* the old me any more,' said Nan. 'I found out that my mother and father separated. He only got custody of me when she died. My picture of her is changing, Megan – and, as that picture changes, so do I.' She saw Sniffle go over to Denise and say something, and then they put their heads together like two schoolgirls.

The movement seemed to catch Nick's eye; he extricated himself from Faith, grabbed Denise by the arm and hustled her into a corner. Denise was shaking her head and smiling. Sniffle stood and watched them. Nick looked angry; then he went over to Tad, and the two of them looked at Denise. Nan heard Nick say, 'I told you.' Tad left the room.

'Gosh,' said Imogen, at Nan's shoulder. 'Hot, isn't it?' The decibel level of the conversations seemed to be rising at the same rate as the temperature.

Nan grabbed an orange juice, and went and stood in a corner. She found herself pressed between Dominic and Trevor. Trevor had his back towards her; he was facing Damon, and Damon had an unnaturally fixed expression on his face. She heard Trevor say in a low voice, 'All packaged up, sweetie. Let's go.' After a moment or two Nan could feel a slight movement, as though Trevor were rhythmically jangling keys in his pocket, only there wasn't an accompanying tinkle of metal. The movements gradually speeded up, and Damon's eyes glazed over. Trevor's wanking him off, thought Nan, right here among all these people. She saw Damon shut his eyes and heard him make some small sound, and the movements stopped.

Trevor cleared his throat, but his voice was still a little husky when he said, 'Now me, darling.'

There was a pause, and the sound of something like someone opening a small tinfoil packet. So that's how they're managing to stay dry, thought Nan: they're wearing condoms. She finished her orange juice. Then Damon whispered, 'All aboard the Skylark, then,' and the movements started again, only this time she could feel Trevor's hips pushing against hers every so often. As he became more aroused he became more careless, until Nan was moving with him, and the friction was making her feel horny herself. She turned her head slightly and caught Damon's eye; Damon grinned.

He knows I know, thought Nan, and he doesn't give a damn. And that was rather titillating too, so she just let herself get carried along with it until the crush in the corner became even more pronounced and found herself transmitting the pass-it-on sex-dance to Dominic. She saw Dominic colour, but he made no attempt to get out of the way; he was obviously enjoying it. It's like a Mexican wave, thought Nan, and if she hadn't been feeling quite so turned on she'd have giggled. Who's Dominic in contact with on the other side? she wondered, and she tried to peer round him.

Just then, Trevor gave a particularly hard thrust, and the material of Nan's dress caught between her legs and started to pull backwards and forwards over her clitoris. She gulped; she'd been enjoying the mild stimulation in a laid-back kind of way, but this was much more inflammatory – her knees were feeling weak and watery, and if she hadn't been sandwiched between the men she'd have had trouble standing up. Dominic's breathing was getting a bit irregular, and she heard him mutter *sorry* to whoever was on his other side. She caught a glimpse of some white-blonde hair and a pair of glasses. It's Faith, she thought, and then she wasn't thinking any more because Trevor had upped the momentum and that tingly feeling had started in her buttocks. When she came, it wasn't the orgasm to end all orgasms, but she felt that it was quite an achievement, under the circumstances. She realised that Trevor had come as well – and possibly Dominic, because he rushed off to the Gents and Faith was left standing there, looking annoyed.

And then the door opened again, and after a moment the room went absolutely silent.

'Hello, everyone,' said Simone cheerfully.

Cheng was standing right behind her, and Nan knew that Simone was drunk.

There was a scattering of hellos. Denise looked absolutely delighted; she was actually smiling. Faith's mouth had dropped open, and Imogen was grinning like an idiot. Gladys, with no sense of propriety, went straight over and said, 'I was hoping I'd get to meet you. What's the difference between what you're painting and pornography?'

Gerald looked absolutely mortified.

Simone smiled sweetly at Gladys and said, 'You can't understand either of them if you're frigid, *chérie*.'

Lettie walked briskly over to Simone and said, 'I love your work. Tell me – how do you make your fantasy elements so realistic? There's a genuine ring of truth about everything you do.'

Cheng said, 'I think Simone's come to a party. She doesn't want to talk about work.'

Nick said, 'I think perhaps you could do with a coffee.'

'*Café*,' said Simone contemptuously. She suddenly spotted Nan and said, 'Nan. I don't need a coffee, do I?'

188

'I'll get her one,' said Nick quietly to Nan. 'Can you keep her talking? Get her off art, for God's sake.' He left the room. Cheng went to get Simone a mineral water as a quick fix.

Oh, well, thought Nan, now or never. 'That photograph we talked about before,' said Nan, 'Felicity. Her mother was a friend of yours.'

Simone tried to focus on Nan, and managed it at the second attempt. 'That was the last photograph I ever took, that one of Felicity in her gypsy dress with the maroon squiggles on it –'

'Maroon?' echoed Nan.

'*C'est à dire* . . . a sort of dark red,' explained Simone helpfully.

'Is there any chance,' said Nan, 'that your friend changed the child's name – and her own – to conceal her whereabouts?'

Simone stared at her.

'Are you still in contact with her mother?'

Simone laughed then. 'I'd need a spiritualist. She died.'

Nan swallowed. 'How?'

'She drowned.'

Nan felt a sudden rush of cold down her back. For a split second she thought it was a physical reaction to the thoughts circling in her head – then she realised someone had spilt something down her. She turned round so quickly that she ricked her neck.

'Sorry,' said Faith.

Nan cursed under her breath, certain it was no accident; Faith had spilt a whole gin and tonic down her, and the dress was clinging to her in a most embarrassing way. Cheng steered Simone away and Faith dabbed ineffectually at her with a tissue, preventing her following.

'I think you'll have to go and change,' said Faith, with a glance in Nick's direction.

'You're even more transparent than this dress,' said Nan, feeling thoroughly annoyed.

Faith looked straight at Nan, her eyes blazing behind her spectacles. 'Nick's just playing with you,' she hissed. 'I've read every word he's written, which is more than you have. I know all about him; I've read every review, every interview. And I know he's only ever loved one woman, and he's been looking for her double ever since. And don't you go getting it into your head it's you, because it *can't* be. You couldn't write to save your life; how could you ever *begin* to understand him?'

'He thinks you're a pain in the arse,' said Nan, feeling angry and upset, 'and what's more, you can't write either.' And with that, she pushed past Faith and made her way to the library door. As she did so, she saw Denise glance at her watch and slip outside in front of her.

She saw Denise heading for the main door. Just as she was about to leave the building, Tad appeared in the doorway, and barred Denise's exit. 'I don't think so,' Nan heard him say.

Nan stopped, stood quite still and watched the pair of them from the shadows of an alcove.

'How did you know?' asked Denise.

'I've got a good memory for faces,' said Tad. 'It just took me a while to remember where I'd seen *yours*. You did a piece on Simone, a few years back, and you trashed her. You were at her private view.'

'Let her go,' said a voice behind Nan.

Nan shrank back against the wall. Cheng passed her without seeing her.

'I might have bloody well guessed,' said Tad. He looked annoyed with himself.

Cheng stopped a few paces from him. He stood there, lightly balanced on his bare feet, his hands free. 'I don't want to hurt you, Tad. I even like you. You're the most genuine person in this whole set-up. But . . .' He shrugged.

'You're a cold-blooded bastard,' said Tad.

'That's right,' said Cheng, and he moved so swiftly that Nan couldn't actually work out what happened, but the next moment Tad was lying on the floor and Denise and Cheng had gone. She ran over to him, and knelt down beside him.

He groaned, opened his eyes and looked at her. 'Hello, nurse,' he said. 'Am I pleased to see you.' He struggled to sit up; Nan supported him and leaned him against the wall. He coughed a couple of times, and shut his eyes again. 'Jesus Christ, can he kick. He's as fit as a bloody tiger.' He coughed again, and smiled weakly.

'You're OK otherwise?'

'Mm.'

'What's going on, Tad?'

He sighed. 'Press. Denise is a journalist. She signed on for Nick's course so that she could do some snooping. She's got a photographer out there somewhere. God knows where he is now; he's been up in Simone's studio taking pretty pictures of everything. I couldn't work out why the door – Oh, I see. Cheng brought Simone down, and left it unlocked.'

Nan began to see the implications. The Sunday supplements. Mike looking a little harder than usual at a double-page spread. Her boss, her stepmother; *Darren, Cassie* . . . 'Oh, my God,' she said.

'Quite. Help me up. I'm OK now . . . I think.'

She got him to a standing position, and he doubled over again. She caught him round the waist, and he leaned on her for a moment before regaining his balance. He breathed deeply for a few seconds, and then stood upright.

'You're going through the wars a bit, aren't you?'

'I feel old,' he said self-pityingly.

'Stop that,' said Nan briskly. 'What are we going to do?'

'Find the bugger, I suppose,' said Tad. 'I've disabled his car, so he can't go far. I just need to expose his film.'

'What's Cheng got to do with it all? What's in it for him?'

'Only one thing it can be,' said Tad. 'Money. He must have sold the story to Denise's newspaper. Guess what's going on at Simone's place? You'll get some amazing piccies.'

'But I thought he was really into Simone's work.'

'So did I,' said Tad.

'Sniffle's been very pally with Denise.'

He looked doubtful. 'Has she?'

'Definitely. They both knew about me modelling. And she doesn't like Simone any more, does she?'

He thought for a moment. Then he said, 'I think we'd better go and find Nick. Then try and get Simone to bed, and go out hunting photographers. They won't have much of a head start, and they don't know the territory.'

'Cheng will be with them,' said Nan.

'Oh, yes,' said Tad, making a face. 'Oh, well. Nick's better at this sort of thing than I am. He'll get the film off them.'

Nan wondered why Tad seemed so certain that Nick could do something.

'I don't imagine they'll try and nick one of the other cars,' he said. 'It's too easy for us to get them intercepted by the police. And Sniffle doesn't have a car. I may not be much good with fuel pumps, but I do know how to let down tyres.' He looked pleased with himself.

'I bet one of them's got a mobile phone,' said Nan.

'Mm. They'll ring someone, get them to come and meet them. So they'll start walking. Which way? If I were them, I wouldn't use the track – too obvious – I'd go across country.'

'In which direction?' said Nan.

'Sod's law,' said Tad. 'The quickest way to the nearest main road is straight through Braithwaite territory. Go and get changed, quick as you can. I'll find Nick and meet you by the main door.' They parted company.

Nan pulled on some army-style fatigues, and chose a

dark patterned T-shirt. It was like playing soldiers: think camouflage, think equipment, think comfort and man-oeuvrability. She put on her boots; then she dropped a torch in one pocket, some string in another, her penknife in a third. She snatched up a bar of chocolate on her way out, and ran back to the main building. Tad was waiting for her. He'd changed his clothes as well – he was wearing a brown leather flying jacket and walking boots, and he was carrying a flashlight and binoculars. He looked different yet again, like a character from a wartime film.

He surveyed her approvingly from head to foot. Then Nick appeared, walking quickly towards them, carrying a rifle. Nan's eyes widened in disbelief. He smiled, put his arm round Nan and kissed her quickly on the cheek.

'Is that thing really necessary?' asked Nan, who had never been so close to a firearm before.

Nick laughed and Nan could hear the bullets jingling in his pocket. 'I won't be using it,' he said, 'but can you think of another way of getting them to hand over the film?'

'Nick is a sickeningly good shot,' said Tad. 'Comes from massacring wildlife in his youth.'

'Don't listen to him,' said Nick. 'I used to shoot things for the pot. Everyone did. That's what you did in India.'

They started off towards the woods. It had stopped raining, but there were puddles everywhere and a lot of mud. Nick was watching the path, Tad scanning ahead. They worked well as a team, Nick tracking, Tad scouting. Nan brought up the rear. Eventually Nick spotted something he said was the imprint of a shoe, although to Nan it just looked as though a wedge of sludge had slipped sideways. But sure enough, there were proper footprints beyond it, and they followed the track into the trees.

'All we want is the film,' said Tad, 'nothing else. They can go where the hell they like after we've got that.'

They crawled under the wire fence and into enemy territory.

'How far is it to the road?' asked Nan.

'Two miles,' said Nick. 'We'd better get a move on.'

'You know what we should have done,' said Tad, 'got Nan to take the car and meet us at the other side.'

'And get left out of this?' said Nan, forgetting how frightened she'd been the last time she'd encountered Braithwaite. 'No way.'

They began to work their way down the other side of the hill, scrambling over the fallen trees and taking short cuts wherever possible. It was easy to imagine that they were all aged eleven or twelve, and playing their own game of soldiers in the woods. Nan kept expecting one of them to show her a conker, or talk about his model railway. And then they *did* see something.

'Light,' said Tad, 'over there.' He raised the binoculars and pointed them at it.

They switched off their own torches. A faint pinpoint of yellow was travelling slowly across the more open ground below them. It disappeared behind a tree every so often, but it was moving in the right direction, and after a while they could make out the dark shapes of the three figures accompanying it.

'We were right,' said Tad.

'OK,' said Nick, 'if we head diagonally east, we should be able to intercept them before they cross the stream.'

They changed direction. It was more difficult now as there wasn't a proper path, and Tad was finding it harder than anyone. He stopped for a breather.

'Did you take your tablet?' enquired Nan.

'Yes,' said Tad, scowling at her.

Nick laughed.

'I'd like to see you tackle this terrain after a gunshot wound and a karate kick,' said Tad bitterly.

'I wasn't implying I could do any better,' said Nick.

'Good.'

'There's one major plus to all this,' said Nick. 'No

Cheng from now on. Surely even Simone can't forgive a betrayal as cynical as this.'

They started off again. The light was stationary now, the figures huddled together. It looked as though they were carrying a fair amount of equipment, and needed a breather themselves. Nan realised that the three of them were a lot closer to the trio than they had been previously.

'Three against three,' whispered Nick. 'I like the symmetry.'

'I'm not sure I do,' hissed Tad. 'Cheng's your department and Denise is too heavy to run fast – that leaves me with the photographer. He could be anything from a total wimp to a finely honed killing machine.'

'I'm the one specialising in melodrama,' said Nick, under his breath. 'Don't usurp my role.'

'Wouldn't dream of it,' said Tad. 'Words lie. Images don't.'

'That's total crap,' said Nick

'Oh, for goodness' sake,' hissed Nan, 'stop it, both of you. And keep your voices down.'

And that was when the shot rang out. The trio below them scattered in different directions, and the little light went out.

'I've had enough of you lot!' Braithwaite shouted, from somewhere between the two groups.

'Oh, shit,' said Nick, 'that's all we need.'

'What do we do?' asked Nan.

'Hang on,' whispered Tad, training the binoculars. 'They've left something on the ground. Could be our lucky day. Looks like a flight-case.' He scanned the trees beyond. 'One of them's hiding in the bushes, waiting till it's clear. Can't see the others.'

'How are we going to get past Braithwaite?' asked Nick.

'With any luck he'll be heading down there as well, moving away from us. Calculated risk, but I think it's worth it.'

They started off again, but more cautiously, not speaking now, treading with care. They stopped when they reached the trees at the edge of the open ground. The moon had emerged from behind the cloud cover, and they could see quite well.

'It *is* a flight-case,' whispered Tad. 'A real piece of luck at last. Who's going to retrieve the thing?'

They all looked at one another.

'We need to know where Braithwaite is,' hissed Nick. 'One of us has to draw his fire.'

'Are you mad?' said Tad. 'He's a good shot. Not *your* standard, I know, but good enough.'

'Maybe one of *them* will try and get it,' said Nan. 'Then, while Braithwaite's attention is on him, one of us can sneak up and whip it.'

They both looked at her as if she had just solved the riddle of the universe.

'Right,' said Nick quietly, 'we wait. We know what we want is down there, so there's no panic.'

They sat down with their backs to a large oak tree. Nan shared out her chocolate. It was back to playing in the woods again; in a minute or two one of them would try to light a fire, and the other would suggest singing the Kookaburra song. They kept their voices very low.

'You're awfully good at this,' said Tad to Nan. 'Were you a member of the SAS in a previous incarnation?'

'The SAS was only formed in nineteen forty-one,' said Nick.

'Picky,' said Tad.

'I just like accuracy.'

'Not in your books, you don't,' said Tad. 'You can't freeze a cat solid in half an hour.'

'When did I say half an hour?'

'You didn't,' said Tad, 'but he put the cat in there at twenty past three, and he used it to brain someone before it got dark. It was January, according to you.'

'January in New Zealand,' said Nick.

Tad looked annoyed.

'Ssh,' whispered Nan. 'Stop bitching and look.'

A figure slipped out of the shadows on the other side of the clearing, lay down on its stomach and inched its way towards the flight-case.

'It's Cheng,' murmured Tad.

They watched him move closer and closer, and still there was nothing from Braithwaite.

'Shit,' said Nick. 'He's going to get the bloody thing. Where's Braithwaite when we need the bugger?'

'Right here,' said Braithwaite from behind them.

Nick grabbed the rifle and rolled into a shallow depression, and Tad stood up as a distraction, his hands spread out placatingly, and said, 'This isn't what you think . . .'

'You,' said Braithwaite. 'I thought I hit you last time,' and then Nick fired and the shotgun leaped out of Braithwaite's hands and fell to the ground a few paces away. Cheng jumped to his feet, seized the flight-case, and ran. Nick swung the rifle round and fired in front of Cheng. There was a sudden spray of mud, and Cheng stopped dead and dropped the case.

'Very wise,' called Nick, reloading.

Nan's ears were still ringing from the shots. She could hardly believe what she'd just seen.

Cheng turned to face him. 'You wouldn't kill me,' he said softly. 'You're English.' And he bent down very slowly and picked up the case again.

Then Braithwaite made a lunge for his shotgun, and Tad dived at his legs. Braithwaite picked up the shotgun and swung it round like a club; Tad was on one knee, raising his hands to his head to protect himself, but the bad arm wouldn't move fast enough. She heard the butt of the shotgun connect. Tad fell over like an object rather than a person and just lay there. Braithwaite swapped the shotgun to his other hand, reversing it in the process, and aimed it at Nick.

'Drop the rifle,' said Braithwaite. Nick dropped it. Cheng had the case now, and he was sprinting across the grass. Braithwaite shouted at him, fired above his head, and Cheng flung himself to the ground. Braithwaite shone the torch at him, and Cheng got up and walked slowly back over. 'All of you,' said Braithwaite, picking up the rifle and slinging it over his shoulder, 'back against the tree.'

Nick, Cheng and Nan did as they were told. Tad hadn't moved. It had all happened so quickly that Nan couldn't really take it in.

Braithwaite turned to Nick. Then his eyes narrowed and he said, 'I remember you. You're that bastard writer, Nicholas Cross. You've been coming here for years. We've met before.'

Nick didn't say anything.

'I've read your books,' said Braithwaite unexpectedly. *'Beyond The Estate.* That was the one.'

Nick stiffened.

'Yes,' said Braithwaite softly, 'you know what I'm on about, don't you? You used me. Turned me into a joke. You described my hair, and my bicycle, and that red T-shirt of mine with an anchor on it. I was a laughing stock in the pub for months when that came out.'

And then Nan remembered the passage of Nick's book she'd read the first evening.

There was a man on an old black bicycle, stationary, one foot on the path, the other foot raised as he adjusted his cycle clip. He was a middle-aged man, muscular – a farm worker maybe. He had a streak of white in his hair, like the crest of a cockatoo, and he was wearing a red vest with a picture of an anchor on it. To the left of the anchor was the letter W . . .

Oh, my God, thought Nan, Nick even *labelled* him a wanker as he wrote about him jerking himself off on that footpath . . .

Braithwaite unlooped a piece of rope from his belt

with one hand and threw it to Nick. Then he turned to Cheng and smiled, the strange little tuft of white hair among the black looking like a shaft of moonlight. 'I think we'll get you secured first,' he said. 'You probably know all that karate stuff.'

Cheng looked back impassively. There wasn't a flicker of anything on his beautiful face.

'Tie him up,' said Braithwaite to Nick, 'and make it good. No slip-knots. I don't like slip-knots. Try anything and you'll end up like him.' He jerked his head in Tad's direction. Nick tied up Cheng, and he made it very good. Nan saw Cheng wince every time Nick tightened something.

'You're a fool,' hissed Cheng. 'If anyone can finish him off, it's me.'

'You,' said Braithwaite to Nan, 'tie *him* up now.' He threw her another piece of rope and nodded his head in Nick's direction. Nan did as she was told, but her hands were shaking. She felt Nick flex his wrists as she tied them, and knew that the rope would loosen once he relaxed. She could see Tad out of the corner of her eye, a very still dark outline on the grass. She was crying now, although she didn't make a sound. The tears just seemed to spill out, misting her vision, uncontrollable. It wasn't a game any more; nobody was going to start handing out pieces of chewing gum or telling smutty jokes. It had tipped over into something so horrible she could hardly believe it was happening. Not to *her*.

'Excellent,' said Braithwaite. 'Well, now. There's two more of you, aren't there? We'd better wait for them. Sit down, you two.'

Nick and Cheng sat down very awkwardly. Braithwaite spaced them out two bodylengths apart. 'You,' he said to Nan, 'go and open that box.' He pointed to the flight-case. Nan went over to it and snapped open the catches. 'Now empty the contents on to the ground.' She turned it upside down and did it. A camera body and a series of lenses fell on the grass, as well as several rolls of film and a few filters. 'Important stuff, no doubt,' said Braithwaite, 'seeing as you're all after it. Film. Filth, more like.'

Nan walked back to the others. Braithwaite stood a little way apart from them, aimed the shotgun at the pile and fired. Then he smiled, ejected the spent cartridges, reloaded, and fired two more times. How ironic, she thought. It was a comprehensive demolition job. Nothing was left undamaged.

Braithwaite turned back to Nan, and reloaded again. 'I don't think I need to bother tying you up,' he said, as though women were an inferior species.

'Please,' said Nan, 'let me go to Tad.'

'Tad, eh,' said Braithwaite. 'And what nationality is that?'

'Tadeusz. Polish.'

A peculiar expression crossed Braithwaite's face. 'Polish?' he said. 'Are you sure?'

Nan couldn't see the relevance. 'Yes,' she said simply.

'Good men in the war, the Poles,' said Braithwaite. 'He shouldn't have sprung my traps, though.'

'He didn't,' said Nick. '*I* did. Now let Nan go and see to him.'

It was a brave thing to say. Braithwaite curled his lip, then he walked calmly over to Nick and kicked him on the shin. Nick screwed up his eyes for a moment, but he didn't say anything. Braithwaite glanced at Nan. 'Go on, then,' he said.

Nan went over to Tad. He was still lying in exactly the same position, hunched up on his side. His face was very white and his eyes were closed. She felt for a pulse, felt again, felt the panic rising inside her. She made herself stop and try again – and there it was after all, faint and fluttery, and then she really was crying.

'Nan,' said Nick, 'Nan. If there's nothing you can do, come away.'

'It's all right,' she said. 'He's alive.' She tried to shift him to the recovery position. He was very heavy. Dead weight, she found herself thinking, but she managed it in the end. His hair was matted with blood.

There was a movement in the trees opposite. Braithwaite swung the shotgun round and fired again. Denise and someone else came out with their hands raised.

'A full half-dozen,' said Braithwaite to himself. 'Sterling work, corporal.' He indicated to Nan with a jerk of his head that she was to leave Tad and join the main group again. She got up and went and stood next to Nick, but her eyes were blurry with tears and she fumbled for a handkerchief.

'You can't treat people like this,' said Denise indignantly when she was close enough. 'This is England, not Bosnia.'

'Shut up,' said Braithwaite conversationally.

'I will not,' said Denise, 'I'm a reporter for –' But she didn't finish because Braithwaite hit her round the face.

'Whore,' he said, 'Take your clothes off in front of men, do you? I know what goes on in that house. I know all about people like you.'

'Wanker!' yelled Denise, completely losing it for the moment.

Braithwaite hit her a lot harder, and she reeled back a couple of paces.

'Inadvisable, Denise,' said the man who was with her, putting out a hand to steady her. Nan knew that voice. She wiped her eyes, and focused on the owner. He was tall and thin, with a curiously old-fashioned look to him. Hugo Forbes. His brow furrowed for a moment; she could see that he knew he'd seen her before, but couldn't quite work out where.

'Tie him up,' said Braithwaite, throwing two more pieces of rope to Nan. 'Then her.'

Nan felt Forbes flex his wrists exactly the same way Nick had done. But Braithwaite wasn't having it; this man was younger than Nick, and he made sure the rope was tight himself.

201

'Well done, corporal,' he said to himself. 'Now then. We're going to have a little execution.'

'What?' said Denise. The side of her mouth was beginning to swell.

Nan heard Hugo Forbes say in a low voice, 'He's a nutter, Denise. Don't rile him, for God's sake. I know a genuine psycho when I see one; I used to teach in a secondary school.'

Denise swallowed, but she didn't say anything more.

Chapter Twelve

'**R**ight,' said Braithwaite, 'let's have a crocodile.'
They all looked at him as he stepped into a puddle of moonlight. He really was a big man, broad, with that strange piebald hair and eyebrows that seemed to be toying with the idea of becoming one. Nan had a sudden flashback to the pub, and Braithwaite's violent reaction to the suggestion he press himself against her.

'Come on, chop chop. Single file.' He jerked the shotgun.

'What about Tad?' said Nan, struggling to keep her voice steady. 'Let me stay with him.' She was trying not to plead, but a wheedling tone was creeping into her voice.

Braithwaite looked contemptuously at her. 'Fucking you, is he?'

Nan was aware that Nick was watching her.

'Certainly not,' said Nan, although she felt the distinction had been a fine one.

'I'd have to tie you up.'

She nodded and Braithwaite tied her wrists behind her, then her ankles, but he didn't jerk the rope tight the same way he had with Hugo Forbes. She copied the others and kept her wrists taut, and then relaxed them when he wasn't watching. She felt the rope give a little.

'You, stay put,' Braithwaite told Nan. 'The rest of you, quick march.' He shifted the rifle back on to his shoulder, and the other four captives preceded him down the path and back into the woods. In less than a minute they had all disappeared.

Nan lay down and did a backstand, rolling on to her shoulders with her feet above her head, and after three tries the penknife fell out her pocket and on to the grass. It seemed to take for ever to open it, and when she finally succeeded the rope was loose enough for her to work the blade underneath it. She sawed and sawed, and when the fibre eventually gave way she had almost given up hope. She massaged her wrists, untied her ankles, and went over to Tad.

His breathing was stronger now, but he was still out of it. Water, she thought, and she looked around for something to carry it in. Then she spotted the flight-case and she went through the contents, making sure each roll of film was completely exposed. The only undamaged container she could find was a lens case. She ran to the stream and filled it with water, and then she carried it over to Tad and moistened his lips. To her relief, he opened his eyes; then he closed them again. She sat with him for a while longer, wiping his forehead with a damp tissue and suppressing her impatience, for she was sure Braithwaite would come back sooner rather than later.

He opened his eyes again and said something in Polish. Then he closed them again and stirred slightly, the first movement she'd seen. She wondered how the party was going, whether anyone had heard the shots. They must have done, but it wasn't an unusual sound round here. And nobody would have thought it odd that she'd disappeared with Tad and Nick; she'd been doing it all the time.

'Why is it always me?' said Tad grumpily.

She felt the most unbelievable sense of relief, and she found she was crying with it.

'Silly bugger,' said Tad. 'Ouch.' He tried to sit up: failed.

'I don't think you should do anything for a bit,' said Nan, 'you've had one hell of crack on the head.'

'Don't remember,' said Tad.

'What's the last thing you *do* remember?'

'Dunno. Walking down a path with you and Nick. Where's Nick?'

'Never mind that,' said Nan.

'What happened?'

'Braithwaite hit you with the butt of his shotgun.'

'Oh. Where is he?'

'Gone. It's OK.'

'Why me?' said Tad again. 'Three times. And Nick doesn't even get thumped once. Maybe I should do something about that.' He sat up, very slowly and groggily. Then he threw up. Nan gave him the rest of the water, and he rinsed out his mouth.

'Funny cup,' he said.

'It's a lens case. Can you see all right? Any double vision?'

'If there were two of you,' said Tad sweetly, 'I'd be in heaven. As it is, I still appear to be on earth.'

She laughed. 'You must have a skull like cast iron.'

He lay down again. 'I know exactly what Simone's less fortunate canvases must feel like,' he said. Then, 'Nan.'

'What?'

'Just hold me for a bit.'

She lay down beside him and put her arms round him. 'Not for long, because we have to move before Braithwaite comes back.'

He closed his eyes and sighed, and they stayed like that for a while. The closeness between them was so sudden and so acute that she felt quite shocked by it.

'D'you know something?' he said.

'What?'

'Performance art isn't really my thing. But I've had this really good idea for an installation. Needs two people, though . . .'

She smiled, and kissed him on the forehead. She was beginning to feel far too fond of him. It wasn't what she'd felt for Nick at all, a sudden rush of real lust, isolated, separate. This was all tied in with him as a person: the narrative, not the image. It was all the wrong way round.

'We can't stay here for too much longer,' she said. 'We ought to get you to hospital.'

'Do you ever get the feeling,' said Tad, 'that life has a cyclical aspect to it?'

'No,' said Nan. 'Nothing like this has ever happened to me before.'

'Like what?'

She knew what she wanted to say, and knew she mustn't say it because it was only true there, then, at that moment, in that setting. She stroked his hair back from his forehead and told him about Braithwaite recognising himself in Nick's book. 'The best thing we can do,' finished Nan, 'is to make our way to the main road and get some help.'

'Give me a hand so I can stand up,' he said. 'God, it seems like I'm always asking you to do that.'

He leaned on her, and they stood up with some difficulty. She could feel him shaking. After a moment or two, the shakes subsided.

'Right,' said Tad, 'which way did they go?'

'Don't be stupid,' said Nan. 'You're in no condition to help anyone.'

'We've got to,' said Tad.

'We've got nothing,' said Nan. 'No rifle, no shotgun, nothing.'

Tad thought for a moment. 'I know where they've gone,' he said. 'There's a hut thing about half a mile away. He keeps his snares there, the ones he's not using.

Come on.' He swayed, and put out a hand to steady himself.

'Tad,' said Nan, 'you are no use to anyone like this. Come on. Let's get down to the main road.'

'I don't think so,' said Braithwaite, shining a light directly at them.

Nan put her hand in front of her eyes. She hadn't expected Braithwaite to come back quite so quickly, but there was no way she could have got Tad out of there any faster. Tad turned his head sharply to one side as though the brightness had struck him physically.

The gamekeeper was on his own, and the shotgun was pointing straight at them. 'Got rid of the rope, then,' he said to Nan. 'Thought I'd better check up on you. Can't have you trotting off to a phone box. Didn't expect *him* to be up and doing for a while yet, mind you.'

They started off along the path the others had taken. Tad was leaning quite heavily on Nan, and Braithwaite allowed them to stop every so often. When they got to the clearing with the hut in it, Nan could see that Braithwaite had rigged up a snare using a small tree, bent right over. He'd used a winch to set it, and it was under extreme tension. The noose was made of wire. Cheng was sitting cross-legged on the ground, tied to some sort of metal structure that looked like the bones of an earlier building.

'The secret,' said Braithwaite, 'is not to kill them straight away. See how many times you can do it before it cuts right through the throat.' He stood and admired his handiwork for a moment.

'Why Cheng?' asked Nan. 'What's *he* ever done to you?'

'Oh, that's not for Karate Joe,' said Braithwaite. 'That's for that bastard writer. Excuse my French.' He tied Tad's hands and then Nan's. After that he went over to the hut and unlocked the door. 'In you go,' he said to Nan. Tad went to follow her, but Braithwaite said, 'No. Not you. You can stay out here with Karate Joe.'

'Does that mean I'm next in line after Nick?' Nan heard Tad say.

'No,' Braithwaite replied, 'I just don't trust you. I've shot you and I've knocked you out and you're still on your feet. So you can stay out here, where I can keep an eye on you.' He shut the door behind Nan, and she heard him shoot a couple of bolts and fiddle with another padlock. He was pretty thorough.

Nick's first reaction was relief to see that Nan was all right, then disappointment that she hadn't been able to go and get help. He obviously had no idea what Braithwaite had rigged up for him outside, and Nan wasn't about to tell him. He had freed his own hands, and then everyone else's, and now he untied Nan's. She told them all that had happened since she'd last seen them.

'I know you,' said Hugo Forbes suddenly. 'It's Nan, isn't it?'

Nan felt herself blush crimson.

'We met fleetingly at Simone's last exhibition,' said Hugo, 'but, alas, there wasn't enough time to get the relationship on to a proper footing.'

Nan glared at him. 'So,' she said, 'what has the escape committee considered so far?'

'There hasn't been an escape committee,' said Hugo, picking a piece of mud off his neat grey flannels. 'Denise and Nick have spent most of the time arguing. We've been through their parentage, their physical appearances and their more personal habits. I suppose, strictly speaking, it's abuse, not argument.'

Nan looked round the hut. Braithwaite had removed anything that might have been of any use. She sat down on the floor with the rest of them. After a while, Denise and Hugo Forbes started to talk about lens filters and light metering. Nan leaned against Nick and said, 'Tell me more about Simone's arty group, when you were all living in Hornsey.'

'Simone and I were only an occasional item,' said

Nick, 'but I fell hopelessly in love with one of her friends.'

This wasn't the way Nan had hoped the conversation would go. She wanted to know whether he had ever met Felicity. But she was intensely curious about this someone Nick had been in love with – especially after what Faith had said – so she bided her time and listened.

'Her mother was Dutch,' said Nick, 'and her father was English. She got married very young, seventeen. But she couldn't settle, couldn't reconcile herself to babies and jam-making. I think her husband realised she'd married the wrong man, and he did everything he could think of to keep her. In the end, he suggested she went to art school, got her restlessness out of her system that way. He made a bargain with her: he'd support her through college, as long as she had his child when she finished. She agreed.'

Nan looked faintly appalled.

'It was a perfectly acceptable form of blackmail at the time,' said Nick. 'It backfired on him, of course. She kept to her part of the bargain, but her college offered her a job and, much to his horror, she accepted, even though she was pregnant. He couldn't bear the idea of the baby being brought up by a childminder; they argued, they fought, he blamed everything on her college course – said it'd turned her head – and he tried to stop her painting. So she left him, left her job as well, and had the luck to be taken on straight away at Hornsey. When I met her at a party at Simone's, it was like walking over a precipice. But she didn't want me; I made a pass at her and got the brush-off. Then, godammit, she fell for my best friend – Alan, a violinist. He didn't realise how I felt about her, and I never told him. But *he* told *me* things. She'd had a pretty boring sex life with her husband, and as soon as she discovered what she'd been missing she wanted it all. He boasted about it. They did it everywhere – graveyards, car parks; everything from bondage to buggery, rubber to roleplay. The jealousy ate away at me like acid, but I never told Alan to keep his private life private. I needed to hear everything. Every detail. The ultimate masochist, emotionally. I wrote about her in an early book of mine –'

'I read it,' said Nan, remembering the artist character and her son, Thomas, who had loved that white shell so much. 'And there was something I wanted to ask you . . .'

'There's a window up there,' said Hugo Forbes suddenly. They all looked up. And sure enough, there was a tiny glint of glass behind a piece of sacking. He stood on tiptoe and pulled away the piece of hessian. It *was* a window – but it was rather small and high up, and Nan was the only one slight enough to get through it.

They all looked at Nan. 'OK,' she said, 'I'm game.'

'I know Cheng wasn't on your side,' said Forbes, 'but actually, he would be a lot of use. Untie Cheng first, and we'll all be out of here in two minutes.'

Nan looked at Nick. Nick seemed undecided. I'll consult Tad on that, thought Nan. 'Right,' she said. 'I need a back to climb on.'

It took a while, but eventually she managed to wriggle through the tiny window. She landed in a heap on some wet manure, but it broke her fall and deadened the sound. Braithwaite was at the far end of the clearing, stoking up a fire with enthusiasm. Cheng and Tad had their faces towards him and their backs towards her, and she crawled across the intervening ground with her heart in her mouth. When she was a few yards from them, Braithwaite turned round, and she sank into a shallow depression and lay there, fairly well camouflaged. Braithwaite lit a cigarette, and Nan knew she was there for its duration.

Tad and Cheng had been sitting in silence. This was finally broken when Tad said quietly, 'You don't seem particularly worried.'

'I'm not,' said Cheng. 'It's not my neck that's going in

the noose. Anyway, that's by the by. I need your assistance.'

'Assistance with what?'

'Getting another set of photographs.'

Tad laughed. 'You're insane.'

'Simone trusted me with her body, but she wouldn't trust me with her keys. Only you have those, don't you, Tad? Not even Nick has a set. And there's no way I could have smuggled a camera up there and taken the photographs myself. One whiff of a Nikon and I'd have been rumbled. In a couple of weeks' time – assuming Nick gets out of this one – he'll be gone and Forbes can come back and you can let him into the studio.'

'Why the hell would I agree to that?'

'Because,' said Cheng, 'Simone would hit the roof if someone told her you've been making canvas babies with Nan. All you have to do is unlock a door. If you're clever she may never find out it was you. And you *are* clever.'

'I'll risk it,' said Tad. 'Photographs of Simone's latest stuff would be hell for Nan. She's got kids, for God's sake.'

'Ah,' said Cheng. '*Nan*. We could always exclude the more incriminating paintings, seeing as you feel so strongly about it. I know quite a lot about Nan. Who her mother was, for instance. I know what her mother got up to, as well. And I know about Nick. Do you think Nan *really* wants her memory back? It may not be all that bad for Simone. She's a recluse, anyway; she doesn't care what the press says about her. She wouldn't even sue. She despises the legal system.'

'How did you find out?'

'I did what you did. Took the book out of the library and aged the photograph. Interesting, isn't it, the people who see it and the people who don't. Nick didn't. I only saw your drawing after I'd done one myself. Then I read Simone's diary. You did exactly the same thing, didn't

211

you, after you read my script? And it was all there: every detail.'

He didn't reply.

'It all fitted, didn't it? Just the names were changed. I rather like that. The words lied, but the picture didn't. Nan was Felicity, all right.'

And there it was, as bald as that. Tad knew I was Felicity all the time, thought Nan, and he didn't tell me. What an utter bastard.

'Why didn't you just ask Simone for the money?' said Tad. 'She'd probably have given it to you.'

'You're kidding,' said Cheng.

'You haven't been around Simone as long as I have,' said Tad. 'What did you want it for, anyway? Anything specific?'

Cheng didn't answer.

'You're sending it back home, aren't you?' said Tad. 'But I bet it isn't to support your dear old mother.'

'My mother's dead,' said Cheng. 'She was shot in front of me when I was five.'

There was a moment of silence. Then Braithwaite stubbed out his cigarette, got to his feet and glanced towards the hut. He picked up the shotgun and sauntered across the clearing, smiling maliciously.

'Done it,' said Cheng.

'Done what?'

'Got free.'

'Untie me, then.'

'I'm going to deal with Braithwaite, first,' said Cheng, and he melted into the long grass at the edge of the clearing.

Nan wriggled forward and touched Tad on the shoulder.

'You took your time,' said Tad, without turning his head. Nan untied the rope. It fell away, and Tad rubbed his wrists with his hands. 'He's got the key to the hut on his belt,' he said softly, 'I think we're going to have to let Cheng do his stuff. How long were you lying there?'

212

'A while.'

'How much did you hear?'

'Enough to know that *you knew I was Felicity all along*, and you didn't tell me. How could you, you fucking *bastard*, you *knew* how much it meant to me . . .'

'I didn't know it all along,' said Tad. 'Not for sure.'

At the other end of the clearing, Braithwaite was separating out his keys in the palm of his hand, the shotgun under his arm. Cheng rose, ghost-like, from the long grass; he reached Braithwaite with one bound, and disarmed him with one kick. The sequence that followed was quite beautiful; Cheng took hold of Braithwaite's right wrist and yanked it, catching the man's calf with his foot at the same time. Braithwaite was off-balance and Nan watched him somersault to the ground, his wrist the pivot. Cheng followed the movement through until he too was on the ground, his body at an angle to Braithwaite's, the man's arm stretched tight across Cheng's bent knee, the hand now palm-upwards. Cheng's knee jerked up, and his arm pressed down. There was a dry snapping sound. Braithwaite screamed. Cheng stood up, leaving Braithwaite writhing on the ground. Then he picked up the shotgun, and hit him dispassionately in the ribs with the butt. 'Keys,' he said. Braithwaite rolled on to his back, and Cheng bent down and took them. He threw them to Tad. Nan stood up.

'That's that, then,' said Tad, and he went over to the hut, slammed back the bolts and unlocked the door. The three captives emerged blinking into the firelight. Braithwaite just lay on the ground, moaning quietly.

'What do we do about him?' asked Denise.

'Leave him,' said Nick. 'But take the shotgun and the rifle.'

'That's a bit heartless,' said Forbes. 'He's got a broken arm.'

'He hit *me*, remember,' snapped Denise.

Forbes smiled into his sleeve.

Cheng turned to Tad. 'Well?' he said.

'Give me time, Cheng.'

'No,' said Cheng. 'I want your decision now.'

'What's going on?' asked Nick.

Tad shut his eyes and shook his head.

'I bitterly regret my involvement with the press, Nick,' said Cheng, with wonderful sincerity. 'I'm asking you both to accept me back as though nothing's happened, for Simone's sake. She need never know about this.'

'No way,' said Nick.

Tad was looking from Nick to Nan to Cheng, his face wracked with indecision.

'You can't be serious, Tad,' said Nick. 'If *you* don't tell Simone what happened, *I* will.'

'You don't understand,' said Tad.

'No,' said Nick coldly, 'I don't.'

'Nan or Simone?' said Cheng. 'Which one, Tad?'

Tad looked at Nan for a long moment. 'I'm sorry,' he said. 'But I can't find a way out of this one.'

'You've made your decision then?' said Cheng. 'You're sticking by Simone?'

'Yes,' said Tad. 'May you burn in hell.'

Cheng turned to Nan and smiled pleasantly. 'You see,' he said, 'there's a lot of money at stake. So I tried to blackmail Tad. Either I reveal what I know about you, Nan, or I keep quiet and I get the key. And I always follow up my threats: it's the way I was trained.'

There was a long pause. They were all looking at Cheng now.

Cheng turned to Nan. 'You really were the child in the photograph, Nan,' he said softly. 'Your mother changed your name to Felicity, to stop your real father finding you.'

'*What?*' Nick had gone as white as a sheet.

'Do you have to do this?' said Tad.

Nick was looking at Nan as though he'd seen a ghost. Then he screwed his eyes tight shut and groaned.

'It's no wonder you can draw,' said Cheng to Nan, 'because your mother changed her name to Harriet

Trent. She was a painter, and a very good one; she exhibited with Simone. And Nick fell for her, in a way he's never fallen for anyone, before or since.'

'No,' said Nan. 'Harriet had a son, not a daughter . . .'

'You read Nick's book, didn't you?' said Cheng. 'He swapped the genders. Poetic licence.'

Nan's mind backtracked to their first ever conversation in the library. *'When you first saw me, you behaved as though you'd seen me before.' 'You reminded me of someone.' 'Who?' 'An old flame, a very long time ago.'* He loved my mother more than he's ever loved anyone, thought Nan. That's the only reason he found me attractive, not because I'm *me*, but because I reminded him of *her*. Second best in spades, this time. Everything makes sense; the things in Nick's book I could picture so well . . . knowing the Latin name of the white crab spider . . .

'Harriet's daughter,' said Nick emptily. 'You're Felicity.'

'And there's more,' said Cheng.

'Don't,' said Tad.

'Some other time, then,' said Cheng, 'but I'll do it. As I said, I always follow up my threats.' He took one pace back, then another. He was smiling. The trees were only a few yards away.

And suddenly, Nan had had enough. She just wanted to be on her own. She simply turned and walked away from the group, back into the woods, back along the path, away. The voices receded; the firelight faded; the woods grew dark and solemn. Nobody followed her. She walked along in a dream, one foot after the other, comfort in automation. She wanted to go home now, find herself in familiar surroundings. She kept on walking, and then she was back on Simone's property. She seemed to have been walking for ever when at long last she saw the lights of the main building in front of her.

And then the shot, distant, unreal.

She glanced at her watch. It was one o'clock, and it sounded as though the party was still in progress. How very strange. She went back to the coach-house and up to her room, and looked at herself in the mirror. There was blood all over her clothes, Tad's blood. Her face looked white and drawn, and she stripped everything off and had a shower. That brought back memories, so she didn't stay under the water for long. Then she dressed herself in jeans and a sweatshirt, and packed her things. She left her bag on her bed, sorted out some change for the phone and went over to the main building. She was going to ask Mike to come and get her. He owed her that, at least.

To her amazement she found Simone, sitting on the stairs, alone. The laughter and the voices and clinking of glasses spilled out from the library like battery acid.

'I *am* Felicity,' said Nan. 'You shouldn't have kept it from me.'

'Is Nick upset?'

'Nick? What about *me*?' said Nan, astounded at Simone's tunnel vision. 'I went to bed with someone who was using me as substitute for my *mother*.'

Simone shrugged. Then she did a double-take. 'You went to bed with him? The studio wasn't the first time?'

'No,' said Nan, wanting to hurt, 'it wasn't.'

'*Bastard*,' said Simone. 'Where are they all, anyway?'

'Killing one another in the woods.'

'*What?* Why?'

Nan told her.

'I see,' said Simone. Then she suddenly seemed to give herself a mental shake. 'I'm sorry,' she said. 'You look a bit fed up about it all, although I can't say it would bother me, particularly. You don't remember anything before you were eight, *n'est-ce pas*?'

'I'm not so sure any more,' said Nan. 'The first time I saw Nick, his face looked strangely familiar. Then I thought it was just the publicity: I'd seen his photograph in the newspaper or something.'

'Bloody photographs,' said Simone. 'They cause nothing but trouble. That one I took of you, all Pre-

216

Raphaelite hair and no inhibitions. When Nick showed it to your father, he said, "Felicity's so like Harriet, isn't she?" And your father said, "She'd better not be." That's when he decided to erase her from your life, when he looked at *my photograph*. He made a snap judgement on a snapshot of time, and treated it as if it were the whole truth. What he did was unforgivable.'

Nan was surprised that Simone was so vehement about it. Empathy hadn't been her strong point up until now.

'I never took another photograph,' said Simone dramatically. 'It was the last one. I saw what a lie it was, taking a fragment of time and saying, this is how it is. What is a fraction of a second on celluloid compared with the months of observation a painting can take? Unforgivable.' She stood up. 'I need a drink. Then I'll be able to decide what to do. You need a drink. Let's go upstairs.'

Nan opened her hand and looked at the coins. Then she put them in her pocket. There were still things she wanted to know. She went up to the studio with Simone.

'You were joking, weren't you?' said Simone as they entered the studio.

'About what?' said Nan.

'Them killing each other in the woods.'

'No.'

Simone stared at her. 'And you just walked away and left them?' She seized the bottle of vodka and poured two large drinks. She finished hers in one go. 'I'm not sure I know what to do either,' she confessed. 'I love all three of them, *chérie*. Tad, Nick, Cheng.'

'Cheng used you.'

'*I* used *him*. I use all of them.'

'You don't mind?' said Nan, aghast. 'You don't mind that Cheng had sold you to a newspaper?'

'He should have said something. I'd have given him the money.'

'So all that was for nothing?'

217

'It's stopped you fancying Nick.'

'Is that all you care about?'

'No,' said Simone. 'I'm more concerned about Tadeusz.'

'What do you mean?'

'You're working together,' said Simone. 'I'm jealous. *Bloody* jealous.'

'You knew?'

'Of course I knew!' shouted Simone. 'I know Tadeusz inside out; I love him. He's an incredible artist. You don't know how lucky you are.'

'It was only because of his arm. He told me what to do, and I did it.'

Simone slammed her glass down on the table. 'He won't ask *me*. Eleven years, and he's done nothing more than a handful of drawing games with me! Eleven years of wanting that sort of – union – and then he does it with *you*, a fucking *student*.'

'I was only his studio assistant,' protested Nan. What am I doing, she thought, defending myself? This is ridiculous. It was his idea, not mine.

'We ought to go out there and find them.'

Nan shook her head.

'Well if you won't, I will. You think Cheng's lethal? Nick's got a temper. One hell of a temper. And he can shoot the pips off a playing card at fifty yards.'

Nan remembered the single shot she'd heard. 'Maybe we ought to call the police,' she said.

'I don't want the police anywhere near Cheng,' said Simone. 'They'd deport him.'

'I can't believe I'm hearing this,' said Nan. 'You still care about him? After everything he's done?'

'He's like a son to me, Nan.'

'You *sleep* with him.'

'So?'

'And you want him back?'

'I want them all back,' said Simone.

'I think I want to go home,' said Nan.

218

Simone stared at her. 'You can't.'

'I can.'

'But . . . the painting . . .'

'God,' said Nan, 'you are so *selfish*.'

Simone began to look restless. 'I need you all back in the studio, I really do. The painting is going so well. We have to get out there, do something. Cheng is a killer, Nan, that's why he's so exciting. Just knowing that someone has that sort of capability . . . intoxicating.' She was tapping her fingers impatiently on the table.

'No,' said Nan.

'*D'accord*,' said Simone. 'I'm going, then.' She pulled on a brown sweater and put on some shoes. 'Stay here if you want. Nan, you don't understand. I do love them, honestly I do. Tad . . . I would trust Tad with my life.'

'He's married, Simone. I don't know how you both just seem to ignore it.'

Simone laughed. 'You don't understand.'

'If anyone says that to me once more,' said Nan, 'I shall scream.'

'You like him, don't you?' said Simone. 'You like him a bit too much, I think.'

'I'm going home,' said Nan.

'Please don't,' begged Simone. 'Don't you want to know what happened? Don't you want to know if they're all right?' She was tugging neurotically at her hair, her eyes bright, her lips shining.

'No,' said Nan. 'I just want to forget I met any of you.' She left the studio and ran down the stairs. She heard Simone following her, but Nan was running away from everything, and it gave her a speed she didn't know she possessed. She sprinted across the courtyard and went into the barn.

Simone came out of the building and stopped. From her hiding place behind a bale of hay, Nan saw her scan the outbuildings like a video camera, left to right. She did two passes, and gave up. Nan watched her head off towards the woods.

It was a much cooler night. After a little while Nan began to shiver, and she knew she couldn't stay there much longer. She felt in her pocket for the coins, found them, cold and unhandled, and closed her fingers round them as though they were the keys out of a prison. Then she slunk out of the barn, and went back into the main building and the telephone. The party seemed to have finished. There was only the sound of a couple of people clearing away glasses. Nan picked up the receiver and dialled her home number.

It rang and rang and rang. She felt every muscle in her head tensing with the effort of holding back the tears, and she named every one in an attempt to pass the time. In the end, she replaced the receiver, and slid down the wall until she was sitting on the floor. She closed her eyes. I'm a quarter Dutch and I never knew it, she thought. Weird. Her head filled with bulb-fields and windmills.

She must have fallen asleep. When she came to with a jerk it was dark; someone had switched off the lights. The telephone was in a slight alcove – nobody would have seen her down on the floor. She ached everywhere. She stood up rather tentatively, and felt her way to the door. Once outside, the moonlight hit her like a search-light. She shielded her eyes as she went back across the courtyard to the coach-house, and felt her way upstairs to her room.

Her bag was still on her bed, packed. She didn't bother to undress; she just got into bed as she was, and fell asleep again immediately.

Chapter Thirteen

*S*unday. For a moment she couldn't work out why she was still fully dressed; then she remembered. She sat up. The sun was shining, and she had no idea what had happened after Simone had headed off for the woods. The desperate urge to get herself home had dulled somewhat. She walked across to the refectory – the first course of action was to see who was left on the staff table.

'Good morning,' said Trevor, coming the opposite way. 'You left the party early.'

'I was tired,' said Nan. This was dreadful. She was going to have to meet people and have normal conversations with them about things like muesli and the weather. Maybe she should just go up to Tad's room, and see if he was there.

She ran up the staircase and turned left at the top. Tad's room was locked. She knocked. Nothing. She looked round, wondering which room belonged to whom. She tried a couple of doors, but they were locked as well. She went along to the studio, but that was also locked.

She trailed outside and sat on the wall behind the refectory. She had no idea what to do; it was all horrible.

Everyone was due to leave at lunchtime, and there were no more classes. She could go home with Megan as though nothing had happened, if she chose. Then an idea struck her – if Braithwaite was the brother of the owner, maybe the brother was in the local telephone directory. She could make up some story, ask if he was going to be in the pub at lunchtime. She found the number, and a woman's voice answered.

'Can I speak to Mr Braithwaite please?'

'Which one?' asked the woman.

Oh, my God, thought Nan, what's his Christian name? It's not going to be Butch, is it? 'The gamekeeper,' she said.

'Rupert Braithwaite has had an accident,' said the woman. 'Who is this, please?'

Nan hung up.

She rang the hospital next. Yes, they did have a Rupert Braithwaite, Sycamore Ward. Was she a relative? She hung up.

At least he was still alive. He must have seen what happened. She had to go to the hospital. She found Megan, and asked her if she could borrow the car – Tad's arm got worse, she said, they kept him in. I'm going to visit – bring him back if he's OK. Megan gave her the keys.

Nan drove down the track, not really concentrating. When she nearly hit a tree she gave herself a sharp talking-to, and drove more carefully. The woods eventually thinned, and she was out on the main road. She could breathe again. She drove to the hospital, parked the car rather badly and took the lift up to Sycamore Ward.

'It's a bit early,' said the sister at the nursing station, 'but never mind. Fitting it in before morning service?'

Nan smiled stupidly.

'He's over there,' said the sister, pointing to a side-ward.

'How is he?' asked Nan, wondering what sort of reception she was going to get.

'Comfortable.'

It told her nothing. She thanked the woman, and made her way across to the room. She looked through the window. Braithwaite was asleep, his arm in plaster, a bandage round his head. Why the bandage? He hadn't injured his head, not that she could remember. She stood there, wondering whether she should wake him up. She couldn't decide, so she went for a walk round the block.

It was a depressing experience. There seemed to be an awful lot of old men: fat ones, thin ones, bright-eyed with medication and disturbingly asymmetrical beneath shapeless pyjamas. The side-wards gave way to general ones, then back to side-wards again. She was nearly back where she'd started. If she could remember where she'd started. The rooms all looked the same, plain white doors with square windows and chrome digits. She hadn't memorised the number. She hadn't even noticed it. She stood there, trying to pinpoint a landmark. There wasn't one. In the end she chose a side-ward at random, and peered through the window.

Tad was lying there. His head was bandaged as well, but he wasn't asleep. He glanced up, and saw her. She opened the door and went in.

'About time, too,' he said. They smiled stupidly at one another, and they didn't seem to be able to stop smiling.

A nurse followed Nan into the room. 'Excuse me,' she said, 'I thought you were looking for Rupert Braithwaite?'

Tad looked rather put out by this unexpected piece of information.

'I'm terribly sorry, Mr Kalinowski,' said the nurse. 'She's got the wrong room.' She glared at Nan, and held the door open for her to leave.

'Have you got the wrong room?' asked Tad.

'No,' said Nan.

'Good,' said Tad.

'But I've decided to go back with Megan after I've left here.'

The nurse was now looking from one to the other.

'Nan's not very sure of her direction at the moment,' said Tad. 'She can stay here until she sorts it out.'

The nurse gave them both an old-fashioned look, and left.

'What happened?' said Nan.

'She's protecting me,' said Tad. 'Some prat wanted me to autograph his plaster cast in the middle of the night. Preferably with a small but apposite illustration.'

'What happened to the *others*, Tad?'

'They decided to wait until my arm got a bit better and my signature was recognisable.'

'Nick and Cheng,' said Nan patiently. 'What happened between Nick and Cheng?'

He smiled. 'Persistent, aren't you? Nick became very reasonable, all of a sudden. I should have smelled a rat. We all decided to head down to the main road, ring Braithwaite's brother and tell him his gamekeeper had had an accident. Then Denise twisted her ankle, and that Forbes fellow gave her a very professional foot massage. But he had to put the rifle down to do it, didn't he, and Nick picked it up.' He leaned back and shut his eyes. 'I can't tell you how nice it is to be in a proper bed. You ought to try it out; I can always move over a bit.'

'Tad. You are infuriating. Get on with it.'

He grinned. 'Nick made sure Denise and I were well out of the way, Braithwaite and Forbes too. He called to Cheng. Cheng turned round, and Nick raised the rifle, very slowly, and aimed it. Rock steady. Cheng knew he didn't have a hope in hell. Nick just stood there, with Cheng in his sights. None of us were close enough to do anything, and I don't think we'd have dared. Cheng was hardly breathing, he was standing so still. "Tell me," said Nick, "when you execute someone, Cheng, how long do you give them to consider the inevitable?" Cheng didn't reply. "One minute? Two? An hour? Two hours? Because that's the real sadism about pointing a firearm at someone, isn't it? Your time is finite; you can tick off the seconds. One less. There goes another, Cheng. Two more." '

Tad glanced round. 'I could murder a glass of water.'

Nan poured him a glass of water. 'There's real sadism in the way you tell a story.'

'Just a bit of coitus interruptus. We'll come to the climax, don't you worry.' He drank some of the water. 'Cheng decided Nick didn't mean it, and he started to walk towards him. Nick fired a warning shot, singed Cheng's hair. But Braithwaite had decided to stagger off on his own. He got in the way, and the shot grazed his head as well. Two for the price of one. He's good, is Nick. Denise freaked; she thought Nick had killed him. Forbes went over and announced Braithwaite was still with us, but out of it for a bit. Nick told the rest of us to bugger off. Denise and her photographer were only too pleased to. They scarpered. Presumably they got to the road OK, and were picked up by whoever they'd rung earlier. I pretended to, then circled back with the intention of retrieving the shotgun. God knows what I'd have done with it if I'd got it; I know which end's which and that's about it. But I couldn't reach it. Nick had it next to him. He kept Cheng standing there for ages, and Cheng started to crack. I didn't expect it; I thought Cheng had nerves of pure spider silk . . .' He closed his eyes for a moment.

Nan felt a bit guilty. 'I'm making you talk too much,' she said. 'Just tell me who's in one piece and who isn't.'

'Come here,' said Tad, patting the coverlet beside him. 'Sit next to me. I need a bit of body contact.'

'I think you're forgetting something,' said Nan, staying where she was.

'What?'

'You knew I was Felicity. And you didn't tell me.'

'I didn't think you needed to have your ego kicked by

225

finding out you were a surrogate Harriet. How much do you know about her?'

'Not a lot.'

'I'd leave it that way, if I were you. I don't think she was an ideal mother.'

What did he know? But now wasn't the time to ask. 'Finish the story, then.'

'Where was I? Oh, yes. Cheng told Nick to get on with it, stop pissing around and finish it. Real fear, for once. Nick started to smile, I think that's all he'd wanted. A crack in Cheng's mask. Then Simone arrived, like some avenging angel. She went over to Cheng and put her arms round him, as though he was a baby, stood between him and Nick, right in the line of fire. She just told Nick he was being silly, and it was such an anti-climax it was almost funny. Cheng was shivering. They all got what they wanted. Simone got to play mummy, Nick established his seniority and Cheng got forgiven. Simone and Cheng just went off, their arms round each other. I imagine they went back to her room and fucked like lunatics.'

'And Nick?'

'Nick just sort of slumped after they'd gone. Then he got his second wind and said, "Let's get Braithwaite to hospital." So we loaded him on to a wheelbarrow and got him down to the main road. I was feeling like death myself, by this point – I think I must have collapsed in the gutter. When I came round, I was here. I said I didn't remember anything, and they told me that both Braithwaite and I had been injured by a hit-and-run driver. I've no idea where Nick went.'

'So what's the prognosis?' said Nan. 'Skull still intact?'

'Nothing fractured,' said Tad, 'but they're worried that it could have had this terrible effect on my libido. I really need someone to put their arms round me, see if I'm still capable of any reaction.'

'Nurse too busy?'

He shifted his body away from her slightly to make

room, closed his eyes, lifted the coverlet and patted the sheet.

'You're impossible,' said Nan.

'Need a cuddle.'

Against her better judgement, Nan sat on the edge of the bed. He put his left arm round her and pulled her against him, so that her head was resting on his bare chest. They sat like that for a while, then his hand slipped down to her thigh and he stroked her rather absently, as though if someone had drawn his attention to it he'd have been surprised and probably apologised for it. She couldn't help it; her left hand slid across his abdomen. She felt the muscles tense with pleasure; he was so capable of just enjoying sensation for its own sake, and he'd made her so aware of the human form that every time she touched him she wanted to explore him in detail, find out what lay where, understand him. Her fingers drifted across him, feeling the point of his hip-bone, the hollow at the side, the pulse in his groin, the texture of hair and skin. There was nothing wrong with his libido. They stayed like that for a while, just touching each other, eyes closed, not speaking.

'Nan,' said Tad.

'What?'

'Before you go home, I want to make love to you. Just once. I don't want to fuck you: I want to make love to you.'

And for once, words were the most inflammatory piece of arousal he could have engineered. She turned her face towards him and he started to kiss her, and if the door hadn't opened she probably would have done it right there, on the hospital bed. But the door did open, and she heard the nurse clearing her throat with embarrassment. She sat up, her face scarlet. Tad kept his arm round her, self-possessed and unapologetic.

'Your wife's here to see you,' said the nurse.

'Oh,' said Tad.

Nan jerked away. The nurse looked from one to the

other, shook her head fractionally with disapproval and left the room.

A tall and beautiful redhead walked in, pulled up a chair, sat down and said, '*O co chodzi?*'

'Nan doesn't speak Polish,' said Tad.

'I'm so sorry,' said the woman to Nan. She was immaculately dressed and made up, and she had a strong accent. Everything about her was tasteful and artistic and expensive.

'Nan,' said Tad, 'meet Grazyna.'

'Hello, Nan,' said Grazyna.

Nan nodded, not trusting herself to speak. The wife was like the Mercedes: another flashy enigma.

'How's Zbiszek?' said Tad.

'Fine.'

Who was Zbiszek? A child?

'How is the arm?' said Grazyna.

'Still attached to the shoulder,' said Tad.

'Will you be able to use it?'

He smiled. 'Oh, yeah.'

'So what happened?'

He told her.

Grazyna shook her head every so often and muttered something in Polish. 'I can't stop for very long,' she said finally. 'Zbiszek's got a big show coming up. Much to arrange. I just wanted to make sure you were still functional.'

'Who rang you?'

'Simone. How long before you can work again?'

'A week, maybe. Nan's been acting as my studio assistant. But she's had enough; she wants to go home.' He sighed dramatically, and looked hard done by.

Grazyna turned to Nan with a dazzling smile. 'If you could stay for a teeny little bit longer,' she said, 'I would be so very grateful. I think Tadeusz needs you.'

Nan stared at her.

'Tadeusz,' said Grazyna sternly, 'you haven't explained anything at all, have you?'

Tad looked sheepish.

'Men,' said Grazyna. 'Hopeless. So many things just never occur to them. I manage artists, I am agent. I live with Zbiszek Milewski, the sculptor. He is married, of course. His wife is Catholic, so no divorce. Seven years ago, I need British passport. Tadeusz offers me his services, I offer him mine. It works very well.' She stood up. 'Don't do anything else stupid, will you Tadeusz? And Nan – look after him. Simone could not look after a cactus.' She gave Tad a quick peck on the cheek, smiled exquisitely at Nan again, said goodbye, and left.

Nan didn't quite know what to think.

'How did you get here?' asked Tad.

'Megan's car.' Nan glanced at her watch. 'I'd better get it back to her. She's going to want to go home in it soon.'

'Are you going with her?'

She took a deep breath. 'Oh, Tad, I'm in a mess,' she said, and then she told him about Mike and Sandra.

He listened. Then he reached over to his locker, and handed her the keys to his Mercedes. 'Take it. If you want to drive home in it at any time, do it. I can arrange to have it picked up. I can't tell you what to do, Nan, but at least you don't have to go back with Megan if you're not sure.'

'When are they going to let you out?'

'Tomorrow, probably. If you stay, you could come and get me. Ring first thing in the morning.'

She stood up. 'I don't know what I'm going to do.'

'You don't want to sit around that place on your own, thinking. Talk to Dominic.'

'Dominic?'

'The wildlife guy. Get him to take you out looking for voles or something. They're a great distraction, voles.'

She smiled.

'Oh, and one last thing.'

'What?'

'Kiss.'

She leaned over the bed, intending to give him the same quick peck on the cheek that Grazyna had, but he caught hold of her wrist with his left hand and pulled so that she overbalanced. Then he started to kiss her, slowly and softly and persistently, so that she couldn't help pressing herself against him. He slid his hand under her T-shirt, and up to her breast. She felt the nipple harden before he even got close and, when he ran his thumb over it, she knew she wasn't going to be the one to pull away. He shifted himself to the far edge of the bed and then she was lying next to him, and he was still kissing her as he slid her trousers down to her knees. I shouldn't be doing this, she thought. It could be extremely embarrassing. And then he was sliding down her pants and playing with her, his finger wet from her response, and it was very difficult to think of anything except the pleasure.

'The window,' said Nan hoarsely. 'Anyone could see.'

'Let them,' said Tad. 'You're not leaving here without an orgasm.'

'And you?'

'I'd quite like one as well,' he conceded, 'just to make sure everything's in working order, you understand. I don't think I'm up to a full-scale installation, just yet, but after I've got you where I want you there's a tube of KY jelly on the locker ... and loads of tissues ...' He thrust his finger right inside her and twisted it before she could reply, and the sudden pressure on her clitoris from the rest of his hand took her breath away, and any chance of remaining coherent. He started to kiss her again, echoing with his tongue what he was doing with his fingers. The pleasure intensified and intensified until she was pushing against him as hard as she could – and then she was swept away by the climax, shuddering against him, hot against his chest, the sweat soaking her T-shirt. He wiped a strand of damp hair from her forehead and kissed her on the nose.

After a moment or two, Nan sat up and glanced at her watch.

Tad turned into a small boy having his sweets confiscated, pouting and looking at the floor. He sniffed. 'If you really do have to go now, I quite understand . . .' he said.

'*Oh*,' said Nan, 'you're impossible. All right.'

She squeezed out a dollop of lubricant, and smeared it over his penis. He sighed with pleasure, and leaned back against the pillow. He really did have a wonderful cock, long and thick, and she closed her hand round it and squeezed gently. He made a purring sound. She started to move the foreskin up and down, feeling him jerk against her fingers every so often under the coverlet. The slipperiness of him was a real turn-on, and she twisted her hand on each downstroke, making him catch his breath.

'Tissues,' said Tad softly. 'I don't think this is going to take very long, and we don't want to add to the hospital's laundry bill.'

Nan smiled, and did as instructed. Then she started to wank him in earnest; his stomach muscles tensed immediately, and he shut his eyes and went with it. She slowed down slightly as he approached his climax, teasing him, delaying the moment to increase the violence of the release.

'Don't piss about,' he whispered, grabbing hold of her hand with his. 'Finish me off.'

'Patience is a virtue,' smiled Nan, slowing down even more. Their hands wrestled but he couldn't get a grip on her; she was too slithery.

'I couldn't give a sod about virtue,' growled Tad, 'just do –'

She suddenly speeded up; his back arched against the pillow and he came, powerfully and copiously. She mopped him up, and he made little animal noises of satisfaction. Then he kissed her affectionately on the lips, and they said goodbye.

Nan had stayed a lot longer than she intended, and she left the hospital and ran to Megan's car, wishing for the impossible. How could life get so complicated so quickly? When she got back to the centre, she phoned Mike again. There was still no reply. What on earth was the point of getting an answerphone, thought Nan? He never remembers to switch it on. She found Megan and gave her the car keys.

'How's Tad?' asked Brian.

'Not too bad,' said Nan. 'Out of hospital tomorrow, probably.' She fiddled with her hair.

'Oh, good,' said Brian, disappearing off somewhere.

'I think you ought to come back with me,' said Megan.

Nan shook her head.

'Nick that good, is he?'

Nick? 'Oh,' she said, offhand, 'that's finished.'

'*Finished*? Why are you staying, then? Simone?'

Nan nodded, glad of an excuse.

'Did you ask her?'

'About the photo? Yes. And it *was* me.'

'Oh, wow,' said Megan, 'how incredible. So Simone really *did* know your mother. What was she like?'

'I haven't had much of a chance to talk to her about it yet.'

'But you're going to.'

Brian came back, carrying Megan's case. He looked drawn this morning; the lines across his forehead were that little bit more noticeable, and his mouth was that tiny bit more pinched. He doesn't want to go home, thought Nan. I wonder what his wife's like. He put the case in the boot of Megan's car, and stood looking at it, his face blank. Nan said goodbye to both of them, and they drove off in their separate cars, back to their separate existences.

The rest of the students left in dribs and drabs around midday. Rather surprisingly, Faith left with Dominic. As she got into his car, Nan heard her say, 'No, I've gone off him as a writer now I've met him. He couldn't even be bothered to say goodbye. But I've always been interested in insects. Spiders are so fascinating aren't they?'

Dominic made a strangled sound in his throat and mumbled, 'Arachnids.'

Lettie and Gerald were presumably saying a long farewell somewhere as Gladys sat in the front seat of the Volvo, tapping the dashboard. Nan was watching her from the window when the door of her room opened.

'I just popped up to say goodbye,' said Lettie.

Nan was touched.

'Take care, won't you?' said Lettie. 'There was something I wanted to say. I've been watching you change over this past week, and ... well ... it suits you. Go for it, whatever it is.' She gave Nan a quick peck on the cheek, and went. A few minutes later there was a screech of tyres and a shower of gravel as Imogen accelerated away.

When everyone had gone, Nan felt an overwhelming sense of relief. She didn't go and look for Dominic; she went down to the lake and had a swim and tried to sort everything out in her head. Her fixation with Nick had quite simply evaporated; she really couldn't handle the idea of being a substitute for her own mother.

The thing that was scaring her the most was how she felt about Tad. She couldn't bear the idea of never seeing him again; then she wondered whether it was just Lavender Hall, and that she'd feel differently once she was back home. After that she considered the prospect of there not being a 'back home'; Mike had, in fact, left her. She didn't know whether she minded or not. No, that wasn't true either. She minded dreadfully one moment – how did you shake off twenty years? How would Darren and Cassie react? The next moment it seemed like the best thing that could happen. Nothing was a simple choice. Everything had at least two sides.

She sat and stared across the lake, watching the waves batting the sunlight from one peak to another. She didn't look at things the same way any more; she searched out

233

the form, tried to find the correlations, the similarities, the differences. She suspected that it wouldn't be a comfortable way of looking at life at home. Home required a soft focus and a number of filters.

'Hello,' said Simone. 'Isn't it nice now that everybody's gone?' She sat down next to Nan. 'Where's Nick?'

'I've no idea,' said Nan.

'He's being very silly,' said Simone. 'What a fuss.'

'Where's Cheng?'

'Knocking up some canvases. I gave him the money. He only had to ask.'

Nan was speechless.

'You are going to carry on modelling for me, *n'est-ce pas*? With Tadeusz?'

'He's agreed to this, has he?'

'I haven't asked him. I expect he will, though.'

'I don't think so,' said Nan.

'Why?'

'Simone,' said Nan, 'Tad has been through one hell of a lot these last few days.'

'Not enough to prevent him working with *you*, though,' said Simone viciously. Then the smile broke through, unpredictable as ever. 'But I've forgiven him for that,' she said, 'because you were right. All he needs at the moment is a studio assistant, not a real collaborator.'

It was a precision-aimed insult, and Nan seethed.

Simone pouted slightly. 'I just want everybody to be friends again,' she said. 'I hate arguments. But it could have been a lot worse. Nobody was killed.' She seemed quite pleased with this conclusion, and decided to change the subject. 'Did you meet Grazyna?' she asked slyly.

'Yes.'

'She's nice, isn't she?'

They didn't say anything for a while, just sat and looked at the water.

'I've known Nick since he was seventeen,' said Simone

suddenly, as though Nan had asked her. She was staring into the distance, a slight smile on her face.

'I didn't think you met until you came over here as a student,' said Nan.

'We didn't,' Simone replied. 'I knew him on paper. I was meant to write in English, and he in French. We did for a while; I told him how I lived in a chateau, and had a tutor. I was so innocent; I knew nothing of life. Nick was two years older than me.'

They both lay down on the grass, resting on their elbows.

'We started to write to one another in our own languages, so that if our parents found the letters they wouldn't be able to translate them. I would write one in English, harmless stuff, and the real one in French. Nick educated me. I had never touched myself; it hadn't occurred to me. Nick told me what to do. We started to write fantasies to one another: I would draw things, he would write. I lived for his letters. Oh, he was experimenting with girls in a practical way by that time, and he described everything. I was a voyeur in that sense from the age of sixteen.' She plucked at a stem of grass and sucked it. 'So: is he any good at it, your Mike?'

'He's OK.'

'OK? Just that?'

'We've been together for more than twenty years,' said Nan. 'What do you expect?'

'I've been with Nick on and off for nearly forty,' said Simone. 'He can still drive me completely insane.' Nan didn't want to think like that about Nick any more, but Simone gave Nan a rather penetrating look and asked, 'Was it better with Nick?'

'Yes,' said Nan.

They didn't say anything else for a while. A pair of swans landed on the lake and sailed along, looking self-satisfied and autocratic. Nan picked a clover-leaf, twirled it between her fingers, and phrased questions about her mother in her head.

'So,' said Simone, 'how do you feel about Tadeusz?'

Nan took a deep breath. 'He's . . . he's got something, hasn't he? Something unique. And he's the best teacher I've ever met in my life.'

'You want to sleep with him, don't you?' said Simone. 'My gosh, a week here and you're at it with everyone.'

'You've got a nerve.'

Simone laughed. 'I can't help it. But Nan, a warning. With Nick it's a performance, and one he knows he can do very well. You can take or leave that sort of thing, like caviar, although it's nice to come back to every so often. But Tadeusz . . . Tadeusz is different. He *makes love*. And he has loved many people – even Grazyna, at the start.'

'Who left whom?'

'They didn't even live together,' said Simone. 'So it wasn't like that.' She smiled. 'I remember the first time I met him. We did a show together; I was just out to shock at that stage, but he was better at it than me. We stood and looked at one of my paintings and he said, you're a Mannerist, aren't you, the way you distort bodily proportions to emphasise things. He was looking at this penis I'd painted – OK, it was a bit on the large side . . .' She laughed. 'I said, I choose my models with great care. He said, from the Guinness Book of Records, no doubt. We talked about the different media you could mix with acrylics to give it texture, body, gloss, and we were sort of talking about how much of yourself you put into your work at the same time. I asked him what he used, and he just said *spunk, ma chérie*, and walked off. I couldn't let that rest, could I? I sent him a painting. He sent me one. We kept that up for a while, getting more and more suggestive, and eventually I invited him down here. I wanted to paint him, and he's been back every summer ever since. But he never liked Nick.'

Nan took the plunge. 'Simone,' she said, 'tell me about Harriet. She was my *mother*, and I don't remember anything about her. What did she sound like? Was she funny, did she have any obsessions, phobias, ailments? Paint her for me, Simone.'

'With words?'

'Yes. With words.'

Simone drew her knees up to her chest and stared across the lake. 'She was like a dragonfly,' she said. 'Beautiful, agile, voracious.' She seemed to think this was a perfectly adequate response, and put her chin on her knees.

'Do you have any of her work?' Nan asked her.

'No,' said Simone bitterly. 'Her husband burned everything after she died.'

'*What?*'

'He made a bonfire in the back garden, and burned the lot. Drawings, paintings, sketchbooks – everything. Even her paints and her brushes. *Naturellement*, it was all my fault,' she added theatrically.

'*Your* fault? How?'

'The photograph. I *told* you what happened. He saw my picture of you, all arty and uninhibited, and that's when he decided to eradicate Harriet's memory, so that you wouldn't have her as a role model. Stupid man. It's not as if keeping her work would have turned you into an artist. Unforgivable thing to do, though; he destroyed something that was utterly irreplaceable.'

Nan suddenly realised that what had upset Simone so much and turned her off photography was the destruction of Harriet's paintings, not the effect on Nan's childhood. She smiled faintly.

Simone brightened. 'There's some paintings of hers in galleries abroad, though,' she said. 'Grazyna would be able to find out. Maybe they'd be able to send you some slides.'

'Oh,' said Nan, 'that would be great.'

Simone looked pleased with herself. 'Harriet was the sexiest woman I ever met,' she said. 'Men fell for her like flies. She had this way of looking at a man that said, I know how to give you an orgasm beyond your wildest dreams.' Then she noticed the expression on Nan's face and said, 'Ah. That is not the sort of information you want about your mother, is it?' She began to describe Harriet more conventionally, and the missing pieces of Nan's own personality started to fall into place. There were so many tastes they had in common, it was uncanny. There were a lot of differences as well, though – Harriet had been much more irresponsible than Nan, and she wouldn't have known an exhaust manifold from an oil filter. Nan had inherited some things from her father, too. The one thing that Nan had hoped would occur didn't happen, however. Simone's narrative didn't open the floodgates of her memory. There was no sudden rush of recollections; the picture Nan was building up of Harriet was firmly rooted in the present, and was entirely dependent on other people's memories. It was a disappointment, but only a small one.

Simone stood up and they both started to walk back to the house. 'Cheng is wonderful, too, you know,' she said, apropos of nothing, 'but in a very different way from Tad and Nick. He doesn't care at all when he makes love, and I like that sometimes. He does it for himself alone, and you feel his spirit, but you can't hold it. I keep trying to capture it in paint, but I have never succeeded.'

'Oh, I don't know,' said Nan, remembering the evil eye in the barn, 'I thought you succeeded rather well, actually.'

Simone fluffed out with pleasure. 'Do you think that? How marvellous. Come and have dinner with Cheng and me. We'll be up in the studio.'

'No, thanks,' said Nan. 'I intend to have a very early night. On my own.'

Chapter Fourteen

Monday. Much to her surprise, Nan woke up feeling refreshed. She had some breakfast, then she walked over to the garages, reversed Tad's car out into the courtyard and drove to the hospital.

He was sitting on a chair by the bed, dressed, ready, reading a newspaper. He glanced up and smiled. 'You stayed,' he said. 'I didn't know if it was going to be you or Nick.'

'Nick hasn't come back.'

He looked surprised.

'Simone wants you to take Nick's place,' said Nan, 'modelling.'

He snorted, and picked up the plastic bag containing his leather jacket. 'I don't think so.'

'That's what I said. Oh – and something I forgot to tell you. She knows about me helping you with your studio work.'

'Oh. And?'

'She wasn't very happy but apparently she's forgiven you,' said Nan, 'because all you need at the moment is a studio assistant, not a real collaborator.'

He laughed. 'Oh, she can be a bitch. Come on. Let's go.' His head was no longer bandaged, and he looked a lot better. The lump had started to go down, although she could see that he'd had a couple of stitches. He stretched himself out in the passenger seat and shut his eyes. 'We could do a bit of painting later today, if you feel up to it.'

'Do *you* feel up to it?'

'Yes, I think so. I want to get on with the dragon shape, and I've had a few ideas for the rest.'

Simone heard the car, and came down to meet them. She threw her arms passionately round Tad, staking a claim, telling him she'd been out of her mind with worry. Tad gently disengaged her, and said he had a headache. Simone was instantly distraught, and suggested he went and lay down for a bit.

'I intend to,' said Tad. 'Come along, Nan.'

Nan followed him into the house. She glanced behind her as she went to shut the door; Simone was standing in the middle of the courtyard, biting her lip. She smiled faintly at Nan, then turned on her heel and walked away in the direction of the barn. As they got to the top of the stairs, Nan heard the sound of splintering wood in the distance.

As soon as they entered his room, he took off his shirt and shoes, and rummaged around for something else to wear; the bandage on his arm had been replaced with a plaster.

'What do you do for the six months you're not here?' asked Nan.

'Travel,' said Tad. 'Sometimes I spend the whole time in Poland, sometimes not. I went to Egypt last year, looking at the temples. I usually have some sort of project. I really fancy Mongolia. I saw a painting once. Sunrise; pink mountains, folded like brains . . . spectacular. And really pink, permanent rose.'

They sat on the edge of the bed and talked about colours.

'Take a colour like intense blue,' he said. 'It's vicious.

Copper phthalocyanine, pure poison. You can't use it on its own: it's too bright, it's one of those pigments you always mix with another. Use it sparingly, use it carefully. Use it unadulterated and you dispense with realism; nothing is actually that colour. But put a tiny drop in with something else and it livens it up, gives it zest.'

They looked at the canvas they'd started two days previously, and discussed the colour scheme. He made her think, he made her laugh, he made her question every assumption about colour she'd ever had.

'What do you know about after-images?'

'Nothing,' said Nan. 'That's next term.'

It was a sudden injection of the outside world – next term implied a continuation of what had gone on before. But she seemed to have progressed way beyond the A level. Not technically – she knew she'd hardly scratched the surface; it was what she wanted to *do* with her painting that had changed. She was thinking about content and theme in a far more complex way, seeing possibilities that would never have occurred to her the previous week.

He got up and went over to the plastic bag he'd brought back from the hospital. He felt inside it and pulled out a tube of Smarties. 'I was thinking about you,' he said. He pulled back the quilt on the bed and smoothed out the white satin sheet that lay beneath. Then he emptied the sweets on it, and selected a green one. 'Lie down,' he said, 'on your stomach.'

She lay down, and he lay down beside her.

He moved the green one directly into their field of vision, so that they couldn't see the others. 'I want you to stare at it,' he said. 'Don't move your head, don't blink, and count up to twenty.'

She did it.

'Don't look up. Switch your gaze to the white sheet.'

The image of a pink Smartie gradually appeared before her and got brighter and brighter, but when she moved her eyes a fraction the image moved with her. She looked at him and smiled. 'Pink,' she said.

He grinned, fed her the green Smartie, and replaced it with a yellow one. This time the after-image was purple. They went through the other colours, leaving the blue until last.

'This colour is very nearly that intense blue I was talking about,' he said.

The after-image was the colour of blood.

They lay face to face on their sides, a little way apart. He told her how staring at something without blinking wasn't the natural way to look at things; eyes flicked from one image to another. The cells became desensitised when subjected to an unnatural barrage of one colour, and stopped seeing it.

'You tired out your blue receptors,' he said. 'Just the ones on that little Smartie-shaped patch on your retina you'd created by staring too hard for too long. Only the red and the yellow were still working, so you saw orange.'

'Orangey-red,' said Nan.

'What sort of blue was it?'

'A cold blue.' It was the colour of a tropical sea beneath an azure sky, unreal, impossible. The wonderful colour you saw when there was silver sand beneath the water, and the light reflected back up through it. A colour that made you want to dive in and submerge yourself in it.

'Oh, I get it,' said Nan, and she smiled. 'I'm seeing the absolute opposite.'

'Known as the complementary.' He stood up. 'You need to understand why it's important in figure painting. Take your clothes off.'

It had become a very ordinary and everyday command. She stripped. He went over to a spotlight in the corner, wheeled it across and put a yellow filter in front of the bulb. Then he switched it on, and shone it on the bed. He pulled down the blind so that the rest of the

242

room was in darkness, then he took off his own clothes and lay down beside her.

'Let your eyes adjust to the light for a moment,' he said. They lay there, looking at one another, not touching. The yellow light caught the top of his hip, his shoulder, his thigh. Once again she thought how beautiful his body was, how she'd never really seen the human form before. 'Now concentrate on the shadows,' he said, his voice very low.

She looked at the purple under his chin, the violet of his arm, the magenta in his hair. 'Yes,' she said. 'I see.'

He got up and changed the filter. This time the light was red. The shadows all became green; there was jade in his hair, and emerald on his hand. 'If you isolated this shadow, saw it against a white background, it would be grey. Shadows are just the absence of light. But we stain them with our after-images, and then we don't paint what we see, we try and paint what we know is there instead. It doesn't work.'

The last filter was blue. 'Look at the cast shadows,' he whispered. 'They're often the brightest.' He moved his hand across and stroked the inside of her arm. She watched the shadow drift back and forth across the sheet, the colour of wine, then blood, then fire. They lay there, making patterns on the sheet with their bodies, joining them and separating them, playing with the idea of union. He untied his hair, and it fell across them both in a shower of carmine, fusing their shadows. She traced the veins in his arm, down to his wrist. His thumb ran lightly backwards and forwards across her palm, shading it with alizarin. He moved his foot across to her leg, sliding it up to behind her knee, creating a crimson triangle below it. She followed his instep with her finger, moving up his leg until he shivered and the burgundy shadows danced on the satin.

They took their time over everything; it was a slow affectionate voyage of exploration. She watched their shadows, inseparable now, a strange new shape created from two others. His lips brushed between her legs, and she felt the rush of a more sharp-edged arousal. They moved head to tail, and she took him in her mouth, delicately, softly, imagining she was a feather, he was eggshell. He teased her with his tongue, soft little strokes, then an increase in pressure, then soft little strokes again. She copied what he did until they were moving in perfect synchrony, licking and nibbling, sucking and blowing. The rhythmic puffs of his breath across her wet clitoris made her writhe with longing, and he seized her hips with his hands to keep her still. She could taste the first leakage of semen on the tip of his cock. His whole body tensed. 'No,' he said softly, after a little while, 'I'll come.' They rolled apart and he handed her a ribbed condom. She put it on for him; it was a statement of intent.

Then he turned her on to her back, and knelt between her legs. He drew the outline of his shadow on her skin with his finger, and then he wrote his signature across her stomach. She watched his face; thoughtful, serious, his painting expression. He smiled and kissed her and she kissed him back; they were in total harmony, and time ceased to exist.

Then he just whispered, 'Now,' and entered her very slowly and deliberately until he was right the way in. He made love to her in slow motion for a long time; smiling now and then, kissing her in unexpected places, refusing to speed up, letting the frustration build to an alarming level and holding her in place by her wrists. The texture of the condom was strange but wonderful, rubbing her in just the right place. She could see how much he wanted her, and how carefully and deliberately he was timing the culmination; his consideration and self-control made her feel like the sexiest woman on earth.

'Tad . . .' she heard herself whisper.

He slowed down even more, and stroked the line of her jaw with his finger; then he let the brakes off altogether. The whole thing escalated with incredible speed. Her hands raked across his back; he held her down; she felt herself strain against him and the tension in her muscles intensified everything even more. The inevitability of their approaching orgasms was inflammatory in itself; his eyes were holding her even more captive than his hands, pinning her against the sheet. Then there was nothing except sensation, and they both climaxed with a violence that left her gasping for breath and with an ache in her abdomen.

He lay on top of her, panting a little, turned her face towards him and said, 'And at the finish, Love And Lust beats Mere Shagging by several lengths.'

She was smiling and crying at the same time. Then she nodded her head in agreement, and held him as tightly as she could. She was remembering what he'd said in the hospital. *Before you go home I want to make love to you. Just once.*

They didn't do any painting. He raised the blind and switched off the spotlight, and they opened a bottle of wine and ate French bread and Brie and did silly things with the rest of the Smarties. He taught her some bits of Polish. 'Say *do widzenia*,' he instructed. 'It's "goodbye", but it means "until I see you again".'

She struggled with the pronunciation, and he found her more and more difficult things to say until she couldn't get her tongue round any of them at all and he was in hysterics.

She showed him how to make an origami swan, and he drew feathers across her skin with a paintbrush. They couldn't leave one another alone. She plaited his hair; he pretended she was a cello, and played Elgar's concerto on her. She retaliated with a Chopin Polonaise, and he threw her on to the bed and kissed her, holding her wrists with his left hand. 'John Cage,' he said. 'Gotcha.' She stroked his thigh with her face and pretended to be a cat. He became a lion. They tussled on the bed, growling and cuffing. He kissed her again and time

245

went haywire. Then they just lay there, watching the clouds through the window and calling out the names of the shapes they saw. Eventually they drifted off to sleep.

When she woke up, Tad was dressed, and removing the teabags from two cups with a palette knife.

Nan picked up Megan's dress and put it on. 'Something you said in the hospital . . .'

He sat down on the bed and put the cups on the floor. 'What?'

'That you wanted to make love to me just once . . .'

'Isn't that what you wanted?'

She hesitated. 'Isn't that what *you* wanted?'

'I asked first.'

'No,' said Nan.

'No as well, then.'

It felt like a dangerous topic of conversation, and they dropped it. They drank their tea, and raided the fridge again for something to eat. The shadows lengthened, and the colours faded as everything grew dark.

'We're going to have to go to the studio and see her,' said Tad.

'What are you going to say?'

He thought for a moment. 'That we're not doing any modelling, and that you're staying on to help me. Her relationship with Cheng is *her* business, I think.'

'I have to phone Mike, first.'

She went downstairs to the payphone and dialled the number with a sick feeling in her stomach. This time he answered. 'Oh,' he said, 'it's you. When are you coming back?'

'I'm not sure,' said Nan.

'There's nothing left in the freezer.'

He sounded different: grumpier than of late, but less distant. I wonder if he's had a ruck with Sandra, thought Nan.

'I'll phone again when I know,' she said.

'Suit yourself.'

246

'Bye, then.'

'Bye.'

'He hasn't left you, then,' said Tad, when she returned.

'No.'

'Pity,' said Tad.

They walked along the corridor to the studio. Tad opened the studio door, and they went in. Simone and Cheng were sitting on the cushions, drinking vodka.

'Oh, good,' said Simone, 'I hoped you'd come round.'

They sat down opposite her. 'We're not going to do it,' said Tad.

'Why not?' said Simone. 'I thought you fancied each other?'

Tad started to laugh. 'You really are impossible, Simone,' he said. 'Of course I fancy her. That's why I won't do it.'

'I don't understand,' said Simone. 'Is it Cheng? You are friends again, *n'est-ce pas*?'

'No,' said Tad.

Simone pouted. 'I've forgiven him. If I have, you ought to be able to.'

Cheng was sitting cross-legged, quite relaxed, his expression unreadable.

'Oh, come on,' said Simone. 'Bury the hatchet. I made a fruit punch. I'll get it.' She left the room looking quite bouncy.

Tad and Cheng regarded one another with caution. 'You won't get anything more than common courtesy out of me,' said Tad, 'and I won't find that easy.'

Cheng smiled. 'We've all got to get along, Tad. Don't make it difficult.'

And then the door opened. Cheng stiffened, so slightly that Nan wouldn't have noticed it if she hadn't been looking at him at the time. She turned to see; it was Nick.

He surveyed Tad and Cheng, and smiled sarcastically. 'Well, well,' he said, 'I didn't expect it of you, Tad.'

Cheng was sitting very still, watching Nick carefully.

Nan got the impression that Nick only had to make one wrong move for Cheng to move like greased lightning.

'Cheng's no friend of mine,' said Tad.

'But you're back here.'

'So are you.'

'I've come to collect my things,' said Nick. 'I'm going.' He turned to look at Nan for the first time. 'I don't know what to say,' he said.

Nan shrugged. She had no idea, either.

Simone appeared in the doorway with a tray. 'Nick,' she shrieked, 'how wonderful.' She put down the tray and ran over, throwing her arms round him.

He shook her off. 'Don't.'

She looked put out. 'Not another one sulking,' she said. 'I really don't know what's wrong with you all.'

'I'm leaving,' said Nick.

Simone looked devastated. 'So early? You can't! At least stay and have a drink. Look, I made some fruit punch. It tastes OK, as well. *Voilà*.' She poured a glass of it and gave it to him. Then she did one for everyone else. 'I won't make any of you stay if you don't want to,' she said, glancing at her watch. 'I just want half an hour. So that I can do one sketch with you all together.'

'I'm not taking my clothes off,' said Tad. 'I've not been well.'

'Costume pose, then,' said Simone, smiling at him. She raised her glass. '*Na zdrowie*.'

Nan was thirsty, and she drank the whole glass. It tasted mainly of blackcurrant, but there were hints of mango and melon with a dash of lime. It was rather nice. No alcohol, which surprised her. Cheng was diplomatic and drank his down in one go, as well. He seemed to be trying quite hard to please.

They sat around on the cushions, no particular arrangement, and Simone started to draw them. Nobody said very much. Quite possibly they were all wondering why they'd agreed to it. Simone finished one drawing and started another. She swore quietly in French a

248

couple times, then said, 'This one isn't working.' She screwed it up and threw it in the bin. 'You're all wearing such boring clothes,' she said. 'Let's dress up.' She went into the store room where she kept her paintings, and Nan heard her start to rummage through bundles of material. 'Come on, all of you,' she called, 'come and sort through this lot with me.'

Cheng got up and strolled over to the store room. Tad shrugged, said, 'Oh, what's the harm,' and followed him. Nan followed Tad.

'Oh, come on, Nick,' said Simone, 'I've got just the thing.' Nick joined them, looking sullen, and sat down on one of the bentwood chairs. Simone passed him a surplice and a dog collar. His face tightened. 'Oh, don't be such a killjoy,' said Simone, and she dropped the surplice over his shoulders. 'This is for you, Cheng,' she said, throwing a black leather codpiece and mask at him. He smiled, took off his trousers, and put them on.

Nick stood up, as though he intended to take the thing off. Then he sat down again, and Nan saw an expression of incomprehension cross his face. It was quite funny; she wanted to laugh. Simone was smiling. She seemed to have been smiling for a terribly long time. Nan began to wonder whether there was something wrong with the perspective in the store room. The vanishing points weren't in quite the right places any more, and the slope of the ceiling seemed strange.

Simone and Cheng looked at one another, and Simone nodded. Cheng left the store room. Tad was fingering a white cotton smock, and looking thoughtful. Simone clapped her hands. 'Oh, *yes*, a pirate. Perfect.' She handed him some knee-length britches and red sash. '*Bon*,' said Simone, turning her attention back to the clothes. She selected a red basque, trimmed with black lace, and some silk stockings. Then she stripped off her clothes until she was quite naked. She still had a beautiful body. Comes from not having children, thought Nan, admiring the smooth tanned flatness of Simone's stomach, the long shapely legs, the neat little breasts. She noticed Nan watching her and said, 'I find women's bodies just as erotic as men's. Different, but equally as sexy.' Then she walked over to Nan, took hold of her hand and placed it on her breast. 'Feels good, doesn't it? You should try women, Nan. Everyone should try everything once, no?'

Simone's breast felt soft and silky. Nan watched the nipple come erect, and marvelled at the fact that she had been the catalyst. Arousing someone else was arousing in itself, whatever their gender. Simone bent towards her, and kissed her lightly on the lips. It was the softest kiss Nan had ever received, and her body reacted accordingly. Simone ran her hand up Nan's leg, underneath the soft chiffon of Megan's dress; the subtlety of it was new and exciting, and Nan felt a tiny trickle of moisture pay homage to it. Simone smiled; then she picked up the basque and the stockings, and put them on. She smoothed everything into place, and fastened the suspenders as sensually as if they were made of flesh.

Tad was having trouble buttoning the shirt, for some reason, and Nick was watching him. Simone put on some red satin stilettos, went over to a mirror and applied some poppy-red lipstick. Nan wondered fleetingly if they were the same shoes she had seen in the picture Hugo Forbes had shown her, in the gallery. Simone turned to her and winked; the wink instantly transformed her into a whore.

And then she heard the studio door open, and tentative footsteps. 'It's OK,' said a woman's voice, 'there's no one here. Right. I suggest we start in the store room.' Footsteps approached. Nan realised that voice belonged to Sniffle. Simone was smiling; then the studio door clicked shut, and there was the sound of a key turning in a lock.

'Cheng!' cried Sniffle. 'What on earth are you doing?'

'Simone felt we all parted on less than favourable terms,' said Cheng. 'She wants to redress it.'

'She's here? But you said –'

Simone smoothed the basque over her hips one more time, and walked back into the studio. The others trailed out after her. Sniffle glared at Cheng, tight-lipped. Standing beside her was Hugo Forbes, carrying a brand new flight-case.

'Cheng told you there would be nobody here,' said Simone, 'that he'd get the key and unlock it for you. You see, I know Denise is going to write about me, photographs or no photographs. So you may as well have a proper interview after all, straight from the horse's mouth. I got Cheng to set it up. More fun with a bit of drama, no?'

Hugo Forbes looked delighted. Sniffle looked dubious.

'Oh, what a long face,' said Simone to Sniffle. 'Have some fruit punch.' She poured her a glass, and then she poured one for Hugo Forbes as well. They both drank; they took their time, and Nan suspected they had accepted because it meant they didn't have to say anything while they were doing it. She turned her attention to Cheng. He appeared to be meditating, staring fixedly at some spot on the other side of the room, motionless. He was rather more motionless than usual. Nan fought the urge to laugh again. How could you be more motionless than motionless?

'Now,' said Simone, 'let's talk about *art*.'

Hugo Forbes was staring at Simone's shoes as though he had just won the lottery. Simone stretched out her leg towards him, and he swallowed. 'They're nice, aren't they?' she said.

'They're divine. They're the ones from *The Naked and the Shod*, aren't they? I adore that watercolour.'

'Do you?' Simone looked pleased. 'It was quite difficult to get the right red. That was the reason I withdrew it from the –' She suddenly looked perplexed. 'Where did *you* see it?'

'Ah,' said Hugo Forbes.

Nan could see Tad staring into his glass, as though it

251

held the meaning of life. She saw him look up, very slowly, saw his eyes meet Simone's. Saw Simone's smile widen even further, and a dawning realisation cross Tad's face. He looked at his glass again. He had only drunk half the contents. He stood up, walked over to the sink and poured the rest of the drink away. Nick looked at his own glass. He'd drunk about three quarters of it. Simone had drunk about a third of hers.

Tad was standing with his back towards them by the sink. He turned to Simone, grim-faced. The music that had been playing in the background suddenly developed an eerie feel to it. There was something not quite right about it. There was something not quite right about everything.

'You idiot,' said Tad to Simone.

Nick put down his drink. Cheng hadn't moved at all. Sniffle looked at her glass, then back at Simone. Hugo Forbes still couldn't take his eyes of Simone's shoes.

'I just wanted us all to be friends again,' said Simone. 'It seemed like the quickest way.'

Nan seemed to be losing the point of the conversation. She looked at Tad. He was still staring at Simone. 'You fucking idiot,' he said.

'What is it?' asked Nan. But her voice sounded different, as though it belonged to somebody else.

'You must have been out of your mind,' said Tad, still to Simone.

'Christ,' said Nick. But he didn't say anything else.

The blind rustled in the breeze. It was far too loud.

'What is it?' repeated Nan.

'Elephants,' said Cheng unexpectedly.

'She spiked the fruit juice,' said Tad.

'Not with anything illegal; I made a concentrate of that aphrodisiac tea stuff,' said Simone, with some pride. 'Effective, isn't it?'

Nick was looking at his hand with considerable interest, separating out his fingers, straightening them and bending them again. 'Very clever,' he said. 'No one can drive anywhere, now. You've got us exactly where you want us, haven't you?'

Tad started the journey from the sink back to the cushions. He got sidetracked very quickly by a smudge of paint on Simone's easel. He just stood there, looking at it.

'Why don't we all just enjoy it?' said Simone.

'I'm enjoying it,' said Hugo Forbes. He was sitting next to Simone, and stroking her ankle. Simone was ignoring him, but she didn't move her foot out of the way.

Tad tore himself away from the easel. He negotiated the last part of the floor as if it were studded with nails, and sat down next to Nan.

Nick stood up. 'Let's do something.'

The others sat and thought about it. Cheng picked up a magnifying glass and looked at the floor. Simone was staring at her drawing. Nan turned to Tad and leaned against him. He put his arm round her. She looked at his hair. Each strand seemed to be a miniature rope, twisted threads of dark blue and purple and turquoise. The closer she looked, the more detail she saw, and the more beautiful and intricate it became. She was getting randy; Tad's proximity was like a green light – the smell of him, the feel of him, the knowledge of what he looked like under his clothes.

'So,' said Simone. 'The vicar, the tart, the pirate, the sex toy.' She smiled fondly at Cheng in his black cod-piece and mask. 'What can we get for Hugo and Sniffle? And what have we got for Nan?'

Nan rather fancied the idea of dressing up like Simone, and seeing what she looked like in something so utterly opposite to what she normally wore. Simone found a Sherlock Holmes hat and cape for Hugo Forbes, and a maid's outfit for Sniffle. Sniffle seemed quite co-operative all of a sudden, and Nan watched Simone undress her. She did it very slowly and sensuously, running her hands over Sniffle's body and pressing her

253

breasts against her to undo the hook on her bra. Sniffle lifted her chin, as though determined not to react, and Simone slid her hands down to Sniffle's hips and left them there. Then she kicked off the red shoes in Hugo Forbes' general direction. Nan watched Hugo retrieve one of them and sit there with it pressed against his lap, stroking it. Simone looked at Nan. Then she said, 'I never ask my models to do anything I wouldn't do myself, *chérie*,' and she started to fondle Sniffle's nipples.

Sniffle looked annoyed. Then a dreamy expression crept over her face and she said, 'You bloody siren, Simone. You know I can't resist that.'

Tad ran his hand down Nan's back, then circled under her arm and touched her breast. Cheng was running his fingers across the black leather bulge of his codpiece. Hugo Forbes was stroking the shoe almost mindlessly by now, his eyes shut and his breathing irregular.

Nick was still standing in the middle of the room. 'We need to *do* something to pass the time,' he said.

Cheng laughed. 'I think the rest of us *are*, Nick.'

Simone stood up as well. '*Le Déjeuner Sur L'Herbe.*' she said. 'A picnic. Down by the lake, all of us, all dressed up. I know what I've got for you, Nan, but you won't want to walk in it so I'll put it in a bag.' She retrieved her shoe from a wistful Hugo Forbes. 'Don't worry,' she said to him, stroking his calf with her foot. 'You can play with them later.' She put the shoes back on, went to another cupboard and bundled things into a plastic carrier. 'Nan, go into the kitchen. You'll find some stuff on the table.'

Nan disentangled herself rather reluctantly from Tad, and went into the kitchen. She hadn't been there before. To her surprise, the requirements for a picnic were neatly laid out in front of her, and a rather exotic one at that. Two bottles of champagne, some crusty rolls, smoked salmon, caviar, a bowl of cherries, champagne flutes – seven of them. She collected all the things together and distributed them in the two baskets that had obviously been placed there for the purpose; there was a blanket and an oil-lamp already in one of them.

They trailed outside and walked across the courtyard. Nan had never seen such a beautiful array of flowers. They glowed, they sparkled, they threw designs into the air like pollen and scattered them across the gravel. Tad bent down and picked up one of the stones. 'Present,' he said, and passed it to her.

She placed it on her palm. Little triangles of green and purple were interwoven with a mosaic of powder-blue and crimson, like a complex glass paperweight. It was the most exquisite thing anyone had ever given her. For the very first time she'd been given a present she really appreciated. She put it in her pocket.

'You're enjoying it, aren't you?' said Simone to Nan. '*Formidable.* I knew it was a good idea.'

'What was a good idea?' said Nan, completely losing the thread of the conversation.

'Elephants,' said Cheng.

And then Nan remembered standing in the woods, watching Lettie and Gerald – and she remembered Tad whispering in her ear, *when elephants do it, the whole herd gathers to watch.*

When they reached the lake Simone spread the blanket on the grass, and lit the lamp. Then she took the basket, and tipped it on its side. A few cherries and a couple of rolls spilled out, and she looked pleased. 'Sit down,' she said. '*Le Déjeuner Sur L'Herbe.* I know there are too many people – but – *pouf!* Who cares!' They sat down. Simone kicked off her shoes again, and once more Hugo Forbes picked them up. Cheng lay down on the grass and trailed his fingers thoughtfully across his codpiece. His eyes looked even more almond-shaped than usual behind the black leather butterfly-mask that covered the upper part of his face. Tad began to caress the nape of Nan's neck with his little finger; only Nick seemed distant and self-contained.

Simone started to caress Sniffle. Sniffle responded by

suddenly and decisively grabbing Simone by the shoulders, pushing her down on the blanket and sitting astride her. She wasn't wearing anything underneath the maid's outfit, and she started to rub herself against Simone's basque. 'Not so fast,' said Simone huskily. 'There's a little something at the bottom of the basket. Cheng, get it, would you?'

Chapter Fifteen

Cheng sat up. His erection was peeping out of the top of the codpiece; he loosened the string slightly and his prick jerked free, pointing at the stars. Then he went over to the basket, pulled out a vibrator, switched it on, and held it against his cock. Satisfied that it was working well, he handed it to Simone.

It had a double attachment. One was a normal penis – of substantial proportions – and the other was a long thin tentacle of rubber, like a greatly elongated finger. Nan found herself staring, imagining what went where. Simone noticed her looking. 'Ah-ha,' she said, 'Sniffle, we have an innocent in our midst. Come here, Nan. And take your clothes off.'

Sniffle made a space between herself and Simone, and Nan undressed and lay down. 'Feel free to have a wank as you watch,' said Simone to the men. 'And if you like, Hugo, you can rub my foot for me while I give Nan the orgasm of the century.'

Nan felt Sniffle's hands on her breasts. They were very skilful, knowing exactly when to press, when to tickle, when to pinch, when to behave like a feather-duster. She let herself drift into a state of pure physical awareness. She felt Simone separate her buttocks with cool, knowing fingers and run her nail delicately along the crease before she placed something very, very lightly against Nan's arsehole. She felt it pucker with pleasure. Something else cool and firm was pressing against her clitoris, and then Simone switched it on and she felt herself rush into the sort of arousal that usually took minutes, not seconds. The vibration against her clitoris was exquisite, and the tickling buzz against her anus was spreading outwards, fermenting inside her, making her press herself against the cool rubber. Then Simone slipped the tentacle right inside the tight little hole. The pleasure strengthened, and Nan moaned with the intensity of it. Sniffle began to lick one of Nan's nipples in a very inflammatory way, and the combination of different sensations all over her body was just too much. She came as though her life depended on it, and the orgasm went on for far longer than usual. As she lay there, mildly astonished, she saw Simone turn the vibrator on Sniffle, saw Sniffle writhe with pleasure. Hugo Forbes was still rubbing Simone's foot – but he had his cock out now, as long and thin as the rest of him, and he caressed her toes with it every so often, making her clench them with delight. Cheng was masturbating with his customary cool precision, his eyes dark pinpricks behind the leather mask, his hand moving up and down with lazy but relentless intent. Nan got up, a little unsteadily, and made her way back to the rakish pirate figure that was Tad. Nick was still just sitting watching them, a statue-like ecclesiastical presence in the background, inscrutable as Cheng.

'Suck me off, cabin boy,' whispered Tad in Nan's ear. Nan laughed. It seemed like exactly the right thing to do at that particular moment. She undid the red sash around his waist, and unbuttoned the fly of his knee-length britches. The fabric felt old-fashioned – rough and unfamiliar and masculine. She found his cock, and slipped it out through the unbuttoned opening. It jerked free, and rose skywards. He lay there on his back, the white cotton smock riding up his chest and revealing his tanned muscles. His long black hair had come loose and fanned out around him, and there was a smile in his eyes. Nan bent her head over him and took him in her mouth, loving the rigidity of him and wanting to make him come as powerfully as she had. She teased him and titillated him and sucked him until he was catching his breath with every sudden movement of her tongue. She stopped, played with his balls and fondled his arsehole. 'Get your head down, cabin boy,' growled Tad. 'Don't bugger about. Not this time, anyway.'

Nan went down on him again, and this time she didn't stop. As the spunk shot into her mouth he cried out; she swallowed it all and then she very gently licked him clean. He ran his fingers through her hair and said, 'Have an extra helping of grog tonight, my lad.'

Sniffle had obviously come a while back, and she was using the vibrator on Simone. Simone was sighing theatrically, and thrashing about on the blanket. Hugo Forbes had let go of her foot and he was holding the shoe against his cheek while having his cock vigorously massaged by Cheng. There was semen on Cheng's thigh; he must have come as well. Hugo Forbes screwed his eyes tight shut and groaned; Cheng speeded up and Forbes came with some considerable force, covering Simone's breasts with spunk and causing her to come with a blood-curdling shriek. Then Nan became entranced by an ear of corn, and time did something strange again.

They had a glass of champagne, and some smoked salmon and asparagus tips. Nick ate silently and sparingly, and kept a little apart. Then Simone up-ended the plastic carrier, and a jumble of clothes fell out, as well as a sketchbook and pencil. 'We've forgotten about Nan's costume,' she said. 'No peeking while she gets dressed.'

Nan watched the men all obediently close their eyes. They're so used to Simone's performances, thought Nan, that following her instructions is second nature to them.

Sniffle didn't bother to shut hers, but Simone didn't seem to mind. She held up a long pale-blue gown with a darker design on the fabric – genuine Victoriana, by the look of it. It had a navy-blue sash around the waist, and there was a hat to go with it, a floppy straw period-piece with a black velvet band and a bow that matched the sash. Nan slipped on the dress and donned the hat, and wished there were a mirror. 'Go and look at yourself in the lake,' suggested Simone. Nan walked to the water's edge and peered at her reflection. It was too dark to see anything but a light shape, but the shape was very feminine – the cinched waist, the tight bodice, the flowing skirt.

'You can look now!' called Simone. The men lowered their hands from their eyes and looked.

Nan saw Cheng smile slightly. She saw Tad's brows draw together, as though he were trying hard to remember something. But Nick had gone quite white. 'Harriet?' he said.

'Oh, Simone,' said Tad, 'why couldn't you just drop it?'

Simone had her sketchbook out, and she was drawing Nick with quick strokes of the pencil.

Nick was sitting there as still as stone, but the hooded wariness had gone and for the first time his face was aflame with naked emotion. Tad stood up, walked over to Nan and put his arm round her. 'It's Nan,' he said. 'Remember? Harriet's *daughter*.'

Nick shook his head in mute disagreement. The tears on his cheeks glittered in the lamplight.

Tad turned to Nan. 'You're wearing the dress your mother wore the day she died. She's even engineered the right backdrop – an expanse of dark satanic water.'

Nan looked down at the Victorian dress, then looked up, confused.

'We went to a fancy dress party,' said Simone, but she didn't stop drawing for a moment. 'Nick, me, Alan, and your mother. I was wearing a basque – not this one,

260

unfortunately – and Nick was wearing a vicar's outfit. The party was on a boat; it hit a submerged tree, and sank. Nick's always seen it as his own fault – if he hadn't persuaded Harriet to meet him on the sly, she wouldn't have been at the sharp end of the collision. Nick was late for his assignation. He survived, she didn't – she couldn't swim. Alan got a crack on the skull during the impact and drowned as well.'

'Harriet?' said Nick again. It was spooky; he didn't seem to be listening to anything anyone else said.

'Harriet's dead,' said Tad. 'This is *Nan.*'

'I never told you how I felt,' said Nick. 'Alan Gordon. My best friend.'

'I'm not Alan Gordon,' said Tad. 'I'm Tadeusz.'

'I'm all for a bit of sexual variety,' said Nick, 'but you got Harriet to prostitute herself, and you watched.'

'I expect she enjoyed it, from what I've heard,' said Tad. Then he looked at Nan, aghast. 'I'm sorry,' he said.

'Harriet was every man's dream, Alan, you told me. She would do just about anything for kicks, anywhere. But that wasn't enough, was it? She did it for money while you watched; went with other men for a small consideration, when I would have given her everything I had without a second thought. I loved her. *Really* loved her. The only time I've ever really loved anyone.'

'No one forced her, Nick,' said Tad. 'You put her on a pedestal.'

'Your father didn't want you to take after her, Nan,' said Simone conversationally. 'Remember? That's why he burned all her paintings, and discouraged you artistically. He didn't want you to find out how she died, either, when the boat went down. Sucking off one of the crew on the bowsprit while she waited for Nick, in exchange for some Navy rum. In those days she did things even I wouldn't do . . . but she was such a brilliant artist.' Her pencil skittered across the page as she completed yet another drawing of Nick.

It wasn't the sort of information you wanted about

your mother, however liberal your views. Nan felt herself retreating from everything, trying to hide inside herself.

'You set this up, didn't you, Simone?' said Tad, sounding distant. 'You've been working towards it right from the moment you first set eyes on Nan, and you saw the resemblance to Harriet. You wanted every last drop of emotion out of Nick; you wanted to do a drawing of him going over the edge. Why?'

'Because he loved Harriet more than me,' said Simone icily, from even further away.

And then the pictures started, inside Nan's head.

First of all it was just the image of a woman standing in a doorway, wearing a dress of pale-blue patterned silk, with frothing petticoats and a dark-blue satin sash. There was a wide-brimmed straw hat on her head, trimmed with a black velvet band and a bow made of the same material as the satin sash. The woman glanced at her watch and looked impatient. My mother, thought Nan. It's the first genuine memory I've ever had of her.

She was a child again, tucked up in bed; she could feel the cool linen of the sheet against her skin, smell her mother's perfume, deep and musky. There was a nightlight beside her ... She could see the laundry basket in the corner, the white wickerwork swan with the yellow beak, identical to the one in Nick's book. And then she could hear her own voice, high-pitched, childish, pleading to be allowed to go to the party as well and her mother laughing and saying *it's not the sort of party you take four-year-olds to, Felicity*.

And there was Alan; tall, dark, dangerously good-looking. And Nick – younger, his hair not white but blond, arguing with Harriet about something. She heard her mother say, *it'll be fine, don't fuss, I've left her on her own before*. Nick kissed Felicity on the cheek, and told her he'd bring her back a present. And then they all went away, and left her quite alone.

Nan shivered. The memories were so clear that she

wasn't quite sure what was reality and what wasn't any more. She heard someone ask her if she was feeling OK, but his voice came from a great distance and his words didn't seem to mean anything. A little bit later, she became dimly aware that someone was carrying her; their bodies jarred together every so often. It didn't seem to be important.

She was lying in the dark, crying. The nightlight had gone out, and the pale shape of the wickerwork swan was the only thing she could see. Felicity didn't know how many hours she'd been lying there, awake; she felt as though she had been there forever when the door opened. Nick came in, his shirt torn, his hair wild, his eyes red-rimmed and tired. He was followed by another man. She sat up. 'You said you'd bring me a present.'

'Oh, Nan,' said the other man, 'I've missed you so much. You've grown. My God, how you've grown.'

Nan? She put her thumb in her mouth, puzzled.

Nick gently removed the thumb, and took her hands in his enormous ones. 'Felicity,' he said, 'your mother won't be coming back. She's ... gone to heaven.' He fought to control his tears. 'This is your father. He's going to look after you now.'

She stared at the strange man, with his funny bow tie and his shiny bald patch. 'And that's my present?' she said.

There was somebody sitting next to her, holding her hand. He was speaking to her, but she couldn't make sense of his words. She looked at him. For a moment she saw someone quite extraordinarily beautiful, and then he dissolved. Things got very confused after that. She seemed to drown, and then to be resuscitated. She froze, and was wrapped in warmth. She was in a bedroom, on a white satin sheet, and the sheet wanted to devour her. She tried to roll away from it, over the precipice, and somebody caught her. She felt there was something she had to escape – and then she *had* escaped it, and the nightmare began to subside.

263

And then there were voices outside, and the door opened, and someone from the real world said, 'What the hell's going on?'

She sat up intact. Her head was clear, and she was in Tad's bedroom.

Mike was standing in the doorway. He was wearing that shirt she hated. She tore her eyes away; it wouldn't do to look at it for too long. The colours tasted too much like a fruit salad.

'Are you OK, Nan?' He didn't move towards her.

'No,' said Nan.

'She's not been very well,' said Tad, from somewhere behind her. 'Someone spiked her drink.'

'Someone?' said Mike.

'Simone,' said Tad.

'Why would she do a thing like that?'

'She's a bit unstable.'

'I see,' said Mike. 'And who are you?'

'Tadeusz Kalinowski. Nan's art tutor.'

'So what happened to *you*?'

'Slipped in the shower,' said Tad.

Mike walked across the room to Nan and sat down beside her on the bed, but he didn't put his arm round her. 'I think I'd better take you home,' he said. He smelled of coal-tar soap and boiled sweets. Nan stood up. She wanted to be told what to do, action by action. She didn't want to have to think for herself. She didn't want to have to make any decisions. She didn't want to think at all.

Mike took her downstairs and sat her in the car. It was so familiar; the broken glove compartment, the grey plastic like shards of glass, the sweet papers on the floor. She watched Tad take Mike across to the coach-house to get her things. They were talking together, and once or twice she saw Mike stop for a moment as though Tad had said something unexpected. Tad had tied back his hair again, and he was wearing a white T-shirt and black trousers. He looked respectable and in control of both

264

himself and the situation. They came back with her bag, and Mike put it in the boot. Tad stood there, expressionless. Mike started the engine, and wound down the window.

'Nice meeting you,' he said.

Tad nodded. He looked at Nan.

'Goodbye Tad,' said Nan.

'*Do widzenia,*' said Tad, but he didn't smile.

Mike put the car into gear. It ground out a mild protest, and lurched away. The gate was already open; Nan didn't get out to shut it. She turned round for one last look as they drove down the track. Tad was standing there in the middle of the courtyard, arms folded, watching them. *I want to make love to you, just once . . .* and just once was all it had been, in the end. She felt the tears begin, but she fought them. By the time they were back on the main road, she'd won.

After a long silence, Mike said, 'Megan came to see me. She was worried about you. She thought the place had turned your head: too much fresh air and intellectual conversation.'

'Oh,' said Nan.

'And she told me you slept with Nick.'

Oh, shit, thought Nan. How *could* you, Megan?

Mike took a deep breath. 'I've got a confession to make as well,' he said. 'I've been having an affair with Sandra – but it's finished now. So let's call it quits and say no more about it.'

A couple of nights, later they had sex. It was like putting on an old jumper; comfortable, predictable, and it was OK. It kept her warm.

Megan left Terry and went to live with Brian. Nan went round to see her.

'I didn't dare come round,' said Megan. 'I am sorry, Nan. Telling Mike about Nick was the only way I could get him to go and pick you up. You'd gone really peculiar, you know. You weren't your old self at all; I was ever so worried about you. I *had* to tell him.'

Nan shrugged.

'Back to the A level on Wednesday,' said Megan. 'Honestly, I had a great time at Lavender Hall but I don't think I learned very much. Did you?'

Within a couple of months, Megan was moaning about Brian. Two weeks after that, she went back to Terry. It was as though the holiday had never been.

Nan drifted back to the same old routine with Mike. The only thing that seemed to have really changed was her painting. Her teacher persuaded her to apply to art college; she got a place and Mike joked about it, and she felt middle-aged and silly.

Megan came round, early one morning. She sat down at the kitchen table and said, 'I've got something for you.' Then she reached into her bag, got out a letter and put it on the table. It was addressed to Nan, but it had been sent care of Megan. 'Where the hell's Ulan Bator?' asked Megan.

Nan seized the letter. Although it was very big, it only seemed to contain one sheet of paper, albeit a thick sheet. 'Ulan Bator's in Mongolia,' she said. She turned her back to Megan and opened it.

It was a watercolour, a straightforward landscape at first glance. There was no writing at all. The painting was very detailed, a range of pink mountains, wild, remote. There were small traces of intense blue here and there. She looked more closely at the shadows, and the more she looked, the more she saw. There was a swan on one peak, and a lion on another. A pile of stones that looked suspiciously like broken Smarties. A gully that could have been a cello, and another one that bore a strong resemblance to a shower faucet. She was smiling like an idiot.

'Let me see,' said Megan. 'What is it? Something from Simone to say thank you for modelling?' She peered over Nan's shoulder and looked at it. 'There's no signature,' she said. 'What a pity. It's really pretty, isn't it? She *is* clever.'

His signature's in every brushstroke, thought Nan, as she put the watercolour away in a drawer, next to a small piece of very ordinary gravel she'd found in her coat pocket. She looked at the painting from time to time when she was on her own. There were references to nearly everything that had happened between them that week, right down to the chanterelles. She painted a picture for him, then another and another, intending to send him the best one care of Lavender Hall. She was on the centre's mailing list, but when the prospectus arrived Tad wasn't teaching the watercolour class any more. Nick's name was absent as well. She phoned Lavender Hall, but the administrator wouldn't give her a contact address. Nan screwed up all the paintings and burned them.

Megan got an E for her A level; Nan got an A. Megan gave up art, took up golf, and began an affair with her instructor.

Mike came in from work one day, looking very pleased with himself. 'Money,' he said, savouring the word as though it had seduced him, ravished him and left him sated. He'd never used that tone of voice about *her*. 'Six-month contract in the States,' he added, and he started to whistle some irritating tune.

'Oh,' said Nan.

'You're going to college,' he said. 'You'll hardly notice I've gone.'

'Who else is going to America?'

'Martin . . . Chuck . . . John Higson . . .'

'Sandra?'

'Oh, for God's sake,' said Mike. 'That's over.'

'But she is going.'

He shrugged.

Nan's eyes narrowed.

'Sandra's a laugh,' said Mike, as though that made it acceptable.

'Her use of English is hysterical,' said Nan, 'I'll grant you that. "My nipples have gone rock-hard in sympathy." Yuk.'

Mike glared at her. 'You don't need a PhD in linguistics to be good in bed,' he said.

'An IQ is a hindrance then, is it?' snapped back Nan.

'It is with you,' said Mike.

Nan turned up the potatoes so that they would boil over, left the kitchen and slammed the door behind her. Then she thought, when was the last time we actually did have sex? And she couldn't remember.

Mike left for Seattle that September, and Nan started college. There were several women in a similar position to her, children off their hands. She made a couple of good friends very quickly, and she loved being a student.

And then Mike came home unexpectedly one weekend.

'How's Sandra?' asked Nan, before she could stop herself.

For once Mike didn't rise to the bait. 'I've been offered a permanent position,' he said. 'And I've accepted.'

'You've *what*? Without a word to me?'

'Nan,' said Mike, 'we've run our course. You know it, I know it. Darren and Cassie are independent now, and –'

'You'd rather be with Sandra.'

'Yes. I'm not into all this art stuff, and I never will be. I'm sorry.'

'Oh, well,' said Nan, suddenly feeling as though a cage door had been opened.

'You can have the house,' said Mike unexpectedly. 'I don't want to end up enemies.'

'Me neither,' said Nan, realising that it was true, and

they spent the rest of the weekend sorting things out in a suprisingly amicable fashion.

As soon as Nan got back from dropping him off at the airport, she tried Lavender Hall again, but this time there was just a recorded message, saying that the centre was closed until the spring. She made a trip to the library, and went through the names of artists' agents until she found Grazyna. She rang the number, but a man's voice answered. 'Grazyna has gone back to Poland,' he said.

'I need to get in touch with one of her clients,' said Nan. 'Tadeusz Kalinowski.'

'He is not with us any more,' said the man. 'Sorry.'

'You don't have a contact number?'

'No.'

She put down the phone and felt so powerless that she burst into tears. Then she suddenly realised that she was late for college and she had to run all the way to the tube. She met her friend Karen in the entrance hall, looking flustered.

'We've got a lecture,' said Karen, 'quick.' And they dashed upstairs and sat themselves at the back.

'God, what a rush,' said Nan, glancing round the raked seating. 'Who is it?'

'Tadeusz Kalinowski,' said Karen.

Nan felt everything drop away, as though some passing eagle had seized her in its talons.

'Kalinowski's stuff's right up your street,' said Karen. 'Clever, but not clinical.'

There were several hundred people in the audience, tier after tier of them; his lecture had appealed to a wider group than just the art students. He probably wouldn't even see her.

He walked in carrying a bundle of drawings and put them on a table in front of him. After a moment or two, he glanced up at the audience and smiled. He'd taking to wearing a small brightly coloured hat, presumably something he'd picked up in Mongolia; it suited him. He looked offbeat, successful and decidedly sexy, but he had real authority.

'Blimey,' said Karen, 'he's *gorgeous*. I had no idea.'

Nan went scarlet, and looked at her shoes.

'What on earth's the matter with you?' whispered Karen. 'You don't *know* him, do you?' She glanced back at Tad, and then at Nan again. 'You do, don't you? Well, well.'

'I'm going to talk about content,' said Tad. 'Themes. Text, I suppose, although I don't think words serve images very effectively. Which makes a lecture on art a bit of a paradox, doesn't it? But there you go.'

He showed them some drawings, and talked about the development of ideas, and he was as amusing and original as ever. The lecture was an hour and a half, and the first hour and a quarter passed enjoyably and uneventfully. He began to talk about his current work, the paintings he'd been doing in Mongolia, and the way he used what he saw in front of him to explore other concerns. He talked about shadows, and how they could be manipulated. He talked about collaborating with Simone, but only in general terms. And then he saw Nan.

For a moment he froze.

He covered it up by dropping one of his drawings, and when he stood up again he was quite composed. But the lecture started to move in another direction, and now there were double meanings in everything he said. He didn't look at her again, he just carried on talking, but she could hear his knowledge of her presence in everything he said. 'So,' he said finally, glancing at his watch, 'keep peering into those shadows.' And then he did look directly at her. 'And if you ever find anyone else who sees the same images, try a bit of collaboration – and if that means using intense blue . . .'

There was ripple of laughter, as everyone knew what Simone's work was like. The lecture was over. Every-

270

body clapped, and some of the students went down to talk to him.

Nan just sat there.

'Nan,' said Karen, standing there waiting to go, 'what is it? How well do you know him?' And when Nan didn't reply, she sat down again and said, '*That* well. I see.'

Nan stood up, and picked up her things. Now it had actually come to it, she couldn't face him. She wanted him too much simply to have a brief exchange of pleasantries. 'Let's go and get drunk,' she said. She could see Tad surrounded by people down on the floor of the lecture theatre. They made their way to the end of the row and headed for the upper exit at the back.

'You're a dark horse,' said Karen. 'Where did you meet him?'

'Simone Garnier's house.'

'Good God, you've met her as well?'

They reached the swing door at the end of the last row of seats. And just as she'd done before, Nan turned for one last look. Their eyes met, and he beckoned to her. When she didn't react, he raised an eyebrow in admonition and beckoned again. She didn't move. The principal went over to him. Tad turned to him impatiently and said something, and she realised he was making his excuses. If she didn't go down to him, he was going to come up and get her. She suddenly felt quite sure that if she tried to leave he would chase her, and to hell with what anyone else made of it.

'Nan,' said Karen, 'it looks to me as though there's something you need to sort out here. Don't mind if I stay and watch, do you?'

They walked down the steps and waited while he dealt rather perfunctorily with the people who wanted to speak to him. It was more than a year since she'd last seen him. The sound of his voice, the angles of his body, his gestures, his smile: every little detail made her ache for him.

Eventually he turned to her and said coolly, 'How's Mike?'

'In America,' said Nan, equally distant. 'How's Simone?'

'Oh,' said Tad, offhand, 'she's got some Nubian guy there at the moment. Face like Nefertiti, rippling muscles and a dick like a donkey's.'

Nan couldn't help it; she laughed. Out of the corner of her eye she could see Karen's reaction; shock, then amusement. Tad grinned at Karen, and she appeared to melt on the spot.

'And Cheng?' said Nan.

'He went back to Cambodia.'

'Cheng went back?'

'Someone shopped him to Immigration,' said Tad innocently. 'He wasn't a postgraduate at all. God knows what he was. Khmer Rouge, probably.'

Karen's mouth dropped open.

Nice one, Tadeusz, thought Nan.

Karen suddenly seemed to realise she was doing a good impression of a haddock. She shut her mouth again rather abruptly, and cleared her throat.

'Oh,' said Nan, 'this is Karen. She's on the same course as me.'

He nodded at her. Then he looked at Nan and said, 'You never replied to my letter. Why? I only said *do widzenia*; I didn't say goodbye.'

'I didn't know how to get in touch with you.'

'You could have written care of Simone.'

'You weren't in the prospectus this year.'

'Only because I was in Ulan Bator.' He picked up his drawings, but he was smiling.

'I loved the Mongolian ones,' said Karen.

'Thanks.' Tad glanced at his watch.

'Don't let us hold you up,' said Nan.

There was a momentary flash of anger. Then he turned very politely to Karen and said, 'Will you excuse us, Karen? I have this overpowering urge to fuck Nan into the middle of next week, and I can't do it here.'

Nan went crimson.

Karen started to laugh. She patted Nan on the back, said, 'See you,' and went.

'Did you have to say that?' said Nan.

He grinned. 'I don't think it'll do my raunchy image any harm. What does it do to yours?'

'I don't have an image.'

'Happily married wife?'

'We've separated.'

He didn't look surprised.

They walked towards the exit. 'What do you want to do?' asked Nan. 'Go for a coffee or something?'

'Oh, yes, very good,' said Tad, opening the door for her. 'Coffee. I don't think so.'

They took the lift to the ground floor, and walked out to the car park. He put the drawings in the boot of the Mercedes.

'Where are we going, then?'

'I've got a studio in Hammersmith. Unless you have some objection.'

It was the first time she'd been in the car with him driving. It felt odd. 'You'll love what happened to Braithwaite,' said Tad, nipping cleverly between two lorries and ending up stuck behind a milk-float.

'Tell me,' said Nan.

'He got religion while he was in hospital. He goes round rescuing every creeping thing that creepeth upon the earth. I blame the head injury, personally.'

'You're kidding.'

'Straight up. He's God's vet to the fowls of the air and the beasts of the earth. He's turned the hut into a sort of animal hospital.'

'I don't believe you,' said Nan.

He just grinned, and she had no idea whether he'd been telling the truth or just made the whole thing up.

The studio in Hammersmith was simply a big room, not too unlike the one he'd had at Simone's. There was a bed in the corner, a fridge, a stove. Piles of papers, canvases. Nan sat down on the bed. He shut the door and leaned against it, arms folded, looking at her. 'I presume you knew it was going to be me, giving that talk.'

'Actually,' said Nan, 'I didn't. I was late. It was a bit of a shock.'

'Not as much of a shock as when I saw you in the audience.'

She smiled.

'I've got a proposition,' he said. 'What are you doing at Christmas?'

'Not much.'

'I want to go to Namibia,' he said. 'Come with me. There's an awful lot I can still teach you. You can be my factotum. Officially. Then next summer we go somewhere else.'

'A sort of Simone arrangement.'

'Phrase it that way if you like.'

'I don't know.'

'We're different things to different people,' said Tad. 'You're the orange to my intense blue. I was the orange to Simone's blue. It's when we use one colour all the time that it takes over, unbalances things. I don't see Simone very often, these days – but she'd be too blue to survive if I didn't see her at all. Nick went to the States, you see. She can't lean on him any more.'

'Complementary colours,' said Nan.

He smiled. 'Together they make a nice safe grey.'

'I miss you dreadfully,' said Nan, 'when I let myself. I try not to think about you. It's the only way to cope.'

He didn't say anything, just locked the door, walked over to the bed and sat down beside her. He still hadn't touched her, not once. 'Before I fuck you into next week,' he said, 'which I shall, I want you to say that you'll come to Africa. That you'll at least try it. If it doesn't work then it doesn't work. But let's give it a go. Anyone other than you would be second best.'

For an artist, she thought, you choose your words

remarkably well. She remembered how he must have looked after her when Simone had spiked her drink; anticipating her terrors, neutralising them one by one, a psychological St George. 'All right,' she said. 'I'll be your colour orange.'

He started to kiss her, but it built very quickly to something so inflammatory that neither of them proved capable of exerting the slightest drop of self-control. She heard one of the buttons on her dungarees pop off and roll into a corner as he wrenched them off her; her T-shirt tore under the arm as he pulled it over her head. Then she was fumbling with his flies as he took off his shoes – and after that she was unzipping him, and trying to slide down his underpants, which had an impressive erection to circumvent. She managed it, and pulled off his socks. He undid her bra, and threw it theatrically across the room. She slipped off her briefs. He ripped off his shirt; then they were both naked, and he threw her on to the bed and yanked her into position by the ankles. There was no preamble; he held her down by the wrists and entered her immediately. The rush of pleasure was instantaneous and acute, and with every thrust it became more impassioned and uncontrollable. She watched his face as he watched hers, noticing every minute change of expression; the lift at the corner of his mouth when she squeezed him, the delight in his eyes when she moaned in response to something, the tilt of his eyebrows when he smiled. She writhed against him, meeting each push with one of her own, letting her body take over, dispensing with all mental activity except the bit that dealt with physical sensation. A curtain of his black hair fell over them, damp with perspiration; he shook it out of his eyes and fucked her even more energetically. And then she was holding him as tightly as she could and she was coming, and so was he.

From two dimensions into three, and from black and white into colour.

With just a touch of intense blue.

BLACK LACE NEW BOOKS

Published in April

SAUCE FOR THE GOOSE
Mary Rose Maxwell
£5.99

Sauce for the Goose is a riotous and sometimes humorous celebration of the rich variety of human sexuality. Imaginative and colourful, each story explores a different theme or fantasy, and the result is a fabulously bawdy mélange of cheeky sensuality and hot thrills. A lively array of characters display an uninhibited and lusty energy for boundary-breaking pleasure. This is a decidedly X-rated collection of stories designed to be enjoyed and indulged in.

ISBN 0 352 33492 4

HARD CORPS
Claire Thompson
£5.99

Remy Harris, a bright young army cadet at a prestigious military college, hopes to become an officer. She understands that she will have to endure all the usual trials of military life, including boot-camp discipline and rigorous exercise. She's ready for the challenge – that is until she meets Jacob, who recognises her true sexuality and initiates her into the Hard Corps – a secret society within the barracks.

ISBN 0 352 33491 6

Published in May

INTENSE BLUE
Lyn Wood
£5.99

When Nan and Megan attend a residential art course as a 40th birthday present to themselves, they are plunged into a claustrophobic world of bizarre events and eccentric characters. There is a strong sexual under-current to the place, and it seems that many of the tutors are having affairs with their students – and each other. Nan gets caught up in a mystery she has to solve, but playing amateur detective only leads her into increasingly strange and sexual situations in this sometimes hilar-ious story of two women on a mission to discover what they really want in their lives.

ISBN 0 352 33496 7

THE NAKED TRUTH
Natasha Rostova
£5.99

Callie feels trapped living among the 'old money' socialites of the Savannah district. Her husband Logan is remote, cold and repressed – even if he does have an endless supply of money. One day she leaves him. Determined to change her life she hides out at her sister's place. Meanwhile Logan has hired a detective and is determined to get his wife back. But she is now treading a path of self-expression, and even getting into the ancient art of Voodoo. Will he want her back when he finds her? And what will she do when she learns the naked truth about Logan's shady past?

ISBN 0 352 33497 5

To be published in June

ANIMAL PASSIONS
Martine Marquand
£5.99

Nineteen-year-old Jo runs away from the strict household where she's been brought up, and is initiated into a New Age pagan cult located in a rural farming community in England. Michael, the charismatic shaman leader, invites Jo to join him in a celebration of unbridled passion. As the summer heat intensifies, preparations are made for the midsummer festival, and Jo is keen to play a central role in the cult's bizarre rites. Will she ever want to return to normal society?

ISBN 0 352 33499 1

IN THE FLESH
Emma Holly
£5.99

Topless dancer Chloe is better at being bad than anyone David Imakita knows. To keep her, this Japanese American businessman risks everything he owns: his career, his friends, his integrity. But will this unrepentant temptress overturn her wild ways and accept an opportunity to change her life, or will the secrets of her past resurface and destroy them both?

ISBN 0 352 33498 3

NO LADY
Saskia Hope
£5.99

30-year-old Kate walks out of her job, dumps her boyfriend and goes in search of adventure. And she finds it. Held captive in the Pyrenees by a bunch of outlaws involved in smuggling art treasures, she finds the lovemaking is as rough as the landscape. Only a sense of danger can satisfy her ravenous passions, but she also has some plans of her own. A Black Lace special reprint.

ISBN 0 352 32857 6

If you would like a complete list of plot summaries of Black Lace titles, or would like to receive information on other publications available, please send a stamped addressed envelope to:

Black Lace, Thames Wharf Studios,
Rainville Road, London W6 9HA

BLACK LACE BOOKLIST

All books are priced £5.99 unless another price is given.

Black Lace books with a contemporary setting

RIVER OF SECRETS £4.99	Saskia Hope & Georgia Angelis ISBN 0 352 32925 4	☐
THE NAME OF AN ANGEL £6.99	Laura Thornton ISBN 0 352 33205 0	☐
BONDED £4.99	Fleur Reynolds ISBN 0 352 33192 5	☐
CONTEST OF WILLS	Louisa Francis ISBN 0 352 33223 9	☐
FEMININE WILES £7.99	Karina Moore ISBN 0 352 33235 2	☐
DARK OBSESSION £7.99	Fredrica Alleyn ISBN 0 352 33281 6	☐
COOKING UP A STORM £7.99	Emma Holly ISBN 0 352 33258 1	☐
THE TOP OF HER GAME	Emma Holly ISBN 0 352 33337 5	☐
LIKE MOTHER, LIKE DAUGHTER	Georgina Brown ISBN 0 352 33422 3	☐
ASKING FOR TROUBLE	Kristina Lloyd ISBN 0 352 33362 6	☐
A DANGEROUS GAME	Lucinda Carrington ISBN 0 352 33432 0	☐
THE TIES THAT BIND	Tesni Morgan ISBN 0 352 33438 X	☐
IN THE DARK	Zoe le Verdier ISBN 0 352 33439 8	☐
BOUND BY CONTRACT	Helena Ravenscroft ISBN 0 352 33447 9	☐
VELVET GLOVE	Emma Holly ISBN 0 352 33448 7	☐
STRIPPED TO THE BONE	Jasmine Stone ISBN 0 352 33463 0	☐
DOCTOR'S ORDERS	Deanna Ashford ISBN 0 352 33453 3	☐

SHAMELESS	Stella Black ISBN 0 352 33485 1	☐
TONGUE IN CHEEK	Tabitha Flyte ISBN 0 352 33484 3	☐
FIRE AND ICE	Laura Hamilton ISBN 0 352 33486 X	☐
SAUCE FOR THE GOOSE	Mary Rose Maxwell ISBN 0 352 33492 4	☐
HARD CORPS	Claire Thompson ISBN 0 352 33491 6	☐

Black Lace books with an historical setting

THE INTIMATE EYE £4.99	Georgia Angelis ISBN 0 352 33004 X	☐
GOLD FEVER £4.99	Louisa Francis ISBN 0 352 33043 0	☐
FORBIDDEN CRUSADE £4.99	Juliet Hastings ISBN 0 352 33079 1	☐
A VOLCANIC AFFAIR £4.99	Xanthia Rhodes ISBN 0 352 33184 4	☐
SAVAGE SURRENDER	Deanna Ashford ISBN 0 352 33253 0	☐
INVITATION TO SIN £6.99	Charlotte Royal ISBN 0 352 33217 4	☐
A FEAST FOR THE SENSES	Martine Marquand ISBN 0 352 33310 3	☐

Black Lace anthologies

PANDORA'S BOX	ISBN 0 352 33074 0	☐
PANDORA'S BOX 3	ISBN 0 352 33274 3	☐
WICKED WORDS	Various ISBN 0 352 33363 4	☐
SUGAR AND SPICE £7.99	Various ISBN 0 352 33227 1	☐
THE BEST OF BLACK LACE	Various ISBN 0 352 33452 5	☐
CRUEL ENCHANTMENT Erotic Fairy Stories	Janine Ashbless ISBN 0 352 33483 5	☐
WICKED WORDS 2	Various ISBN 0 352 33487 8	☐

Black Lace non-fiction

THE BLACK LACE BOOK OF WOMEN'S SEXUAL FANTASIES	Ed. Kerri Sharp ISBN 0 352 33346 4	☐

-------- ✂ --------------------

Please send me the books I have ticked above.

Name ....

Address ....

....

....

.... Post Code ....

Send to: **Cash Sales, Black Lace Books, Thames Wharf Studios, Rainville Road, London W6 9HA.**

US customers: for prices and details of how to order books for delivery by mail, call 1-800-805-1083.

Please enclose a cheque or postal order, made payable to **Virgin Publishing Ltd**, to the value of the books you have ordered plus postage and packing costs as follows:

UK and BFPO – £1.00 for the first book, 50p for each subsequent book.

Overseas (including Republic of Ireland) – £2.00 for the first book, £1.00 for each subsequent book.

If you would prefer to pay by VISA, ACCESS/MASTER-CARD, DINERS CLUB, AMEX or SWITCH, please write your card number and expiry date here:

....

Please allow up to 28 days for delivery.

Signature ....

-------- ✂ --------------------